Books by Miss Read

THE CAXLEY CHRONICLES

THE MARKET SQUARE *and*
THE HOWARDS OF CAXLEY

Miss Read

Drawings by Harry Grimley

HOUGHTON MIFFLIN COMPANY

Boston • New York

First Houghton Mifflin paperback edition 2007

THE MARKET SQUARE
Copyright © 1966 by Miss Read
Text copyright © renewed 1994 by Dora Jessie Saint
Illustrations copyright © renewed 1994 by Harry Grimley

THE HOWARDS OF CAXLEY
Copyright © 1967 by Miss Read
Copyright © renewed 1995 by Dora Jessie Saint

For information about permission to reproduce
selections from this book, write to Permissions,
Houghton Mifflin Company, 215 Park Avenue South,
New York, New York 10003.

Visit our Web site: www.houghtonmifflinbooks.com.

Library of Congress Cataloging-in-Publication Data
Read, Miss.
The Caxley chronicles / Miss Read ; drawings by Harry
Grimley.— 1st Houghton Mifflin pbk. ed. 2007.
p. cm.
ISBN-13: 978-0-618-88429-2
ISBN-10: 0-618-88429-7
1. Country life—Fiction. 2. England—Fiction.
I. Title.
PR6069.A42C39 2007
823'.914—dc22   2006103553

Printed in the United States of America

MP 10 9 8 7 6 5 4 3 2 1

THE MARKET SQUARE

To Olive and Philip with love

THE HOWARDS OF CAXLEY

To Pat and John with love

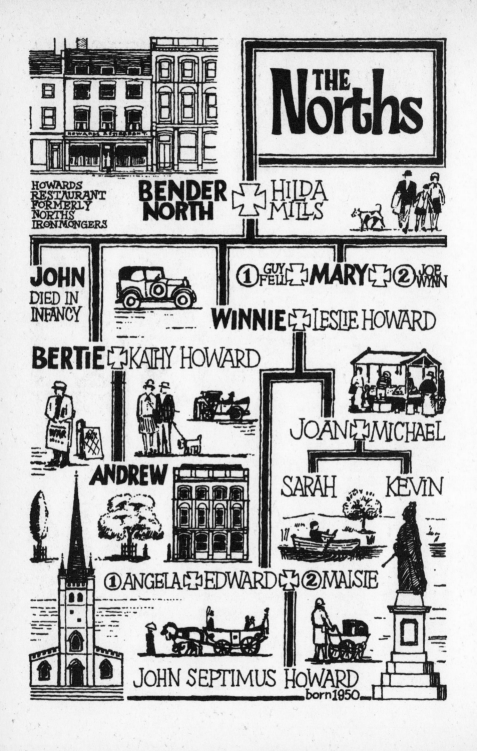

CONTENTS

The Market Square

The Howards of Caxley

THE MARKET SQUARE

PART ONE

I

A June Morning

IT HAD been raining in Caxley, but now the sun was out
again. A sharp summer shower had sent the shoppers into
doorways, and many of the stallholders, too, from the
market square, had sought more shelter than their flimsy
awnings could provide.

Only fat Mrs Petty remained by her fish stall, red-faced and
beaming through the veils of rain that poured from the covers
above the herring and hake, the mussels and mullet. She
roared a few rude and derisory remarks to her more prudent
neighbours sheltering across the road, but the rain made such
a drumming on the canvas, such a gurgling in the gutters, that
it was impossible to hear a word.

It spun on the stones of the market square like a million
silver coins. Office windows were slammed shut, shop-keepers
braved the downpour to snatch in the wares they had been
displaying on the pavement, and even the pigeons took cover.

It ended as suddenly as it had begun, and people emerged
again into the glistening streets. The pigeons flew down from
the plinths of the Corn Exchange and strutted through the
shining puddles, their coral feet splashing up tiny rainbows as
iridescent as their own opal necks. There was a fresh sweetness
in the air, and Bender North, struggling out of his ironmongery shop with a pile of doormats in his arms, took a
great thankful breath.

'Ah!' he sighed, dropping his burden on the pavement from which he had so recently rescued it. He kicked the mats deftly into a neat pile, and, hands on hips, breathed in again deeply. He was a hefty, barrel-shaped man and had been feeling the heat badly these last few days, and his much-loved garden was getting parched. This refreshing shower was welcome. He surveyed the steaming awnings in the market with an approving eye.

No one – not even Bender himself – could quite remember how he had come by his odd name. He had been christened Bertram Lewis thirty-five years earlier at the parish church across the market square. Some said that as a youth he had liked to show off his outstanding muscular strength by twisting pieces of metal in his great hands. Others, who had shared his schooldays at the old National School in Caxley High Street, maintained that he was so often called upon to 'bend over for six' that some wag had decided that 'Bender' was the perfect name for this boisterous, lusty rebel against authority. Whatever the reason, now long forgotten, for dubbing him thus, the name stuck, and if any stranger had asked in Caxley for Bertram North, rather than Bender North, he would have been met with blank countenances.

Bender watched the stallholders resuming their activities. The man who sold glue was busy smashing saucers deftly, and putting them together again with equal dexterity, while a crowd of gaping country folk watched him with wonder and amusement. Fat Mrs Petty shook a shower of silver sprats from the scale-pan into a newspaper. Tom and Fred Lawrence, who ran a market garden on the outskirts of the town, handed over bunches of young carrots and turnips, stuffed lettuces into

already overcrowded baskets, weighed mounds of spring
greens, broccoli, turnip tops and potatoes, bawling with lungs
of brass the while. This was Caxley at its best, thought Bender!
Plenty of life, plenty of people, and plenty of money changing
hands!

'A mouse trap, North,' said a voice behind him, and the
ironmonger returned hastily to his own duties. He knew,
before he turned to face his customer, who she was. That
clipped authoritative boom could only belong to Miss Violet
Hurley, and it was a voice that commanded, and unfailingly
received, immediate attention.

'This way, ma'am,' said Bender, standing back to allow
Miss Hurley to enter. He inclined his broad back at a respectful
angle, for though the lady might buy nothing more than a
mouse trap, she was a sister of Sir Edmund Hurley at Springbourne, and gentry needed careful handling.

'Sharp shower, ma'am,' he added conversationally when he
was again behind the broad counter confronting his customer.
She stood there, gaunt and shabby, her scrawny neck ringed
with a rope of beautiful pearls, her sparse grey locks sticking
out from under her dusty feathered hat like straw from beneath
a ruffled hen.

'Hm!' grunted Miss Hurley shortly. Her foot tapped
ominously on Bender's bare boards. This was not the day for
airy nothings, Bender realized. Miss Hurley was in one of her
moods. She should have found him in the shop, not dallying
outside on the pavement. He reached down a large box from
the shelf behind him, blew off the dust delicately, and began
to display his wares.

' "The Break-back", "The Sterling", "The Invincible",

"The Elite",' chanted Bender, pushing them forward in turn. He took a breath and was about to extract more models from the bottom of the box but was cut short.

'Two "Sterling",' snapped Miss Hurley. 'Send them up. Immediately, mind. Book 'em as usual.'

She wheeled off to the door, her back like a ramrod, her bony legs, in their speckled woollen stockings, bearing her swiftly out into the sunshine.

'Thank you, ma'am,' murmured Bender, bowing gracefully. 'You ol' faggot!' he added softly as he straightened up again.

He wrapped up the two jangling mouse traps, tied the parcel neatly with string, and wrote: 'Miss V. Hurley, By Hand' with a stub of flat carpenter's pencil.

'Bob!' he shouted, without looking up from his work. 'Bob! Here a minute!'

Above his head the kettles, saucepans, fly swats and hob-nail boots which hung from the varnished ceiling, shuddered in the uproar. A door burst open at the far end of the shop, and a black-haired urchin with steel spectacles fell in.

'Sir?' gasped the boy.

'Miss Hurley's. At the double,' said Bender, tossing the parcel to him. The boy caught it and vanished through the open door into the market square.

'And wipe your nose!' shouted Bender after him. Duty done, he dusted the counter with a massive hand, and followed the boy into the bustle and sunshine of the market square.

The first thing that Bender saw was Miss Violet Hurley emerging from Sep Howard's bakery at the corner of the square. Sep himself, a small taut figure in his white overall, was showing his customer out with much the same deference as the ironmonger had displayed a few minutes earlier. He held a square white box in his hands, and followed the lady round the corner.

'Taking a pork pie home, I'll be bound,' thought Bender. Howard's raised pork pies were becoming as famous as his lardy cakes. There was something particularly succulent about the glazed golden pastry that brought the customers back for more, time and time again. Pondering on the pies, watching the pigeons paddling in the wet gutter, Bender decided to stroll over and buy one for the family supper.

He met Sep at the doorway of the baker's shop. The little man was breathless and for once his pale face was pink.

'Been running, Sep?' asked Bender jocularly, looking down from his great height.

'Just serving Miss Violet,' replied Septimus. He paused as though wondering if he should say more. Unwonted excitement nudged him into further disclosures.

'She's as good as promised me the order for Miss Frances' wedding cake,' he confided. 'You could've knocked me down with a feather.'

He hurried into the shop in front of Bender and scurried behind the counter. Beaming indulgently, Bender followed with heavy tread. The air was warm and fragrant with the delicious odours from steaming pies, pasties, scones, fruit cakes and a vast dark dish of newly-baked gingerbread, glistening with fat and black treacle.

Mrs Howard was serving. Her hands scrabbled among the wares, dropped them in paper bags, twirled the corners and received the money as though she had not a minute to lose. Howard's bakery was patronised by the stallholders as well as the town people on market day and trade was brisk.

'A pork pie, please, Sep,' said Bender. 'A big 'un. I'll pay now.'

He watched the baker inspecting the row of pies earnestly and felt amusement bubbling up in him. Same old Sep! Dead solemn whatever he was doing! Why, he'd seen him at school, years before, studying his sums with just that same patient worried look, anxious to do the right thing, fearful of causing offence.

'They all look good to me,' said Bender. 'Any of 'em'll suit me.' Lord love Almighty, he thought, we'll be here till Christmas if old Sep don't get a move on!

The baker lifted a beauty with care, put it in a bag and came round the counter to give it to Bender.

'I'll open the door for you,' he said. 'So many people pushing in you might get it broken.'

'That's what you want, ain't it?'

'You know that,' said Septimus earnestly.

They found themselves in the doorway, Sep still holding the bag.

'I should be able to let you have the last of the loan at the end of the week, Bender,' he said in a low voice.

'You don't want to fret yourself about that,' answered Bender, with rough kindness. 'No hurry as far as I'm concerned.'

'But there is as far as I am,' said Sep with dignity. 'I don't like to be beholden. Not that I'm not grateful, as you well know—'

'Say no more,' said Bender. 'Hand us the pie, man, and I'll be getting back to the shop.'

The baker handed it over and then looked about the market square as though he were seeing it for the first time.

'Nice bright day,' he said with some surprise.

'Expect it in June,' replied Bender. 'It'll be the longest day next week. Then we'll start seeing the trimmings going up. They tell me the Council's having bunting all round the square and down the High Street.'

'Well, it's over sixty years since the last Coronation,' said Septimus. 'About time we had a splash. It seems only yesterday we were decorating the town for the old Queen's Diamond Jubilee!'

'Four years ago,' commented Bender. 'That was a real do, wasn't it, Sep? Beer enough to float a battleship.'

He dug his massive elbow into the baker's thin ribs, and gave a roar of laughter that sent the pigeons fluttering. Septimus's white face grew dusky with embarrassment.

'Ah! I was forgetting you'd signed the pledge,' chuckled his tormentor. 'You'll have to change your ways now the war's over and we've got a new King. Be a bit more sporty, and enjoy life, Sep! Once we've crowned Edward the Seventh on June the twenty-sixth you'll find Caxley'll start fizzing. Keep up with the times, Sep my boy! You're not a Victorian any longer!'

Muttering some excuse the little baker hurried back to his customers, while Bender, balancing the fragrant white parcel on his great hand, strode back through the puddles and the pigeons, smiling at his secret thoughts.

* * *

Septimus stepped down into his busy shop, trying to hide the agitation this encounter had caused. Why should a brush with Bender always give him this sick fluttering in his stomach? He had known him all his life – been born within a few yards and in the same year as this man. They had shared schooldays, celebrations, football matches, and all the life of the little town, but always the rift remained.

'You're nothing but a yellow coward,' Sep told himself disgustedly, stacking hot loaves in the window. 'Why can't you meet Bender man to man? He's no better than you are. His joking's only a bit of fun, and yet you are all aquake the minute he starts to take a rise out of you.'

He watched Bender stopping to speak to one of the stall-holders. He saw his great shoulders heave with laughter as he turned again and vanished into the murk of his shop. At once Sep's tension relaxed, and he despised himself for it. Did Bender ever guess, he wondered, how much he affected other people?

Take this morning, for instance, thought the little baker, threading his way through the customers to the comparative peace of the bakehouse at the back. Bender could never have known how much he would upset him by talking of Queen Victoria like that. The death of the old Queen had shaken many people. Septimus Howard was one of them. She was more to him than a reigning monarch. She was the mother of her people, a symbol of security, prosperity and order. She offered an example of high-minded principles and respectable family life. She was the arch-matriarch of a great nation. And Septimus loved her.

He loved her because, in his eyes, she had always been right and she had always been there, safely on the throne of England. His father and mother, staunch Methodists both, had revered the Queen with almost as much piety as the stern God they worshipped, thrice every Sunday, at the Wesleyan Chapel in the High Street. Their children, with the possible exception of flighty Louisa, shared their parents' devotion.

Septimus knew he would never forget the shock of that terrible news which Caxley had heard only a few months before. It was a dark January afternoon, the shop was empty and Sep had been engaged in cutting wrapping paper ready for the next day's supplies. He saw Tom Bellinger, the verger of St Peter's across the square, hurry up the steps and disappear inside. Within three minutes the tolling bell began to send out its sad message.

Sep put aside his knife and went to the door.

'Who's gone?' he asked Sergeant Watts, the policeman, who was striding by.

'The Queen, God rest her,' he replied. For one moment they stood facing each other in silence, then the policeman hurried on, leaving Septimus too stricken to speak. He made his way to the quiet warmth of the bakehouse and sat down, stunned, at the great scrubbed table where he made the loaves, letting the tears roll unchecked down his cheeks. Not even when his father had died had he felt such a sense of loss. This was the end of life as he knew it. An England without Queen Victoria at its head seemed utterly strange and frightening.

Septimus disliked change. He was not sure that he wanted to be an Edwardian. Something in that new word made him as nervous as he felt in Bender's presence. He suspected that the new monarch had some of Bender's qualities; his gusto, his

19

hearty laugh, his ease of manner and his ability to know what the other fellow was thinking. The new King loved life. Septimus, his humble subject, was a little afraid of it. He mourned Victoria, not only for herself, but for all that she stood for – a way of life which had lasted for decades and which suited him, as it had suited so many of his fellow countrymen.

At the time of the Queen's Diamond Jubilee in 1897, a fund had been opened in Caxley to provide a lasting memorial of this outstanding reign. Septimus Howard was one of the first contributors. He gave as much as he could possibly afford, which was not a great deal, for times were hard with him just then, and his fourth child was about to be born. But he was proud to give, and prouder still when he stood in the market place, later that year, and watched the fine drinking fountain, surmounted by a statue of Her Majesty, being unveiled by the Mayor in his red robe of office.

Now four years later, the statue stood as an accepted landmark in Caxley. Children played on its steps and drank from the four iron cups chained at each corner of the plinth supporting the sovereign. The cheerful rogue who sold bunches of roses in the market, sprinkled his wilting blooms with water from the great basin, and Mrs Petty dipped in an enamel mug and sloshed the contents over the fish stall before the afternoon customers arrived. The fountain was much appreciated, and Caxley folk often wondered how they had managed so long without it.

But to Septimus, the statue above it gave greater comfort. He looked down upon it every morning whilst he shaved at the mahogany stand in the bedroom window. The view, it is true, was shrouded a little by the lace curtains which modestly covered the windows, but that morning glimpse of Victoria meant much to the little baker.

And now, on this hot June morning, with excitement mounting everywhere at the thought of the Coronation so soon to come, Sep looked again at the small bronze crown just showing above the flapping awnings in the market square. The shop was more crowded than ever, the heat was intense, the noise deafening, but Sep had found new strength.

Bender's visit, the thought of the money he owed him, the staggering news from Miss Violet about the order for her niece's wedding cake, suddenly seemed to matter less. Somehow, Sep knew, he would be able to face everything. Surely, to have spent all the thirty-five years of one's life with the example of the Queen to follow must give a chap enough strength to recognise and perform his duties, and to welcome her son without trepidation!

He squared his shoulders, dropped six sugary buns into a paper bag and handed it down to a waiting urchin.

'Threepence, my dear,' said Mr Howard the baker briskly.

All fears had gone, and Sep was himself again.

2

The Norths at Home

'NASTY ACCIDENT over at Beech Green,' observed Bender to his wife Hilda that evening.

'What's happened?' asked Mrs North, putting down the vast pair of trousers, belonging to her husband, which she was mending.

'Some youngster – forgotten his name – fell off the top of one of Miller's hay wagons. Young Jesse Miller was in the shop this afternoon. He told me. Just been up to see the boy at the hospital. Wheel went over his shoulder, so Jesse said. Pretty bad evidently.'

'People have no business to allow children to get into such danger,' said Hilda North firmly. 'Asking for trouble.'

Bender laughed.

'What about our kids and the boat?' he replied.

'I'm always saying,' retorted his wife, 'that I don't hold with it. One of these days one of ours will be drowned, and you'll only have yourself to blame, Bender.'

'You fret too much,' said Bender good-naturedly. 'They can all swim. What's the point in having a fine river like the Cax at the end of the garden if you don't have a bit of fun on it?'

His wife made no reply. This was an old argument and she had too much mending to get through to waste her energies that evening. Bender turned back to his desk and silence fell again in the sitting-room.

It was a vast, beautifully proportioned room on the first floor. It ran across the shop below and had three fine Georgian windows overlooking the market square. During the day, the room was flooded with sunlight, for it faced south, but now, at nine o'clock on a June evening, the room was in shadow, the gas lamp hissed gently in its globe on the ceiling, casting its light on Hilda's needlework and the great back of Bender bending over his crowded and untidy desk as he wrote out some bills.

Through the window before him he could see the last of the stallholders packing up. Two men with brooms were brushing up cabbage leaves, pieces of paper, orange peel and all the market day débris. The setting sun shone pinkly on the upper parts of the buildings at right angles to Bender's shop. Septimus's bedroom window gleamed like a sheet of gold as it caught the last hour or so of dying sunlight. Soon its light would be doused by the creeping shadow of St Peter's spire, which lengthened and climbed steadily up the west-facing shops and houses in the market square, like some gigantic candle snuffer.

It was quiet in the great room. Bender hummed now and again and shuffled his papers, a faint squeaking from Mrs North's well-laced stays could be heard when she moved to reach more thread from her work-box, and occasionally the whirring of a pigeon's wings as it returned to roost on the parapet of the North's roof.

At last, Bender pushed his papers carelessly to the back of the desk, anchored them with a small ancient flat-iron, and threw himself, with a contented grunt, into the arm chair opposite his wife.

23

'Why you use that ugly old thing for a paper-weight I can't think!' commented Hilda. 'What's wrong with the glass one we bought at Weymouth last summer?'

'Too fiddle-faddle,' answered Bender easily. 'I like my old dad's flat-iron.'

He began to fill his black Turk's head pipe with deliberation. The fragrance of strong tobacco crept about the room as the great china tobacco jar beside him stood un-stoppered. His big roughened fingers worked delicately at his task, and when the tobacco was tamped down exactly as he liked it Bender took a long paper spill from a vase on the mantel-piece and, crossing to the gas lamp, held it above the globe until it caught fire.

Soon the room was wreathed in clouds of blue smoke, the stopper was replaced and secured with a massive brass screw on the top of the tobacco jar, and Bender was prepared for his evening relaxation.

He looked about him with pleasure. His possessions – the dearest of them still busy with her mending – gave him enormous quiet pride. He liked the grey watered silk wall-paper that had been new when they married twelve years ago, and was now comfortably grubby. He liked the sofa, the arm-chairs and the two prim little occasional chairs, flanking the sofa, all upholstered in good dark red velvet. He liked the heavy mahogany sideboard, richly carved, and crowded permanently with silver, china, bronze, as well as the ephemera of daily living such as letters awaiting answers, bundles of knitting, indigestion tablets, and spectacle cases.

There was something particularly satisfying too about the octagonal mahogany table which stood always by his armchair. His niece had worked the pink and red silk roses on the black satin mat, which stood plumb in the table top's centre. It was a handsome piece of work for a twelve-year-old to have accomplished, thought Bender approvingly, and she had finished it with a splendid silky fringe a good two inches in length. She had also made a companion piece which ran the length of the top of the walnut piano against the wall. Its beauties were somewhat hidden by Hilda's group of naked china cherubs and the two great nautilus shells which stood on each side of them, but the little girl's workmanship was much admired by those waiting to sing, one elbow lodged nonchalantly on the black satin runner while the accompanist was propping the music on the music rest.

No doubt about it, thought Bender puffing dreamily, it looked rich, and he liked richness. His eye roamed indulgently over the crowded room, the wide wooden picture frames, the chenille curtains looped back with fine brass bands, and the cases of dried grasses and sea lavender on the corner brackets near by. It looked the sort of place a prosperous tradesman deserved, and he was indeed prospering. His wandering gaze came to rest upon his wife, now snipping busily at a frayed lining. It was to Hilda, as much as anything else, that he owed his growing prosperity. She worked as hard – harder maybe, thought Bender candidly – than he did himself. When they were first married they had thought nothing of being in the shop at seven in the morning until nine or ten at night. Somehow she had still managed to clean and cook, to sew and knit, and to bring up the family to be as industrious as she was herself.

She was a small plump young woman, fair-haired, and grey-eyed, with a pink button of a mouth, not unlike the old queen in her younger days. The bearing of three children – the first tragically stillborn – had thickened her waist a little, but tight lacing kept her figure still trim and shapely. To Bender's delight, she loved bright colours, unlike many matrons of her own age and times, and tonight she wore a lilac print frock decorated with bands of purple braid. Beneath its hem Bender could see her small black shoes adorned with cut steel buckles.

She looked across at him quickly, aware of his gaze.

'Where was Jesse Miller off to?' she enquired, harking back to the snippet of news.

'Never asked him. Beech Green, I should think. He'd done his buying at market and seen the young chap in hospital.'

'More likely to have gone up to my home,' commented Hilda. 'Pa says he's been calling to see our young Ethel lately.'

'Why not?' said Bender, smiling lazily. 'He must be twenty-odd, going to have a good farm with his brother Harold, when the old man goes aloft, and I reckon Ethel'd be lucky to get him.'

'He's a bit wild, they say,' responded Hilda, letting her mending fall into her lap and looking into the distance.

'Who's "they"?' asked Bender testily. 'There's too much gossip in Caxley. People here mind everyone else's business but their own! Makes me sick!'

He tapped out his pipe irritably.

'I'd sooner see young Ethel wed to Jesse Miller,' he continued, 'than that waster Dan Crockford she's so sweet on! What's the future in painting pictures for a living? He wants to get down to a job of work and keep his paint brushes for the week-end. If I were Dan Crockford's father I'd chuck him out to fend for himself! No, our Ethel's better off as a farmer's wife, and I hope she'll have the sense to see it!'

'Well, well, well! Don't get ratty about it,' replied his wife equably. 'They're both old enough to know their own minds, and it's time Ethel settled down.'

She rolled up the trousers briskly, and stood up, picking ends of thread from the lilac frock with quick pink fingers.

'Let's take a turn in the garden before we go up,' she said. 'It's still so hot. I wonder if the children are feeling it? Bertie was tossing and turning when I went up just now.'

Bender lumbered to his feet.

'They'll be all right. The girl's up there if they want anything. Come and look at the river, my dear.'

She led the way down the staircase, pausing on the landing, head cocked on one side for any sound from above. But all was silent. They made their way through the little parlour behind the shop, and the great shadowy store shed which housed ironmongery of every shape and size, and smelt of paint and polish, tar and turpentine, and the cold odour of stone floors, and cast iron girders.

It was almost dark when they emerged into the garden. It was small, with a brick wall on each side, and a lawn which ran gently down to the banks of the Cax. The air was soft and warm, and fragrant with the roses which climbed over the walls and the white jasmine starring the rustic arch which spanned the side path. Bender's shop might be villainously untidy and his desk chaotic. His neighbours might scoff at his muddles there, but here, in the garden, Bender kept everything in orderly beauty.

27

The river, lapping at the bank, kept his soil moist even in the blazing heat of such a spell as this. The Norths had always been great gardeners, and Bender was one of the best of his family. He looked about his trim flower beds with pride.

A rustic seat stood close by the river and here the two sat, while the midges hummed and a bat darted back and forth above the water. Sitting there, with the peace of the summer evening about them, was pleasantly relaxing.

'Where does it go?' asked Hilda suddenly.

'What? The river?'

'Yes. Does it go to London?'

'Must do, I suppose. The Cax runs into the Thames about fifteen to twenty miles east, so they told us at school, if I recall it aright.'

'Seems funny, doesn't it,' said Hilda dreamily, 'to think it goes past our garden and then right up to London. Sees a bit of life when it gets there. Specially just now with the streets being decked up for the Coronation. It said in the paper today that no end of royalty have arrived already, and troops from Canada and Australia for the procession. Wouldn't it be lovely if we could go, Bender? I'd give my eye teeth for a sight of the Coronation, wouldn't you?'

Bender smiled indulgently at this womanly excitement.

'I'm quite content to watch the Caxley flags and fairy-lights next week,' he replied. 'Maybe have a drink or two, and keep a lookout for the bonfire up on the beacon. We'll give the King a good send-off, you'll see, without having to traipse to London for a bit of fun.'

His wife sighed, and was about to speak when she caught

sight of something white glimmering in the shadows of the fuchsia bush, and went over to investigate.

'What is it?' asked Bender following her. Hilda was turning a little white yacht in her hands.

'It must be the Howard children's,' she said. 'Bertie asked them over to bathe after tea. They've forgotten it. Another trip to make, running after them.' There was a tartness in her tone which did not escape her husband's ear.

'Only child-like,' he commented easily. 'I'm glad Bertie thought of asking them. They've nowhere to play in their baker's yard. Not much fun there for kids this weather.'

'Oh, I don't mind the *children*,' said Hilda, a trifle pettishly. 'And Septimus is all right.'

It's strange how she always calls him Septimus and not Sep, as everyone else does, thought Bender. These little primnesses about his wife never failed to amuse him. The fact that she could never bring herself to ask the butcher for belly of pork, but always asked delicately for stomach of pork, delighted Bender perennially.

'It's Edna I can't take to,' went on Hilda. 'Try as I might there's something about her – I don't know. I can't think what Septimus saw in her, respectable as he is.'

She had picked a tasselled blossom from the fuchsia bush and now tossed it petulantly into the darkening water. Bender put a massive arm round her plump shoulders.

'Are you sending your contribution to the Coronation decorations?' he asked jocularly, nodding towards the floating flower. 'It should get to Westminster in a couple of days.'

'And keep fresh in the water,' agreed his wife, smiling. Bender congratulated himself on his success in changing the subject. Once embarked on the ways of Edna Howard, Hilda could become mighty waspish for such a good-natured wife.

At that moment, the quarters chimed across the market square from St Peter's, and Hilda became agitated.

'Gracious me! That must be half past ten, and I've not had a word with Vera! You lock up, Ben, while I run upstairs.'

She flitted away from him across the grass, as light on her feet as when he first met her, thought her husband watching her depart.

He turned for a last look at the Cax before following her into the house. The twilight had deepened now into an amethyst glow. The river glided slowly round the great curve which swept eastward, shining like a silver ribbon beneath the darkening sky. Say what you like, Bender told himself, Caxley in June took a lot of beating! Let the whole world flock to London to see the King crowned! This was good enough for Bender North!

He picked up the toy boat from the rustic seat. Tomorrow he'd take it back himself to Sep's youngsters. No point in upsetting Hilda with it.

He left it on the bench in the store shed, where his eye could light on it in the morning, locked and bolted the doors of his domain, and made his way contentedly to bed.

3

Consternation in Caxley

THE BUNTING was going up all over England, under the bright June skies. In the villages round about Caxley there was a joyful bustle of Coronation preparations. At Fairacre School an ambitious maypole dance was causing heartache to the infants' teacher there, and bewilderment to the young fry who lumbered round and round, ribbons in hand, weaving the biggest and brightest tangle ever seen in the history of the parish.

On the downs above Beech Green a great pile of faggots was outlined against the clear sky, waiting for a torch to be plunged into its heart on June the twenty-sixth. The blaze would be visible from four counties, the old men told each other, and some said that they could remember their fathers talking of the blazing beacon, on the self-same spot, which had celebrated the end of the Napoleonic Wars.

The drapers in Caxley were running short of red, white and blue ribbon, and the little saddler in West Street was surprised to find that his horse-braid in these three colours was in demand, not only for plaiting manes and other orthodox uses, but also for decorating trestle tables, oil lamps in village halls, and even for tying patriotic children's hair now that all the ribbon had been snapped up by early shoppers.

The market square at Caxley blossomed like a rose. Strings of fairy lights were festooned round the sides of the square and tubs of red and white geraniums, edged with lobelia, flanked the steps of Queen Victoria's plinth. Less happy was the arrangement of red, white and blue ribbons radiating from an erection on the crown of Her Imperial Majesty. Like the spokes of a wheel they formed a circular canopy rather like that of Fairacre's maypole in readiness for the troublesome dance. Septimus Howard looking down on it from his bedroom window, cut-throat razor in hand, thought it looked as garish as the market place at Michaelmas Fair. He overheard an old countryman observe to his crony as he surveyed this centrepiece:

'Fair *tawdry*, 'ennit, Ern?' and, privately, Sep heartily agreed with him.

It was on the evening of the twenty-fourth that the blow fell. King Edward had been stricken with appendicitis. He was dangerously ill. The Coronation would have to be postponed. This was no time for rejoicing, but for earnest prayer for the King's recovery. There were those who said that was doubtful – but, as Bender North said stoutly – there are dismal johnnies everywhere at such times, and they should not be heeded.

It was Edna Howard who had brought the dire tidings to North's shop, and thus added yet another misdeed, in Hilda's eyes, to those already committed. The shop was closed, but Bender was still tidying shelves and sweeping odd scraps from counter to floor with a massive hand.

Hilda stood at the door, and watched Edna Howard advance across the square, with that lilting gait, and proud turn of her dark head, which irritated Hilda so unaccountably. Edna was a tall woman, large bosomed, and long-legged, with a mass of black silky hair. Her eyes were quick and dark, starred with thick black lashes, and with an odd slant to them which told of gipsy blood. For Edna Howard had been a Bryant before her marriage, the only girl among a tribe of stalwart boys. Her mother had been a true gipsy, who had left her wandering family when she married a doting farm labourer and settled near Fairacre to produce a family of her own.

There was something foreign and wild about Edna Howard which stolid Caxley inhabitants could not understand. In the country, memories are long, and despite Edna's respectable marriage, her industry in the shop and home, and her devoted care of her children, Edna's exotic streak was the first thing to be mentioned when the worthies discussed her.

'Plenty of the ol' gyppo about that 'un,' they said. 'Remember her ma? Used to come round with a basket o' pegs not so long ago.'

Edna knew very well the sort of remark that was made behind her back, and gave no hint of caring. She dressed in colours that were gaudy in comparison with those worn by her sedate neighbours. Sometimes she knotted a bright silk scarf about her throat, gipsy fashion, as though flaunting her origin, and on her wrist she jangled a coin bracelet which had once been her gipsy grandmother's.

Two other qualities added to Edna's colourful character. She possessed a thrillingly deep contralto voice and she could play the banjo. For some reason, Caxley approved of the first gift but was somewhat shocked by the second. Occasionally, Mrs Howard was invited to sing at charity concerts, by ladies who were organising these affairs. The fact that she was an accomplished banjoist was known, but ignored, by the organisers. 'Sweet and Low', rendered by Mrs Septimus

Howard to the decorous accompaniment on the pianoforte by the Vicar's son was permissible in the Corn Exchange. Edna Howard, let loose with her banjo, might prove a trifle vulgar, it was felt.

How meek little Septimus had ever managed to capture this wild bright bird was one of the mysteries of Caxley history. That Edna Bryant was 'one for the boys' was well-known. She could have picked a husband from among dozens who courted her from the time she was fifteen. Perhaps Sep's wistful shyness was the main attraction, contrasting so strongly with her own vivid confidence. In any case, the marriage had flourished, despite much early head-shaking, and Edna Howard was outwardly accepted in Caxley life.

Hilda unbolted the shop door and let Edna in with a polite smile. Bender's was considerably more welcoming. He liked a handsome woman, and he didn't much mind if Hilda knew it.

'Come on in, Edna,' he shouted heartily. She rewarded him with a warm smile and a provocative glance from under her dark lashes which Hilda did her best to ignore.

'Just brought the pattern I promised you,' said Edna, holding out an envelope. 'It turned out fine for Kathy, and you only need a yard and a half.'

'Thank you,' replied Hilda. 'You shouldn't have bothered, 'specially leaving the children in bed.'

This was a shrewd blow, and was not missed either by Edna or Bender. Under the surface solicitude, the sentence managed to imply parental neglect and to draw attention to the fact that Edna had no resident help in the house to mind her offspring, as Hilda herself had.

'Sep's there,' said Edna shortly. She put up a dusky thin

hand to brush back a wisp of hair. The coin bracelet jingled gaily.

'You heard the news?' she continued. There was a hint of excitement in her casual tone.

'What about?' said Bender, coming forward. He was frankly interested to know what was afoot. Hilda assumed an air of indifference. Really, local tittle-tattle did not interest her! She blew some dust from a box of screws with an expression of distaste.

'The King!' said Edna. 'They say he's been took bad, and the Coronation's off.'

Hilda was shaken from her lofty attitude. Her mouth fell open into a round pink O.

'You don't say! The poor dear! What's the matter?'

'The King!' echoed Bender, thunderstruck. 'You sure this is true?'

'Gospel! Had it from Lord Turley's coachman. He told him himself. Lord Turley's just got back from London on the train.'

This was news indeed.

'But what about all this 'ere?' spluttered Bender, waving a large, dirty hand at the bedecked market place.

'And the parties? And the concerts and all that?' echoed Hilda, all dignity forgotten in the face of this calamity.

'And what about poor Sep's baking?' retorted Edna. 'He's got a bakehouse chock full of iced cakes, and sausage rolls, and a great batch of dough ready for the buns. I tell you, it's ruination for us, as well as bad luck for the King!'

Bender's face grew grave. He knew, only too well, the narrow margin between Sep's solvency and his business downfall. He spoke with forced cheerfulness.

'Don't you fret about that, Edna. It won't be as bad as you think. But do the Council know? Has the Mayor been told? And what about the vicar? Ought to be summat done about a service pretty sharp.'

Edna did not know. Her cares were all for the King's condition and her husband's set-backs.

'I'll be getting back,' she said, putting the paper pattern on the counter. There was a hint of sadness now in her downcast countenance which stirred Hilda's conscience.

'Now, Edna, don't you worry,' she said, with unaccustomed gentleness. 'It's a sore blow for everyone, but the one who's suffering most is poor Queen Alexandra, and the Family too. There'll be another Coronation as soon as the King's fit, you'll see, my dear, and then all our troubles will be over.'

She walked with Edna to the door and let her out, watching her walk back across the square beneath the fluttering flags. Hardly had she closed the door when one of the Corporation's carts, drawn by two great carthorses, clattered to the centre of the market square. Two men jumped down and began to remove the ribbons which bedizened the statue of the old Queen. At the same moment the bell of St Peter's began to ring out, calling all parishioners to prayer.

'Let's go, Bender,' said Hilda suddenly.

Without a word, Bender removed his overall, and accompanied his wife aloft to fetch jacket, hat and gloves.

Within three minutes, the Norths with other bewildered Caxley folk, crossed the market square, fast being denuded of its finery, and, with heavy hearts, entered the sombre porch of the parish church.

*   *   *

From a top floor window, high above the ironmonger's shop, young Bertie North looked down upon the scene, unknown to his parents.

It is difficult to go to sleep on summer evenings when you are eight years old and put to bed firmly at seven o'clock. Bertie resented this early bed-time. Just because Winnie, two years his junior, had to go then, it seemed mighty unfair to expect a man of his advanced age to retire simply because it saved trouble for Vera, the girl. He did not make a fuss about the matter. Bertie North was a peace-loving child, and did not want to upset Vera, the fourteen-year-old country girl from Beech Green, who worked hard from seven in the morning until the North children were in bed at night.

But the injustice rankled. And tonight, as he stood at the high window in his cotton night-shirt, he felt even more resentful, for there, far below, he could see the two Howard boys. They were hopping gaily about the statue, watching all the activity of taking down the ribbons and fairy lights. Bertie had seen them bob down behind the stone plinth to hide from their mother as she made her way home from visiting his own parents.

They weren't made to go to bed so early! Of course, thought Bertie reasonably, they were much older than he was; Jim was twelve, and Leslie was ten. His particular friend, Kathy, who was only seven, had to go to bed when her little brother did, just as he did. This crumb of cold comfort went a small way towards consoling the boy gazing down at the enviable freedom of the older children.

The bell stopped ringing, and the everyday noises could be heard once more. The clop of the horses' great shaggy hooves, as they moved across the cobblestones of the market square, mingled with the screaming of swifts round the spire of St Peter's. Behind him, in one of the back bedrooms looking across the river Cax, he could hear Vera singing to herself as she darned socks.

There were four little bedrooms at the top of the tall old house. Bertie and Winnie had one each overlooking the square. Vera had another, and the fourth was known as 'the boxroom' and was filled with the most fascinating objects, from a dress-maker's model, with a formidable bust covered in red sateen and a wire skirt, to a dusty pile of framed portraits of North ancestors complete with cravats, pomaded locks and beards.

These old be-whiskered faces intrigued young Bertie. He liked to think that he belonged to the same family; that they too had once been his age, had run across the market square with their iron hoops as he did, and floated their toy boats on the placid face of the river Cax. His father and mother had been patient in answering his questions, and he already had an idea of his respectable background. Brought up in a community which recognised the clear divisions of class, Bertie knew the Norths' place in the scale and was happy to be there.

The Norths were middle class. They were respected trades-people, church-goers and, best of all, comfortably off. Bertie was glad he was not in the class above his – the gentry. Their children were sent away to school or had stern governesses. Their fathers and mothers seemed to be away from home a great deal. It would not have suited Bertie. Sometimes a passing pang of envy shot through him when he saw his betters on ponies of their own, for Bertie loved horses dearly. But there was always the sturdy little cob that pulled Uncle

Ted's trap in the High Street, and on this the boy lavished his affection.

He was even more thankful that he did not belong to the class below, the poor. The people who lived in the low-lying area of Caxley, called 'The Marsh', were objects of pity and a certain measure of fear. Respectable children were not allowed to roam those dark narrow streets alone. On winter nights, the hissing gas lamp on the corner of the lane leading from the High Street to the marsh, simply accentuated the sinister murk of the labyrinth of alleys and small courtyards which were huddled, higgledy-piggledy, behind the gracious façade of the Georgian shop fronts.

Other people – far too many of them for Bertie's tender heart – were also poor. He saw them in his father's shop, thin, timid, unpleasantly smelly, rooting in their pockets or worn purses for the pence to pay for two screws, a cheap pudding basin, or a little kettle. They were pathetically anxious not to give any trouble.

'Don't 'ee bother to wrap it, sir,' they said to Bender deferentially.

'It don't matter if it's a mite rusty,' said another one day. ' 'Twill be good enough for I.'

It seemed strange to the listening boy, his head not far above the counter, that the poor whose money was so precious, should be content to accept shoddy goods, whereas those with plenty of money should make such a terrible fuss if there were the slightest fault in their purchases.

'What the hell d'you mean, North, by sending up this rubbish?' old Colonel Enderby had roared, flinging a pair of heavy gate hinges on to the counter, with such force that they skidded across, and would have crashed into young Bertie's chin if he had not ducked smartly. 'They're scratched!'

His father's politeness, in the face of this sort of behaviour, brought home to his son the necessity for knowing one's place on the social ladder. But it did not blind the child to a certain unfairness in his world's structure.

Standing at the high window, his bare feet growing more and more chilly on the cold linoleum, a new thought struck Bertie, as he watched Jim and Leslie far below. Were the Howards poor? They certainly had plenty to eat, delicious pies, new crusty loaves, and cakes in plenty; but they had very few toys, and Bertie's mother often gave Mrs Howard clothes, which Winnie had outgrown, for Kathy.

He remembered too, with some shock, that Jim's and Leslie's grandmother was old Mrs Bryant, the gipsy, who sometimes came into the shop, bent under her dirty black shawl. She certainly was poor. She spoke in a whining nasal voice and Bertie had heard her ask his father to take less than the marked price.

Did this mean that the Howard boys were on a par with the marsh children? His mother certainly spoke with some condescension about the Howards, Bertie recalled, but he knew very well that he would not be allowed to play with the marsh folk. Obviously then, the Howards were acceptable as play fellows.

It was all very puzzling, thought Bertie, resting his forehead against the cold glass. As far as he was concerned, Jim and Leslie were friends, even heroes, for when one is only eight one looks up to those of ten and twelve, especially when they are gracious enough to accept one's homage.

Through the window-pane, now misted with his breath, Bertie saw Mrs Howard appear at the shop door and beckon her sons inside. Reluctantly, with backward glances, they obeyed and Bertie watched them vanish indoors. The shop door closed with a bang.

'Now *they've* got to go to bed!' said Bertie with satisfaction. And with this comforting thought he bounded into his own and was asleep in five minutes.

4

First Encounter

THE KING recovered, and the nation rejoiced. Now the Coronation would be on August the ninth. The decorations, so sadly taken down, were restored to their places, and Queen Victoria peered once more from beneath her ribbon umbrella. The bells of St Peter's rang out merrily, calling across the countryside to a hundred others pealing from tower or soaring spire, among the downs and water meadows around Caxley.

Septimus Howard was doubly thankful for the King's recovery. On the morning after Edna's visit to Bender's shop he had called there himself, pale with anxiety. Bender had ushered him into the shop-parlour and closed the door.

'Say nothing, Sep,' he said. 'I know how it is.'

'I've got to say something,' burst out poor Sep. 'I haven't had a wink all night. I stand to lose nigh on forty pounds with cancelled orders, I reckon, and I can't see my way clear to paying you back what I owe for many a week.'

He passed an agitated hand over his white face.

'Look here, Sep,' rumbled Bender, 'you've got nothing to worry about. I know my money's safe enough. It'll come back one day, and it don't matter to me just when. Your business is coming along a fair treat. These 'ere set-backs happen to us all – but you keep plodding on, boy.'

He smote the smaller man a heartening blow on the shoulder

which made his teeth rattle. Sep managed to produce a wan smile.

'It's good of you, Bender,' he began, but was cut short.

'More to the point, Sep – have you got enough to tide you over? Do you want a mite more till this business is straightened out?'

Sep's pale face flushed. His eyes were unhappy. He looked through the glass partition between the parlour and the shop and gazed at the kettles and saucepans, dangling from the ceiling there, with unseeing eyes.

'I think so. I think so, Bender. I'll know more tomorrow, and I don't want to borrow from you if I can help it. You've been generous enough already.'

He rose from the horse-hair chair and made his way to the door.

'Must get back to the shop. Plenty to do over there. People want loaves even if they don't want Coronation cakes.'

He turned and put out a timid hand. Bender gripped it painfully and pumped his arm vigorously up and down.

'Don't let things get you down, Sep,' boomed Bender cheerfully. 'That shop o' yours will be blooming gold mine before you know where you are. Keep at it, old chap!'

'I only hope you're right,' poor Sep had replied, hurrying back to his duties.

But by August the ninth, with Coronation orders renewed, Sep had recovered his losses and made a handsome profit besides. By the end of that month, when he settled down, with Edna beside him, to cast up his accounts, he found that for the first time he was out of debt. Bender's loan had been repaid, so that the shop, furnishings, bakehouse and machinery, were now entirely their own. It was a day of thankful celebration in the Howard household.

From that moment, it seemed, fortune began to smile upon Sep and his family. The wedding cake for Miss Frances Hurley had been a creation of exquisite fragility, much commented upon by other well-born matrons at the wedding with daughters in the marriage lists. Sep's handiwork, and his competitive prices, were noted, and many an order came his way. Howard's bakery was beginning to earn the fine reputation it deserved. Sep himself could hardly believe his luck. Edna, excited by more money, needed restraining from gay and frivolous expenditure.

'Don't fritter it away,' begged poor Sep, bewildered but still prudent. ' 'Tis wrong, Edna, to be too free. There'll be plenty more rainy days to face. One swallow don't make a summer.'

With these and other cautious warnings Sep did his best to cool Edna's excitement. His strong chapel-guided principles deplored show and waste. Thrift, modesty and humble bearing were ingrained in the little baker. He thanked his Maker for blessings received, but was too apprehensive to expect them to continue indefinitely. Nevertheless, a tidy sum began to accumulate steadily in the bank, the Howard boys had a new bicycle apiece, Edna glowed from beneath a pink hat, nodding with silk roses, as the Howards, as well as the Norths, began to share in the genial prosperity of Edward's golden reign.

It was a perfect time to be young. As the serene years slipped by, as slow and shining as the peaceful river Cax, the young

Howards and Norths enjoyed all the wholesome pleasures of a small and thriving community. There was always something going on at the Corn Exchange, for this was the era of endless good works 'in aid of the poor' who were, alas, as numerous as ever. Concerts, plays, tableaux vivants, dances, socials, whist drives and even roller-skating, followed each other in quick succession. The talent was local, the organisation was local, and the appreciative audiences and participants were local too. There was something particularly warming in this family atmosphere. It had its stresses and strains, as all family relationships have, but the fact that each was known to the other, the virtues, the vices, the oddities and quirks of each individual were under common scrutiny, made for interest and amusement and bound the community at large with ties of affection and tolerance.

Bertie North now attended the town's grammar school daily and Winnie was one of the first pupils at the new girls' county school. Neither was outstandingly academic, but they were reasonably intelligent, obedient and hard-working, and became deeply attached to their local schools, an affection which was to last a lifetime.

Despite the modest fees asked by these two establishments, and the diverse backgrounds of the pupils there, Sep could not bring himself to send his children to either, and they walked daily to the same National School in the High Street where he and Bender had been educated. The schooling was sound and the discipline strict. Bender, knowing something of Sep's finances, often argued with him to send his children elsewhere, but Sep was unwontedly stubborn on this point.

'The old school was good enough for me, Bender,' he

replied. 'It'll do for my boys. No need for them to get ideas above their place.' And no amount of argument could budge him.

The children did not worry their heads about such distinctions. Life was much too full and fascinating. Every Thursday the market square's usual hum rose to a crescendo of shouting and clattering as the weekly market took place. The North and Howard children loved Thursdays. The day began very early, for long before breakfast time at seven o'clock the rumble of carts and the clop of horses' hooves woke the square. By the time the children set off for school everything was in full swing. Prudent town shoppers had already filled their baskets with fresh fruit and greens from the surrounding countryside before the country dwellers themselves arrived by trap or carrier cart to fill their own baskets with more sophisticated things. Everywhere was the sound of hooves and the sweet-sharp smell of horses.

For this was the golden age of the horse. Family coaches, some with fine crests on the doors, still rumbled through Caxley from London to the west. Glossy carriages, with equally glossy high-steppers, bore the local gentry from one tea-party to another. Broughams and landaus, gigs and phaetons, traps and governess carts tapped and stuttered, rattled and reeled, round the square and onward. In the dusty country lanes, massive hay carts and wagons piled high with sacks or sheaves, swayed like galleons, with slow majesty, behind the teams of great cart horses, shaggy of hoof and mild of eye. The music of the horse and carriage was everywhere, the thunder of wheels and hoofs acting as bass to the treble of cracked whip and jingling harness. And always, as added accompaniment, there was the cry of man to horse, the encouraging chirrup, the staccato command, the endearment, with the appreciative snort or excited whinny in reply. It was an age when the horse was king, and his stabling, fodder and well-being were paramount. He provided transport and labour, and the calm bright world was geared to his pace. The animal kingdom from man himself, who harnessed that willing and beautiful energy, down to the lowliest sparrow which fed upon his droppings, acknowledged the horse as peer. The thought that the smelly and new-fangled motor-car might one day supersede the horse never entered the heads of ordinary folk. Wasn't it true that London made the carriages, and England supplied the horses, for all the world? Nothing could alter that invincible fact.

It was the horse, in all its infinite variety, that the three boys chiefly encountered on their bicycle rides. Within five minutes of leaving the throbbing market place, they could be in the leafy lanes that led north, south, east and west from Caxley. The wide fields were fragrant with cut hay or bean flowers, freshly ploughed earth or ripe corn according to the season. The hedges were snowy with blossom or beaded with shiny berries. Blackbirds darted across their path. Speckled thrushes sang their hearts out from sprays of pear blossom in cottage gardens. There were butterflies of every hue fluttering on the flowered verges of the roadside, and when the boys rested in the cool grass under the shade of a hedge, they could hear all around them the tiny quiet noises of the countryside. Somewhere, high above, a lark carolled. In the dark thickness of the hedge a mouse scuffled the dry leaves stealthily. A bee bumbled lazily at the orange lips of toadflax flowers, and little winged insects hummed in the sunlight. These were the long happy hours of childhood which the boys were never to forget. The gentle countryside and its quiet villages were theirs to explore, and Caxley, small and secure, the beginning and the end of every adventure. Nothing, it seemed, could ruffle Caxley's age-old order.

But something did. In the midst of this halcyon period an event occurred which was to have far-reaching consequences. It began innocently enough, as such things so often do. It began with Dan Crockford's sudden hunger for one of Sep Howard's lardy cakes.

Daniel Crockford had lived in Caxley all his life, as had generations of Crockfords before him. The family had supplied woollen cloth to the town, and to all England – and parts of Europe for that matter – from the time when Caxley, in the sixteenth century, was building its prosperity from this industry. The family still owned a mill, but now it was a flour mill, some half-mile along the bank of the Cax from the market square.

Crockfords had played their part in the town's history and were well-liked. They had been Mayors, churchwardens, sidesmen, councillors, magistrates and generous benefactors to many causes. But not one of them, until Dan appeared, had ever had anything to do with the arts. It would be true to say that the world of the imagination was looked upon with considerable suspicion and complete lack of interest by the worthy Crockfords.

It was all the more shocking, therefore, when the adolescent

Daniel proclaimed that he intended to be an artist. His father was impatient, his mother tearful. What would the neighbours say?

'They'll say you're plain stark mad,' announced his father flatly. 'The mill needs you. There's a living waiting for you. If you must paint, then have the common sense to do it in your spare time!'

'They'll say you're no better than you should be,' wailed his mother. 'You know how wild and shameless artists are! It's common knowledge! Oh, the disgrace to us all!'

The young man remained unmoved. A few uncomfortable months passed and at last his father paid for him to go to an art school in London for two years.

'Let him work it out of his system,' he growled to his wife. But Dan throve on the work, his reports were reassuring and he returned to his home determined to make painting his career. His father, seeing that the boy's mind was made up, had a studio built at the back of the house in Caxley, and let him have his way. There were other sons to take an interest in the mill, and Dan had a small income from an indulgent uncle and godfather which covered his essential needs. The Crockford family was resigned to the black sheep among the rest of the flock.

Dan sold an occasional landscape to various local people who had wall space to fill. His views of the Cax were considered very pretty and life-like. His portraits were thought unflattering, and rather too garish in colour. With photography becoming so cheap and reliable it seemed sinful to spend so much money on having a portrait painted which might not please when it was done.

But Dan worked away happily, and did not appear to mind that the stacks of paintings grew in his studio and very seldom sold. He was a large handsome man of flamboyant appearance, with a wealth of red hair and a curling red beard. He loved food, and he loved drink even more. Tales of Dan Crockford's prowess in the bars of Caxley and the country inns near by grew tall in the telling. He wore a dark wide-brimmed hat and big floppy silk ties. He had taken up the work of an artist, and he intended to make it plain. Needless to say, he was looked upon in Caxley as a somewhat worthless character, and his family, everyone said, was to be pitied.

On this particular morning, Dan had spent over an hour in cleaning his brushes and his nostrils were filled with the reek of turpentine. It was a soft May morning and the door of the studio was propped open with an old velvet-covered chair. On it, asleep in the sunshine, the family tabby cat rested a chin on its outstretched paws.

The turpentine had run out, and intrigued with the texture and markings of the cat's leonine head, Dan took a piece of charcoal and began to sketch intently. He brushed in the soft ruff, the upward sweep of grey whiskers and the fluff protruding from the pricked black ears. Delicately he sketched in the intricate frown marks of the forehead, the rows of black dots from which sprang whiskers on the upper part of the muzzle, and the bars which ran, echelon fashion, along each jaw.

He began to feel excitement rising. The sketch was good. He selected a firmer piece of charcoal and began the difficult job of emphasising the streak of each closed eye and the puckering of the mouth.

Suddenly, the cat woke, yawned, leapt down and vanished. Furious, Dan swore, flung away the charcoal and burst from the studio into the garden. He found that he was shaking with fury. He would take a brief walk to calm himself. He picked up the empty turpentine bottle, resolved to get it filled at North's, have a quick drink and return to work.

Swinging the bottle, his great hat crammed on the back of his red head, he strode through the market place. There were several people outside the baker's shop and he was forced to step close to the window in order to pass them. A wave of spicy fragrance floated from the open. Sep was putting a trayful of sticky brown lardy cakes in the window, and Dan realised that he was desperately hungry. He stepped down into the shop, and saw, for the first time, Edna Howard.

It was a shock as sudden and delightful as a plunge into the Cax on a hot afternoon. Dan knew beauty, when he saw it, by instinct and by training. This was the real thing, warm, gracious, dynamic. In one intent glance he noted the dark soft wings of hair, the upward sweep of the cheekbones, the angle of the small pink ears, and the most beautiful liquid brown eyes he had ever seen. Dan gazed in amazement. To think that this beauty had remained hidden from him so long!

'Sir?' asked Sep deferentially.

Dan wrenched his eyes away.

'Oh, ah!' he faltered. He fumbled in his pocket for a sixpence. 'One of your lardy cakes, if you please.'

While Sep busied himself in wrapping up his purchase in fine white paper, Dan looked again. Edna had walked across the shop to a shelf where she was stacking loaves. Her figure was as exquisite as her face, her movements supple. There

51

was something oddly foreign about her which excited Dan.

He found Sep holding out the bag. He was looking at him curiously.

'Thanks. Good day to you,' said Dan briskly, and departed towards the river bank.

There, sitting on the grassy bank beneath a may tree, he devoured his fresh, warm lardy cake and made plans.

She must sit for him. He must go back again and ask her. She was the perfect subject for his type of portrait – full of colour, warmth and movement. She must be Sep Howard's wife. He groped in his memory.

Of course! What had the old wives said? 'He married beneath him – a *Bryant*, you know!'

Dan leapt to his feet, and banged the crumbs from his clothes.

' "The gipsy",' he cried. 'That's what we'll call it: "The Gipsy Girl"!'

5

Domestic Rebellion

DAN FOUGHT down the impulse to return at once to Sep's shop and hurried home instead. By judicious questioning of his mother, he confirmed that the beautiful girl was indeed Sep Howard's wife.

In his studio, he wrote a brief note to say that he would give himself the pleasure of calling upon Mr and Mrs Howard that evening at eight o'clock, on a matter of business, and dispatched it by the little maid-of-all-work. The hours until that time seemed excessively tedious to the impatient artist.

'I can't think why he didn't say anything in the shop this morning,' said Sep, much puzzled, as he read the note.

'Maybe it's only just come to his mind,' suggested Edna, busy mending baby clothes and not much interested in the letter.

'Seems funny to address it to *both* of us,' went on Sep. Dan Crockford's open admiration of his wife had not escaped Sep's sensitive eye.

'He probably only wants you to do a bit of catering for a party or something,' said Edna off-handedly. She snapped the cotton with her white teeth, and folded up the baby's gown.

Prompt at eight, Dan arrived. Edna and Sep received him in the first floor parlour which was at the back of the house overlooking the yard and the distant Cax. The willows lining the banks were shimmering green and gold in their new May finery, and Edna wore a dress which matched their colour. In her presence Dan felt strangely shy, as he was introduced. Sep, who had known the Crockfords slightly for many years, was obviously ill at ease. Edna was quite unperturbed.

'I believe you want to discuss business matters,' she said, rising. 'I'll be with the children if you need me.'

Dan leapt to his feet in alarm.

'Don't go! Please, Mrs Howard, don't go! The business concerns you too, I assure you.'

Wonderingly, Edna slowly resumed her seat. Dan, still standing, wasted no more time but swiftly outlined his proposal. It would be doing him a great honour. He realised that she was very busy. Any time which would suit her convenience would suit his too. It was usual to pay sitters, and he hoped that she would name her fee. He would try to do justice to her outstanding good looks.

The words tumbled out in a vast torrent now that he had begun. Edna gazed upon him in amazement, her beautiful eyes wide and wondering. Sep grew paler as the scheme was unfolded. What impudence, what idiocy, was this?

At last Dan came to a halt, and Edna spoke shyly.

'It's very kind of you, I'm sure. I don't quite know what to think.' She looked at Sep in perplexity. Clearly, she was a little flattered, and inclined to consider the project.

Sep found his voice.

'We'll have nothing to do with it,' he said hoarsely. 'I'm not having my wife mixed up in things of this sort. We don't want the money, thank God, and my wife wouldn't want to earn it that way, I can assure you. I mean no offence, Mr

Crockford. Your affairs are your own business, and good luck to your painting. But don't expect Edna to take part.'

Dan was frankly taken aback by the force of the meek little baker's attack. The thought that there would be such fierce opposition had not entered his mind. He spoke gently, controlling his temper, fearing that Edna would be surely lost to him as a sitter, if it flared up now.

'Don't close your mind to the idea, please,' he begged. 'Think about it and talk the matter over with your wife, and let me know in a few days. I fear that I have taken you too much by surprise. I very much trust that you will allow me to paint Mrs Howard. She would not need to sit for more than three or four sessions.'

Calmer, but still seething inwardly, Sep acknowledged the wisdom of discussing the matter. His old timidity towards those in the social class above him began to make itself felt again. One could not afford to offend good customers, and although his face was firmly set against Edna's acceptance, he deemed it wise to bring the interview to an outwardly civil close.

He accompanied Dan to the door and showed him out into the market square.

'We will let you know,' he said shortly, 'though I must make it plain that I don't like the idea, and very much doubt if Edna will agree.'

He watched Dan swing across the square on his homeward way. His red hair flamed in the dying sun's rays. His chin was at a defiant angle. Dan Crockford was a handsome man, thought Sep sadly, and a fighting man too.

Suddenly weary, conscious that he must return to face Edna,

he caught sight of Queen Victoria, proudly defiant, despite a pigeon poised absurdly on her bronze crown.

'And what would she have thought of it?' wondered Sep morosely, turning his back on the market place.

The scene that ensued was never to be forgotten by poor Sep.

'Well, that's seen the back of that cheeky rascal!' announced Sep, on returning to the parlour. He assumed a brisk authority which he did not feel inwardly, but he intended to appear as master in his own house.

'Who says we've seen the back of him?' asked Edna, dangerously calm.

'I do. I've sent him about his business all right.'

'It was my business, too, if you remember. Strikes me you jumped in a bit sharp. Never gave me time to think it over, did you?'

'I should hope a respectable married woman like you would need no time at all to refuse that sort of invitation.' Sep spoke with a certain pomposity which brought Edna to her feet. She leant upon the table, eyes flashing, and faced her husband squarely.

'You don't appear to trust me very far, Sep Howard. I ain't proposing to stand stark naked for Mr Crockford—'

'I should hope not!' broke in Sep, much shocked.

'It was me he wanted to paint. And I should have had the chance of answering. Made me look no better than a stupid kid, snapping back at him like that, and leaving me out of things.'

Sep buttoned his mouth tightly. He had become very pale and the righteous wrath of generations of staunch chapel-goers began to make his blood boil.

'There's no more to be said, my lady. It was a shameful suggestion and I'll not see my wife flaunting herself for Dan Crockford or anyone else. I don't want to hear any more about it.'

If Sep had been in any condition to think coolly, he must have realised that this was the best way to rouse a mettlesome wife to open rebellion. But he was not capable of thinking far ahead just then. He watched the colour flood Edna's lovely face and her thin brown hands knot into tight fists.

'You don't want to hear any more about it, eh?' echoed Edna. Her voice was low, and throbbing with fury. 'Well, let me tell you, Sep Howard, you're going to! I should like to have my picture painted. Dan Crockford don't mean anything more to me than that chair there, but if he wants to paint my picture, I'm willing. You can't stop me, and you'd better not try, unless you wants to run the shop, and the home too, on your own. I won't be bossed about by you, or anyone else!'

It was at this dangerous moment in the battle that Sep should have given in completely, apologised for his arrogance, told Edna that he could not do without her, and that of course she could sit for Dan Crockford if she wanted to so desperately. Edna's defiance would have abated at once, and all would have been forgotten. But Sep made the wrong move. He thumped the table and shouted.

'I forbid—' he began in a great roaring voice which stirred the curtains.

'Forbid?' screamed Edna. 'Don't you take that tone to me, you little worm! Who d'you think you're talking to – our Kathy? I'm going up to bed now, and tomorrow morning I'm going round to Dan Crockford's to tell him I'll sit for him!'

She whirled from the room, her gold and green dress swishing, leaving Sep open-mouthed. Here was flat rebellion, and Sep knew full well that he had no weapon in his armoury to overcome it.

Morning brought no truce, and Edna set out purposefully across the square as soon as her house was set to rights. Sep watched her go, dumb with misery.

By the time market day came round again the whole of Caxley buzzed with this delicious piece of news. Fat Mrs Petty, chopping cod into cutlets, shouted boisterously above the rhythmic noise of her cleaver.

'No better'n she should be! Once a gyppo, always a gyppo, I says! And us all knows what Dan Crockford's like.'

'It's her poor husband I feel so sorry for,' nodded her customer lugubriously. Her mouth was set in a deprecating downward curve, but her eyes were gleaming with enjoyment. Gossip is always interesting, and this was a particularly exciting snippet for the good folk of Caxley.

'It won't surprise me to hear that Sep Howard turns her out,' continued the customer with relish. 'Been brought up proper strict, his lot – chapel every Sunday, Band of Hope, and all that. You never know, it might all end up in the court!'

She looked across at Caxley's Town Hall, standing beside

St Peter's. Two magistrates were already mounting the steps, dignified in their good broadcloth, for the weekly sitting. Mrs Petty broke into loud laughter, holding up two fat hands, sparkling with fish-scales.

'Court?' she wheezed merrily. 'Ain't no need to take Edna Howard to court! All her husband needs is to take a strap to her!'

In this, Mrs Petty echoed most people in Caxley. If Sep's wife behaved like this, they said, then Sep was at fault. He knew what he'd taken on when he married her. He should have been firm.

The Norths watched the affair closely, and with dismay. Bender was inclined to dismiss it as 'a storm in a tea-cup'. Edna would come to her senses in time. But Hilda felt some inner triumph. Hadn't she always said that Edna wasn't to be trusted?

'One thing,' she admitted, 'it's bringing our Ethel round to seeing the truth about Dan Crockford. Pa said she was quite cool with him when they met in the street. And Jesse Miller's no fool. He's been up at Pa's every evening this week, hanging up his hat to our Ethel.'

'It don't do to make bad blood anywhere,' rumbled Bender, especially in a little place like Caxley. We've all got to rub along together, come fair, come foul, and the sooner this business blows over the better. No need to fan the flames now, Hilda.'

His wife bridled, but said no more.

But the flames ran everywhere, fanned smartly by the wind of gossip. That this should have happened to meek little Septimus Howard, strict chapel-goer, diligent baker, and earnest father, made the affair even more delectable. It was said that Edna went twice a week to Dan's studio, unchaperoned, in the evening, and that no one could really tell what happened there, although, of course, it was easy enough to guess.

Even the children heard the tales, and young Bertie asked the two Howard boys if their mother really had let Mr Crockford paint her picture. To his everlasting horror, one boy burst into tears and the other gave him such a swinging box on the ear that he fell into the thorn bush and was obliged to lie to his mother later about how he had become so severely scratched. Certainly, Edna's portrait created enough stir.

In actual fact the sittings were few and rather dull. They did occur, as rumour said, twice weekly and in the evening, but after six sessions Dan assured his model that he could finish it without troubling her further. Her beauty delighted him, but her dullness bored him dreadfully. Her independence having been proved, Edna was quite willing to make things up with her unhappy husband, and outwardly at least, harmony once again prevailed in the Howards' household.

But the matter did not end there.

The picture was enchanting. Dan knew in his bones that this was the best piece of work he had ever done. Edna glowed from the canvas, gay and vivid, in her gipsy costume. She made a compelling figure, for Dan had caught her warmth and grace magnificently. Furthermore, he had painted a perfect woodland background in minute detail. All the fresh haziness of a May morning sparkled behind Edna – a smoke-blue wood, with pigeons like pearls sunning themselves in the branches, above a grassy bank, starred with daisies, and almost golden in its May newness. He had caught exactly the spirit of wild young life in all its glory. Dan put it aside carefully to be sent to the Academy early next year. This one, surely, would find a place on those august walls.

Meantime, while the gossip ran rife, Howard's bakery suffered a temporary decline. A few self-righteous families refused to deal with a baker whose wife behaved so loosely. Others were embarrassed at facing Sep and preferred to slip into other bakers' establishments until the family affairs were righted. It was an unfortunate set-back for poor Sep who felt his position keenly. There were times when he longed to shut up the shop and flee from Caxley, from the sidelong glances, the whispers behind hands, the wretched knowledge that all knew his discomfiture.

He had said little to Edna after that first terrible encounter. There was so little to say which did not sound nagging, pompous and bitter. Sep told himself that 'the least said soonest mended' and continued doggedly with his business affairs. Apart from a certain coolness, Edna continued her household duties unconcerned. When the sittings came to an end, tension between the two relaxed slightly, but, for Sep at least, things could never be quite the same again.

In time, of course, Caxley began to lose interest in the affair as other topics took the place of the portrait painting as a nine days' wonder. The scandal of the erring alderman, the bankruptcy of an old family business, the elopement of a local farmer's son with a pretty dairymaid, and many other delightful pieces of news came to the sharp eyes and ears of Caxley folk and engaged their earnest attention. It was not until the following year that the Howard scandal was suddenly revived and bathed now in miraculous sunlight instead of shadow.

For Dan Crockford's picture was accepted by the Hanging Committee of the Royal Academy and was one of the paintings of the year. *The Caxley Chronicle* printed this wonderful news on the front page, with a photograph of Dan Crockford and another of the portrait. The headline read: 'Well Deserved Success for Distinguished Local Artist', and the account mentioned 'the beauty of Mrs Septimus Howard, captured for posterity by the skill of the artist's brush.'

This put quite a different complexion on the affair, of course. If *The Caxley Chronicle* thought Dan Crockford was distinguished, then the majority of its readers were willing to believe it. And say what you like, they told each other reasonably, when they met the following week, he'd made a proper handsome picture of Sep's wife and it was a real leg-up for Caxley all round.

People now called at the bakery to see the celebrated Mrs Howard, and poor bewildered Sep found himself accepting congratulations in place of guarded condolences. It was a funny world, thought Sep, that kicked you when you were down, and patted you when you were up again, and all for the same reason.

Nevertheless, it was pleasant to find that the takings had risen sharply since the news came out. And he readily admitted that it was pleasanter still to be greeted warmly, by all and sundry, as he carried his hard-earned money across the market square to the bank. Pray God, thought Sep earnestly, things would now go smoothly for them all!

6

Local Election

THINGS WENT very smoothly indeed in the early part of the century. Trade was brisk generally, and despite the high new motor-cars which began to sail majestically down Caxley High Street like galleons before the wind, though with somewhat more noise, the stablemen, coachmen, farriers and the multitude of men engaged in ministering to the horse, still thrived.

It was true that Bill Blake's cycle shop at the marsh end of the High Street had begun repairing cars, and had taken over a yard at the side of the premises for this purpose. Under the shade of a vast sycamore tree against the rosy brick wall, Bill and his brother investigated the complicated interiors of the newcomers, surrounded by the enthusiastic small fry of Caxley. But the idea of the motor car ever superseding the ubiquitous horse was never really considered seriously by those who watched with such absorption.

The Howard boys had been among the keenest students of the early motor car, and as they grew older did their best to persuade Sep to discard the two horse-drawn vans, which now took his expanding business further afield, and to buy a motor-van. But Sep would have none of it. It would cost too much. It would break down. He preferred his horses.

By the time King Edward died in 1910 and his son George was made King, both boys were in the bakery business. Jim was now twenty-one and Leslie nineteen. Jim was like his father in looks and temperament, neat, quiet and industrious. His presence in the shop was invaluable, and as Sep grew older, he was glad to give more responsibility to his first-born.

Leslie took after Edna, dark, volatile and with the same devastating good looks. To be seen dancing the polka with Leslie at the Corn Exchange was something the girls of Caxley thoroughly enjoyed.

It was Leslie who bowled round the country lanes in the baker's van, touching his cap politely to the gentry as he edged Dandy the mare into the hedgerow to let a carriage – and sometimes a brand-new tonneau – pass by. It was Leslie who won the hearts of the old country women with his cheerful quips as he went on his rounds.

'A real nice lad,' they would say to each other, a warm loaf held in the crook of their arms as they watched Leslie and the mare vanish in a cloud of dust. 'Got his ma's looks, ain't he? But takes after his pa, too, let's hope.'

The growth of Sep's fortunes had brought him into the public eye. He had been persuaded to stand as a candidate in the local elections, and, much to his surprise, was successful in gaining a seat on the council. Caxley recognised the integrity and strength of character which was hidden behind his diffident appearance. His family and his business flourished, and his conduct over the portrait affair, which had been so severely criticized at the time, was now spoken of with praise.

'Sets a real example to that family of his! Look how forbearing he was with his Edna! Some would've kicked her out of doors, behaving that way. But you see, it's all turned out for the best, and she've quietened down into a thorough good wife.'

Edna certainly gained dignity as the years passed. She still sang in public, and still played her banjo in private. But memories are long in the country, and Edna was still looked upon with some suspicion by the good ladies who organized charity events. Not so Hilda North, whose help was asked for on many occasions. It gave Hilda much private satisfaction to be invited to serve on committees with the local gentry, particularly as Edna was never so invited. Their children remained firm friends, and their husbands too, but the two wives grew cooler with each other as the years passed.

Hilda, in the early days of the new reign, now had three children. Bertie was seventeen and intended going into the motor trade, Winifred fifteen, still at the High School and longing to finish there and start training as a nurse. It was on Winnie's twelfth birthday that Hilda had discovered that she was having another child – an event which she greeted with mingled dismay and pleasure, for she had thought her family complete and was looking forward to an end to cots and prams and all the paraphernalia of babyhood. But Bender was whole-heartedly delighted with the news.

'Always the best – those that aren't ordered,' he assured his wife. 'You mark my words, she'll be a beauty.'

Amazingly enough, it was indeed a girl, and a beauty. At four she was as pretty as a picture with fair curls and eyes as blue as speedwell flowers. She was also thoroughly spoilt by all the family and hair-raisingly outspoken.

When Lady Hurley called to enlist Hilda's aid in raising money for a Christmas fund for the poor of Caxley, the tea table had been laden with the best china, the silver teapot and wafer-thin bread and butter. The lightest of sponge cakes crowned a silver dish, and three sorts of jam, flanked by Gentlemen's Relish, added distinction to the scene.

While Hilda was plying her honoured guest, young Mary put her head round the door and interrupted the genteel conservation.

'Our cat sicked up just before you came,' she volunteered in a clear treble voice. 'He sicked up half a mouse and a—'

'That'll do!' said poor Hilda hastily. She rang the bell and Mary was removed, protesting loudly, to the kitchen. It was a scene which the family remembered with pleasure for years, and Hilda with the deepest mortification.

Hilda's sense of propriety was strongly developed. She enjoyed her position in Caxley society and was proud to be the wife of a well-to-do tradesman, churchwarden and well-known public figure. She liked to be seen entering St Peter's for Matins, clad in her best gown and mantle in suitably quiet colours, dove-grey perhaps, or deep mauve, with a sedate hat to match, trimmed with pansies or a wide watered-silk ribbon. She retained her trim figure over the years, and tight lacing contributed to her neat appearance.

She was proud too of her family, good-looking and robust, even if not over-blessed with brains. Winifred, now growing up fast, would never be the beauty that little Mary promised to be, but she had a fresh fairness which the boys seemed to find attractive. Somewhat to Hilda's annoyance, she suspected that Leslie Howard, old enough to have chosen someone among his numerous admirers for his particular choice, cast a roving eye upon his friend of a life-time. An alliance with the

Howard family was not to be borne. Winifred was to do much better for herself. Climbing the social ladder was an exercise which Hilda accomplished with ease and dexterity. There was no reason on earth why a girl like Winifred should not marry happily into the gentry, if the cards were played with discretion.

As for Bertie, Hilda's heart melted whenever her eye rested upon him. He had always been particularly dear, perhaps because he followed so soon upon the stillborn son who was their first child, and gave them so much comfort when it was sorely needed. At eighteen Bertie was as tall as his massive father, but long-limbed and slender. His fair hair had not darkened much with the years, and his quiet grave good looks were much admired.

There was a reserve about Bertie which set him a little apart from the rest of the Norths. Always cheerful in company, he also loved solitude. He liked to dawdle by the Cax, or hang over the bridge, watching the smooth water glide below, whispering through the reeds at the bank side and weaving ever-changing patterns across the river bed. Perhaps he had noise enough at his work at Blake's, for he had just started a course of motor engineering with that firm. It was work that absorbed him. He had patience and physical strength, and a ready grasp of mechanics. He was certain, too, in his own mind, that the motor-car had come to stay despite the scoffings of his elders. Above all, he was secretly thankful that he was not in the family business, for Bender's somewhat slap-dash methods irked him, and he was too respectful a son to criticize his father.

On the face of it, the business flourished. The Norths now owned their own horse and trap, for Uncle Ted's little cob had been sold when the old man grew too frail for driving, and it was now Bender's turn to take his elder brother on an occasional visit in the family trap. A freshly-painted skiff was moored at the end of the North's small garden, and once every year the shop was left in charge of Bob, now second-in-command, still with a mop of unruly black hair and steel spectacles set awry, while the family took a week's holiday at the sea. Caxley never doubted that Bender's business was as flourishing as ever.

But Bender himself knew otherwise. His turnover had not increased in the past few years, and now there was a serious threat to the business. The great firm of Tenby's, which flourished in the county town, opened a branch next door to Blake's at the marsh end of Caxley High Street. Their premises were far grander and far larger than Bender's, and the new agricultural machinery, which was beginning to make its way on to the market, was displayed and demonstrated with great ease in the commodious covered yard behind the shop.

It was Jesse Miller who brought the seriousness of the position home to Bender. He was a frequent caller now at the Norths', for he had succeeded in persuading the vacillating Ethel, Hilda North's sister, to marry him a few years earlier when Dan Crockford's behaviour appeared so reprehensible to the sterner eyes of Caxley.

The two men sat smoking in the snug murk of the shop parlour one November evening. Outside the pavements were wet with the clinging fog which wreathed its way from the Cax valley to twine itself about the gas lamps of the market place.

Above their heads the gas hissed, and a bright fire flickered cheerfully in the little round-arched grate.

'Got a good fire there,' observed Jesse, watching Bender's ministrations with the steel poker.

'Coal's cheap enough,' answered Bender, widening a crack with a smart blow. 'Can still afford that, thank God!'

Jesse Miller blew a long blue cloud towards the ceiling. He watched it disperse reflectively and then took a deep breath.

'Look, Bender! I've had something on my mind for some time and I reckon it's best to speak out. Am I right in thinking the shop's not paying its way?'

Bender's face flushed and the deep colour flooded his bull neck, but he answered equably.

'I'd not go that far, Jesse. We're not bankrupt yet, if that's what's on your mind.'

'But it's not as good as it was?' persisted Jesse, leaning forward.

'Well, no,' admitted Bender, with a sigh. He thrust out his long legs and the horse-hair chair creaked a protest. 'Bound to be a bit of a drop in takings when a shop like Tenby's first opens. People like to bob in and see what's there. They'll come back, I don't doubt.'

'I do,' said Jesse forcefully. 'You might as well face it – Tenby's are here for good, and they'll offer more than you ever can.'

Bender was about to protest, but Jesse Miller waived him aside.

'It's not only the room they've got; they've got keen chaps too. And another thing, they're quick with getting the stuff to the customer. I've had a couple of harrows on order here since Michaelmas, and where are they?'

'You know dam' well where they are,' rumbled Bender,

beginning to look surly. 'Down in Wiltshire where they're made, and where they're too idle to put 'em on the railway! I've written to them time and time again!'

'Maybe! It don't alter the fact, Bender, that Tenby's have got a dozen stacked in their yard now, and if you can't get mine here by next week – I'm telling you straight, man – I'm going there for a couple.'

The two men glared at each other, breathing heavily. They were both fighters, and both obdurate.

'Oh, you are, are you?' growled Bender. 'Well, I daresay the old business can manage without your custom for once, though I think it's a pretty mean sort of thing for one friend to do to another.'

Jesse relaxed, and tapped his pipe out on the bars of the grate.

'See here,' he said in a softer tone, as he straightened up, 'I'm not the only chap in these parts who's feeling the same way. If you want to keep your customers you'll darn well have to put yourself out a bit more, Bender. You're too easy-going by half, and Tenby's are going to profit by it.'

'Maybe, maybe!' agreed Bender.

'And what's all this I hear about you putting up for the council? Can you spare the time?'

'That's my business. I was asked to stand, and Hilda agrees it's a good thing.'

'Against Sep Howard? He's had a good majority each time.'

'Why not against Sep Howard? We know each other well enough to play fair. Sep's quite happy about it, that I do know.'

Jesse Miller sighed, and pocketed his pipe.

'Well, Bender, you know what you're doing, I suppose, but if this business were mine, I wouldn't waste my time and energy on anything else but putting it back on its feet again.'

He rose to his feet and lifted his greatcoat from the hook on the door.

'What does young Bertie think about it all?' he asked, shrugging himself into the coat.

'He knows nothing about it,' replied Bender shortly. 'I'm not panicking simply because the takings are down a bit on last year. The business will be as good as ever when it's time for me to hand it over.'

'I wonder!' commented Jesse Miller, and vanished round the door.

Bender had cause to remember this conversation in the months that followed. Trade began to wane to such an extent that it was quite clear that many people, particularly farmers, were transferring their custom to Tenby's and would continue to do so. It was not in Bender's nature to be alarmed, but he went about his business very much more soberly.

The local election did much to distract his mind from the depressing state of affairs. The third contestant was a local schoolteacher of advanced ideas, with a fine flow of rhetoric when unchecked, but having no ability to stand up to bucolic hecklers. Sep and Bender agreed that he would constitute no great menace to either of them.

When Sep had first heard that Bender was opposing him, he felt the old sick fluttering in his stomach which had afflicted him in Bender's presence ever since his schooldays. It was absurd, he told himself for the hundredth time, to let the man affect him in this way. Sep was now a man of some substance, although his way of life had changed little. He attended chapel as regularly as ever, accompanied by Edna and the family. Sometimes, it is true, Leslie was not present, but when you are twenty, and as attractive as Leslie Howard, it was not to be wondered at, the more indulgent matrons of Caxley told each other.

Sep had been a councillor now for several years. He looked upon this present fight as a private challenge – not between Bender and himself – but to his own courage. In chapel, his head sunk upon his hands, Sep prayed earnestly and silently for help in overcoming his own fears. He did not pray that he might win – it would have been as despicable as it was pre-sumptuous to do so; but he prayed that he might fight the fight bravely and honourably.

There was no doubt about it, Bender was going to be a formidable opponent. He was well-liked, he had a com-manding presence, and a breezy sense of humour which stood him in good stead when the heckling began. Sep knew he could not compete with Bender in this field, but he could only hope that his record of steady service to the town would keep his supporters loyal.

The boys and girls of the two families thoroughly enjoyed the excitement. They cycled up and down the Caxley streets, stuffing pamphlets through letter-boxes and nailing up election posters on doors and railings. There was no hostility between the two parties, as far as the younger generation was concerned. Winifred North and Kathy Howard accompanied each other on these expeditions, and were not above taking one side of each road and posting both notices through the boxes, with superb magnanimity.

Sep and Bender approached their electioneering in typical fashion. It was the custom to take turns in having the market place for an open-air meeting. Bender addressed the crowd in a hearty voice which could be heard clearly. His eyes sparkled, his arms waved in generous and compelling movements. Here was a man who enjoyed the publicity, the excitement and the fight. His hearers warmed to him.

The evenings when Sep took the little platform, close by Queen Victoria, were much more sedate. Small, pale, his gentle voice scarcely audible, Sep nevertheless managed to command attention. There was a sincerity about him which appealed to his listeners, and moreover his past work was generally appreciated. It was hard to forecast which of the two men would win the election. Caxley seemed fairly equally divided in its loyalties.

On the great day, the schools were used as polling stations, much to the gratification of the local children. Bender and Sep, taking brief spells off from their businesses, ranged the town in their traps to take the infirm to register their votes. It happened to be market day in Caxley, and so the bustle was greater than ever.

By the time polling ended both men were tense and tired. Counting went on at the Town Hall next door to St Peter's. This edifice, built in the middle years of the old Queen's reign, was of a repellent fish-paste red, picked out, here and there, with a zig-zag motive in yellow tiles. It contrasted sadly with the mellow honey-coloured stone of the noble church beside it, but on this day its architectural shortcomings were ignored, for here, on the red brick balcony would be announced the name of the victorious candidate.

It was almost eleven o'clock when at last the Mayor and other officials made their entrance high above the square. The upturned faces grew suddenly still, and the noise of a distant train could be clearly heard chuffing its way rhythmically out of Caxley Station a mile away.

The three candidates stood self-consciously beside the scarlet-clad Mayor.

'John Emmanuel Abbott, two hundred and thirty-four,' read the Mayor sonorously. There was a mingled sound of cheering and booing. The little schoolteacher preserved a dignified and tight-lipped silence and bowed slightly.

'Septimus Howard, six thousand, nine hundred and two.' More cheers arose, hastily checked as the Mayor lifted his paper again.

'Bertram Lewis North, four thousand, seven hundred and twenty-two,' intoned the Mayor.

Now the cheering broke out anew, and when Septimus Howard, elected once more, stepped forward shyly, someone began to clap and shout: 'Good old Sep!' It was taken up by almost all the crowd, a spontaneous gesture of affection which was as touching as it was unexpected.

Sep bowed his thanks, spoke briefly of the honour done him, and promised to do his best to be worthy of the confidence shown in him. He turned to shake the hands of his opponents, first that of John Abbott, and then Bender's.

At that moment, their hands tightly clasped, Sep experienced a shock. Bender's smile was as broad as ever, his complexion as ruddy, but it was the expression in his eyes, the look of hurt

74

wonderment, which shook Sep so profoundly. For the first time in his life, Sep felt pity for the great giant of a man before him, and, as well as pity, a new deep and abiding peace.

Amidst the tumult of the crowd and the dazzle of the lights, Sep became conscious of one outstanding truth. Within him, born suddenly of this strange new feeling, was an inner calm and strength. Somehow, Sep knew, it would remain there, and would colour his relationship towards Bender in the years ahead.

7

Love Affairs

LIKE MANY other bluff, hearty men who seem to ride boldly through life, Bender was easily upset. The outcome of the election was a considerable shock to him. That his fellow townsmen preferred Sep's services to his own was particularly humiliating. Not that Bender disparaged Sep's industry and sincerity, but he could not help feeling a certain condescending amusement at what he called 'Sep's bible-thumping' attitude to life. As a lifelong church-goer, Bender tended to underestimate the strength of Methodism in Caxley, and though this did not influence the outcome entirely, yet he could not help realising that many chapel-goers had voted for Sep. His easy tolerance of nonconformists now suffered a change. Smarting secretly from his hurt, Bender was inclined to view the chapel-goers with a little more respect and, it must be admitted, with a twinge of sourness.

It was not surprising, therefore, that he was unusually waspish when Hilda told him of her fears about Leslie Howard and Winifred.

'I'm beginning to think,' Hilda said, 'that there's more to it than just being friendly. Our Winnie's at a silly age, let's face it, and Leslie's had plenty of practice turning young girls' heads.'

'Probably nothing in it,' replied Bender, pacifying womanly doubts automatically. 'But we certainly don't want our girl mixed up with the chapel lot.'

'It's not "being mixed up with the chapel lot", as you call it,' retorted Hilda, with unwonted spirit, 'but Leslie's been mixed up with too many girls already! Besides,' she continued, 'there are better fish in the sea for our Winnie than Sep Howard's boy.'

'You've no call to speak like that about Sep,' admonished Bender, secretly regretting his hasty disparagement of the Howards' religion.

'But surely you don't want anything to come of this?' demanded Hilda, putting down her crochet work as though about to do battle. Bender began to retreat. He had enough worries with the uncertainties of the business and the shock of the election without adding this problem to the list. He took a man's way out.

'You have a quiet word with Winnie, my dear. You'll handle it better than I can. And if I get a chance I'll just mention it to Sep and he can speak to Leslie. But ten chances to one, you're worrying yourself about nothing. Damn it all Hilda, our Winnie's not nineteen!'

'I married you at that age,' pointed out Hilda tartly. She picked up her crochet work again, and stabbed sharply, in and out, with unusual ferocity.

As might be expected, Bender said nothing to Sep or anyone else about Leslie's attentions to his daughter. But Hilda approached her task with circumspection one evening when she and Winifred were alone in the kitchen. Her daughter blushed a becoming pink, twirled a tea-cloth rapidly round and round inside a jug, but said remarkably little.

Hilda, washing up busily at the sink, went a trifle further.

'Not that there's anything against the Howards, dear, or you would never have been allowed to be such good friends with the family, but it's as well to let it remain at that.'

'How d'you mean?' asked Winifred.

Really, thought Hilda, fishing exasperatedly for a teaspoon lurking in the depths, Winnie was sometimes very awkward!

'What I say! People are beginning to notice that you and Leslie dance a great deal together, and go for walks alone – all that sort of thing – and naturally they wonder if they're going to hear of an engagement.'

'You'd hear first,' said Winnie briefly.

It was not the sort of answer which gave Hilda any comfort. She began to feel that she was not making much progress.

'So I would hope! It doesn't alter the fact that Leslie is paying you a great deal of attention. He's in his twenties now, and he'll be thinking of marriage before long. You're only eighteen.'

'You were married at nineteen,' pointed out the maddening girl. Hilda tipped out the washing-up water, advanced upon the towel on the back door, and sent the wooden roller rumbling thunderously as she dried her hands energetically. It seemed that the time had come for plain speaking.

'What I'm trying to make you see, Winnie, is that there are other young men in Caxley – and *better placed* young men – who would most certainly make you happier than Leslie Howard when the time comes. Just be warned, my dear, and don't get entangled before you've had a chance to look round you. Leslie's well known as a charmer, and you don't want to be left high and dry, as so many of the others have, when Leslie's lost interest.'

Winifred continued to polish the jug. Her eyes were downcast. It was difficult to know just how she was taking this little homily, but at least she was not reacting violently. Hilda thanked her stars that Winifred had always been a placid girl. Some daughters would have answered back, or burst into tears, or flounced from the room, thought Hilda with relief.

'And you think Leslie will lose interest in me too?' queried the girl quietly.

'That's up to you,' responded Hilda. 'You certainly shouldn't encourage him. You don't want to find yourself married to a Howard, I hope.'

'Why not?' asked Winnie, setting the jug carefully on a shelf. Her back was towards her mother, so that Hilda could not see her face, but her voice was as calm as ever.

'Why not?' echoed Hilda, now too confidently embarked upon her mission. 'Because your father and I have hopes of something better for you than becoming a baker's wife when you decide to get married. We've always done our very best to introduce you to nice families. You can look higher than the Howards for a husband. Surely you can see that?'

The girl wheeled round and the determined look upon her face shook her mother into silence.

'There's one thing I can see,' said Winnie levelly, 'and that is that I've got a snob for a mother.' And before Hilda could get her breath back, Winnie walked, head-high and unhurried, from the room.

*　　*　　*

It was not only Hilda who had been perturbed by the fast-growing attachment between Leslie and Winnie. Bertie too had watched the pair with misgivings quite as strong, but of quite a different nature. His affection for the Howard boys was unchanged by the years. He was now approaching twenty-one, a thoughtful, intelligent young man, but still harbouring traces of that hero-worship he had felt as a child for the two boys who were his seniors. Jim at twenty-four, and Leslie at twenty-two, seemed to be grown men, and Leslie certainly was experienced in the ways of women. Bertie, of shyer disposition, felt that he knew too little of the world to question the Howards' actions. Nevertheless, his deep affection for Winnie put him on his guard, and he observed her growing awareness of Leslie's charms with uneasiness.

If Jim had been Winnie's choice, Bertie would have been delighted. Bertie and Jim had much in common, both being peace-loving young men, thoroughly engrossed in their jobs and enjoying the pleasant social life of Caxley in their spare time. There was a steadiness about Jim which Leslie lacked. He might be incapable of sweeping a girl off her feet, but he would make a thoroughly reliable husband. Bertie, inexperienced as he was, could not fail to see that Leslie might prove far too volatile for such a lasting institution as marriage.

But this was not the only thing which worried Bertie. He knew, only too well, that there was a streak of cruelty in Leslie. There had been birds' nesting expeditions, when they were boys, when Jim and Bertie had seen Leslie throw a young bird wantonly over a hedge. Bertie had once come upon Leslie in the baker's yard chastising their old spaniel with unnecessary severity because it had chased a cat. Both Bertie

and Jim had made their disgust plain on these occasions, but
Leslie appeared unrepentant. Bertie himself remembered many
a twisted arm and painful kick delivered by Leslie, for no
apparent reason but self-indulgence. As he grew older, and
enjoyed his successes with the girls, the same callousness
showed in his attitude to those of whom he had tired. He
showed not a quiver of compunction. For Leslie, when the
affair was done, it was finished completely, and he passed to
his next willing victim without one glance behind. It was small
wonder that Bertie trembled for Winnie, so young and so
vulnerable. Should he say anything to her, he wondered? Or
would it simply add fuel to the fire?

He salved his conscience with the thought that almost
always the pair were in company with other young people.
Besides, Winnie was a sensible girl and had known Leslie and
his ways long enough to realise that his affection would
certainly not last long. He decided that it would be prudent to
keep silence.

Other matters engaged Bertie's attention at this time,
distracting him from the affairs of his sister. Kathy Howard,
now nineteen and working in the family business, had long
been taken for granted by Bertie as an occasional tennis
partner or a useful team member when they played 'Clumps'
at parties. But during the summer of 1913 Bertie began to
find her presence curiously and delightfully disturbing. She
was as vividly beautiful as her mother had been at the same
age, and attracted as much attention from the boys. Her hair
was a dusky cloud, her eyes large and luminous. She could
dance all night without flagging, and had a gay recklessness
which, until now, Bertie had dismissed as 'showing off'.

When young Mary North, aged eight, had dared her to jump from their garden bridge fully clothed into the Cax, Kathy had done so immediately, and been reproved by Bertie. When the attic curtains blew out from the windows, high above the market square, and became caught in the guttering, it was Kathy who stood on the window-sill to release them before the three boys had pounded up the stairs after her. And it was Bertie again who remonstrated with her.

But these things had happened a year or two earlier, before Bertie's feelings had suffered a change. The very thought now of the risks that Kathy ran made Bertie tremble with apprehension. She was becoming incredibly precious to him, he realised with surprise. Meanwhile, oblivious of his feelings, Kathy continued her carelessly happy way, as dazzling as a butterfly, flitting from one pleasure to the next, with no thought of settling down. And Bertie was content to watch her with increasing delight, and to accustom himself to these new tremors which her presence excited.

He had another cause for concern. He strongly suspected that things were not well with the family finances and only wished he could ask his father openly about the situation. Somehow, it was not easy to speak to him. Bertie awaited an opportunity, half-hoping, half-fearing that his father would broach the subject, but time passed and nothing was said. It did not escape Bertie's notice, however, that his father was more preoccupied than usual, and that some of the stock was not being replaced when it was sold. He had a pretty shrewd idea that Tenby's had hit his father's trade more seriously than he would admit.

Nevertheless, the staff still numbered six, presumably were

being paid, and were content with their lot. Bob, who had been at North's since leaving school, was now head assistant and Bender left more and more responsibility to him. He had grown into a harassed vague individual with a walrus moustache. His steel-rimmed spectacles screened myopic brown eyes which peered dazedly at the world about him. Despite his unprepossessing appearance the customers liked him and the staff treated him with deference. Unmarried, he lived with his old mother and seemed to have no particular vices, unless whist at the working men's club, and occasional bets on a horse, could be counted against him. Poor, plain Miss Taggerty, who was in charge of the kitchen ware at North's, openly adored him, fluttering her meagre sandy eyelashes, and displaying her distressingly protruding teeth and pink gums, in vast smiles which Bob appeared not to see. Only the very lowliest member of North's staff, young Tim, aged thirteen, sniggered at Miss Taggerty's fruitless endeavours and was soundly cuffed by the other assistants when so discovered. To them, disrespect towards Bob was tantamount to disrespect to Bender and the family. If Bob seemed satisfied with conditions in the business, Bertie told himself, why should he perturb himself unduly?

Summer slid into autumn, and the picnics and river parties gave way to concerts and dances as the days drew in. It was in October that the Caxley Orchestra gave its grandest concert each year, and in 1913 Winnie North appeared for the first time among the violinists.

Her family turned up in full force to do her honour. They sat in the front row of the balcony at the Corn Exchange.

'In case Mary wants to go out during the performance – you know what she is,' said her mother.

Mary, dressed in white silk with a wide sash of red satin, was beside herself with excitement. This was better than going to bed! Her eyes sparkled as she gazed about the crowded hall. Hilda, matronly in black velvet, did her best to quell her youngest's volatile spirits. Bender, at the end of the row, smiled indulgently upon his handsome family and their friends.

For the Howard family had been invited to join the party, and although Sep and Edna had excused themselves, and their youngest was in bed with the mumps, yet Leslie and Kathy were present and were to take Winnie and Bertie to their home for supper after the show.

As the performance went on the air grew warmer and more soporific in the balcony. Bertie found his attention wandering as the orchestra ploughed its way valiantly through Mozart's 'Eine Kleine Nachtmusik'. Along the row he could see Kathy's bronze leather shoe, wagging in time with the music, beneath the hem of her yellow skirt. Below the balcony, ranged neatly in rows each side of the wide gangway he could see the heads of almost two hundred worthy Caxley folk.

There was the mayor's bald pate, shining and pink, gleaming in the front row. Beside him were the glossy black locks, suspiciously lacking any silvery flecks or light and shade, of his sixty-year-old wife. Near him Bertie could see the bent figure of old Sir James Diller from Beech Green, his ear trumpet well in evidence and his shaking head cocked to hear every in-distinct sound. Immediately behind him sat his manservant, ready to aid his ageing master if need be. In the same row were the manservant's sister and her husband, the local butcher, there to hear their two sons performing, one as a flautist and the other as a violinist.

Bertie's eyes wandered farther afield. There was the postmaster, whose son had just lost a leg as the result of a train accident. There was the cobbler who drank, the schoolmistress who sang like an angel and the elderly curate of St Peter's who was father-confessor to half the parish. There was Mrs Gadd, the watchmaker's wife, who was aunt to Bob at the shop, and refused to have anything to do with him, for reasons unknown, and always demanded to be served by Bender himself. There was her cousin, known to young Caxleyites as 'old Scabby' because of his unfortunate complexion, and the chastiser of Bertie, aged six, when he had trespassed into the old man's garden in search of a lost ball. And beyond him was Louisa Howard, aunt to Kathy, and a thorn in the side of the Howard family because of her rebellious ways. Her flaming red hair and flaming red nose matched the flaming temper which scorched all with whom she came in contact.

'A vixen,' Bender called her, 'and a vicious vixen at that. If she'd been a boy she'd have been packed off to sea.'

Bertie's eyes strayed back to the platform. Husbands, wives, sons, and daughters, nieces and nephews scraped and blew, banged and squealed to the pride of their relatives in the audience. Bertie watched his sister's smooth fair head bent above her violin. Her pretty plump arm sawed energetically up and down as she concentrated on the music propped up before her.

How closely they were all tied, thought Bertie! Not only by the bonds of kinship which enlaced most of those in the Corn Exchange, but also by the bonds of shared experience.

They not only knew each other, their faults and their foibles, they shared the town of Caxley. They knew the most sheltered spot to stand in the market square when the easterly wind blew sharp and keen across the cobbles. They knew where the biggest puddles had to be dodged on dark nights, and where the jasmine smelt sweetest on a summer evening. They knew where the trout rose in the Cax, where a nightingale could be heard and where lovers could wander undisturbed. They knew who sold the freshest meat, and who the stalest. They knew who made the stoutest boots, the smartest frocks and the best pork pies. In short, they were as closely knit as a family, and as lucky as villagers in a village, in that Caxley was small enough, and leisurely enough too, for them to appreciate each other and the little town which was home to them all.

Nodding gently, in the pleasant stuffiness of the balcony, Bertie gazed through half-closed eyes at his fellow-citizens and found them good.

Some chaps, mused Bertie to himself, would be itching to get away from all this at my age, but Caxley suits me!

He caught sight of Kathy's tapping toe again and sat up straight.

Yes, Caxley would certainly suit him, he decided, as 'Eine Kleine Nachtmusik' crashed triumphantly to a close, and he joined enthusiastically in Caxley's generous, and wholly biased, applause.

8

A Trip to Beech Green

WINNIE WAS flushed with excitement after the performance. Bertie had never seen her looking so pretty, nor had Leslie, it was plain.

They sat at the Howards' supper table and Bertie, hungry after three hours of Caxley music, looked with pleasure at the magnificent pork pie which stood before Sep at one end of the table, and the huge bowl of salad before Edna at the other. One of Sep's superb bread rolls, with a carefully plaited top, lay on each side plate, and Bertie broke his in two, savouring its delicious fresh scent.

'Let us call a blessing on the food,' intoned Sep sonorously, and Bertie hastily put his erring hands in his lap and bent his shamed head. It was bad enough to look greedy. It looked even worse to appear irreverent. Cursing his luck, Bertie could only hope that the whole table had not seen his actions. But, catching the eye of Winnie across the table, he soon saw that one member of the family would tell the tale against him later on.

'Lord bless this food to our use and us to Thy service,' droned Sep, his thin hands pressed together and eyes tightly shut.

'Amen,' murmured the rest of them, and there was an uncomfortable silence, broken at last by Sep himself who picked up a large knife and fork flanking the pie and began to cut the golden crust, with almost as much reverence as his saying of grace.

Bertie, anxious to reinstate himself, passed the butter dish to Edna and complimented her on the superb vase of late roses which were the centrepiece of the table.

'Your ma gave them to me,' replied Edna. Bertie fell silent and studied the tablecloth.

It was a white damask one similar to those used in the North household, but much greyer, and badly ironed. Bertie could not imagine his mother allowing such a cloth on their own table, and certainly not such thick white plates, chipped here and there, and covered with minute cracks across the glaze where they had been left too long to heat in the oven. His knife blade wobbled on its handle, and the tines of his fork were so worn that it was difficult to spear the slippery pieces of tomato on his plate. He wondered why Sep and Edna endured such shabby adjuncts to their superb food, and also, as a rich crumb of pastry fell into his lap, why they did not think to provide table napkins. But it was positively churlish, he told himself, to think in this way at his host's table, and he set himself out to draw Edna into conversation about young Robert's mumps. He felt Kathy's eyes upon him across the table, and hoped she did not think too badly of his early gaffe.

'It's a funny thing,' Edna began energetically, 'but one side of his neck don't hardly notice, but the other's up like a football. Of course he can't swallow a thing, and his poor head's that hot you could poach an egg on it!'

Once launched, Edna sailed along readily enough, and Bertie allowed his mind to wander.

Only Winnie seemed to sparkle and Leslie too was at his

gayest. Their end of the table, where Sep presided, seemed considerably livelier than Edna's where Bertie was doing his best to woo the subject from infectious diseases, but with small success. Edna had no small talk, and, as Dan Crockford had found years before, very little of interest in her beautiful head. But she liked to chatter, and the subject of mumps had led, naturally enough, to measles, whooping cough, diphtheria and other children's ailments which had caused Edna dramatic alarm over the years.

'And that young Dr Martin, whose gone over to Fairacre now – and a good thing too if you ask me – he came and had a look at our Leslie. And I said to him: "He's got yellow jaundice, doctor," and do you know what he said?'

Bertie murmured politely.

'He simply said: "And how do you know?" With that poor little ha'porth as yellow as a guinea! It didn't need much to tell a mother what was wrong with him, but doctors don't give no one any credit for having a bit of sense. Though I must say, speaking fair, he give Leslie some very strong medicine, which did him a world of good.'

She gazed down the table at her second-born, and sighed happily.

'Make a lovely couple, don't they?' she said artlessly, and Bertie felt his heart sink. Was it really becoming so obvious to everyone? Could it be that a marriage would be arranged between the two? Bertie felt cold at the thought, and even Kathy's smiles and cheerful conversation after supper could not quite dispel the chill at his heart.

They made their farewells soon after eleven and emerged into the quiet market square. The stars shone brightly from a clear sky above the tumbled Caxley roofs. In the yard of the public house a horse snorted, as it awaited its master. A few late home-goers straggled past Queen Victoria's upright figure, and somewhere, in the distance, a cat yowled in a dark alley.

Leslie had accompanied them down the stairs and opened the door at the side of the shop for them.

'Goodnight, Leslie, and thank you again,' said Bertie. But Leslie was not listening. Bertie saw that his hand held Winnie's tightly, and that the two were exchanging a look of complete love and understanding.

The Norths crossed the square, turned to wave to Leslie silhouetted against the light from his open door, and entered their own home.

Bertie made his way to bed that night with much food for thought.

It was soon after this that Bertie acquired his first motor-car, and it did much to distract the young man from his cares. It was a small two-seater, an A.C. Sociable, by name, and had been owned by young Tenby, the son of the flourishing iron-monger in Caxley High Street, since 1909 when it was in its first glory. Young Tenby, now married, with one son and another expected, had bought a larger car. It was the envy of all Caxley, a glossy new Lanchester, and Bertie was able to buy the old one at a very favourable price. One of his first trips was to Beech Green to take his mother to visit Ethel, now happily married to Jesse Miller, and also awaiting the birth of her second child.

Hilda, her hat tied on with a becoming grey motoring veil, sat very upright beside Bertie trying to hide her apprehension. But once the terrors of Caxley High Street were past, and they entered the leafy lane which climbed from the Cax valley to the downs beyond, her fears were calmed, and she looked about her at the glowing autumn trees with excited pleasure. Speech was well-nigh impossible because of noise and dust, but once they had drawn up, with a flourish, outside the farmhouse door, she complimented Bertie on his driving.

'Thank you, mamma,' said Bertie, secretly amused, 'but it's what I've been doing ever since I left school you know. I'm glad you weren't too frightened.'

While the two sisters exchanged news, Jesse Miller took Bertie round the farm. Harvest was over early that year and the stubble in Hundred Acre Field glittered like a golden sea. The two men crunched their way across it, Bertie envying his uncle's leather leggings which protected his legs from the sharp straw which pricked unmercifully through his own socks. He was glad when they approached the hedge of a cottage garden and Jesse paused to speak to the family who were working there. He bent down and removed some of the cruellest of the tormentors from the tops of his boots and his socks, and caught a glimpse through the bare hedge of a pretty girl, with her father, and a tall young man with red hair.

'Our thatcher,' said Jesse Miller, as they resumed their tour of the farm. 'Francis Clare. Just had to let him know the barn roof needs patching after last week-end's gale.'

'And the girl?'

'Dolly, his daughter. And the copper-nob's her young man, Arnold Fletcher. Getting married next year, I hear. Time you thought of it yourself, Bertie.'

'I'll remember,' promised Bertie.

The air was pure and refreshing, up here on the downs, and scented with the sweet-sad smells of autumn, the damp earth underfoot, and the dying bracken growing in the rustling hedge. Bertie paused to look about him in this lovely open place. In the Cax valley such exhilaration rarely seized him. There was something strong and uplifting in the great sweep of hills with the moving clouds gliding across their tops. He would like to live here, savouring their tranquillity, one day. Perhaps with Kathy for company, he wondered? The thought was as heady as the winds about him.

They returned to the farmhouse for a gigantic tea. A bowlful of freshly boiled brown eggs, set in the centre of the table, was only a prelude to the ham sandwiches, hot buttered scones, home made plum jam, Victoria sponge, Dundee cake, custard tartlets and half a dozen dishes of assorted small cakes.

Ethel pressed her sister and nephew to eat heartily as they had such a long cold drive before them, and Hilda returned the compliment by persuading Ethel to eat equally well as she was 'feeding two'. Between them they managed to dispatch quite half the food arrayed on the table before setting off for home behind the hissing acetylene lamps.

Half-way between Beech Green and Caxley, a fine hare leapt from a high bank and zig-zagged along the road in front of the car, bewildered by the lights. Bertie slowed down and it stopped. He moved gently forward again and the hare continued its erratic and terrified course. At length, Hilda could bear it no longer, and motioned Bertie to stop completely, which he did in a convenient farm gateway.

The hare made off across the fields. It was very quiet with the engine at rest, and Hilda gave a little sigh.

'Bertie,' she began, 'we don't often get a little time on our own, and before we get home I want your advice.'

'My advice?' queried Bertie, genuinely startled. 'It's usually the other way round, mamma.'

'I'm worried about so many things, Bertie, and I can't discuss them all with your father. Winnie and Leslie Howard is one worry, and there's another.'

She stopped, and her voice had a little tremor which did not escape Bertie.

'There's not much one can do about Winnie,' said he gently. 'She's got plenty of sense, and father will surely have a word with Leslie if he's worried.'

'I doubt it,' responded Hilda, with a flash of spirit. 'He's got worries of his own, I suspect, which are more serious than he'll admit to me.'

She turned to him suddenly.

'Bertie, do try and talk to him. You're a man now, and can help. Something's going very wrong with the business, and he won't discuss it with me. But he's getting so unusually tight with money these days, and only this morning he said he didn't think we'd have the staff Christmas party.'

'No party?' echoed Bertie. Things must be serious indeed if this annual jollity, which Bender so much enjoyed, were to be cancelled.

'And there's a lot of other things. This car, for instance. He's really cross that you've bought it, and says we can't afford it.'

93

'But it's my own money,' protested Bertie, with justifiable heat. 'I saved every penny of it! Father knows that! And in any case, it's a dashed sight cheaper to run this little A.C. than to keep our horses in fodder and the trap in repair. Really, it's a bit thick!'

'Forget what I said,' said Hilda hastily, patting her son's hand. 'It's simply that he's terribly worried, and if you can help him, Bertie, he'll be so grateful, and so will I.'

'I'll do what I can, mamma,' replied Bertie, a trifle huffily, starting up the car again.

He drove home, fuming secretly at his father's criticism. Can't afford it indeed! Anyone would think he'd badgered the old man into parting with his money! For two pins he'd have it out with him the minute he got home!

But the words were never said. For when he and his mother entered the drawing-room above the shop, they found Bender white-faced, his sparse hair on end, and papers and account books in confusion on the desk and floor.

'Bender,' cried Hilda, hurrying towards him, 'what on earth has happened?'

'Plenty!' replied Bender grimly. 'Bob's gone off with the cash box, and I've sent the police after him!'

9

Thoughts in the Snow

THE NEWS of Bob's disappearance swept through Caxley with the speed and commotion of a forest fire.

'I've never liked the look of that fellow,' wheezed fat Mrs Petty, wise after the event. 'Had a look in his eye like this 'ere cod. Proper slimy customer, I always thought.'

The square buzzed with the gossip on that market day. Both stallholders and customers knew Bob and Bender well. It seemed a shameful thing for a man to serve his master so shabbily, wagged some of the tongues.

'We ain't heard Bob's side yet,' replied the more cautious. 'Catch the fellow first, I says. Maybe 'e never took it after all. Who's to say?'

As soon as Sep Howard heard of the affair he went across the square to see Bender. He did not relish the encounter. Bender hurt could be Bender at his most truculent, as Sep well knew, and the age-long tremors still shook the little man as he entered the ironmonger's shop.

Bender was rummaging in one of the many small drawers ranged on the wall behind the counter.

'Can you spare a minute?' asked Sep.

Bender led the way, without a word, into the shop parlour behind the shop, where private transactions were carried out. He motioned Sep to a high office stool and sat himself heavily on another.

'S'pose you've heard?' grunted Bender. 'Fine old how-d'you-do, ain't it?'

'I'm sorry,' said Sep. 'Was much taken?'

'The week's takings.'

Sep drew in his breath with a hiss. He knew what it was to face such disasters in business.

'Any chance of getting it back?'

'I doubt it, Sep, I doubt it.' Bender passed a gigantic hand over his face and head, as though to wipe away the cares that clung to him. 'There's no doubt about one thing though. The blighter's been helping himself off and on for two or three months now, and I hadn't twigged. Been too careless by half, Sep. Left too much to him, you see.'

He pushed a ledger across to him.

'See that eight? That was a three. See that nine? That was a nought. Oh, he's been having a high old time among the books just lately!'

'But what's behind it? He got a decent wage, lived pretty small, never seemed to flash the money about.'

'Betting,' said Bender briefly. 'Always liked a bob on a horse, and now it's turned into a sovereign. I've been round to see his old ma, and it all came out. I feel sorry for the poor old girl, I must say. Come to that, I feel pretty sorry for myself, Sep.'

This seemed Sep's chance to speak up, and he took it.

'If I can help, I hope you'll let me. I don't forget all you did for me, you know. You gave me a hand when I needed it most and I'd like to have the chance to help, if there's any mortal way of doing it.'

Bender's great face flushed red. There was no doubt that he

was touched by the offer. He cleared his throat huskily before answering.

'Good of you, Sep. I appreciate it very much, and you'd be the first I'd turn to, if it came to it. But I ain't pushed for a pound yet, and I reckon North's will make it, Bob or no Bob.'

There was a heartiness about this reply which did not ring quite true to Sep. Bender was making light of a situation which was far more serious than he would admit. But Sep could do no more in the circumstances.

'Well, I'll be over the way if you want me any time, Bender. You know that. I hope it'll all get cleared up satisfactorily.'

He made his way from the shop feeling very worried. But in the midst of his doubts and fears, he took comfort from the words still ringing in his ears.

'You'd be the first I'd turn to, if it came to it!'

He never thought to hear Bender North utter those words to him.

A week passed, and still the villain was at large. The police had found that he was seen on the London-bound train on the evening of his disappearance. Two Caxley ladies, returning from a day's shopping in town, also remembered seeing him at Paddington station. Beyond that, there was nothing. Somewhere, Bob was lying very quietly indeed, waiting for the hue and cry to die down, it seemed.

It was almost November and a bitingly cold east wind bedevilled the town, raising tempers as well as dust. Doors banged, windows rattled, and fires smoked indoors. Outdoors it was even worse. The wind whipped off hats, stung cheeks, inflamed eyes, and screamed through the awnings of the market stalls. Dust eddied in miniature whirlwinds, raising paper, leaves and straw, and depositing them where they were least wanted. Coughs and colds, sore throats and chapped lips plagued the populace, and it was generally agreed that it would be 'a darned good thing when the wind changed'.

Unscathed by the hostile world about them, Leslie and Winnie continued to rejoice in each other's company. Bertie had dutifully spoken to his sister, saying that their mother was worried, and that he too hoped that she was not serious about Leslie. Winnie had answered briefly. They had known the Howards all their lives. She knew what she was doing. She also knew that her mother was worried, and they had spoken about it before Bertie was approached. Bertie, having fired his warning shot, retreated in some disarray before Winnie's level defence.

Sep had suddenly realized what was afoot and secretly approved of their union. What could be more fitting than a wedding between the two families? It would be a happy bond between Bender and himself. He recalled Bender's comforting words. Sep's heart warmed to the young people. His Leslie was a fine boy and it was time he settled down. Winnie would make a good wife. As far as Sep could see the outlook was rosy. He liked the idea of the young couple finding happiness together. He liked too the idea of becoming closer to Bender. He said as much to Edna, and was disconcerted by her reply.

'You don't think *he'll* like it, do you? Nor our Hilda! She's got her eye on the gentry for her Winnie! Nothing less than a belted earl for Hilda's daughter!'

'What's wrong with Leslie? Fine upstanding youngster with

a share in the business – you don't tell me that the Norths will disapprove?'

'That I do!' responded Edna flatly. 'Say what you like, Sep, the Norths have always looked down on us, and they won't let their Winnie marry Leslie without a fight.'

'You're fancying things!' muttered Sep, turning away. There was too much truth in Edna's sallies to please him, but he refused to be daunted.

'Let the young 'uns find their own way,' he pronounced at last, and hurried into the bakery before he heard any more unwelcome home truths.

There was plenty of work to distract Sep's attention from his son's affairs of the heart during the next few weeks, for Christmas was approaching, and there were scores of Christmas cakes to be made and iced.

Although Sep now employed several more workers, he still did as much himself in the bakery. The fragrance of the rich mixture, the mingled aroma of spices, candied fruits and brown sugar, cheered Sep afresh every year. It was his own personal offering to the spirit of Christmas, and he enjoyed the festive bustle in the warmly scented bakery. It was like a sheltered haven from the bleak winds in the market square beyond the doors.

The cold spell was lasting longer than expected, and the weather-wise old folk prophesied a white Christmas in Caxley. Sure enough, in the week before Christmas, a light fall whitened the ground and powdered the rosy-tiled roofs of the town, and the lowering grey skies told of more to follow.

On Sunday afternoon, Bender set off for Beech Green with two large saw blades for Jesse Miller.

'He won't get much done in the fields,' commented Bender wrapping the blades briskly in brown paper. 'The ground's like iron. He'll be glad to set the men to sawing firewood tomorrow, and I promised him these as soon as they came.'

'Give them all my love,' said Hilda. 'I won't come with you with the weather like this. And wrap up warmly, do, my dear. Put your muffler on, and your thick gloves.'

'Never fear,' answered Bender robustly. 'I've known the downs long enough to know how to dress for them. I'll be back before dark.'

The horse trotted briskly through the town. There were very few people about and Bender was glad to be on his own, in the clean fresh air. Now he could turn over his thoughts, undisturbed by family interruptions or customers' problems. He always felt at his best driving behind a good horse. He liked the rhythm of its flying feet, the gay rattle of the bowling wheels, and the clink and squeak of the well-polished harness.

The pace slackened as Bill, the horse, approached Beech Green. The long pull up the downs was taken gently and steadily. The reins lay loosely across the glossy back, and Bender reviewed his situation as they jogged along together through the grey and white countryside.

Things were serious, that was plain. Bob had been picked up by the London police ten days earlier, and now awaited his trial at the next Assizes. He had been in possession of fourteen shillings and ninepence at the time of his arrest, and could not – or would not – give any idea of where the rest of the money had gone. Clearly, nothing would be restored to his employer.

What would he do, Bender asked himself? He could get a further loan from the bank, but would it be of any use? Had the time come to take a partner who would be willing to put money into the firm? Bender disliked the idea. He could approach both Sep Howard and Jesse Miller who had offered help, but he hated the thought of letting Sep Howard see his straits, and he doubted whether Jesse Miller could afford to give him the sum needed to give the business a fresh start. Jesse was in partnership with his brother Harry at the farm, and times were hard for them both at the moment.

The other course was a much more drastic one. Tenby's had approached him with a tentative offer. If he ever decided to part with the business would he give them first offer. He would of course be offered a post with the firm who would be glad of his experience. They were thinking of housing their agricultural machinery department on separate premises. North's, in the market square, handy for all the farmers in the district, would suit them perfectly. They asked Bender to bear it in mind. Bender had thought of little else for two days, but had said nothing to Hilda. He knew well enough that she would be all in favour of the action, and he wanted to be sure that it was right before making any final decisions.

Hilda, for years now, had been pressing Bender to move from the shop to one of the new houses on the hill at the south side of the town.

'It's so much healthier for the children,' asserted Hilda. 'You know how chesty Mary is—she takes after you, you know—and it's so damp right by the river here.'

'She looks all right to me,' Bender said.

'Besides,' continued his wife, changing her tactics, 'everyone's moving away from the businesses – the Loaders, the Ashtons, the Percys—'

'The Howards aren't,' pointed out Bender. Hilda tossed her head impatiently.

'Don't be awkward, Bender! Who cares what the Howards do anyway? It would be far better for Bertie and Winnie, and Mary too, later on, to have a place they can ask their friends to without feeling ashamed.'

'*Ashamed?*' echoed Bender thunderously. 'What's wrong with this place?'

'We could have a tennis court if we had a bigger garden,' said Hilda. Her blue eyes held that far-away look which Bender had come to realize was the prelude to some expense or another. 'The children could invite all sorts of nice people to tennis parties.'

'They're free to invite them here to parties – boating and otherwise – as far as I'm concerned,' said Bender. 'Don't tell me that it's the children who want to move. It's entirely your notion, my dear, and a mighty expensive one too.'

Hilda had fallen silent after that, but returned to the attack many times until Bender had begun to wonder if there was something in the idea after all. It was not social progress, though, that caused Bender to give the matter his attention, but the financial possibilities of the move.

If Tenby's made him the substantial offer he expected, he could well afford to buy Hilda the house of her dreams. There was no doubt about it that the market place living quarters were rambling and far too large for their needs. Bertie and

Winnie, it was reasonable to suppose, would be married and away before long. It would be more economical, in every way, for those who were left, to live in a smaller and more up-to-date house where repairs and upkeep would probably be less than half the present sum. Also, Hilda was right in saying that they would find it healthier. Not only would they be on higher ground; it would be a good thing to leave the business behind at night and get right away from its responsibilities.

He presumed that he would be offered the managership. In that case there would be a steady income, with no worries attached. Bender, gazing unseeingly across the snowy fields, lulled almost into slumber by the rhythmic swaying of the trap, began to feel that selling North's might be the best way out of his many difficulties. But not yet, he told himself. He would hang on as long as he could, and who knows? Something might turn up. He'd been lucky often enough before. There was still hope! Bender North was always an optimist.

He put Billy into the shelter of a stable and tramped across the snowy yard to the Miller's back door.

He was greeted warmly by the family, and he was put by the fire to thaw out. The usual vast tea was offered him, but Bender ate sparingly, with one eye cocked on the grey threatening sky outside.

'I mustn't be too long,' said Bender, his mouth full of buttered toast. 'There's more snow to come before morning, or I'll eat my boots.'

They exchanged family news. Ethel's youngest was running a temperature, and was upstairs in bed, 'very fretful and scratchity', as his mother said. Jesse's pigs were not doing as well as he had hoped, and he had an idea that one of his men was taking eggs. 'Times were bad enough for farmers,' said Jesse, 'without such set-backs.'

He accompanied Bender to the stable when he set off.

'And how are your affairs?' he asked when they were out of earshot of the house. Bender gave a reassuring laugh, and clapped the other man's shoulders.

'Better than they have been, Jesse, I'm glad to say. I hope I shan't have to worry you at all.'

The look of relief that flooded Jesse's face did not escape Bender. It certainly looked as though Tenby's would be the only possible avenue of escape if the business grew worse.

Ah well, thought Bender, clattering across the cobbled yard, we must just live in hope of something turning up! He waved to Jesse and set off at a spanking pace on the downhill drive home.

The snow began to fall as Bender turned out of Jesse's gate. It came down thickly and softly, large flakes flurrying across mile upon mile of open downland, like an undulating lacy curtain. It settled rapidly upon the iron-hard ground, already sheeted in the earlier fall, and by the time Billy had covered half a mile the sound of his trotting hoofs was muffled. He snorted fiercely at the onslaught of this strange element, his breath bursting from his flaring nostrils in clouds of vapour. His dark mane was starred with snow flakes, and as he tossed his head Bender caught a glimpse of his shining eyes grotesquely ringed with glistening snow caught in his eyelashes.

His own face was equally assaulted. The snow flakes fluttered against his lips and eyes like icy moths. It was difficult to breathe. He pulled down the brim of his hard hat, and hoisted up the muffler that Hilda had insisted on his wearing, so that he could breathe in the stuffy pocket of air made by his own warmth. Already the front of his coat was plastered, and he looked like a snowman.

A flock of sheep, in a field, huddled together looking like one vast fleece ribbed with snow. The bare hedges were fast becoming blanketed, and the banks undulated past the bowling trap smoothly white, but for the occasional pock-mark of a bird's claws. The tall dry grasses bore strange exotic white flowers in their dead heads, and the branches of trees collected snowy burdens in their arms.

And all the time there was a rustling and whispering, a sibilance of snow. The air was alive with movement, the dancing and whirling of a thousand thousand individual flakes with a life as brief as the distance from leaden sky to frozen earth. At the end of their tempestuous short existence they lay together, dead and indivisible, forming a common shroud.

There was a grandeur and beauty about this snowy country-side which affected Bender deeply. Barns and houses, woods and fields were now only massive white shapes, their angles smoothed into gentle curves. He passed a cow-man returning from milking, his head and shoulders shrouded in a sack, shaped like a monk's cowl. He was white from head to foot, only his dark eyes, glancing momentarily at the passing horse, and his plodding gait distinguished him from the white shapes about him.

Bender turned to watch him vanishing into the veil of swirling flakes. Behind him, the wheels were spinning out two grey ribbons, along the snowy road. He doubted whether they would still be visible to the fellow traveller, so fast were they being covered from above.

He turned back and flicked the reins on Billy's snow-spattered satin back.

'Gee up, boy!' roared Bender cheerfully. 'We both want to get home!'

Sep Howard watched the snow falling from his bedroom window. His hair was rumpled from a rare afternoon nap on the bed, and he had awakened to find the window darkened with flying flakes.

He judged that it was two or three inches deep already. The steps of St Peter's and the Town Hall were heavily carpeted. The snow had blown into the cracks and jambs of doors and windows, leaving long white sticks like newly-spilt milk. A mantle of snow draped Queen Victoria's shoulders and her bronze crown supported a little white cushion which looked like ermine. Snow lay along her sceptre and in the folds of her robes. The iron cups, in the fountain at her feet, were filled to the brim with snow flakes, and the embossed lions near by peered from snow-encrusted manes.

There were very few people about for a Sunday afternoon. An old tramp, carrying his belongings in a red-spotted bundle on a stick, shuffled disconsolately past St Peter's, head bent, rheumy eyes fixed upon the snow at his feet. Two ragged urchins, no doubt from the marsh, giggled and barged each other behind him, scraping up the snow in red, wet hands to make snowballs.

Sep watched them heave them at the back of the unsuspecting old man. At the moment of impact he swung round sharply, and raised his bundle threateningly. Sep could see his red, wet, toothless mouth protesting, but could hear no word through the tightly-shut bedroom window. One boy put his thumb to his nose impudently: the other put out his tongue. But they let the old man shuffle round the corner unmolested before throwing their arms round each other's skinny shoulders and running jubilantly down an alley-way.

Momentarily the market square was empty. Not even a pigeon pattered across the snow. Only footprints of various sizes, and the yellow stain made by a horse's urine, gave any sign of life in that white world. Snow clothed the rosy bricks and sloping roofs of Caxley. It covered the hanging signs and the painted nameboards above the shops, dousing the bright colours as a candle snuffer douses a light.

What a grey and white world, thought Sep! As grey and white as an old gander, as grey and white as the swans and cygnets floating together on the Cax! The railings outside the bank stood starkly etched against the white background, each spear-top tipped with snow. There was something very soothing in this negation of colour and movement. It reminded Sep of creeping beneath the bedclothes as a child, and crouching there, in a soft, white haven, unseeing and unseen, all sounds muffled, as he relished the secrecy and security of it all.

There was a movement in St Peter's porch and a dozen or so choirboys came tumbling out into the snowy world, released from carol practice. The sight brought Sep, sighing, back into the world of Sunday afternoon.

He picked up a hair-brush and began to attack his tousled locks.

'Looks as though the weather prophets are right,' said Sep to his reflection. 'Caxley's in for a white Christmas this year.'

10

Trouble at North's

THE WEATHER prophets were right. Caxley had a white Christmas and the good people of the town walked to church and chapel through a sugar-icing world sparkling in bright sunshine.

Edna, wrapped warmly in a new black coat trimmed with fur at the neck and hem – Sep's Christmas present to her – felt snug and happy, as she composed herself to day-dreaming whilst the minister delivered his half-hour's exhortation. Even his stern countenance was a little softened by the joyous festival, she noticed.

'New hope, a new life, a New Year,' declaimed the minister, and Edna thought how queer it would be to write 1914 so soon. It would be a relief too, in a way. She had felt a little uneasy through 1913. It was an unlucky number. Gipsy superstitions played a larger part in Edna's life than ever her husband suspected.

Yes, there was something reassuring about the sound of 1914. She was going to enjoy this beautiful Christmas and her beautiful new coat, and look forward to an even more prosperous New Year than ever before!

'Peace on earth, goodwill toward men,' the minister was saying, one finger upraised for attention.

Edna stroked her new fur trimming and sighed contentedly.

*   *   *

Hilda North also welcomed the New Year. In its early months Bender, with his mind now clear, told her of Tenby's offer and the possibility of buying the house of her dreams on Caxley's southern slopes.

Hilda was joyful and triumphant.

'Have you told Bertie?' was her first question. 'He ought to know. After all, this would have been his one day.'

Bender promised to speak to his son that evening. It was a mild spring day with soft rain falling, straight and steady over Caxley and the countryside. In his waterside garden, Bender watched the rain collecting in the cups of his fine red tulips, and dripping, drop by drop, from leaf to leaf, down the japonica bush against the workshop wall. The Cax was dimpled with rain, the rustic bridge glistened. There was a soft freshness in the whispering air that soothed, and yet saddened, the watching man. He was going to miss all this, after so many years. Would Bertie miss it too?

Bertie, at that moment, was also watching the rain. He was at Fairacre where he had been summoned by old Mr Parr whose automobile refused to start. Bertie had spent the morning repairing it, and now sat in the thatched barn which housed the car, munching a sausage roll which was his lunch. A robin splashed in a puddle near by, flirting wings and tail, bobbing its thumb-sized head, as it gloried in its bath.

A veil of drops fell steadily from the thatched roof, splashing on to the washed gravel surrounding the building. In the field next door Bertie could see sheep moving slowly and unconcernedly, their wool soaked with rain. Steam gently rose from their backs as they cropped. An old cart-horse, streaked with the wet, nodded under a horse chestnut tree, its back as shiny as the sticky buds bursting from the branches above it.

It was a good life thought Bertie, looking across at the motor-car restored to usefulness. He hoped he might never leave this absorbing occupation. It would be a sad day for him if his father decided that he should take over the family business! No – motor-cars were his own choice!

He brushed the crumbs from his clothes, stood up, and decided to visit the 'Beetle and Wedge' for a drink, before returning to Caxley.

It was a relief to the young man when Bender spoke of his affairs that evening, and he said so.

'I haven't liked to question you, Father, but I guessed things were getting more and more difficult. That business of Bob's seems to have put the lid on it.'

'Well, he's safely inside for twelve months,' replied Bender, 'and we're all a sight better off without the rascal. But North's will have to go, as far as I can see, and perhaps it's as well. I shall still be able to work here, and not have the responsibility. I tell you frankly, Bertie, I shouldn't like to go through the last year or so again.'

'You'll miss the garden,' said Bertie, looking out at the wet evening.

'There'll be another on the hill,' said Bender robustly. 'And I'm glad for your mother's sake we're making the move. It means a lot to her.'

He clapped his son on the shoulder in a dismissive way.

'Glad to have told you, Bertie. You've taken it very well.

There's times I've felt I've let you all down. This used to be a real warm business, as you know. I've been a bit of a bungler, it seems to me.'

'You can put that idea out of your head,' replied Bertie. 'It's just the way things have fallen out. I, for one, won't miss the business. My heart's never been in it, as you well know.'

He made his way up to his room to change. His spirits rose as he mounted the stairs, for he was going to the Howards' and would spend the evening in Kathy's company.

He stood at the window looking down upon the glistening market square, and, for the first time since hearing the news, he felt a sudden pang.

This he would miss. He had not realized quite how much it meant to him. He could not imagine living in another house which did not look upon the market square. This scene had been the background to his entire life. He could remember being held in Vera's arms, clad in his scratchy flannel nightshirt, to watch the pigeons wheeling across the striped awnings of the market stalls. He had stood at that window in tears of fury after being banished from below for some misdemeanour. He had stood there, in quiet contemplation, soothed by the familiar shapes of the clustered buildings and the comings and goings of well-known Caxley folk. His fears and doubts, his hopes and joys, had been experienced here in the market square. Here were his roots, here was his entire past. How would he live without the market place around him, its sights and sounds, and its bustle of people?

He looked across at Howard's bakery. How could he live so far from Kathy? The thought was insupportable. He flung away from the window and tore off his working jacket in near panic. Then he recovered his control.

He was behaving like a child. He would still be living in Caxley. Kathy would still be there, lovely and loving. Who knows? One day he might come back to live in the market square, in a house of his own, with Kathy to share it.

The news that the North family was leaving the market place came as a great shock to Caxley. The business had been there for three generations, and Bender was popular. It was sad to think of that vast figure filling a doorway no longer his own. A few self-righteous and mean-spirited citizens announced that Bender had brought this humiliation upon himself by slackness and indolence. But Bender's friends rose to his support, and cried them down.

The move was a leisurely one, much to Hilda's exasperation. She would have liked to pack up and go immediately, once the decision was made, but it was not to be. Tenby's had much to arrange with Bender, and Hilda had to content herself with daily trips up the hill to supervise the painting and decorating which went on in the red-brick villa so soon to be the family home.

As usual, on these occasions, nothing in the old house seemed to fit the new one. The curtains and carpets were either too small, too large, or too shabby. Hilda nobly did her best to keep expenses down, knowing now the truth of their financial circumstances, but she fought a losing battle. Colours clashed, walnut warred with oak, the vast mahogany dining table had to be left behind because it would not go through any door or window, and a new one bought. New chintz covers became a necessity, shrouding odd chairs in a more pleasing harmony. Two fireplaces had to be replaced, and it was deemed necessary to overhaul the gas system from the attics to the cellars. Bender began to wonder if the tidy sum from Tenby's would be enough to cover the cost of the new villa, let alone leaving him a nest egg in the bank.

His own time was occupied in clearing out the main part of the premises for Tenby's agricultural equipment. A mammoth sale of kitchen hardware took place and was long remembered in Caxley in the years to come. Many a stout bread crock or set of saucepans became known in cottage homes in the Caxley district as 'one of North's last bargains'.

Most of Tenby's men were local fellows, well known to Bender, and he found no difficulty in getting on with them in the weeks that followed. Tenby himself he disliked. He was a shrewd business man, originally from the north, and thought far more quickly than Bender ever could. His beady dark eyes ran over the possibilities of the old house, and Bender could not help feeling a qualm when he heard him discussing the advantages of ripping out the first floor walls to make one large showroom above the shop. His grey and white striped drawing-room, now standing empty, seemed to breathe a mute appeal. Where now were the red velvet chairs, the wall brackets bearing sea-lavender, and all the other familiar furnishings of his best-loved room? Bender had to admit that the new house gave him small satisfaction compared with the spacious shabby comfort of the old premises. It would be sad to see the place so altered.

It made him sadder still when he discovered that later on the firm proposed to flatten his beautiful little garden, cement it over, and to erect an enormous structure on the site to house new tractors and other large pieces of equipment. Bender could hardly bear to think about it. The pinks bordering the river bank were particularly fine in the summer of 1914, and their heady fragrance held a doomed poignancy which Bender never forgot. What had he done when he had parted with his heritage? Was it all to be destroyed?

The family was now installed on the hill. The new house was called 'Rose Lodge' which Hilda felt was refined. It took Bender years before he could write it automatically at the head of his rare letters. Somehow he always put 15 *The Market Square*, before remembering the change of address.

The top two floors of the old premises were to be refurbished, 'for future staff use', as Jack Tenby said. Meanwhile, they stood empty. Sometimes Bender climbed the stairs and had a look at the bare dusty rooms. Against the walls were marks where furniture had stood for years. Here the paper had peeled where young Mary's prying fingers had been busy through the bars of her cot. There was the pale circle on the wall where Winnie's mirror had hung. And there on the corner pane were Bertie's initials, cut with his mother's diamond ring. That little escapade had earned the young ten-year-old a severe spanking, Bender recalled.

There was something infinitely pathetic in the ghostly rooms. They were full of memories. Every creak of the floorboards, every rattle of the windows, was familiar to Bender. He had not realized how tightly the old house had entwined them all, until he had cut the bonds, only to find himself still imprisoned in memories. He threw himself into the work of supervising the changes in the shop, glad to be able to forget the silence above in the hubbub of activity below.

It was not easy, as Bender discovered, as the summer slipped by. For one thing, it was excessively hot. The market place basked in one golden day after another. The Cax seemed the only cool spot in the town, and was besieged by boys and girls swimming and paddling in the evenings. For a man of Bender's weight, the weather seemed torrid, however much the younger ones might revel in it. He took to slipping out into the doomed garden to enjoy the air and to gain refreshment from the sight of the cool water rippling by. But again the pleasure was tempered by the oppressive knowledge that this might well be the last summer in which the garden would enchant him.

It was towards the end of July that the first blow came. Bender's managership had been tacitly understood, and for three months now he had done his best to get things working smoothly, under the eye of Jack Tenby, and one or two other directors of the firm, who called in from time to time to see how things were shaping.

One morning, Bender found a letter waiting for him at the office, and he read it with mounting indignation. It said that the firm had now had a chance to make plans and were reorganising their business, both in Caxley and elsewhere. Their young Mr Parker, of Trowbridge, who had been with the firm since leaving school, would be transferred to the agricultural department of the Caxley firm and would take up residence on the premises, as soon as possible. He would be in charge of the department, and they felt sure that Mr North would give him all the co-operation he had so readily shown to the firm in the last few months. They would be pleased to maintain Mr North's present rate of pay, and hoped to have the advantage of his experience for many years to come. They were 'his faithfully'.

'Faithfully!' snorted Bender, in the privacy of the shop parlour. Was this faith? Was this trust? Was it plain honesty? The truth was that it was a dam' dirty trick, to foist a young man over him in his own shop.

'His own shop.' The words echoed in his ears. Oh, the misery of it all, thought Bender! He ground one gigantic fist into the palm of the other hand, as he read the letter anew.

This was treachery. He would have it out with Jack Tenby. They should not treat Bender North like this. For two pins he would chuck the job in and let them muddle on without his help! That would show them!

But would it? Is that what they wanted? Was he simply a nuisance to be got rid of? And if he threw up this job, where would he get another? There was the family to consider. The new house was still running away with the money at an alarming rate. Dammit all, Bender groaned, ramming the letter back into its envelope, he must try and face the stark and unpleasant fact that he was no longer his own master. It was a bitter pill to swallow at any age. At forty-eight, it was doubly bitter, Bender mourned.

All that day, Bender went mechanically about his affairs in a daze. He decided not to mention the matter to Hilda until his mind was calmer. He felt that he could not bear Hilda's protestations on his behalf, her hurt pride and her ready tears. It was a day or two later, that the second unpleasant happening occurred.

Bender was adding up figures in the shop parlour with the door open into the shop. Near by, Miss Taggerty, and another woman assistant, Miss Chapman, dusted shelves and gossiped together, imagining that they were unheard.

Miss Taggerty, still faithful to the imprisoned Bob, was as plain as ever. The increasing years and private grief had speckled her sandy hair with grey, but had not added discretion to her virtues. She rattled on, blissfully unconscious of Bender's presence so close at hand, telling of scandals past and present. Bender, used to this sort of thing, let it flow over him, until a familiar name caught his attention.

'Of course it's Les Howard's! Why should the girl say it is if it isn't? A lovely boy, old Ma Tucker told my pa. Weighed nigh on ten pounds at birth, and the spitting image of Leslie – same dark eyes and all.'

'But it might be her husband's surely?' objected Miss Chapman. 'He's dark too.'

'Not *this* dark!' pronounced Miss Taggerty triumphantly. 'And it's common knowledge that Les Howard spends far too much time there on the rounds. It's pretty lonely up Bent way. I bet she was glad of a bit of company.'

'But there's not another house in sight!' protested Miss Chapman. 'How do people know Les Howard went in?'

'There's such people as hedgers-and-ditchers, and ploughmen, and the like,' retorted Miss Taggerty. 'And they've got eyes in their heads, and wasn't born yesterday, for that matter. Besides, as I told you, the girl swears it's Leslie's and the husband swears he's going to take him to court over it.'

Bender felt it was time he made his presence known. He

dropped a heavy ledger on the floor, swore and picked it up. The clear voices stopped abruptly, to be replaced by some agitated whispering, and a muffled giggle. He heard no more of the matter, but he thought about it a great deal. If this were true, then it was time his Winnie dropped the young man pretty quickly.

In the next two days he heard the same rumour from other sources. There seemed to be some foundation for the story, and Bender's worries increased. He had half a mind to have a word with Sep about the matter, but decided to let the matter rest for a few days until he was surer of his facts.

As it happened, things came to a head precipitately within the next day or two. Although Winnie and Leslie sought each other's company still, Bender had fancied that they had seen rather less of each other since the move, and hoped that the affair might be dying a natural death. Winnie was extra busy these days at the local hospital where she was doing very well as a nurse. Her free time was scarce, and quite often she spent it lying on her bed to rest her aching legs, in the unusually hot weather.

It was now August, and as close as ever. Hilda and Bender sat in their new drawing-room with all the windows open. A pale yellow moth fluttered round the gas bracket, its wings tap-tapping on the glass globe. Bender found the noise distracting.

He was still mightily aggravated by the letter from Tenby's, and had come to realize that he was in no position to protest. Naturally, this added to his fury. He wondered, as he listened to the moth and turned the newspaper in his hands, if this were the right time to tell Hilda what had occurred. She would have to know some time about 'our young Mr Parker from Trowbridge'.

At the memory, Bender grew hotter than ever. The room seemed stifling. He undid the top button of his shirt, and turned his attention once more to the newspaper. He'd tell Hilda tomorrow. It was late. She might not sleep if he broke the news now.

There seemed mighty little comfort to be had in the paper, he reflected. All this trouble in Europe! Germany at war with Russia, and the ambassador recalled from Petersburg, and the Frenchies getting the wind up and looking to us for help! Not likely, thought Bender! Let them all get on with their squabbling safely on the other side of the English Channel!

It was at that moment that the door burst open and Leslie Howard and Winnie appeared, bright-eyed. Winnie ran to her mother, holding out her hands.

'Mummy, Leslie and I have got engaged! Look at my ring!'

Hilda's face grew rosy with mingled pleasure and wrath. What could be said in the face of such combined triumph and joy? Hilda, tears in her eyes, looked at Bender for assistance.

Something seemed to burst in Bender's head. The rumours flew back to buzz round him like stinging wasps. The heat, his private worries, the depressing newspaper, and his deep love for Winnie pressed upon him unbearably.

He flung the newspaper upon the floor and turned on Leslie.

'Engaged? That you're not, my boy, until I've had a word with you in private. Step across the hall, will you? No time like the present!'

He stormed past the young man, pale-faced, into the empty dining-room, leaving Winnie and her mother trembling.

Sep Howard did not hear of the unknown young Mr Parker's promotion until the day after Leslie's uncomfortable encounter with Bender. He did not hear, either, about that piece of news, from his son.

He was very perturbed on Bender's account. This was going to hurt him very much, and it might well mean that he would be very poorly off. Should he go once again, and offer any help that he could? It needed a certain amount of courage to face Bender at any time, but Sep remembered those words: 'You'd be the first I'd turn to, Sep,' and took heart.

He had heard the news from Jack Tenby himself, and so knew that there was no doubt about it. He decided to step across to the shop as it opened, and to do what he could.

A little nervous, as he always was when approaching Bender, yet glowing with the consciousness of doing the right thing, Sep entered North's shop. Bender glowered at him over his spectacles. His voice was gruffer than ever.

'Whatcher want?' he growled.

'A word with you, please,' answered Sep.

He followed Bender's broad back into the privacy of the shop parlour, and began, diffidently, without further ado.

'I've heard the news about the new manager, Bender. Jack Tenby mentioned it. It's very hard lines on you. Is there anything I can do?'

Bender wheeled to face him, face down, like a cornered bull,

his eyes blazing and his breathing noisy. Sep began to step
back in horror.

'Clear out!' said Bender, dangerously calm. 'That ain't the
only news you've heard, I'll lay! You heard about that son of
your'n and his goings-on?'

He threw his head up suddenly, and began to roar.

'I don't want no mealy-mouthed help from you, Sep
Howard, and I don't want to see hair or hide of you or your
dam' kids ever again! If Leslie comes crawling round our
Winnie once more, I'll give him the hiding of his life. Clear
off, clear out! And dam' well mind your own business!'

He flung open the door, bundled Sep outside, and slammed
the door shut again in the little man's face. Two or three
interested assistants peered furtively from behind shelves. Sep
pulled his jacket straight, and walked past them with as much
dignity as he could muster.

His legs trembled as he crossed the market square, and his
head buzzed with the echo of Bender's shouting. He must see
Leslie at once and hear his side of this shocking story. Shaken
though he was by the encounter, Sep felt more pity and
concern for Bender than fear, and rejoiced in his own
confidence.

His eldest boy, Jim, stood immersed in the newspaper at the
bakery door. His hair was white with flour, his sleeves rolled
up, and his white apron fluttered in the breeze from the river
near by. The boy's face was excited. His eyes sparkled as he
looked up from his reading.

'Well, dad, it looks as though we're ready for 'em! Les and
I should be on our travels pretty soon according to this!'

He held out the paper so that Sep could read the headlines.

'Ultimatum to Germany. War at Midnight.'

Sep's face grew graver as he read.

'I never thought it would come to this,' he said in a low voice, as though speaking to himself. He looked soberly across the paper at his son.

'But it is the right thing to do,' he said slowly. 'No matter what the consequences are, a man must always do what he knows is right.'

He turned to enter, and his son turned to watch him go, a small erect figure, bearing himself with a dignity which the young man had never noticed before.

Across the square, Bender paced up and down the shop parlour, quivering with rage. The calendar caught his eye, and he stopped to tear off yesterday's date. What had he done, he asked himself, crumpling the paper in his hand? His world seemed in ruins. He had upset Hilda, and poor Winnie, and now he had thrown his old friend from him. What straits a man could find himself in! What depths of despair still lay ahead?

Automatically he bent to read the daily motto on the new date. It said: Aug. 4, 1914 'Be strong and of a good courage'.

It was the final straw. Bender sank upon the office stool, dropped his burning head to the cold leather top of the desk, and wept.

PART TWO

11

Over by Christmas

THE PEOPLE of Caxley greeted the declaration of war against Germany with considerable jubilation and a certain measure of relief. Tension had been mounting steadily throughout the past week. Now that the die was cast, excitement seized them.

'That Kaiser's bin too big for 'is boots for time enough. 'E needs taking down a peg or two!' said Mrs Petty.

'Us'll daunt 'em!' declared a bewhiskered shepherd nearby.

'Ah! He've got the Empire to reckon with now!' agreed his old crony, spitting a jet of tobacco juice upon the market place cobbles, with evident satisfaction. The air rang with congratulatory greetings. August Bank Holiday may have been upset a little by the news of war, but spirits were high everywhere.

The papers were full of cartoons depicting Belgium as a helpless maiden in the grip of a strong, brutal, and lustful conqueror. Chivalry flowered again in the hearts of Caxley men. Justice must be done. The weak must be protected, and who better to do it than the British, with all the might of a glorious Empire to support them? There was no possibility of failure. It was simply a question of rallying to a good cause, throwing down a despot, succouring the victims, and then returning to normal life, with the glow of work well done, and a reputation enhanced with valour.

If war had to be, then it was inspiring to be so resolutely on the right side. There was no doubt about this being a righteous cause. It was the free man's blow against slavery. It was even more exhilarating, at this time, for the common man to realize how wide-flung and mighty were the bonds of Empire. There was a sudden resurgence of pride in the colonies overseas. For some years now the word 'imperialism' had seemed tarnished. Kipling's jingoistic exhortations were out of fashion. But the older people in Caxley, including Sep and Bender, remembered the show of might at Queen Victoria's Golden and Diamond Jubilees in 1887 and 1897, and remembered it now, with fierce pride, and considerable comfort.

'You see,' Bender told Hilda, 'they'll come flocking from all over the world – black, brown, and every other colour! Wherever they salute the old Union Jack! The Kaiser hasn't a hope! It'll all be over by Christmas!'

It was the phrase which was heard on all sides: 'Over by Christmas!' As the troop trains poured through Caxley station on their way to the coast, the men shouted it jubilantly to the waving mothers and wives on the platform. Caxley had never seen such a movement of men before. This was the first European war in which England had taken part for generations, and the rumble of road and rail transport, as Haldane's Expeditionary Force moved rapidly towards France, was an inspiring sound. Between August 7th and 17th, in a period of blazing sunshine, it was said that over a hundred thousand men crossed the Channel. To the people of Caxley it seemed that most of them made their way southward through their reverberating market square.

A recruiting centre had been opened at the Town Hall and

the queues waiting outside added to the noise and excitement. From all the surrounding villages and hamlets, from tumble-down cottages hidden a mile or more down leafy cart tracks, the young men found their way to the market square. They came on foot, on bicycles, on horseback and in carts, farm waggons, and motor-cars. One of the most splendid turn-outs came from Fairacre and Beech Green. Two coal-black cart horses, gleaming like jet, drew a great blue-painted waggon with red wheels into the market place. Harold Miller held the reins. His whip was decorated with red, white and blue ribbons, and the brass work on the vehicle and the horses' harness shone like gold.

About a score of young men grinned and waved cheerfully as they clattered into the market square. Jesse Miller sat beside his brother, and among the sun-tanned men aboard could be seen the bright auburn head of Arnold Fletcher, fiancé of Dolly Clare of Fairacre. Bertie North, who had already added his name to the lengthy list, waved enthusiastically to his fellow-comrades from the doorway of his father's shop.

He had never known such deep and satisfying excitement before. Ever since he and the Howard boys had volunteered, life had assumed a purpose and meaning so far unknown to him. It was as though he had been asleep, waiting unconsciously for a call to action. Now it had come, vibrant and compelling, and Bertie, in company with thousands of other young men, responded eagerly.

Their womenfolk were not so ardent. Hilda was openly tearful. She had never made a secret of her great love for Bertie. He held a special place in her heart, and the thought of her eldest child being maimed or killed was insupportable.

Winnie, though outwardly calm, was doubly anguished, for Leslie was involved, as well as Bertie.

Edna Howard, with two sons enlisted and Kathy worrying to leave home to nurse or to drive an ambulance, had her share of cares, but there was a child-like quality about her which rejoiced in the general excitement and the flags and uniforms, military bands and crowds, which enlivened Caxley at this time. It was Sep who went about his business white-faced and silent, suffering not only for his sons, but also because of his years, which denied him military action.

He grieved too for the rift which had parted him and Bender. The rebuff which he had received hurt him sorely. He was too sensitive to approach Bender again, and a quiet 'Good morning' had been greeted with a grunt and a glare from the ironmonger which froze poor Sep in his tracks. As things were, with everything in turmoil, it seemed best to leave matters alone and hope that time would bring them both some comfort.

The Corn Exchange had been turned into a medical centre, and the young men went straight there from the Town Hall. The Howard boys and Bertie were passed fit and swore to serve His Majesty the King, his heirs and successors, and the generals and the officers set over them, kissed the Bible solemnly, and looked with awed delight at the new shilling and the strip of paper bearing their army number, which each received.

'Do we get our uniform yet?' asked Jim hopefully.

'Old 'ard,' replied the sergeant, in charge of affairs. 'You ain't the only pebbles on the beach. You clear orf back to your jobs till you're wanted. You'll hear soon enough, mark my words. Now 'op it!'

Thus began the hardest part of this new adventure. Carrying on with an everyday job was galling in the extreme to these young men. But at least, they told each other, they were in. Some poor devils like Jesse Miller, for instance, had been found medically unfit.

Jesse was heart-broken.

'Flat feet and varicose veins, they said,' Jesse cried in disgust. 'I told 'em I could walk ten miles a day behind the plough without noticing it, but they'd have none of it. Makes me look a proper fool! But I'm not leaving it there. I'll try elsewhere, that I will! I'll get in by hook or by crook! If Harry goes, I go!'

He received a great deal of sympathy, as did other unfortunate volunteers who had been unsuccessful. It was Kathy who shocked everyone by stating a startling truth at this time.

'You'd think they'd be glad really. After all, I suppose lots of the others will be killed or wounded. I think *they're* the lucky ones.'

Her hearers looked at her aghast. What treason was this? Her brothers, and Bertie too, rounded on her abruptly. Had she no proper pride? Did patriotism mean nothing? Of course it was a deprivation for men like poor old Jesse Miller to be denied the glory of battle. They were amazed that she should think otherwise.

Kathy shrugged her pretty shoulders and tossed her dark head.

'It seems all topsy-turvy to me,' she replied nonchalantly. And, later, amidst the chaotic horror of a French battlefield, Bertie was to remember her words.

*   *   *

The sun blazed day after day throughout that golden August. The corn fields ripened early and there would be a bumper harvest. The lanes round Caxley were white with dust. The grass verges and thick hedges were powdered with the chalk raised by the unaccustomed volume of army traffic making its way southward.

It seemed unbelievable that within less than a hundred miles of Caxley, across a narrow ribbon of water, men were blasting each other to death.

Now and again in the noonday heat, which bathed the quiet downs in a shimmering haze, a shuddering rumble could be heard – the guns of distant battle. News of the retreat from Mons came through. It sounded ugly – *a retreat*. Surely, the Caxley folk told each other, the great British army should not be in *retreat*?

It was easy to explain away the unpleasantness. The army was simply moving to a better strategic position. They were luring the Kaiser's men to a sure defeat. There was nothing really to worry about. It would all be over by Christmas, they repeated.

But it was news of the retreat which resulted in action at last for the Caxley volunteers, for they were called up and sent to a training camp in Dorset at the beginning of September.

Winnie North was among those who crowded Caxley station to wave good-bye to Bertie and the Howard boys. She kissed them all in turn, but clung longer to Leslie. As the train drew away her gaze lingered upon his dwindling hand until it vanished around the great bend of the railway line. She returned, pale but calm, to Rose Lodge and her mother's tear-blotched face.

Three days later she broke some news to her father and mother.

'I'm being transferred to a naval hospital,' said Winnie abruptly. She had just come in from work, and still wore her nurse's uniform.

Her mother looked up, wide-eyed with shock. The khaki sock which she was knitting for Bertie fell neglected into her lap. Bender emerged from behind his newspaper and shot her a glance over the top of her spectacles.

'Oh, Winnie dear,' quavered Hilda, her lip trembling.

'Now, mother,' began Winnie firmly, as if speaking to a refractory patient, 'I volunteered for this as soon as war broke out, and I'm very lucky to be chosen. You must see that I can't stay behind when the boys have already gone.'

'Where is this place?' asked Bender.

Winnie told him. Bender's mouth took a truculent line.

'But that's near Bertie,' cried her mother, looking more cheerful.

'And Leslie Howard,' grunted Bender. 'It don't pull the wool over my eyes, me girl.'

'Dad,' said Winnie levelly, 'we've had all that out until I'm sick of it. Once and for all, I am engaged to Leslie, whatever you say. That disgusting rumour you persist in believing hasn't a word of truth in it –'

'Winnie,' broke in Hilda, 'you are not to speak to your father like that. He acted for the best.'

'When I need your support,' bellowed Bender to his wife, 'I'll ask for it! She's nothing but a love-sick ass, and refuses to face facts. I never thought a daughter of mine would be such a fool – but there it is!'

There was an angry silence for a moment, broken at last by Winnie.

'I'll believe Leslie, if you don't mind,' she said in a low voice. 'And it may interest you to know that I didn't choose to go to this hospital – glad though I am, of course. I'm simply being drafted there, and probably not for long.'

'When do you have to go?' asked Hilda.

'Next Saturday,' said Winnie, 'so let's bury the hatchet for these few days and have a little peace.'

She rose from the chair, went across to her mother and kissed her forehead. Five minutes later they heard the bath running and Winnie's voice uplifted in song.

Bender sighed heavily.

'I'll never understand that girl,' he muttered. 'Blinding herself to that waster's faults! Leaving a comfortable home! Defying her parents!'

'She's in love,' replied his wife simply, picking up her knitting.

Rose Lodge seemed sadly quiet when Winnie had departed to her new duties. Mary, the youngest, attended a sedate little private school near her home, and seemed to spend her time in fraying old pieces of sheet for army dressings.

'Pity you don't learn your multiplication tables at the same time,' commented Bender. 'Strikes me that you'll know less than the marsh lot at the National School, when it comes to leaving. And a pretty penny it's costing us too!'

'Why can't I leave then?' urged Mary. 'I could help at the

hospital, couldn't I? Sweeping, and that? Kathy Howard's started there as a nurse. Did you know?'

Bender looked at Hilda. Hilda turned a little pink. Since the row with Sep he had not spoken a word to any of the Howards if he could help it, but Hilda kept in touch.

'Well, I did just happen to run across Edna at the butcher's yesterday,' admitted his wife, 'and she mentioned it. I should think she'd make a good little nurse; cheerful and quick to learn. And it does mean she can live at home,' added Hilda, rather sadly, her thoughts with her distant Winnie.

Bender made no comment, but his frown deepened, and Hilda's heart sank. If only things could be as they used to be before that horrid little Mr Parker from Trowbridge took charge of their shop! If only Bender could shake off the cares which seemed to bow him down! In the old days, nothing had worried him, it seemed. She remembered their early troubles, their set-backs, the loss of their first baby, the financial struggles of their early years in business, Bob's duplicity, and a hundred other problems. Somehow Bender had always faced things cheerfully, his great laugh had blown away her cares throughout their married life, until this last disastrous year. If only he could recover his old spirits!

She made a timid suggestion, hoping to distract his mind from the Howards' affairs and turn it to happier things.

'Shall we go and have a look at the dahlias, dear?'

'No thanks,' said Bender shortly. 'Nothing seems to do as well here as in the old garden. It's disheartening.'

He slumped back into his armchair and closed his eyes. It was, thought Hilda, as if he wanted to shut out the sight of the pretty new drawing room at Rose Lodge. Was he, in spirit, perhaps, back in the old room above the shop where they had spent so many evenings together? How helpless she felt, in the face of this silent unhappiness! Would there never be an end to it?

Letters came regularly from Winnie and Bertie during the following months. They met occasionally. Both looked extraordinarily well, they assured their parents separately. Bertie had put on almost a stone in weight, and there were rumours that his unit would be off to France before Christmas. If so, there would be leave, of course. Bertie said he would let them know just as soon as he knew himself. Hilda was buoyed up with hope, and hurried about making a hundred preparations, refusing to think further than the homecoming.

Winnie mentioned Leslie in her letters, but did not speak of her feelings. Hilda guessed that she did not want to upset her father by introducing the contentious subject.

At the beginning of December two letters arrived at Rose Lodge. Bertie's said that his week's leave began on the following day, and would his mother cook a really square meal? Winnie's said that she too had leave, and would be arriving three days after Bertie. She too could do with a square meal. Singing, Hilda made her way to the kitchen to make joyful preparations. Bender, smiling at last, stumped down the hill to the shop, which he had come to loathe, to embark on the day's work with rather more eagerness than usual.

Across the market square, Sep Howard stood in the kitchen reading a letter from Leslie. He too was smiling. Edna waited anxiously for him to finish, so that she could read it for herself.

He handed it over with a happy sigh.

'Read that, my love,' he said gently.

Edna's eyes widened as she read, and her pretty mouth fell open.

'Married?' she whispered.

'Married!' repeated Sep huskily. To Edna's surprise, she saw that there were tears in his eyes. She had never realized that Leslie had meant so much to him.

But it was not Leslie, nor his bride, that occupied Sep's thoughts. This, Sep told himself thankfully, must heal the breach between Bender and himself. At last his earnest prayers had been answered.

12

An Unwelcome Marriage

BERTIE'S HOMECOMING was such a joyful occasion, he looked so fit and happy, that neither of his parents noticed a certain constraint in his manner. His appetite was enormous, his eagerness to visit his Caxley friends so keen, that Hilda was kept busy providing meals and entertainment.

Winnie was expected the following Wednesday.

'Did she tell you what time she would arrive?' asked Hilda at breakfast. 'I must go shopping this morning, but I don't want to be out when she comes.'

'I don't think she'll be here much before this evening,' said Bertie slowly.

'How late!' exclaimed Hilda. 'Won't she catch the same train as you?'

'I doubt it,' replied Bertie briefly, and escaped from the room.

All that day, Hilda went about her affairs, humming cheerfully. Bertie watched her carry a vase of late chrysanthemums up the stairs to Winnie's room. When darkness fell, she refused to draw the curtains in the drawing room, hoping to catch the first glimpse of Winnie coming up the path.

It was very quiet that evening. Bender dozed in his armchair, Hilda was stitching braid on a skirt, and Bertie flipped idly through the pages of the *Caxley Chronicle*. It was nearly eight o'clock when they heard the sound of footsteps on the gravel outside, and before Hilda could fold up her sewing and hurry out, the door opened and, Winnie, smiling and radiant, blinking in the unaccustomed light, stood on the threshold. Behind her was a tall figure.

'Leslie!' exclaimed Hilda involuntarily. The joy in her face faded to a look of apprehension. The couple came into the room and Bender awoke.

'What the devil – ' he rumbled truculently, eyeing the young man. Winnie went forward swiftly, kissed him, and pushed him back again into the armchair.

'Don't say anything, Dad dear, just listen,' she pleaded. She turned to face them.

'Leslie and I are married. It's no good scolding us, either of you. So, please, *please*, forgive us and say you hope we'll be happy.'

Hilda moved forward, her face working. She took Winnie in her arms and gave her a gentle kiss, but there were tears in her eyes.

'You should have told us,' she protested. 'You should have written. This hurts us all so terribly.'

Bender had struggled to his feet. His face was red, his head thrust forward like an angry bull.

'This is a fine way to treat your mother and me,' he growled thickly. 'You'll get no forgiveness from me – either of you – whatever your mother does.'

He glared round the room and caught sight of Bertie's pale face. Something in it made him start forward.

'You knew about this,' he said accusingly. Bertie nodded.

'I stood witness, Dad,' he said. 'I'm sorry.'

There was a dreadful silence, broken only by Bender's

laboured heavy breathing. At last he gave a great gasp, shouldered his way blindly across the room, and burst through the French windows into the garden, leaving them to clang behind him.

'Bender!' cried Hilda, beginning to follow, but Bertie caught her arm.

'He's better alone, mamma,' he said quietly. 'Sit down, and I'll bring you a drink.'

He turned to the young couple.

'No doubt you'll need one too.' He moved a chair forward for Winnie and motioned the silent Leslie to another. There was an authority about him which cooled the situation.

'It would have been nice to drink a toast to your future happiness,' said Bertie, when the glasses were filled, 'but this does not seem quite the time to do it.'

Hilda, trembling, took a sip and then put down her glass carefully on the work-box beside her.

'This has been such a shock – such an awful shock! You know how your father has felt, Winnie. And as for you, Leslie, I don't think we shall ever be able to forgive you. So underhand, so sly – !' She began to fumble for a handkerchief.

'Mamma, it was no use telling you anything. Neither you nor Dad would listen. We knew that. We were determined to get married. Now we have. In a registry office. You'll simply have to get used to the idea.'

Leslie spoke at last.

'I wanted to write, but Winnie felt it was far better to come and tell you ourselves when it was all over. I promise you I'll take care of her. You must know that.'

'I don't know that,' responded Hilda with a flash of spirit, 'which is why we opposed the match. But now it's done, then all I can say is that I sincerely *hope* you will take care of her.'

Practical matters now came to the front of her distracted mind. Winnie's room lay ready for her, but what should be done with Leslie? If only Bender would return from the garden! If only he would give her some support in this dreadful moment!

As though divining her thoughts Winnie spoke.

'We're not going to stay, Mamma, as things are. Father's too upset, and it will take him a little while to get used to the idea. Aunt Edna has offered us a room and we'll call here again tomorrow morning. We'll try to have a word now with Dad before we go.'

She kissed her mother again and squeezed her gently.

'Cheer up, my love. We're so happy, don't spoil it for us. And try to persuade Father that it isn't the end of the world.'

'I'm afraid it *is* the end of the world for him,' replied Hilda sadly.

The young couple made their way into the dark garden followed by Bertie.

'Dad!' called Winnie.

'Dad!' called Bertie.

But there was no reply. Bender was a mile away, walking the shadowy streets of Caxley, his mind in torment as he looked for comfort which could not be found.

Hilda, alone in the room, wept anew. 'Aunt Edna!' It was hard to bear. That Edna Howard should be the one to whom her Winnie turned in trouble was a humiliation she had never imagined.

She thought of all her own loving preparations during the day. Winnie's bed was turned down, the sheet snowy and smooth above the pink quilt. A hot water bottle lay snugly in the depths. The late chrysanthemums scented the room with their autumnal fragrance.

Winnie married! And in a registry office too! Some dim sordid little room with no beauty about it, she supposed. All her plans for Winnie's wedding had shattered before her eyes. Where now were her dreams of a blue and white wedding, white roses, lilies and delphiniums decorating the church, and Winnie herself a vision in bridal white?

It had all been so clear, even down to Mary's blue and white bridesmaid's frock and the posy of white rosebuds with long blue ribbons streaming from it. Somehow the bridegroom had always been a shadowy figure – just someone pleasant and kind, with a good bank balance, of course, and a natural desire for a reasonably sized family, sensibly spaced for dear Winnie's sake. That anything as catastrophic as this could happen threw Hilda's world into utter chaos. How would she ever face the other Caxley matrons? And worst of all, how could she face Edna Howard?

But this was in the future. The first thing was to comfort poor Bender. He must, somehow, be made to see that the situation must be accepted, regrettable though it was. Winnie, foolish and disobedient, was still their daughter, after all.

She mopped her eyes resolutely. All that was left for them now was to be brave, and make the best of a very bad job.

But Hilda's efforts were not to begin until the next day, for

Bender did not return until the small hours of the morning, long after Hilda had taken her aching head to bed. And, as she feared, when she broached the painful subject after breakfast, Bender refused to discuss it.

'Don't speak to me about it,' he said warningly. 'I've had enough at the moment. To think that Winnie's behaved like this! And that Bertie knew about it all the time! A fine pair of children! I'd expect no more from a Howard than Leslie's shown us, but that Winnie and Bertie could treat us so shabby – well, it's like being betrayed!'

Hilda's lip began to tremble and Bender began to speak more gently.

'Let me go to the shop now, there's a love. I'll work it off, maybe, and feel better when I come home. But I can't face my family – nor that dam' scoundrel Leslie – yet awhile.'

It was Bertie who made his father face him, later that day. In these last few hours Bertie seemed to have become very grown up, and might almost be the head of the house himself, thought Hilda wonderingly, watching her son shepherd Bender into the dining room for a private talk.

'I won't keep you long, father,' said Bertie, closing the door behind him, 'but I've only three or four days' leave left and I'm not having it spoilt by this affair. I'm sorry to have deceived you, but Winnie insisted, and frankly, I'd do it all over again, in the circumstances.'

'Bad enough deceiving me,' retorted Bender, 'but a sight worse to let a Howard marry your sister.'

'I think I know Leslie better than you do,' replied Bertie calmly. 'He's not the man I should have chosen for Winnie, but it's her choice, and I honestly think he loves her.'

141

Bender snorted derisively.

'He's ready to settle down,' continued Bertie levelly, 'and Winnie's the one to help him. Dash it all, father, we've known the Howards all our lives! How would you have felt if she had run off with a complete stranger? It's happening often enough in wartime! For your own sake, as well as Winnie's and Mamma's, do try and accept this business sensibly. It does no good to keep up a useless feud, and to make the whole family unhappy.'

'It's easy to talk!' replied Bender. 'I can't forget what I know about that young man, and I can't believe he'll treat Winnie properly.'

'All the more reason why you should stand by her now,' retorted Bertie. 'If she's in trouble she'll need her home.'

'You're right, I don't doubt, my boy,' said Bender sadly. 'I'll ponder it, but I can't see much good coming of it. I wonder what Sep and Edna think of it all?'

'They're delighted,' Bertie told him. 'Made them very welcome when they arrived, Winnie said.'

A thought struck Bender. He looked shrewdly at Bertie over his spectacles.

'They knew, did they?'

'Leslie wrote on his wedding day,' said Bertie shortly. 'He knew they'd be pleased.'

'But Winnie didn't,' murmured Bender, as if to himself.

'She knew you wouldn't be,' Bertie said simply, and left his father alone with his thoughts.

That evening there was a dance at the Corn Exchange. Bertie

dressed with unusual care and studied his reflection in the mirror with considerable misgivings. What a very undistinguished appearance he had! He disliked his fair hair and his blue eyes. To his mind they appeared girlish. He wondered if a moustache might improve his looks. Too late to bother about that now, anyway, he told himself, looking at his watch.

The newly-weds and Jim and Kathy were to be of the party, and Bertie was relieved to leave the heavy atmosphere of Rose Lodge behind him and stride down the hill to the market square. It was a crisp clear night, full of stars. Now and again the whiff of a dying bonfire crossed his path, that most poignant of winter smells. It was good to be back in the old town. It was better still to be on the way to meeting Kathy. Tonight he would ask her.

The Corn Exchange was gay with the flags of all nations. Ragtime music shook the hall, and there was an air of determined hilarity about the many dancers, as though, for this evening, at least, they would forget the horrors of war, and simply remember that music and rhythm, youth and excitement, also had a place in the scheme of things.

Leslie and Winnie danced together, heads close, oblivious to all about them. They had always danced well together, thought Bertie, gazing at them over the dark hair of Kathy, his own partner. They looked happy enough, in all conscience. If only he could quell the little nagging doubt at the back of his own mind! He looked into Kathy's eyes and forgot his sister's affairs.

It was agony to part from her and to watch other partners claim her. Kathy's dance programme was much too full for Bertie's liking. There was no one else in the room that he wanted to partner, but Caxley eyes were as sharp as ever, and he dutifully piloted a few young ladies about the floor, his eyes on Kathy the while. She was lovelier than ever – vivacious, sparkling, light as a feather. Had he any hope at all, wondered Bertie, stumbling over his partner's foot and apologising abstractedly?

She was dancing with one of the Crockford boys. How unnecessarily damned handsome they were, thought Bertie crossly! When the Crockfords were not large and red-headed, they were tall, elegant and dark. This one had hair oiled till it shone like jet, a handsome black moustache, and an enviable turn of speed when he reversed. Kathy was gazing at him in a way that Bertie found infuriating. As soon as the dance was over he hurried to her side.

'Come outside for a moment,' he begged.

'Why?' asked Kathy. Her bright eyes darted everywhere about the hall. Her little satin slipper tapped the floor in time to the music. *'Hullo! Hullo! Who's your lady friend?'* throbbed through the hall, and the refrain was taken up by many voices. The noise was unbearable to Bertie.

'It's quieter,' he shouted, above the din. Kathy rose rather reluctantly, and followed him outside into the market place. It was deliciously fresh and cool after the stuffiness of the Corn Exchange, but Kathy shivered and pulled her silk shawl round her.

'Let's go and look at the river,' said Bertie.

'We'll miss the dancing.'

'Only this one,' promised Bertie. He put his arm through hers and led her past her own house and down the narrow lane leading to the tow path. The noise behind them died away.

Only the plop of a fish and the quiet rippling of the Cax disturbed the silence. They made their way to the little bridge and leant over. Now that Bertie had succeeded in bringing Kathy here, he became horribly nervous. So much depended on the next few minutes. He took a deep breath and began.

'Kathy, I've wanted to ask you often. You must know how I feel about you. Do you care about me at all?'

'Of course I do,' said Kathy, with a cheerful promptness that made Bertie despair. 'I care very much about you. And Leslie and Jim, and all my friends who are fighting.'

Bertie sighed and took her hand. It was small and thin, and very cold.

'Not that way, Kathy. I meant, do you love me? I love you very much, you know. Enough to marry you. Could you ever think about that?'

Kathy laughed and withdrew her hand. It fluttered to Bertie's hot cheek and patted it affectionately.

'Oh, Bertie dear, don't talk so solemnly! I'm not thinking of marrying for years yet! Not you – or anyone else! There's too much fun to be had first! Take me back, Bertie, it's cold, and I want to dance.'

He tried once more, putting his arms round her, and tilting up her chin so that he could look into her lovely face.

'Please, Kathy,' he entreated, 'think about it. I know you're young, but I love you so much. Say you'll think about it!'

She pushed him away pettishly.

'I'm not going to promise any such thing. I want to be free, and you ought to be too!' She took his arm again and began to pull him back towards the market square.

'Come on, Bertie, I shall miss the next dance and it's a

military two-step. Don't be stuffy, there's a love. You're a dear old stick really!'

They walked back to the Corn Exchange, Bertie in silence, Kathy chattering of he knew not what. At the doorway he stopped.

'I won't come in,' he said. 'I've a headache. Go and enjoy yourself.'

She tripped in without once looking back, arms outstretched to her waiting partner.

Bertie turned away, and made his way blindly to the drinking fountain in the middle of the square. He filled one of the iron cups and drank the icy water. The feel of the cold iron chain running through his hot palm reminded him of the times he had sought refreshment here as a boy.

He leant his head against the comforting cold plinth beneath the Queen's bronze skirts, and looked across the square towards his old house. If only he could turn back the years! If only he could be a boy again, with none of a man's troubles to torture him!

It was almost a relief to return to his unit. The prospect of going overseas was one to look forward to after the unhappy events of this disastrous leave. He was glad to let other people make the decisions for him. Whatever the future held could give Bertie no more pain, he felt sure, than the grief of his family and the bitter disappointment of Kathy's complete disregard of his feelings.

In the crowded railway carriage rattling to Dorset through the darkening winter afternoon, Bertie re-lived again those moments with Kathy. To be called a 'dear old stick!' He shuddered at the remembrance. What hope was there ever for him, if those were her feelings? He remembered his last glimpse of her at Caxley Station. To his surprise she had come to see off the three of them, for Winnie and Leslie too were on the train.

She had kissed them all in turn. He felt her kisses still upon his cheek, as cold and light as moths, and his heart turned over. One thing he knew, whatever happened to him here, or in France, now or in the future, there would be nobody else for him but Kathy. Always, and only, Kathy.

He closed his eyes. The train roared through a cutting, carrying him unprotesting to whatever the future might hold.

13

Caxley at War

THE BELLS of St Peter's rang out across the market square and the rosy roofs of Caxley on Christmas morning. Bender, Hilda and Mary hurried up the steps and made their way to their usual pew.

The church was unusually full. Across the aisle the Crockford family filled two pews. They must have a houseful for Christmas, thought Hilda, with a pang of envy. Dan was making one of his rare appearances in church, his leonine head glowing against the murky shadows of the old building.

As the organ played the voluntary, Hilda gazed up the long nave and let her sad thoughts wander. If only Bertie and Winnie were here! But Bertie and the Howard boys and the rest of their company were somewhere in France, and Winnie was still nursing at the hospital in Dorset.

If only Winnie could have chosen someone else to marry! What a wedding Hilda had planned for her, with this noble church as its setting! She could see it so clearly in her mind's eye – the lilies on the altar, where now the Christmas roses and the scarlet-berried holly glowed, the smilax and white rosebuds where now the glossy ivy trailed its dark beauty. And there, at the altar, her dear Winnie in the beautiful wedding gown with the long train which she had so often visualized!

Tears blurred Hilda's eyes. The nave and chancel swam mistily before her, and she was glad to hear the gentle meanderings of the organist turn to the loud joyful strains of 'Adeste Fideles' as the choir entered, singing, and the congregation rose to join in praise.

'Please, God,' prayed Hilda desperately, as she struggled to her feet, 'let us all be together next Christmas, and let us all be happy again!'

Not far away, Edna Howard, beside Sep in the chilly chapel, wondered too about her two children in a foreign land. To think that this time last year she was positively looking forward to 1914! It had brought nothing but trouble!

The minister's voice droned on, but Edna did not attend to his exhortations. Sometimes she doubted if there were really any God to speak to. Sep said there was, and seemed to be comforted by the knowledge, and Edna had never expressed any of her own doubts. It would have upset Sep so much. But when you heard of the terrible things that the Germans were doing, then surely there couldn't be a God or he would never let it happen?

Edna mused vaguely on her uncomfortable bench, until her attention was caught by a white thread on the sleeve of her coat. She plucked it away neatly, let it flutter to the scrubbed floor boards so near her painful knees, and stroked the fur of her cuffs lovingly. It was wearing very well, she thought. After all, she had had it a whole year now, and it still looked as good as new. How kind Sep was to her! She stole a glance at his pale face beside her. His eyes were shut fast, his dark lashes making little crescents. His lips were pressed together with the intensity of his concentration. He was in communion with his Maker, and for Sep the world had ceased to exist.

Perhaps, thought Edna, returning to the contemplation of her coat, it could be turned in a few years' time. It was good stuff . . .

It was during the next week that Hilda heard how Bertie had spent his Christmas Day in the front line somewhere south of Armentières. His letter read:

Dearest Mamma,

I opened your parcel on Christmas morning and everything in it was first-class. Thank you all very much. The cake was shared with some of the other Caxley chaps who appreciated it very much.

The queerest thing happened here. Just before dawn we heard the Germans in their trench opposite singing carols. They sang 'Peaceful Night, Holy Night' – only in German, of course, and we joined in. After a bit, one of our officers went into no-man's-land and met one of theirs, and gradually we all climbed out and wished each other 'Happy Christmas' and exchanged cigarettes. Some were from your parcel, mamma, and I hope you don't mind a few of them going to the enemy. I can assure you, they did not seem like enemies on Christmas morning. We kept the truce up long enough to bring in our dead.

Further down the line, we heard, both sides had a game of football together. It makes you realize what a farce war is – nobody wants it. But it looks as though it will drag on for a long time yet, I'm afraid.

My love to you and to all the family,
Your loving son,
Bertie

Bertie's fears were echoed by all at home. The cheerful cry: 'Over by Christmas' was heard no more. Fighting was going on in all parts of the world, and the news from the western front grew grimmer weekly. It was here that the local men were engaged, and anxious eyes read the columns of 'Dead, Wounded and Missing' which were published regularly in the *Caxley Chronicle*. It was a sad New Year for many families in Caxley, as 1915 came in, and the knowledge that losses must continue to be very heavy was too terrible to contemplate.

For Bender, at least, the war had brought one small consolation. He was again in charge of the old shop, and all alterations had been postponed. Young Mr Parker was serving in the Navy, one or two of the assistants had also gone to the war and Bender struggled on with Miss Taggerty and a chuckle-headed boy from Springbourne, called Ralph Pringle, as his only support.

It suited Bender. Trade was slack, so that he was not overworked, and he had time to look after the shabby empty rooms of his late home, and to keep the beloved garden tidy. It was a reprieve for North's, Bender thought, and he was thankful.

He had recovered some of his old zest, doing his best to cheer Hilda now that Bertie was away from home. They spoke little of the disastrous marriage. The subject was too painful, but time and the background of war did much to lessen the tension. Hilda held weekly sewing parties in her new drawing room and busied herself in packing up the results to be sent to the Front.

Bender joined the local branch of the Home Defence Corps and thoroughly enjoyed his evenings at the Corn Exchange or in the Market Square. He, in company with other Caxley men too old for military service, drilled rigorously. Stiff joints and creaking knee-caps gave off reports as loud as the guns they longed to have, and although they knew in their hearts that their contribution was pitifully inadequate, yet they enjoyed the comradeship, the exercise, and the feeling of being alert.

Sep Howard was not among them. He had joined the Red Cross at the outbreak of war, and spent many nights at Caxley Station tending the wounded on their way to hospital from the battle front. He never forgot those tragic hours.

Between trains, Caxley station lay dim and quiet in the hollow by the river. The waiting room had been turned into a canteen. Urns bubbled, sandwiches were stacked and the helpers' tongues were as busy as their willing hands. Sometimes Sep left the warm fugginess to pace the deserted dark platform. Alone under the stars he walked up and down, watching the gleam of rails vanishing into the distance, and listening for the rumble of the next train bearing its load of broken men. His compassion had quickly overcome the physical nausea which blood and vomit inevitably aroused. He had become used to limbs frighteningly awry, to empty sleeves, and to heads so muffled in cotton wool and bandages that nothing emerged from them but screams.

Sep was recognised as one of the most tireless workers, with an uncanny gift of easing pain.

'I'm used to working at night,' he said simply, 'and I try to move the chaps the way my mother handled me when I was ill. She was a good nurse.'

He gained great satisfaction from the voluntary work. He recoiled from the martial side of war and even more from the pomp and glory of its trappings. Military bands, flags fluttering, soldiers in splendid array, all gave Sep a cold sickness in his heart. He had viewed with tears the jubilant crowd outside the Town Hall at the outbreak of war. The boisterous zeal of the elderly Home Defence Corps was not to Sep's liking. He found himself nearer the truth of war in those dark pain-filled hours at Caxley station.

He had seen Bender stepping out bravely with his fellows as they marched through the streets of Caxley to some military exercise on one of the surrounding commons. After the terrible scene in Bender's office, Sep had purposely kept out of his way, but had longed for things to be easier between them.

He had never been able to find out the truth about the ugly rumour of the girl at Bent. Leslie had denied the whole thing roundly when he had asked him about the matter. Sep was still troubled about the affair, and could not wholly believe his son, but was too proud to do more than accept Leslie's word. In any case, both he and Edna were delighted with his marriage to Winnie, and welcomed the couple whenever they could manage a brief visit. One must look forward, not back, Sep told himself.

As the early weeks of 1915 passed, Sep was relieved to see Bender looking more cheerful. Now they spoke when they met. Topics were kept general, enquiries were made about each other's families, but no mention was ever made of Winnie and Leslie between the two men. There was still a constraint about each meeting, but at least the ice was broken, and Sep hoped earnestly that one day he and Bender would be completely at ease with each other. The families did not meet so readily these days. Since the move, and since the war began, they had grown apart. The younger children did not mix as readily as the older ones had done when they lived so near each other in the market place, and the marriage had proved another barrier, much to Sep's grief.

It was in February that the Howard family had its first blow. Two local men had been killed near the Ypres Canal, and one of them was Jim Howard. The other was Arnold Fletcher, the gardener at Beech Green, and the fiancé of Dolly Clare who taught at Fairacre.

Sep received the news with numbed dignity, Edna with torrents of tears and furious lamentations. Sep grieved for her, but secretly envied the ease of her outbursts, for they were so exhausting that she slept soundly at nights. He went about his affairs pale and silent, and refused to give up his Red Cross vigils, even on the night of the news. Each man that he tended was Jim to him, and from this he gained strength.

Bender heard the news as the wintry sun was setting behind St Peter's. Without a word he made his way across the square, still clad in his shop overall, and went into the bakehouse in the yard. As he had suspected, Sep was there alone, stacking tins automatically, his face stricken.

'Sep,' muttered Bender, putting one massive hand on each side of Sep's thin shoulders and gazing down at him. 'What can I say?'

Sep shook his head dolefully. He did not trust himself to speak.

'I feel it very much,' went on Bender gruffly. 'And so will Hilda. We were always very fond of your Jim – a fine boy.'

Sep bit his quivering lip but remained silent. Bender dropped his hands and sat down heavily on the great scrubbed table, sighing gustily.

'This bloody war,' he growled, 'is going to cause more heartache than we reckoned, Sep. Who'd have thought, when our kids were playing round the old Queen out there, that it would have come to this?'

He gazed unseeingly at the brick floor and his two great black boots set upon it. After a minute's silence he shook himself back into the present, and began to make his way to the door. It was then that Sep found his voice.

'It was good of you to come, Bender. I've missed you.'

'Well, we've had our ups and downs, Sep,' replied Bender, turning in the doorway, 'and there's some things we'll never see eye to eye about. But in times like this we forget 'em.'

His voice dropped suddenly.

'God's truth, Sep, I'm sorry about this. I'm sorry for all of us with sons these days.'

And before Sep could reply he had turned the corner and vanished.

The war dragged on. Food was getting short, and the posters everywhere exhorted men and women to save every crumb and to guard against waste. Caxley did not feel the want of food as harshly as the larger towns. Set amidst countryside, with the Cax meandering through it, vegetables, fruit, eggs, milk and river fish were comparatively easy to come by. There was a shortage of sugar, and sweets, and Mary North was told never to ask for such things when they were visiting.

'People haven't enough for themselves,' pointed out Hilda. 'Just say you aren't very hungry.'

'But I'm *always* hungry for sweets,' protested Mary. 'You wouldn't want me to lie?'

'There are such things as *white* lies!' responded Hilda. 'And in wartime you'll have to make use of them.'

Certainly there were minor hardships as well as the dreadful losses overseas which cast their shadows. But the spirit of the people was high, and many of the women were tasting independence for the first time. They set off daily to munitions factories or shops, enjoying company and the heady pleasure of earning money of their own. They did not intend to throw this freedom away when the war ended. As they worked they talked and laughed, as they had never done cooped up in their own homes, and snippets of news about local fighting men were always the first to be exchanged. So often they were sad items, but now and again there was good news, and there was great excitement in 1916 when Caxley heard that Harold Miller had been commissioned at Thiepval after displaying great gallantry. His brother, Jesse, still struggling with the farm and with very little help, received many congratulations on market day that week.

It was towards the end of the same year that Hilda had a letter from Winnie to say that a baby was expected the next summer. She sounded happy and well. She was living in a small flat near the hospital, where she was going to remain at work for as long as possible. There were also plans for her to have the baby there in a small maternity wing attached to the main hospital.

Leslie was still in France and had taken to army life very well. He made a good soldier, quick, obedient and cheerful, and had received his commission about the same time as

Harold Miller. He did not write to Winnie as often as she would have liked, but as things were, she readily forgave him. Now that the baby was coming, she longed for the war to end, so that they could settle down together as a family.

Hilda was delighted with the news and even Bender softened at the idea of a grandchild in the family. The Howards were even more pleased, but Sep had the sense to resist mentioning it when he and Bender met. Let him make the first move, thought Sep!

One wet November day when the market square was lashed with rain and the wet leaves fluttered about the garden of Rose Lodge, the postman arrived at the Norths' door with another letter.

Bender took it in and tore it open. His face grew pale as he read the message and he put a hand on the door for support.

Hilda came up the hall to him, perplexed. He handed her the flimsy paper in silence.

Trembling, Hilda read it aloud.

'We regret to inform you that your son has been wounded and is receiving medical attention at the above military hospital. He may be visited at any time.'

Wonderingly she raised her face and looked at her husband. His expression was grim and determined.

'Put on your coat, my dear. We'll go at once.'

14

Caxley Greets the Armistice

THE HOSPITAL lay a little way from Bath, some sixty miles or so from Caxley. Bill Blake, who owned the motor firm where Bertie worked in peace time, drove them there himself.

There was little talking on the journey. Hilda gazed through the rain-spattered windscreen at the wind-blown countryside. The sky was grey and hopeless, the trees bowed, the grass flattened. Long puddles lined the road reflecting the dull skies above. They passed little on the long agonising journey, except an occasional army lorry which only reminded them more sharply of their purpose.

In happier days the hospital was a country mansion. The three mounted the long flight of steps, dreading what lay ahead. Within a few minutes, formalities were over and they found themselves at Bertie's bedside. He was barely conscious and very pale, but he smiled when he saw them.

They had been told that one leg was badly shattered and that a bullet had gone clean through his upper arm. Loss of blood was the chief cause for concern. He had lain for several hours in the mud before he had reached a field station.

Bender never forgot Hilda's bravery at that time. Not a tear fell. She smiled as encouragingly at her son as she had done years before when he was bed-bound by some childish ailment.

'You'll be home again soon, my dear,' she whispered to

him, as she kissed his waxen face gently. 'Back safely in Caxley, you remember?'

He nodded very slightly, his blue eyes bemused. She could not know that the word 'Caxley' brought back a vision of the market square to him, framed in the familiar curtains of his old Caxley bedroom.

They were only allowed to stay for two or three minutes before being ushered out by the nurse.

'The doctor thinks he will be able to operate tomorrow or the next day,' the sister told them later. 'Of course he's gravely ill, but he's a strong young man and all should go well, we hope.'

With this guarded encouragement to give them cold comfort, the three made their farewells, and returned sadly along the road to Caxley.

The hours seemed endless when they reached home, and there was little sleep for Hilda and Bender in the next two nights. Bender rang the hospital twice a day, and at last he spoke to the surgeon who had operated that afternoon.

'He's doing fine,' said the voice, warm and hearty at the other end of the line. 'The arm should be as good as new in a few weeks. Just a little stiffness maybe.'

'And the leg?' Bender pressed the receiver closer to his ear. Hilda stood beside him and he clasped her hand with his free one. She could only hear the distant murmur of the surgeon's voice, but her eyes scanned Bender's face anxiously. His grip tightened, he swallowed noisily, and his voice was husky when he said the final words.

'I'm sure you did. Quite sure you did. It's a sore blow, but you know we're grateful to you. Good-bye.'

He hung up and turned to his wife.

'The leg is not as bad as they feared, but his foot, Hilda . . .
His foot has had to come off . . . '

Bender had expected tears, but they did not come. For all
her pallor, Hilda looked calm.

'I'm thankful,' she said in a low tone. 'Honestly thankful!
Now he'll never have to go back. He'll be safe at home for
always.'

Women, thought Bender in wonderment, were truly
unpredictable.

Bertie's lengthy convalescence took place at a riverside
nursing home within fifteen miles of Caxley. He made slow
but steady progress, but endured great pain, and had to learn
to walk again with an artificial foot.

Lying in bed, or in a chair on the green lawn sloping down
to the river, he had plenty of time for thought. In many ways
he regretted the end of his soldiering days, but he was realistic
enough to be grateful that he need not return to active fighting.
He had seen enough of war's squalor and agony to sicken him,
and had often remembered Kathy's remarks about 'the lucky
ones who were left at home'. He did not think she was wholly
right, but he could see her point more clearly now.

But what of the future? Bill Blake had guaranteed him a job
in the firm – possibly a partnership after the war. He looked
forward to returning. There was no place like Caxley and no
business like the motor business. It should be more flourishing than ever when the war ended. He supposed he would
live at Rose Lodge as before, but he longed to have a

place of his own. If only he could have gone back to the old home!

He thought, as he so often did, of Kathy. He had never met another girl to touch her, and felt positive that he never would. But how could he ask any girl to marry such an old crock? He was irritable when he was in pain, which was most of the time, and devilish slow in making progress with the new foot. He must simply persevere and hope that things grew easier. Meanwhile, he received many Caxley friends, and learnt all he could about Kathy's circumstances. She was still nursing at Caxley Hospital, he heard, and having as gay a time as war allowed in the evenings.

Bill Blake, who knew what was in Bertie's mind without being told, offered to bring Kathy over one afternoon when she was free, and was as good as his word.

Bertie watched the clock anxiously all the morning. By two o'clock when she was due, he was in a state of feverish excitement. He sat in a wicker chair on the lawn waiting impatiently.

She was as lovely as ever when she finally arrived, clad in a pink fluttery frock with pearls at her throat. Her dark hair was piled on top, her great eyes danced as gaily as ever. She gave him a light kiss, making his head swim, and settled herself in a chair beside him. Bill, the soul of tact, vanished to make some imaginary adjustment to the car which had brought them.

They fell into conversation as easily as ever. Kathy told Bertie all about her life at the hospital. She chattered of the patients, the staff, the doctors. She talked of the Howards and the fun of looking forward to being aunt to Leslie's baby. Only when she spoke of Jim did her lovely face cloud over, and she let Bertie take her hand. But within a minute she was happy again, and Bertie thought how like her mother she was, with the same gaiety and the same ability to throw off trouble. Could it be lack of feeling? Sadly, listening to the welcome prattling, Bertie realized that it could, but he would not have her any different. Kathy was perfect.

'Want to see me walk?' asked Bertie suddenly. Kathy leapt to her feet. They made careful progress along a path beside the river.

'It reminds me of the Cax,' said Bertie, shading his eyes with his hand and gazing along the shining water. 'It makes me think of you. I still do you know.'

Kathy squeezed his arm, her smile mischievous.

'Bertie, don't think of me any more. I wasn't going to say anything. Nobody knows – not a soul. But I'm going to tell you, because somehow I can tell you everything. I'm going to be engaged any day now. We shall tell our families this week.'

It was as well that Kathy's arm supported him for Bertie could have fallen with the shock. It was really no great surprise. He had known that Kathy must marry one day and that his own case was now doubly hopeless. She had never felt for him in that way, and now his injuries made him shy of asking her again. But now that the blow had fallen it was hard to bear.

'Say you're pleased, Bertie dear. I shall be so miserable if you're not pleased. I'm very fond of you. I want you to like Henry. Shall I bring him next time?'

Bertie did his best to rally. She was gazing at him anxiously for his approval. He could deny her nothing, and told her sincerely that he hoped she would always be happy. The unknown Henry he loathed with all his being at the moment, but supposed he would feel less savage when he got used to the idea. But God help him if he was not good to Kathy!

He let Kathy tell him more, glad to be silent to regain his composure. Henry was very tall, and big, with red hair. He was in a Scottish regiment. (That damned kilt, groaned Anglo-Saxon Bertie inwardly! What havoc it caused among susceptible young women!) He was as brave as a lion, and always happy. (Who wouldn't be with Kathy beside him, thought poor Bertie?) His home was in Edinburgh and he had shown her pictures of the great castle there. He would take her to see it, on his next leave, and then she would stay with his parents. They hoped to marry in the spring.

It was small wonder that Bill Blake thought Bertie looked a bit off colour when he returned to take tea on the lawn. He commented on it with some concern, adding that there were bound to be ups and downs in a long illness.

'In life too!' agreed Bertie simply, smiling across at Kathy.

Winnie's baby, a boy, was born soon after Kathy's visit to Bertie, and he was glad to hear of this event for his mother's sake as well as Winnie's. It diverted attention from his own affairs and enabled him to get a grip on life. Now that Kathy was irretrievably lost to him, he set his mind on getting back to his unit as quickly as his tardy body would allow.

But it was autumn before he was discharged, and no medical board would pass him fit for military service. Philosophically, Bertie returned to Rose Lodge, the raptures of Hilda, and the welcome routine of the motor trade. He undertook more voluntary work than Hilda felt he should, but he gained in strength and seemed happy enough in his sober way.

The Norths received an invitation to Kathy's splendid wedding in the spring, and surprisingly, Hilda insisted on going, but she went alone. Bender pleaded overwork. Bertie simply stated flatly that he was unable to accompany her. There was a stricken look about Bertie's face, when he told her this, that gave Hilda her first suspicion of his feelings towards Kathy. Not another Howard, surely! She dismissed the thought almost as soon as it had come to life, and dwelt with relief on Kathy's union with another and her probable abode in the northern fastness of Edinburgh. The further away the better, thought Hilda privately. The Howards brought them nothing but trouble, one way or another.

As it happened, Kathy did not move away immediately. Whilst the war still ground on remorselessly, Kathy lived with her parents in the market square and continued nursing. Bertie often saw her as he drove his little A.C. to work in the morning, and his heart turned over as disconcertingly as it had ever done. She looked so pretty and trim in her nurse's uniform, and Bertie envied the lucky patients who would spend their day in her presence.

In the early days of November 1918 it became apparent that, at last, victory was near. After four years of suffering it was hard to believe, but on Monday, November 11th, there were excited murmurs in the streets of Caxley.

'It's true, Mr North,' said an old woman across the counter in his shop. 'The war's over!'

'Who told you that yarn?' quipped Bender. 'The papers don't say so.'

'The paper shop does though,' she retorted. She shook her umbrella at Bender's unbelieving face. 'He's put up a notice saying "Yes! Yes!" that must mean it's true!'

After she had departed Bender made his way out into the drizzling morning. Little knots of people had gathered and were asking questions. A cheer went up as several bell-ringers were seen to run up the steps into St Peter's.

'Where are the flags?' yelled one. As if in answer to his question the cross of St George began to mount the flag staff on top of the church.

'The Post Office should know if it's true,' Bender said to fat Mrs Petty who stopped to get news. He resolved to walk there and make enquiries. Miss Taggerty and young Pringle could cope with slack Monday morning trade for once.

There was no confirmation yet of the rumours, the official at the Post Office said austerely. As soon as anything was known it would be posted publicly. Bender made his way back across the market square. By now there was quite a crowd. Some wag had lashed a Union Jack to Queen Victoria's hand and tied a red, white and blue bow on her crown. Sep, standing at his shop window, would normally have felt shocked at such sacrilege, but today he was sure Her Majesty would have forgiven this little frivolity had she known the circumstances.

The children began to pour out of school. It was twelve o'clock, and they gathered round the statue to enjoy the fun before racing home to Monday's meagre cold meat or war-time rissoles. At twelve-thirty the suspense was over. A notice was put up in the Post Office window. It said: 'Armistice signed.

Hostilities ceased this morning.'

Now Caxley rejoiced. The flag was run up over the Town Hall. The bells of St Peter's rang out and people left their homes to run through the streets to the market square. The crowd joined hands and danced in a gigantic ring round Queen Victoria. Overhead, an aeroplane flew back and forth, very low, over the town, the pilot waving madly to the crowd. Someone had wrapped himself in a Union Jack and rode majestically through the streets on a high old-fashioned bicycle, acknowledging the cheers of the throng.

The town band was gathered hastily and marched through the pouring rain, blowing away at their instruments with gusto. Outside the hospital, an effigy of the Kaiser dangled from the portico, and a bonfire was being prepared for his funeral pyre in the grounds by enthusiastic patients.

Union Jacks waved everywhere. Buttonholes and hair ribbons of red, white and blue blossomed on all sides. The pouring rain did nothing to dampen the spirits of Caxley folks on their great day. After dark came the greatest thrill of all – the street lamps were lit for the first time for years, and children gaped in amazement at the wonderful sight. Fireworks were let off by the river, and as the rockets soared and swooshed, and the Catherine wheels whirled in dizzy splendour, Caxley celebrated victory with frenzied excitement which lasted till the small hours. Now it was over – the suffering, the parting, the misery! Let all the world rejoice!

But not all could rejoice. Not all could forget. Some like Sep, thankful though they were that the war was over, mourned the loss of a son. Standing outside his shop in the dark market place that night, Sep watched the surging crowds with mingled joy and sorrow. The flags fluttered bravely, the bells rang out, beer flowed freely, singing and laughter echoed through the square. And above all, indomitable and unchanging, Queen Victoria surveyed her people from beneath her beribboned crown. She too, thought Sep, had seen war and victories. She too had lost sons. She would have understood his own mixed feelings.

Poor Jim, dear Jim! But it was no use grieving. Leslie was still spared to him, and Winnie, and the new baby. Kathy too and her husband, and young Robert at large somewhere in the town, and enjoying all the fun with a twelve-year-old's zest for it.

He turned to go in and caught sight of Bertie North limping resolutely along the pavement towards the firework display. What was Bender feeling, Sep wondered as he mounted the stairs? Despite the jubilation in the streets, Sep guessed that there was mourning in many hearts today, not only for a million dead, but for many more damaged in mind and body.

It was going to be hard, thought Sep, to build the new world the papers spoke of so hopefully, but somehow it must be done. Resolutely, Sep looked to the future.

15

Post-War Troubles

THE MEN came back with relief and with expectations of unalloyed bliss. But things were not as simple as that. The first flush of joy necessarily cooled a little. Wives who had enjoyed freedom found the kitchen routine irksome. Children born during their father's absence resented the intrusion of the stranger in their homes. Food was still short and jobs were hard to get. But families shook down together again as well as they could, and it was good to see young men again in the fields and on the farms and working in the shops, and in the market square of Caxley.

About a third of them did not return, and some came back only to succumb to the plague called Spanish influenza which swept the country in 1918 and 1919. Among them, tragically, was Harry Miller so recently returned to his Beech Green farm, covered in honours. Once more Jesse Miller was left to farm alone.

Sep Howard, his Red Cross work having dwindled, threw himself with added concentration into his council duties. He had been made chairman of the local housing committee and found plenty to occupy him, for many new homes were needed for the returning men. Leslie was back in the business and doing well. He and Winnie were living in a small cottage which Sep had bought some years earlier for Edna's mother. Now that the old lady was dead it provided the young couple with an attractive little home, strategically placed at a distance from the parents of both.

The Howards had cheerful letters from Kathy now settled in Edinburgh with the stalwart Henry and expecting their first child. Henry was the only son of a fairly prosperous printer in the city, and Kathy enjoyed some social standing at the local functions. It looked as though Kathy was lost to Caxley for ever, and Bertie tried to persuade himself that it was all for the best.

His father was less quixotic about his circumstances. Young Mr Parker had returned from the war, full of zeal, and was turning North's upside down with his plans for the business. Worse still, from Bender's point of view, his wife and family had joined him and all were to live above the shop in Bender's old premises. It was some comfort to know that his children were numerous and that, for the time being, anyway, he would need all the living accommodation available. At least, thought Bender, his old drawing room would remain intact, and not house dairy equipment and rolls of chicken wire as had once been suggested.

It was in 1921 that Winnie's second child was born. Hilda had begged her to come to Rose Lodge for the confinement, but Winnie preferred to remain at the cottage attended by the local district nurse and a good-natured neighbour. Family affairs were difficult for Leslie and Winnie. The Howards always welcomed them and they visited the market square house frequently, but Bender refused to have Leslie at Rose Lodge although he wanted Winnie as often as she could manage it, and adored his grandchild, Edward. Winnie paid most of her visits home in the afternoon, when Leslie was at work, or called at the shop to see her father whenever she was in town.

A pair of enterprising brothers had started a motorbus service from Caxley to the surrounding villages, after the war, and this proved a blessing. Winnie frequently used it to travel to Caxley, and Edna often hopped on the bus outside her door and paid a surprise visit to her mother's old cottage.

Hilda came less often. It grieved her to see Winnie living in such modest surroundings.

'You can perfectly well afford something better,' she scolded her daughter. 'Leslie's a partner now, and Howard's is an absolute gold-mine.'

'There's time enough for something bigger when the family grows,' replied Winnie. 'Besides, I love it here, and it's healthier for Edward.'

She did not add that money was not as plentiful as Hilda supposed. Leslie never seemed to have much, despite the modest way they lived, and she too had wondered if Howard's were as flourishing as local people asserted. If so, just where was the money going? It made Winnie uneasy.

All through the long hot summer of 1921 she had plenty of time to think. Leslie had never been a home-lover, and now he seemed to spend most of his evenings out. He pleaded work at the shop, but Winnie wondered. She lay in a deck chair in the shade of the damson tree in the cottage garden and tried to put these tormenting questions out of her mind, as she awaited the birth of the baby.

The heat was overpowering. Day after day of blazing sunshine scorched the grass and turned the chalky lane outside the gate into a white dust bath for the sparrows. Streams dried up, and the Cax shrank to half its size, leaving muddy banks criss-crossed with cracks and smelling abominably.

Water was short everywhere. Wells ran dry, and water carts trundled the lanes doling out a little to each householder. People ran down their paths, buckets in hands, and watched jealously to see that they received as much as their neighbours.

Edward, now a lively four-year-old, grew fractious in the heat and demanded more attention than his unwieldly mother could give him. It was a relief to Winnie when at last her pains began and Leslie took Edward to work with him, as arranged. She knew Edward would be thoroughly spoilt and happy with his grandparents, and she was free to get on with the vital job in hand.

The birth was easy, and by tea-time Leslie was at home again with his new daughter in his arms. She was to be called Joan.

For a few months after the baby's arrival, things seemed to be happier. Leslie was kinder and more thoughtful, and Winnie began to hope that Leslie was beginning to take his family responsibilities more seriously. But, as the autumn approached, his absences from home became more and more frequent. Winnie found herself sitting by the fire, the two children in bed above, alone with her thoughts from six o'clock until eleven or twelve when Leslie returned. He was always in good spirits, with ready and plausible excuses, but Winnie was fast becoming aware that her husband was a glib liar, and that her father, and Bertie too, had known more about his true nature than she had done.

One afternoon, just before Christmas, Hilda was busy decorating the Christmas tree at Rose Lodge. She was alone in the drawing room. On the table beside her was the box of bright baubles which had appeared annually ever since her marriage. Here was the spun glass bird with the long red tail which was Bertie's favourite. She hung it carefully towards the front of the tree. Here was a tiny silver lantern made by Winnie as a child. If only they were all young again! How they had always enjoyed dressing the tree! Now she was doing it alone. She threaded the little lantern on to a dark branch. The broken needles of fir gave out an aroma in the warmth from the crackling fire. At that moment the door opened, and Winnie appeared with the baby in her arms and Edward beside her.

'What a lovely surprise!' cried Hilda. She settled Winnie by the fire. The girl looked cold and shaky. Edward made straight for the box of bright decorations. Hilda removed it hastily, and then began to take off the baby's shawl.

'We'll have tea now, dear,' said Hilda. 'You look tired. Vera's here this afternoon, polishing the silver ready for Christmas. I'll get her to make it.'

'I've got a lot to tell you, mamma,' said Winnie. Edward's bright eyes were fixed upon her hopefully. 'But little pitchers you know . . .'

'Edward, you can have tea with Vera in the kitchen,' said his grandmother promptly. 'Come along, and we'll see her.'

Ten minutes later, while the baby slept on the sofa, and Winnie neglected her tea, the tale unfolded. To Hilda, it came as no great surprise, but she grieved for Winnie telling it with a stony face.

She had taxed Leslie last night with his neglect of her and the children. Without a trace of shame he had admitted that there was another woman and that he fully intended to leave home to live with her.

'His actual words,' said Winnie bitterly, 'were: "I owe it to her. She was always first with me." He goes there today.'

'Very nice!' commented Hilda drily. 'I suppose it's the woman at Bent?'

Winnie nodded. Her hands turned her teacup round and round ceaselessly. A little muscle twitched by her mouth, but her eyes remained dry.

'Well, this has shown him in his true colours,' said Hilda grimly.

'For God's sake don't say "I told you so!",' cried Winnie. 'I don't think I could bear it! The thing is – what happens to me and the children?'

'You come here,' said Hilda promptly.

Winnie shook her head.

'It would never do, mamma, and you know it. Father might not say anything in front of me, but I should know he was thinking about Leslie. It's not fair to either of you. Besides there's not enough room.'

'What would you like to do?' asked Hilda. 'Are you prepared to have him back if he can be persuaded?'

'He won't be. He said so, and he means it.'

There was silence. A robin outside whistled in the grey afternoon and the fire rustled companionably.

'Do the Howards know?' asked Hilda.

'I've no idea. I doubt it. But I shall tell them, of course. Tomorrow probably. I can't face much more today.'

'You must stay the night here. Tomorrow too. For as long as you like, my dear. This is your home.'

'No, mamma, it isn't,' replied Winnie gently. 'The cottage is my home, even if Leslie's left it. I must go back.'

'Not tonight,' said Hilda with all her old authority. 'This has been a terrible shock. We'll look after the children, and you must have an early night.'

'Very well,' agreed Winnie, in a low tone. She passed her hand across her face, with the same gesture as her father's when he was worried and bemused.

Hilda began to stack the tray. Before it was done she looked across at Winnie. The girl lay back, eyes closed, as white as death and as quiet as the baby asleep nearby.

Hilda lifted the tray and crept stealthily from the room.

But the Howards knew already – at least Sep did. At about the same time as Winnie's arrival at Rose Lodge, Sep and Leslie were alone in the bakehouse.

'You may as well know, Dad, that Winnie and I have parted company,' announced Leslie. He was wiping shelves and kept his back carefully towards his father.

Sep stood stock still by the great scrubbed table. Had he heard aright?

'Whose idea is this?' he asked.

'Well, mine I suppose,' said Leslie with assumed lightness.

'Am I to understand,' said Sep thunderously, 'that you are seriously proposing to leave your wife and children?'

Leslie continued to rub at the shelves. For once he was silent.

'Face me!' commanded Sep. Obediently, Leslie turned. He was a child again, caught out in some misdemeanour, and awaiting retribution. Sep, filled with righteous wrath, commanded respect, despite his small stature.

'What lies behind this? What has happened?'

'Well, Winnie and I haven't seen eye to eye for some time. She's been off-hand most of this year. She – '

'She has been carrying a child,' Sep broke in. '*Your* child. What do you expect?'

Leslie flushed. He opened his mouth to speak, but Sep was first.

'There is another woman.' It was a statement not a question. Leslie nodded, eyes cast down.

'The one at Bent?' asked Sep, his voice dangerously calm.

'Yes, dad.'

There was a dreadful silence, broken only by the heavy breathing of the older man. His hands were clenched on the surface of the table.

'Then you did lie to me. I feared it.'

Leslie threw up his head. Now he was angry, with the anger of a cornered animal. He shouted wildly.

'So what? Why shouldn't I lie? I was driven to it, in this bible-thumping house – and so was Jim, if you did but know it! He wasn't the stained-glass saint you tried to make out!'

'You'll do no good trying to blacken your dead brother's name,' cried Sep. 'Answer for yourself! What hold has this woman on you?'

'She's got my child – '

'Winnie's got two of your children.'

'She came first. She always did. We suit each other. And now her husband's left her. I've got to help her.'

Suddenly, the younger man crumpled, slumping on to the

wooden stool by the table. Sep, standing, surveyed him grimly.

'You knew your responsibilities before marrying Winnie North. You've wrecked her life, and this woman's – and her husband's too. No good ever came of giving way to sin.'

Leslie raised his head from his arms.

'It's too late for chapel talk now,' he said bitterly.

'It's never too late for true repentance,' said Sep gravely. 'You must think again. Don't break up your marriage. Go back to Winnie. She'll forgive you. Break with this woman for good. If she knows there is no chance of seeing you, their marriage may be mended. For pity's sake, Leslie, think about it!'

'I have thought. I will never go back to Winnie. She'd never forgive me. At heart she's her father all over again. I'm starting afresh, and taking Milly with me. I should have married her years ago.'

Sep began to pace the bakehouse.

'I'm not going to discuss it with you further today. Go home and turn over my advice. Think of Edward and Joan. What sort of life will they have without a father? And tomorrow we'll talk again. I shall say nothing to your mother about this.'

Leslie struggled to his feet.

'Whatever you say, dad, will make no difference. I'll see you tomorrow morning as usual. But there's no hope, I tell you.'

'There's always hope,' said Sep soberly, as his son went through the door.

There was little sleep for Sep that night, while Leslie packed his bags in the empty cottage and Winnie tossed and turned under her parents' roof.

The next morning father and son faced each other again. Leslie's expression was mutinous.

'I've nothing to add,' he said with finality. His jaw was set at an obstinate angle.

'But I have,' responded Sep. He leant across the table and spoke firmly. 'If you have decided to go forward with this wickedness, then you must leave the business and leave your home too.'

Leslie looked up, startled.

'I won't have you setting a bad example to the workmen or to young Robert. You know my views. I won't countenance such behaviour. Finish the week here, and meanwhile look for another job.'

'But, dad – ' began Leslie.

'I am putting a hundred pounds into your bank account today,' went on Sep. 'Our partnership will be dissolved. You must make your own way. Don't appear here for help if you find yourself in a mess. You've chosen your own road – you must travel it alone.'

Later that evening he had to break the news to Edna and face the expected storm. She could not believe that Leslie had behaved so badly. It would pass. This other woman could be paid off. Why didn't Sep think of it? After all, lots of boys had these passing infatuations. The war had unsettled poor Leslie.

Sep let her ramble wildly on for a time, and then spoke sternly. Leslie was a man. He knew what he was doing. He, as his father, was not prepared to connive in such despicable conduct. He had his duty to Robert, to his wife and to his work people. Leslie must go.

Edna looked up at him with wet eyes. Another thought had flitted through her head.

'What will happen to poor Winnie and darling Edward and the baby? How will they live if you've stopped Leslie's wages? Why should they suffer?'

'I have thought of that,' replied Sep. 'They will be looked after.'

Unable to bear more he made his way upstairs to the peace of the bedroom. In the market square they were erecting the town's Christmas tree. The season of peace and goodwill towards men, thought Sep bitterly, and he had just banished a son!

Beside the tree, dwarfed by its dusky height, Queen Victoria gazed regally across the cobbles.

'She would have approved,' Sep murmured aloud. 'Yes, she would have approved.'

Nevertheless, it was cold comfort.

16

Bertie Finds a Home

CHRISTMAS WAS a muted affair, for both the Howard and North families. There was the usual visit to church and chapel, the mammoth Christmas dinner, the ritual of the tree at tea time, and for those at Rose Lodge the welcome diversion of Edward's excitement.

On Boxing Day Winnie and the children went to tea in the market square and it was then that she learnt of Sep's generous provision for her family. Leslie's salary would be paid automatically into her bank account. The cottage was hers, rent free, for as long as she cared to make use of it.

Sep explained it all to her in the privacy of the dining room when the rest of the party were playing 'Hunt the Thimble', for Edward's benefit, next door. The table was still littered with the remains of Christmas crackers and tea time debris. The magnificent cake, made by Sep's own hands, towered amid the wreckage, the candles still gave out a faint acrid whiff.

Winnie was greatly touched by this overwhelming generosity, and tried to say so, but Sep would not hear her.

'It's little enough,' he said, 'and my pleasure'.

Winnie broke the news to her parents as soon as she returned home. They too were loud in their praises of Sep's conduct. Secretly, Hilda felt a pang of shame for her past off-handedness towards Sep and Edna. She must do what she could to make amends, she determined.

Bender's first feeling was of great relief. He had been much worried by his responsibilities towards Winnie and her children. She was welcome to make her home with them, though the house would be devilishly cramped, he had to admit. But his salary simply could not be stretched to giving Winnie an allowance, and the thought of Edward's education and Joan's in the years to come had made him shudder. He was on the point of going to Sep and telling him to force his son to pay a weekly maintenance sum. Thank goodness he had never done it! In the face of this liberal open-handedness, Bender was overcome. He had never thought to be beholden to Sep Howard, but he was glad to be, in the circumstances.

It was now that Bertie came forward with his proposal. He had been thinking for some time of buying a house. Now that Mary was growing up, and her hobbies took up a large amount of room, he felt that it was time he provided for himself. Hilda began to protest when he broached the subject, but Bertie was firm.

'Mamma, I have reached the ripe old age of twenty-eight. You were good enough to take me in and look after me when I really needed it. But I've no excuse now. I'm as fit as the rest of you and I should dearly love to have a little place of my own to invite you to whenever you wanted to come.'

Hilda was partly mollified, and when he went on to point out that he would need advice on furnishing his establishment, she began to be quite reconciled to the idea.

Bertie went on to suggest that Winnie might like to house-keep for him. They had always got on well together, and he would do his best to keep a fatherly eye on Edward and Joan. He had been told of a house for sale just off Caxley High Street, with a small garden sloping down to the Cax. It was not far from his work, and would be convenient for Winnie for shopping and visiting her Caxley friends.

'And remember,' continued Bertie, 'young Edward will be starting school in a few months' time. There is plenty of choice in Caxley. He's a good two miles to walk if he stays at the cottage.'

This was perfectly true, and had not occurred to Winnie in her present distraught condition. She liked the idea immensely, and appreciated Bertie's kindness. There would be no quarrelling in the household, she felt sure.

And so it was arranged. The house that Bertie had found was approached from a little lane off the busy High Street. It was a red-brick, four square house, solidly built with good rooms and large windows. It was certainly more commodious than a bachelor would normally choose, and Winnie realized that it had been bought mainly for her benefit.

She told Sep at once about Bertie's proposal and he agreed that it was the best possible arrangement. The cottage would be welcomed by one of his men, he knew, but Winnie's needs had come first.

She had hardly left him before Bender crossed the market square and entered the shop.

'Come through,' said Sep, guessing his errand. The two men settled themselves in Sep's tiny office. It was hardly big enough to house the neat oak desk and the rows of books on the shelves around the walls, but at least they had privacy.

'You know why I'm here, Sep. You're being uncommonly

good to our Winnie. It's appreciated, you know. To tell the truth, I couldn't help her much myself, as things are.'

'Say nothing, please. I'm too much ashamed of Leslie's behaviour to talk about it. This is the least I can do. She may be your daughter, Bender, but her children are my grandchildren. I do it for their sakes as much as Winnie's.'

'Ah! It's a bad business!' agreed Bender, shaking his massive head. 'And no hope of patching it up, as far as I can see.'

'Perhaps it's as well,' replied Sep. 'I blinded myself to the boy's faults. I face that now. He'll be no good to any woman, as that poor creature he's with will soon find out. No, I think Winnie's well rid of him.'

'And you've heard of Bertie's plans?'

'Yes, indeed. Winnie's just been here, and I'm all in favour! That boy of yours is solid gold, Bender.'

'He's a good chap,' nodded Bender. 'Bit of an old stick-in-the-mud, I sometimes think, but better that way than the other!'

'Definitely,' replied Sep, with a little chilliness. Bender felt that he may have put his foot in it. He rose hastily.

'Must get back to the shop.' He held out his hand and ground Sep's small one painfully in it.

'Bless you, Sep. We've got every reason to be grateful. Winnie's happiness means a lot to us.'

'I'm glad to be able to help,' said Sep sincerely, putting his damaged hand behind him and opening the door with the other.

He watched the vast figure cross the market place, then hurried back soberly to his duties, well content. For the first time in his life he had been able to succour Bender.

* * *

After weeks of occupation by bricklayers, carpenters, plumbers, plasterers, decorators and their assorted minions, the house was ready and Bertie and Winnie moved in.

The garden was still a tangle of weeds and overgrown plants, but tall tulips peered from the undergrowth in the borders and the lilac was in fine bloom. Bertie strolled about his new kingdom in proud happiness. It was a fine place to own and the neglected garden would give him a rewarding hobby. He paced down the mossy gravel path to the tall hedge at the end. Let into it was a wooden gate, in sore need of painting, which opened on to the tow-path of the winding Cax.

It was this aspect of his property that gave Bertie the greatest satisfaction. All his life he had loved the river. Its rippling had soothed him to sleep as a boy. In the dark, pain-filled nights of the war, when his absent foot throbbed and leapt as though it were still in the bed with him, he had imagined himself sitting by the shining water, cooling his feet among the waving reeds and the silver bubbles which encrusted them. Its memory had helped to keep him sane in the nightmare world. Now it was here for him to enjoy for the rest of his life. He gazed at it with affection. Here he would saunter in the evenings while the gnats danced above the surface and the swallows skimmed after them. Here he would sit on long hot afternoons listening to the noisy boys splashing in the distance. He might take up fishing seriously. It was a good occupation for a man with a gammy leg and young Edward already had a taste for trout.

He returned to the garden and made his way towards the house. Someone was hanging curtains upstairs and for one wild ecstatic moment he imagined that it was Kathy. If only it could be! But he thrust the thought from him. No use crying for the moon! He was damned lucky to have all this – and dear old Winnie to keep him company.

He waved affectionately to the figure in the window and limped into his own house thankfully.

Thus began a period of great pleasure and tranquillity, for the brother and sister. It gave them both time to recover from the shocks they had received, and to gain strength to enjoy the pleasant familiar world of Caxley again.

They had always been fond of each other. They were both placid and good-natured in temperament, and shared the same circle of friends. Occasionally they went to a concert or spent an evening with neighbours or at Rose Lodge or at Sep's. Vera, their old maid, lived close by, and loved to bring her knitting and sit with the children. To many people in Caxley it seemed a remarkably hum-drum existence. Why on earth didn't they each find a partner, they wondered? Bertie was charming, gentle and handsome – eminently suited to matrimony, the speculative matrons with daughters told each other. Winnie was free now that her divorce from Leslie had gone through.

The older generation, including the Howards and the Norths, could not help being rather shocked at divorce. To their minds, attuned to good Queen Victoria's proprieties, a woman – even if she were the injured party – was somehow besmirched if she had appeared in the divorce court. Happily, those of Winnie's generation took a more realistic view of her position and sincerely hoped that in time she would find a partner who would appreciate her company and prove a good father to her two attractive children.

There was little news of Leslie and his new wife. They had moved far west into Devon where he was working as a car salesman. With his smart good looks and plausible tongue, Winnie felt he was well equipped to make a success of this career. She never ceased to be thankful that he had gone, and hoped never to set eyes on him again.

Every year that passed made the children dearer to her. Edward attended a small school in the High Street and was to go to Caxley Grammar School when he was nine. One of his friends was Tim Parker, the youngest child of the Parkers at his grandfather's old home.

He had always known the shop well, for he had visited Bender there for as long as he could remember, but he had not been familiar with the premises above until he was invited to play with Tim. From the first, he was enchanted. To stand at the windows of the great drawing room and to look out at the bustle of the market square was a constant joy. There was so much to watch – the cheapjacks, flashing cutlery and crockery, their wives spreading gaudy materials over their buxom arms and doing their best to persuade cautious housewives to part with their money.

And even if it were not market day when the square was gay with stalls, there were always familiar figures to be seen going about their daily affairs. He saw the tall dignified figure of the Town Clerk enter the Town Hall, the vicar running up the steps of St Peter's, the one-legged sweeper wielding his besom broom round the plinth of the Queen's statue. Sometimes he saw his grandfather in his white baker's clothes, or Grandma

Howard in one of her pretty hats, tripping across to buy chops for dinner. In sunshine, or rain, winter or summer, the view fascinated him. There was always something happening there. It was as good as a serial story – a story which would never end.

He tried to tell his Uncle Bertie about his feelings, and found a sympathetic listener. Bertie told him old tales of their childhood above the shop, and on his next visit Edward searched for, and found, the scratched initials on the window pane which had resulted in a beating for poor Uncle Bertie. He told the child about the beauties of the old drawing room – the red plush furniture, the sea lavender on the wall brackets, the hissing gas lamps, and Edward longed to be able to go back in time and see its ancient glory.

He was, naturally, more familiar with the Howard's house for here he was one of the family and not just a guest. He adored Sep and Edna, and felt much more at ease with them than with Bender, of whom he was a little afraid. Grandma North he was fond of, but conscious that he must behave 'like a little gentleman'. Ears were inspected, nail-biting was deplored, and his dress had to be immaculate at Rose Lodge. At the baker's house so much was going on that such niceties were overlooked. Here he was happy with the company, but the house itself had not the same power of enchantment for him as the rooms above North's old shop. With a child's disconcerting frankness he said as much to Sep one day.

'It's a lovely house,' agreed Sep gravely. 'And your grandpa and grandma North always made it very pretty and comfortable. But we have the same view, you know. In fact, I often think there is a better view of the market square from here.'

Edward pondered the point, and lit upon the truth.

'But the sun's wrong. You only get it when it's going down behind the church. Over there, at Tim's, it shines into the rooms from morning till afternoon. That's what makes it so nice.'

Sep agreed again. The child was right. North's aspect was much more favourable than their own. He was amused to see how much the old house meant to the boy. Of course, he had heard all sorts of tales from his mother and uncle about the good old days there and this must lend a certain fascination to the place. But it was not a good thing to dwell too much in the past, thought Sep. A young boy should be living in the present, and looking forward to the future.

'What about giving me a hand in the bakehouse?' asked Sep. The child's eyes shone. He loved the warmth, the fragrance and the bustle as dearly as he loved the square outside. And, who knows? There might be a hot lardy cake or a spiced bun waiting for him.

He danced ahead of Sep towards the treasure house, and Sep, following sedately, recalled with a pang the days when two small boys, now lost to him, had led the same way to happiness.

17

Sep Makes a Decision

IT WAS in the January of 1930 that Bender had his first
serious illness. Hilda found him a most refractory patient.

'It's only a chest cold, I tell you,' he wheezed, waving
away inhalants, cough sweets and all other panaceas that his
poor wife brought. The very idea of calling the doctor sent
up his temperature.

'He'll only send me to bed,' he gasped. 'I'm much better off
down here by the fire. Don't fuss so, Hilda.'

But after a day or two he had such violent pains in his chest,
and his breathing was so laboured that Hilda slipped out of the
house and rang up the doctor from a neighbour's. Within an
hour Bender was in Caxley Cottage Hospital.

Sep heard about it at dinner time and rang the hospital
for news. He was in some discomfort, he was told, but
making progress. He would not be allowed visitors for some
time.

Sep was deeply shaken. For the next few days he went about
his affairs silent and depressed. The market square was not the
same without Bender's huge figure in the doorway of North's,
and his great laugh sending the pigeons flying. Sep rang Hilda
and kept in touch. He did not like to call at the house. Since
the Norths had moved he had seldom visited them. Any
meeting with Bender had taken place at the shop, or, by chance,
in the market place or street.

As soon as Bender was allowed visitors Sep went to see him. It was a cold night of sharp frost, and the railings and lamp posts were hoary with rime. It was good to get inside the warmth of the hospital, despite the reek of disinfectant which always upset Sep's stomach.

Bender looked mountainous in bed. His face against the pillow had an unnatural pallor which shocked Sep. Clearly, Bender had been very ill indeed. Beside his bed was another visitor, and as Sep approached he saw that it was Jack Tenby. The man rose as Sep came near.

'Don't go, Jack,' said Bender. 'Sit you down, man. I'm allowed two visitors at a time. Stay till Hilda comes.'

He held out a hand to Sep and gripped him with the same old firmness with which Sep was familiar.

'Good to see you, Sep. How's things?'

The three men exchanged news of Caxley friends. Someone had moved, someone else had taken up motor-racing, a third was to be made Mayor next year. The bridge was being repainted. A new bus service had been started to the county town. There was talk of a housing estate in the field behind the park.

Bender listened eagerly to all these topics, but he seemed tired, Sep thought, and when Hilda appeared bearing fruit and flowers, the two men made their farewells and left the hospital together.

The cold air caught their breath as they emerged. Above them the stars were brilliant. Their footsteps rang on the frosty pavement as they descended the gentle slope into the town together.

'How d'you think he looks?' asked Jack Tenby.

'Pretty weak,' admitted Sep.

'I agree. His wife was telling me the other day that the doctor says he should retire.'

They had reached the crossroads where their ways divided and paused beneath the lamp post to continue their conversation. In the light from the gas above them their breath rose in clouds.

'I haven't said anything to Bender about this yet, but I know it will go no further if I tell you about my plans. I'm pulling out of the market place.'

Sep was taken aback.

'For good, do you mean? What's gone wrong?'

'Nothing particularly. It's time I retired myself. It's been thought over and it seems best to sell up all but the original shop. Things aren't easy and are going to get worse. Staffing's a constant headache. I'm not getting any younger. If I collect the cash now and bank it, I reckon I can tick over comfortably until I die. The family's out in the world and it's time my wife and I had a bit of a rest.'

Sep nodded. All this was sensible. But what would Bender feel about it? And what would happen to his old home?

'What about North's?' he asked.

'It'll be put on the market,' replied Tenby. 'Good position like that should help its sale.'

'Jack,' said Sep suddenly, laying a hand on the other's arm, 'let me know when you finally decide. I should like to think about it.'

'I'll do that,' promised Tenby. 'It's going to happen before long. You shall be the first to know my plans.'

He raised a hand and set off at a brisk pace, leaving Sep to gaze at his dwindling figure.

Sep moved off more slowly. He had plenty of food for thought, and he would digest it undisturbed as he walked the streets of Caxley.

How oddly things had turned out! For over a year now Sep had been trying to find new premises in which to expand his thriving business. All Caxley said that Howard's was a gold mine. Only Sep knew how prosperous the business really was. He had saved regularly. His way of life had altered little over the years. As a result of this, and of his foresight and industry, Sep's bank account was extremely satisfactory. It was time that he put some of this money into another business, he decided, and it looked now as if one of his pipe dreams might come true. If North's were to come on the market it would be the perfect place for Howard's restaurant which he and Edna had thought about for so long.

He turned aside down a quiet lane which led to the river. Firelight flickered on the curtains of a cottage. A tabby cat streaked across his path. The smoke from Caxley's chimneys rose straight into the motionless night. Sep seemed to be the only person abroad as he paced along deep in thought.

He could see it all so clearly in his mind's eye. There would be one great room running from front to back on the ground floor, with french windows leading into Bender's garden. A garden had always been one of the highlights of Sep's dream. Here, in the summer, the Caxley folk could eat at little white tables, sipping their coffee or tea and choosing those delectable pastries made at Sep's shop over the way. There had been a need for a good class restaurant in Caxley for many years. Who better to supply it than Sep, who could provide the best cakes and pies in the neighbourhood?

If this property really became his how wonderful it would be! His own premises had been cramped for many years now. True, he had been able to buy the yard next door which belonged to the old herbalist who ran the dusty little shop beside Sep's own. Here he was able to keep the vans and some of his stores. He had often thought about buying out the herbalist, but the property was small and inconvenient, and although old Mr White was in his seventies, and looked as though a puff of wind would blow him away like thistledown, he continued to bumble about among his elixirs and nostrums with remarkable energy for one so frail.

Strangely enough, the possibility of North's ever becoming free had never occurred to Sep when thinking about his restaurant. Somehow, North's belonged to Bender still in Sep's mind, and was inviolate. If it should become his, thought Sep, quickening his pace as he reached the tow path, he would see that Bender's garden was restored as nearly as possible to its former glory. It would be a perfect setting for teas on the sloping lawns with the Cax rippling by.

And what about the house above the restaurant? He and Edna would not want to live there. They were far too comfortable in their own home, and even such a short move would be repugnant to Sep. Would Bender want to return? Would he rebuff any offer of Sep's yet again, if he were to suggest it?

Sep stopped by a willow tree, stretching its skinny arms to the stars above. Bender's waxen face as he had seen it that evening, floated before him. It was no use blinking the fact, thought Sep, suddenly becoming conscious of the icy cold, Bender had not many years before him, either at Rose Lodge or anywhere else. But if it lay in his power, Sep swore to himself, Bender should have his old home again, if he so wished.

And after? Sep turned up his coat collar and set his face towards the market square. Well, if this dream should become reality, then one day, far in the future, Bender's home should go to one of his own – one who would love it as Bender had done.

It should be Edward's.

Sep kept his thought to himself, and said nothing of Tenby's disclosures to Edna or anyone else. Bender made very slow progress, and the crocuses were out before he was allowed to return to Rose Lodge.

He found convalescence even more tedious than hospital life. At least there had been a routine there, a succession of small happenings and a constant stream of people, nurses, doctors, fellow-patients, and visitors. It was too cold to go in the garden. He was forbidden to work in the greenhouse, which was his latest joy, in case he lifted something too heavy or stood too long on his weak legs. Books tired his eyes, radio programmes his ears. Food was a bore, drink was restricted, and smoking too. Visitors were his only distraction, and Hilda welcomed them for it gave her a brief respite from her patient's claims on her time.

Bertie and Winnie and the children called in every day.

Occasionally Winnie stayed the night and Bertie took his mother out to friends or for a drive in the countryside to refresh her. She had borne up wonderfully during these tiring months, but to Bertie's eyes she looked years older.

'He frets to get back to the shop,' said Hilda on one of their outings, 'but the doctor won't hear of it yet. I do so wish he would retire. Do try and make him see sense, Bertie.'

'I'll have a word with him when I can,' promised Bertie dutifully.

But there was no need for Bertie to exercise his persuasive powers. When they returned they found that Jack Tenby had called and had told Bender all his plans for the future. So there had been something in the rumours flying round Caxley, thought Bertie.

His father looked pale and shaken.

'That settles it,' he said heavily. 'I'm finished for good now. The old place to be sold, and no job for me even if I could do it.'

Hilda straightened the cushion behind his aching head, and spoke with spirit.

'Don't be so full of self-pity! This is the best news I've heard for a long time. Now perhaps you'll make the best of being a retired man, and stop worrying about that wretched shop.'

'What have I got to look forward to?' asked Bender, half-enjoying his sad plight.

'Looking after me,' said his wife promptly. 'Pottering about in the greenhouse. Planning the garden for the summer. Helping your grandchildren with their homework. Being a little more welcoming to Mary's boy friends when she brings them home. Dozens of things.'

Despite himself, Bender had to smile.

'Have I been such a trial?' he asked.

'You've been *terrible*!' cried Hilda, with such fervour that Bender laughed aloud, and then began to wheeze. Bertie went forward in alarm, but was waved back vigorously.

'I'm all right, boy. Haven't been so right for weeks! Dammit all, now it's come to it, I believe I'm going to settle back and enjoy my old age!'

It was a month later that Sep called at Rose Lodge – a month that had been hectic for the little baker. He and Edna had talked far into the nights about the restaurant. There had been discussions with the bank, with surveyors, builders, solicitors, and dozens of people concerned in the exchange of property. Meanwhile, his own business had to be carried on, and all the time the problem of broaching the subject to Bender was uppermost in Sep's mind. Now the time had come. The deal was virtually done, and the property his.

He had gone about the affair as discreetly as possible and was confident that Bender had heard nothing. He wanted to break the news himself. It was unthinkable that he should hear of it from any other source.

Hilda let him in with a smile.

'He'll be so glad to see you. He's in the greenhouse watering the plants.'

Sep made his way into the garden. The greenhouse was warm and scented. Little beads of perspiration glistened on Bender's forehead. He put down the watering can and sank on to an upturned wooden box, motioning Sep to do the same.

'Good to see you, Sep. What's the news?'

'I'm not sure how you'll take it. But it's news you're bound to hear before long, and I wanted to be the one to bring it.'

'Well, get on with it then. Is it about Edna? Or has that new baby of Kathy's arrived?'

'Not yet – any day now, I believe. But it's not exactly family affairs I've come to talk about, but business ones.'

'Oh ah!' said Bender, yawning.

He did not seem to be particularly interested. At least, thought Sep, it should not be too great a shock.

'It's about your shop, Bender.'

'Has it gone yet? Jack Tenby said something about an auction if it didn't sell.'

'It has been sold,' said Sep. He ran a finger round the rough rim of a flowerpot, his eyes downcast.

'That's quick work!' commented Bender with more interest. 'Anyone we know bought it?'

'As a matter of fact,' said Sep, looking up from the flowerpot, 'I've bought it.'

There was silence in the heat of the greenhouse, and then Bender took a deep breath.

'Well, I'm damned,' he said softly. Then, leaning forward, he smote Sep's knee with something of his old heartiness.

'Well, don't be so deuced apologetic about it, boy! I'm glad you're having it, and that's the truth! Could have been bought by some sharp lad from London, simply to sell at a profit. Tell me more.'

Sep began. Once started it became easier to tell of his search for premises, for the hope of a restaurant and the general expansion of Howard's. Bender listened intently.

'And the garden?' he asked, when Sep paused to take breath.

'I want to keep it as you used to have it,' said Sep, 'when the children played there. It was at its best then, I always think.

'It was,' agreed Bender. 'Tell you what, I'll try and remember how it was we had it, and let you have the plants to set it up again. I'd like to do that for the old place.'

His face was cheerful, and he picked up the watering can again.

'Well, well, well!' he muttered bending over his seedlings. 'So you're going to be the owner of North's!'

He looked across at Sep.

'Ever going to live there?'

'No,' replied Sep. 'Young Parker is going to set up on his own in the High Street. Starting a china shop, evidently, but there's no accommodation there. I've told him he can stay where he is for the time being.'

Bender nodded, and continued his watering. Was this the time, Sep wondered, with a beating heart, to broach the question of Bender's return? Not yet, perhaps. Enough had happened today. He would wait a little.

But Bender forestalled him.

'It's a good house. We had some happy times there, didn't we, Sep? And some rotten ones too, but that's how it goes – and somehow it's only the happy ones we remember, thank God. I wouldn't want to go back there – not for all the tea in China. Too many memories, Sep. Far too many! Hilda and I are better off here.'

He put down the can resolutely.

'But it's good to think of it going to friends, Sep. I'm glad things have turned out this way.'

He opened the door of the greenhouse and gulped the cool air.

'Let's go and get Hilda to give us a cup of tea. Ain't no point in offering you anything stronger, I suppose?'

Wheezing and laughing, he made his way to the house, relishing the news he had to give his wife. And behind him, thankful in heart, followed Sep.

That night, lying sleepless in bed, Bender pondered on the changes of fortune. Who would have thought, when they were boys together in the rough and tumble of the old National School, that frightened little Sep Howard with holes in his boots would beat him – the cock o' the walk – as he had done?

There was Sep now, hale and hearty while he lay a crock of a man. Sep was a prosperous tradesman, a councillor, a pillar of the chapel, and now the owner of his old home. Not that he grudged him any of it. He'd earned it all, he supposed – funny little old Sep!

Well, that's how it went on life's see-saw, thought Bender philosophically. One went up, while the other went down! Nothing to be done about it, especially when you were as tired as he was. But who would have thought it, eh? Who would have thought it?

He turned his cheek into the plump comfort of his pillow, and fell asleep.

18

What of the Future?

A S USUAL, there were innumerable delays in starting
work on Sep's new restaurant. But one windy autumn
day the workmen moved in and the sound of picks
and shovels was music in Sep's ears.

It was market day, and he watched the first stages of the
work to the accompaniment of all the familiar market noises.
Cheapjacks yelled, awnings flapped and crackled in the wind,
leaves and paper rustled over the cobbles, dogs barked, children
screamed, and everywhere there was bustling activity.

Caxley was becoming busier than ever, thought Sep, picking
his way through the debris underfoot. Cars and vans streamed
along the western side of the square to continue on their way
into the High Street. There would be plenty of travellers
needing refreshment at the new restaurant, particularly in the
summer. By that time it should be going well. There were
plenty of local people too who would fill the tables at midday.
He had already planned to have a simple three-course luncheon,
modestly priced, to suit the time and tastes of the business
people nearby. This should provide steady trade for all the
year, and he hoped that he would be able to cater for evening
functions as well. As Caxley expanded – and it was doing so
fast in the early thirties – there should be plenty of scope for
Howard's restaurant.

Sep made a daily inspection of the work. Never before had

he felt such deep satisfaction in a project. This was building for the future. The thought of Edward living in the house in the years to come filled Sep with joy. The union of the two families, which Bender had refused to recognize in the marriage of Leslie and Winnie, would be assured when Edward took his joint heritage in the property.

One foggy November afternoon Sep returned from his inspection to find the evening paper on the counter as usual. His eye was caught by a photograph of two trains, hideously telescoped, toppling down the side of an embankment. The headline said: 'Scottish Rail Disaster'. Sep read on.

'In the dense fog which covered the entire British Isles this morning, an express train from London crashed into the rear of a local train three miles outside Edinburgh. Twenty-four people are known to be dead. It is feared that almost fifty are injured.'

It went on to describe the valiant efforts of volunteers who scrambled up the steep embankment to help the victims. Fog and ice hampered rescuers. Survivors were being treated at local hospitals. It was estimated that it would take twenty four hours to clear the wreckage from the track.

A terrible affair, thought Sep. So many other people affected too – wives and mothers, husbands and sons. A number of children were among the dead, for the accident had occurred soon after eight in the morning, when people were going to work and children to school.

The shop bell tinkled, and Jesse Miller came in to buy buns to take back to the farm for tea. Twisting the corners of the paper bag, and asking Jesse about his affairs, Sep forgot the news he had been reading.

What of the Future?

It was not until the next day that the Howards learnt that Kathy's Henry, on his way to the printing business, had been killed and now lay in an Edinburgh mortuary with the others so tragically dead.

It was young Robert Howard who escorted Edna to Scotland to comfort Kathy, and to attend the funeral, for Sep could not leave the business or the supervision of the new building.

The news was soon known in Caxley and Sep received many messages of sympathy. Kathy had always been popular, and Henry, so stalwart and handsome, had impressed the neighbourhood during his short time there. It was Winnie who told Bertie the news. His face turned so ashen that she thought that he would faint, but he remained calm and very quiet.

Inwardly he was in turmoil. He would like to have snatched his coat, leapt in the car and headed for Scotland to comfort her. The thought of Kathy in trouble, in tears, lonely and broken, was insupportable. But it could not be. Instead he sat at his desk and wrote, offering all help possible. He would come at once if it were of any assistance. Please let him help in any way possible. He wrote on, feeling all the time how inadequate it was, but the best that he could do in the circumstances.

Kathy's reply arrived in a few days. She was so touched by everyone's kindness, Bertie's particularly, but she was being well looked after. Her mother and Robert were still with her, and Henry's family lived close by and were taking care of everything. She was planning to come to Caxley when the weather improved and looked forward to meeting all her friends again.

This letter, Winnie noticed, was put into Bertie's pocket-book and was carried with him, but she made no comment.

Some days after Robert's and Edna's return, Sep walked up the hill to visit Bender. The shops were beginning to dress their windows for Christmas. Blobs of cotton wool, representing snow flakes, adorned the grocer's, tinsel glittered in the chemist's, and a massive holly wreath was propped tastefully against a grave vase in the local undertaker's. Sep shuddered as he passed. Death was too near just now.

He found Bender sitting in his high-backed winged arm-chair by the fire. He looked suddenly very old and his massive frame seemed to have shrunk, but his eyes lit up when he saw his visitor and his greeting was as hearty as ever.

'Hilda's down at Winnie's,' said Bender. 'They're making a party frock or some such nonsense for young Joan. She won't be long. Nice to have a bit of company, Sep.'

The two men warmed their feet by the fire. The kettle purred on the trivet. Chrysanthemums scented the firelit room. Hilda had always had the knack of making a house attractive, thought Sep. It was something that Edna had never really managed to do.

'Terrible business of Kathy's,' said Bender. 'I can't tell you how shocked we were to hear it. How's the poor girl getting on? And the children?'

Sep gave him what news he could. The little boy was the

hardest one to console – just old enough to understand things. The baby girl was thriving. She should be a great comfort to Kathy. They hoped to see them all in the spring for a long visit. They might even persuade Kathy to stay for good, but she was very attached to Edinburgh and to Henry's people. It was too early to make decisions yet.

Bender listened and nodded, sipping a glass of brandy and water.

'And the shop?' asked Bender, turning the conversation to more hopeful things. Sep's face lit up.

'We've taken down the wall between the shop and the parlour,' began Sep enthusiastically and went on to explain the plans he had for the interior decoration. Bender thought he had never seen him so animated. Howard's restaurant would not lack care and affection, he thought, as he listened to Sep running on.

'You're looking ahead,' he commented when Sep paused for breath, 'and a good thing too! Young Robert will have a fine business to carry on when you want to give up.'

'The business will be his,' agreed Sep, 'but not the house. Our own place will go to him, no doubt.'

'And what about North's?'

'He doesn't know yet,' said Sep slowly, 'but it's to be Edward's.'

A long silence fell. A coal tumbled out of the fire, and Bender replaced it carefully. The tongs shook in his hands, his breathing was laboured. At last he sat back and gazed across at Sep.

'That pleases me more than I can say, Sep. The old house will stay in the family – in *both* our families – after all!'

He picked up his glass again, raised it silently to Sep, and drained it.

It was at that moment they heard a car draw up at the front door and the sound of voices. Hilda hurried into the room followed by Bertie and Edward.

'Bertie brought me back,' said Hilda, when greetings were over, 'and I want him to stay to supper, but he won't.'

'I can't, mamma. I've three business letters to write and young Edward has his Latin prep. to do. We promised Winnie we'd go straight back.'

Hilda looked rather put out, but made no further demur, and Sep watching them all, thought how well Bertie handled his parents. He was, in truth, the head of the family now, with an air of authority which was not entirely hidden by his gentle and affectionate manner. Edward began to make obediently for the door.

'Can I sit in the front, Uncle Bertie? I wish I could drive! I could if it were allowed, you know. Uncle Bertie says he'll let me have a go in a field one day.'

'You must take care –' began Hilda.

'Don't worry, Grandma. A car's easy. I'm going to fly an aeroplane as soon as I get the chance.'

'Really, Edward!' expostulated Hilda, laughing.

'No, I mean it. I've told Uncle Bertie, haven't I? I'm going into the Air Force, and in the next war I shall be a pilot.'

'Time enough to think of that later,' put in Sep. 'You're only fourteen. You may change your mind.'

'Can I give you a lift?' asked Bertie, turning to Sep.

They made their farewells to Hilda and Bender and went out into the starlit night. An owl was hooting from a nearby garden, and another one answered from the distant common. The scent of a dying bonfire hung in the air. It smelt very wintry, thought Sep, as they drove down the hill to the market square.

Bertie dropped him by St Peter's and drove off. Obeying an impulse, Sep mounted the steps and opened the door. He rarely went inside the church, but was proud of its history and its beauty. It was dimly lit and Sep guessed that the cleaners were somewhere at work. There were sounds of chairs being moved in the vestry at the far end of the church.

Sep sat down in a pew near the door and gazed up at the lofty roof. Tattered flags hung there, relics of the Boer War and earlier wars. He thought of Edward's excitement as he talked of a future war in which he proposed to fly. Would there ever be an end to this misery and wrong thinking? Would the League of Nations really be able to have the last sane word if trouble brewed?

And there certainly was trouble brewing, if the papers were right. Not only between nations, but here on our own doorstep. What would be the result of these desperate hunger marches, some of which Sep had seen himself? It was an affront to human dignity to be without means to live. A man must have work. A man must have hope. What happened if he had neither? Life, thought Sep, chafing his cold fingers, was a succession of problems, and only some of them could be solved by personal effort.

He sighed and rose to his feet. His boots made a loud noise on the tiled floor as he made his way to the door. Across the market place the lights of his home glowed comfortingly. On his left shone the three great windows of young Mr Parker's drawing room above the gaunt black emptiness of the future Howard's Restaurant.

Warmth suddenly flooded Sep's cold frame. A man could only do so much! He had set his hand to this particular plough and he must continue in the furrow which it made. What use was it to try to set the whole world to rights? He must travel his own insignificant path with constancy and courage. It might not lead to the heights of Olympus, but it should afford him interest, exercise and happiness as he went along. And, Sep felt sure, there would be joy at the end.

As Sep was crossing the market square to his home, Bertie sat at his desk, pen in hand, and a blank sheet of writing paper before him.

His thoughts were centred on Edward who sat at the table, head bent over an inky exercise book. His dark hair shone in the light from the lamp. His eyes, when he looked up, were just as Bertie remembered Leslie's at the same age. He was going to have the good looks of his father and his grandmother – vivacious, dusky and devastating.

And so he wanted to fly, mused Bertie! There was no reason on earth why he shouldn't. Bertie thought it was an excellent idea and would do all in his power to help him. Flying was going to develop more rapidly than people imagined. With the world shrinking so fast, surely the nations must settle down amicably together! Edward's calm assumption that there would be another war did not fill Bertie with quite the same horror as it had Sep. Bertie could not believe that the world would go to war again. The memory of 1914–18 was too close. Even now, years after its ending, scenes came back to Bertie as he drifted off to sleep at nights, waking him again. It had been a war to end war. Thank God, Edward's flying would be used for more constructive ends!

He pulled the blank paper towards him and began to write the neglected letter.

19

Sep Loses a Friend

CHRISTMAS CAME and went. The tree in the market square grew bedraggled, the tinsel in the shop windows tarnished. It was a relief when Twelfth Night came and everything could be tidied away. Down came the brittle holly, the withered mistletoe. Into the rubbish bins went the dusty Christmas cards, the broken baubles, and the turkey bones, and into the cupboards went some unwanted Christmas presents, placed there by the more frugal for future raffles and bazaars.

It grew iron-cold as the New Year broke and little work could be done on the site of the restaurant. Sep did his best to be patient, but it was almost more than he could endure. This was the great year when he would open his new venture. He wanted everything ready by the spring, down to the napkins and the flowers on the tables. From Easter onwards he looked forward to a growing volume of trade. These delays irked Sep sorely.

In the midst of his frustration he heard that Bender was again in hospital with pleurisy. Sep went at once. He was deeply shocked at Bender's appearance. He had not seen him since his visit to Rose Lodge before Christmas. His eyes were sunken, and he moved his head restlessly on the pillow. His hand, as he took Sep's, felt hot and damp. Now there was no vigour in his grip. He could barely speak.

Sep tried to hide his distress, and talked gently of things which he felt might interest the sick man. Bender scarcely seemed to hear him. He began to wheeze alarmingly, and a young nurse hurried towards him and tried to hoist him higher on the pillow.

'Let me,' said Sep, sliding an arm under Bender's shoulders. All his memories of wounded men at Caxley station in wartime flooded back to him.

'You've got a good touch, Sep,' wheezed Bender. 'Got a knack you have. That's better now!'

'That's the spirit!' rallied the young nurse, tucking in the bedclothes with painful vigour. 'Not dead yet, you know!'

'It's not death I'm afraid of,' responded Bender, with a flash of his old spirit, 'but living on – with this dam' pain!'

He put a hand to his side and lay silent for a minute.

'Tell me,' he managed to say at last, 'tell me, Sep, about the shop. The plants are ready in the greenhouse whenever it's fit to put them out in the garden. Hilda'll let you have them. And Sep, the jasmine wants trimming back at that old arbour. Makes a deal of growth every year, that stuff.'

Sep promised to attend to it. Suddenly Bender's eyelids drooped and his head fell back. The nurse hurried forward.

'He's asleep again. I think you'd better leave now, Mr Howard. He's having drugs, you know, to relieve the pain.'

Sep nodded and rose to go. There was something pathetic and defenceless about the sleeping man, a look of the boy that Sep remembered years ago. He stood silent, loth to leave him, loth to turn away.

The nurse touched his arm, and he moved unseeingly towards the door. He knew now, with utter desolation, that he would not look upon Bender's face again.

*   *   *

It was very cold that night. The market square glistened with frost. Icicles hung from the lions' mouths on the old Queen's fountain. The pigeons, roosting on the ledges of the Town Hall, tucked their heads more deeply into their feathers. The stars above were diamond-bright, the air piercingly sharp.

The ward where Bender lay was dim and shadowy. The young night nurse, on duty, sat at the table at the end near the corridor, a pool of light upon her papers. She shivered in the draught and wrapped her cloak more tightly around her.

It was deathly quiet. Only the sound of laboured breathing, and an occasional moan from the red-blanketed beds, broke the stillness. It was the time of night, as the nurse well knew, when life was at its lowest ebb.

She raised her head, suddenly aware of a change in the ward. Someone, somewhere, had ceased breathing. There was a chill in the air which was not wholly natural.

Quietly she rose and glided swiftly to Bender's bedside. His eyes were closed, his mouth slightly open in a smile which was infinitely young and gentle. The nurse held the warm wrist and put her ear to the quiet breast.

At last, she straightened herself, crossed Bender's arms and covered his face with the sheet.

The day of Bender's funeral was cold and bright. It happened to be market day, and Sep, as he crossed the bustling square, thought how Bender would have liked that last touch.

St Peter's was crowded with mourners, many of them from the stalls outside. Bender had been known and respected, not only in Caxley, but for many miles around. His great figure was as much a part of the market scene as the bronze statue which dominated the place. Bender was going to be sadly missed.

The church looked very lovely. The candles wavered and flickered – now tall as golden crocuses, now small and round as buttercups, as the breeze caught them. On the coffin, at the chancel steps, a great cross of bronze chrysanthemums glowed in the candlelight. The family mourners sat, straight-backed and sad-faced. Among them, Sep was surprised to see, was young Edward.

Winnie and Bertie had not wanted the children to be present, feeling that the occasion was too harrowing for them, but Edward had pleaded passionately to be allowed to attend.

'He's my grandfather. I want to be with him till the end,' announced Edward, his mouth stubborn. 'I'm not a child any more. You must let me go.'

Winnie had been about to protest, but Bertie restrained her.

'The boy's right,' he said quietly. 'He's part of the family. Let him take his place.'

And so Edward was the youngest mourner present. Sep and Edna sat towards the back, and Sep couldn't help noticing how old and bent many of the congregation were. It was a shock to realize that he would be seventy in a few years' time and that these people were his and Bender's contemporaries. Did he too look so old, Sep wondered? He did not feel any older than he had when he had first taken his lovely Edna to live in the market square, and together they had worked so hard to build up the business.

And that would not have been possible, thought Sep, his eyes on the coffin, if it had not been for Bender's timely help.

He had a debt to him which he could never repay – and it was not only a material debt. His whole life had been inextricably bound up with that of the dead man. Bender's influence upon him had been immeasurable. To say that he would miss him was only stating a tenth of the effect which Bender's passing meant to him.

What was it, Sep mused in the shadowy church, that created the bond between them? They had shared schooldays, manhood and all the joys, troubles and setbacks of war and peace. Together they had played their parts in the life of Caxley. The market square had been their stage – the kaleidoscopic background to tragedy and farce. Their families had intermarried, their grandchildren were shared.

But that was not all.

Sep felt for Bender – and always had – a variety of emotions: fear, affection, pity, hero-worship, and, at times, distaste for his ebullience and ruthlessness. Perhaps he could best sum up these mingled feelings as awareness. Whatever happened to Bender affected Sep. Whatever had happened to Sep was measured for him by Bender's possible reaction to it. He could never remember a time when he had been entirely independent of the other man. Bender mattered. What Bender thought of Sep mattered, and reason, principles, codes of conduct – even religion itself – could not entirely guide Sep's actions while Bender lived.

A vital part of Sep had died too when Bender died. From now on the stuff of Sep's life would be woven in more muted hues. The brightest, the strongest, and the most vivid thread in the fabric would be missing.

* * *

That afternoon Sep made his way alone to the old garden behind the restaurant. It was sadly neglected. The workmen had trodden down the borders, the lawn was bare and muddy, the shrubs splashed with lime and paint where the men had plied their brushes carelessly.

Sep stood in silence, taking stock. With care, before long, it should look as it did in Bender's day. The grey spiky foliage of pinks still lined the edge of the path. The lilac bushes already showed buds as large and green as peas. Dead seed-pods of irises and lupins made rattling spires above the low growing pansies and periwinkles at their feet. It should all be as it was, vowed Sep silently surveying the scene of decay.

He made his way to the ancient arbour which was covered with jasmine. It had been made years earlier for Bender's mother to sit in and enjoy the sunshine. Now it was damp and mouldering. Sep sat down on the rickety bench. Bright spots of coral fungus decorated the woodwork, and splashes of bird droppings made white arabesques on the floor. An untidy nest spilt grass and moss from the rustic work at the corners of the doorway. Broken snails' shells surrounding a large flint by the entrance showed where the thrushes used their anvil. The brick floor was slimy and interlaced with vivid lines of green moss and the silver trails of slugs.

It was very tranquil. The river whispered nearby and the overgrown jasmine rustled gently in the little breeze from the water. Tomorrow, thought Sep, he would bring his shears and trim back the waving fronds as Bender had directed.

He rose to go, and then caught sight of something white half-hidden in the shadows under the seat. He bent down to retrieve it and carried it into the dying light of the winter afternoon.

It was a toy boat. It must belong to one of the Parker children, he supposed, but it was exactly like the boat he had once bought for Leslie long ago. Money had been short, he remembered, but the boy had looked at it with such longing in his dark eyes, that Sep had gone into the shop and paid a shilling for the little yacht. How it brought it all back!

Sep stroked the rusty hull, and straightened the crumpled sail. How many generations had sailed their boats on the Cax's placid surface? And how many more would do so in the future?

With the first flush of warmth that he had felt that day, Sep remembered Edward. One day his children – Sep's great-grandchildren – would carry their boats across this now deserted garden and set them hopefully upon the water.

Smiling now, Sep made his way from the peace of the riverside to the noise and confusion of the emerging restaurant. He paused to set the little yacht on the foot of the stairs leading to Bender's old home, where its young owner would find it – safely in harbour.

The short afternoon was rapidly merging into twilight. The stall holders were beginning to pack up now. The children from the marsh were already skimming round the stalls, like hungry swifts, and screaming with much the same shrill excitement. This was the time when the stall holders gave away the leavings, when a battered cabbage or a brown banana or two were tossed to eager hands. Many a prudent Caxley housewife was there too, glad to get a joint or some home-made cheese or butter at half price.

The dust vans were already beginning to collect the litter.

The dustmen's brooms, a yard wide, pushed peelings, straw and paper before them. Colour from all over the world was collected and tossed into the waiting vans – squashed oranges from Spain, bruised scarlet tomatoes from Jersey, yellow banana skins from Jamaica, the vibrant purplish-pink tissue paper which had swathed the Italian grapes – all were mingled with the gentler colours of the straw, the walnut shells and the marbled cabbage leaves from the Caxley countryside.

Already the sun had sunk behind St Peter's, where earlier in the day Sep had watched part of his life put quietly away. The air was beginning to grow chilly, and the market people redoubled their efforts and their clamour to get their work finished before nightfall.

Sep turned at his doorway to watch them. For them, it was the end of just another market day. For him, it was the end of an era. He let his eyes roam over the darkening scene. In an hour's time the market folk would have departed – folk as colourful and ephemeral as summer butterflies.

But the market square would remain, solid and enduring, a place of flint and brick, iron and cobbles, shabby and familiar, ugly and beloved. There was no other place quite like it. Caxley life might pulse throughout the network of streets and alleys on each side of the slow-running Cax, but here, in the market square, was the heart of the town.

Here sprang the spirit, here the hope. Sep looked across at the dark shell of Bender's old shop, awaiting its future life, and was comforted.

20

Hopes Realized

IN THE weeks that followed, Sep's spirits rose. An unusually mild spell gave the workmen a chance to make progress unhindered by frost. If things continued at this pace, he would certainly open on time.

Whenever he could spare a few moments from his own shop, Sep was at the new premises watching with a keen eye all that was being done. He took a particular interest in the remaking of the garden. He knew little about gardening. He had never owned one, and had been too busy to acquire much knowledge of plants and flowers, but Bertie proved to have the North flair for gardening, and he and Edward offered to help in the work.

Bertie's own garden was a constant joy to him. He was very proud of his property and liked to do jobs himself. Since his father's death Winnie was often at Rose Lodge with the children, and Bertie was left undisturbed to enjoy his gardening and his attempts at carpentering and decorating.

Bertie had tried to persuade his mother to make her home with him, but she disliked the idea of becoming dependent upon the next generation. She had always felt a fierce pride in possessions, and would not consider parting with any of the things which made Rose Lodge so dear to her.

'It would break my heart to have to sell, Bertie, and that's what I'd have to do. There simply wouldn't be room for everything, and every single piece means so much to me. That desk of your father's, for instance – and that ugly old flat-iron to hold down his papers! Why, I can't throw that away! And that chair – I used to sit on it to change your nappies, dear. Just the right height for me. No, it can't be done! I shall stop here until I'm too old and doddery to cope, and you must all come and see me as often as you can.'

And so it had been settled. After the first shock of grief had gone, Hilda set about running the house and her many charitable activities with all her old zest and efficiency. She went out and about to friends and relations in Caxley, and delighted in her grandchildren, but she was thankful to settle by her own fireside at Rose Lodge each evening, with all the dear souvenirs of a happy life around her.

Bertie was glad to see her so independent and was relieved too that she need not face the upheaval of another move. His own house was pretty full and he would have had to sacrifice his sitting room to accommodate his mother if she had wanted to come. This he was prepared to do willingly. Winnie had suggested that she should go and live with Hilda, so that she would not be alone, but it was done half-heartedly for she did not want to leave Bertie, and the children were happy in the house. It seemed best to let things go on as they were, and so far everything had gone very smoothly.

Winnie heard from Kathy occasionally. They usually wrote when one of the children had a birthday, and then exchanged news of Caxley and Edinburgh. Kathy had been left comfortably off, and her parents-in-law were kind and understanding. She was beginning to meet people again. Her visit to Caxley was planned to coincide with the opening of Sep's restaurant in April, and she told Winnie that she hoped to stay with her parents for several weeks.

Winnie never suspected the turmoil which went on behind her brother's calm countenance when she read these letters to him. Kathy was never far from Bertie's thoughts. Henry's parents, whom he had never met, he viewed with mixed feelings – gratitude for their care of Kathy and alarm at their solicitude for her future. It sometimes seemed to Bertie that they were busy looking for another handsome Scot for his Kathy. Would she never return? Should he take the plunge and go north to see her? Natural shyness restrained him. Her loss was so recent. She must be given time to find herself again. He must await her coming to Caxley with all the patience he could muster, and speak to her then. He had nothing to lose: everything – everything in the world – to gain! Bertie watched the calendar as avidly as a homesick schoolboy.

She came soon after Easter, three days before the party to celebrate the opening of Howard's restaurant. Winnie and Bertie were invited to supper the day after her arrival, and as they sat at the great table, waiting for Sep to carve a handsome round of cold beef, Bertie remembered all the other meals he had eaten in this room and with this family. Robert sat now where Jim used to sit. Mary was beside him. Kathy sat opposite, lovelier than ever, but thinner than he remembered. Life had dealt both of them some pretty shrewd knocks, thought Bertie, and they were both a good deal older and more battered than when he had sat there bringing shame upon the Norths by starting to eat his roll before Sep had said grace. Bertie smiled now at the recollection – but how he had smarted then!

Kathy's children were asleep in her old bedroom, but Winnie insisted on creeping up to see them and Bertie went with her. The boy was a Howard, dark and handsome. The baby already displayed a few wisps of auburn hair and the fresh complexion of her Scottish father.

'What do you think of 'em?' asked Sep proudly, when they returned. 'I'm all for having 'em at the party, but Kathy won't hear of it. Everyone else in the family will be there. Seems a pity to me!'

Excitement was in the air. The party was to take place on Saturday evening. The restaurant opened on Monday. All those connected with the building and creation of the new premises were invited. Old Caxley friends and the whole of the Howard family would be present. This grand affair was to start at seven o'clock, and the party would sit down to a superb dinner of Sep's devising at seven thirty.

'Now, do keep an eye on the time, Edward,' begged Winnie at lunch time. He was going fishing with Tim Parker, and when thus engaged the hours flew by unnoticed. 'You must be back by six at the latest to get cleaned up.'

Edward nodded absentmindedly. Uncle Bertie had promised to enquire about a rod in Petter's shop window. Had he done it, asked the boy?

'Sorry, Edward. It slipped my mind. I have to go out this afternoon. I'll call in then. If he's asking a reasonable price you can come in with me later on and see if it suits you.'

Edward's face lit up. The rod he used now had once been Bender's and was sadly the worse for wear. A new one was the height of Edward's ambition. He could scarcely wait to tell Tim the good news.

As Winnie had feared, it was half past six before the boy returned on his bicycle, drenched, muddy but supremely happy. He was pushed swiftly into the bathroom and exhorted to hurry. Winnie fluttered back and forth between her own room and Joan's, arranging curls, fastening necklaces, and smoothing stockings.

At last the party set off, Edward still damp from his bath, his hair as sleek as a seal's. He gazed in admiration at his uncle's neat figure.

'You've got a new suit!'

'Do you like it?'

'Very much. It makes you look quite young, Uncle Bertie.'

'Thank you, Edward. How do I usually look?'

'Well, not exactly old, but – '

'Middle-aged?'

'That's it! But not in that suit. I suppose it's because it's more up-to-date than your others.'

And with this modified praise, Bertie had to be content.

The restaurant was ablaze with lights, although the evening was bright with sunshine. Sep had chosen white and gold for the interior of his new premises, and vases of daffodils added to the freshness. The tables had been put together to form two long ones down each side of the room with another across the end. The new table linen glistened like a fresh fall of snow, the glass winked like diamonds, the silver reflected the gay colours of the women's frocks and the golden lamps on the tables.

Through the french windows could be seen the green sunlit lawn running down to the Cax. More daffodils nodded here, and a row of scarlet tulips stood erect like guardsmen. The Cax caught the rays of the sun, flashing and sparkling as it wound its way eastward under Bender's rustic bridge. There was no doubt about it, Sep's dream had come true, and this evening he rejoiced in its fulfilment.

The meal was as sumptuous as one might guess with Sep as host, and although he himself drank only lemonade, he saw that his guests were served generously with wine. One of the waiters poured out some sparkling white wine for Edward, unnoticed by his elders, and the boy drank it discreetly. It looked remarkably like Joan's fizzy lemonade across the table, he noticed with considerable complacency, but tasted very much better. This was the life!

He caught sight of his Uncle Bertie at the other end of the table and remembered his fishing rod. He was too far away to call to—he must catch him later. Meanwhile it was enough to sip his wine, and see if he could find room for cheese and biscuits after all the courses he had managed already. He eyed the pyramids of fruit ranged down the tables for dessert. Somehow he doubted if he would have room for fruit as well . . .

Now his grandfather was standing up to make a speech – and heavens! – how loudly the people were clapping and cheering him! And how pretty grandma Howard looked tonight in her pink silk frock – as pretty as she looked in the picture Dan Crockford had painted long before Edward was born. Edward leant back in his chair and let the room revolve gently round him, too dizzy and happy to listen to speeches, too bemused to see anyone in focus.

When, finally, the guests moved from the tables and coffee

was being served, Edward was obliged to look for the lavatory. His head throbbed so violently that he could not be bothered to seek out the luxurious accommodation provided for the restaurant, but slipped up the familiar stairs to the Parker's bathroom. It was blissfully cool there after the heat and cigar smoke below. Edward splashed his burning face with cold water and began to feel better.

He leant his forehead against the cold window panes and gazed at the market place below. Queen Victoria was bathed in a rosy glow from the setting sun. Her bronze features gleamed as though she had been rubbed with butter. A car or two went by, and a girl on a piebald pony. A man with a violin case hurried into the Corn Exchange. How peaceful it was, thought Edward!

Below him he could hear the hum of the party. He must go back again before he was missed . . . back into that strange noisy grown-up world where men smoked and drank wine and clapped his pale little grandfather. It was good to have escaped for a few minutes, to have found a brief refuge in the old familiar quietness above.

But it was good, too, to go back, to join his family, to be one of the Howards and one of the Norths too, to be doubly a man of Caxley. He belonged both upstairs and down in this ancient building.

Swaggering slightly, Edward descended the stairs.

An hour or so later, as the guests were beginning to depart, Edward remembered his fishing rod and looked for his Uncle Bertie.

'He went into the garden,' said his mother. But Edward could not find him there.

'Maybe he stepped into the market place,' suggested Grandma North. There was no sign of him there either.

'Have a piece of crystallized ginger,' advised his sister Joan. 'You can see Uncle Bertie any day. You won't see this gorgeous stuff tomorrow.' Edward shelved the problem of his Uncle Bertie's disappearance and joined his sister at the sweet dish.

At last only a few of the family were left. It was beginning to get dark. The evening star had slid up from the Cax and hung like a jewel on the dusky horizon.

'Cut along home, my boy,' said his grandfather's voice. 'To our place, I mean. Your mother's just gone across. I'll be there in a few minutes.'

Obediently, he set off across the darkening square. A child was filling one of the iron cups with water, and Edward realized how thirsty he was himself. He made his way to the next lion, and pressed the cold button in its head. Out gushed the water from the lion's mouth, giving him the same joy which it had always done.

He let it play over his sticky fingers and hot wrists before filling the cup. He tilted it against his parched mouth and enjoyed the feeling of the drops spilling down his chin. Wine was all right to boast about, but water was the real stuff to drink!

At that moment he heard his grandfather approach and turned to greet him. At the same time he saw Uncle Bertie and Aunt Kathy emerge from the doorway of Howard's Restaurant. How young Uncle Bertie looked tonight! It must be the suit. And how happy! That must be the wine, surmised Edward, unusually sophisticated.

He suddenly remembered his fishing rod.

'Uncle Bertie!' he shouted towards the couple. 'What about my fishing rod? *Uncle Bertie? Uncle Bertie!*'

Sep's hand came down upon his shoulder.

'He doesn't hear me!' protested Edward, trying to break free.

'No, he doesn't,' agreed Sep equably.

The boy stopped struggling and watched the pair making their way towards the river. There was something in their faces that made him aware of great happenings. This was not the time to ask about his fishing rod, it seemed.

He gave a great tired sigh. It had been a long day.

Sep took his wet hand as he had done when he was a little boy. They turned to cross the market square together.

'There's always tomorrow, Edward,' Sep said consolingly. 'Always tomorrow . . .'

THE HOWARDS OF CAXLEY

PART ONE

1939—1945

I

Happy Independence

IT WAS six o'clock on a fine May morning.

The market square was deserted. Long shadows lay across the cobblestones, reaching almost to the steps of St Peter's church. Pink sunlight trembled across its old grey stone, gilding the splendid spire and warming the hoary saints in their niches. A thin black cat, in a sheltered angle of the porch, washed one upthrust leg, its body as round and curved as an elegant shell. Not even the pigeons disturbed its solitude, for they still slept, roosting in scores on the ledges of the Corn Exchange and the Victorian Town Hall.

A hundred yards away, the river Cax, swollen with spring rains, swept in a shining arc through the buttercup fields. The haze of early hours lay over all the countryside which surrounded the little market town, veiling the motionless clumps of elm trees in the fields and the cottages still sleeping among their dewy gardens.

The minute hand of St Peter's clock began its slow downhill journey from the gilded twelve, and Edward Howard, pyjama-clad at his bedroom window nearby, watched it with mounting exhilaration. This was the life! How wonderful to be alive on such a morning, to be twenty-one and – best of all – to have a place of one's own!

He flung up the window and leaned out, snuffing the morning air like a young puppy. The sun touched his face with gentle warmth. It was going to be a real scorcher, he thought to himself happily. He laughed aloud and the thin cat, arrested in the midst of its toilet, gazed up at him, a tongue as pink as a rose petal still protruding from its mouth.

'Good morning!' called Edward civilly to the only other waking inhabitant of the market square. The cat stared at him disdainfully, shrugged, and then continued with its washing.

And Edward, turning towards the bathroom, followed its good example.

Lying in warm water, he ran an appraising eye round the bathroom and mused upon his good fortune. At this time last year he had been living at Rose Lodge, a mile away on the hill south of Caxley, with his mother and grandmother North. It had been his home for seven or eight years, and he had, he supposed, been reasonably happy there in the company of the two women. But these last few months of bachelor independence made him realise the restrictions which he had suffered earlier. Now there was no one to question his comings and goings. If he cared to stay out until two in the morning, there was no waiting tray, complete with hot chocolate in a vacuum flask, to reproach him. No parental note reminded him to bolt the door and switch off the landing light. It wasn't that he didn't love them, poor dear old things, thought Edward indulgently as he added more hot water to his bath, but simply that he had outgrown them.

'God bless Grandpa Howard!' said Edward aloud, as he sank back again.

It was good to be living in Caxley market square where his

grandparents on both sides had built up their businesses. Here, in this house, of which he was now the proud owner, Bender North and his wife Hilda had lived for many years over their ironmongery shop. Edward could see his grandfather clearly now, in his mind's eye, a vast figure in a brown coat overall striding among the coal scuttles and patty pans, the spades and milking pails, which jostled together beneath the pairs of hob-nailed boots and hurricane lamps that swung from the ceiling above him. Soon afterwards, Bender and his wife had moved to Rose Lodge – a far more genteel address to Hilda's mind – and the glories of the great drawing room over the shop were no more. But Winnie, Edward's mother, and his Uncle Bertie North had described the red plush furniture, the plethora of ornaments and the floral arrangements of dried grasses and sea-lavender, with such vivid detail, that he felt quite familiar with the Edwardian splendour which had now vanished.

He knew, equally well, the sad story of the decline of Bender's business. It had been bought by a larger firm in the town and, later still, his grandfather Septimus Howard had taken it over. Sep still lived in the market square above his thriving bakery. The whole of the ground floor at North's he had transformed into a restaurant, almost ten years ago. It was, according to Caxley gossip, 'an absolute gold-mine', but there were few who grudged Sep Howard his success. Hardworking, modest, a pillar of the local chapel, and a councillor, the little baker's worth was appreciated by his fellow townsmen.

The business was to go to his son Robert, already a vigorous partner, when Sep could carry on no longer. Sep was now, in the early summer of 1939, a spry seventy-three, and there was no sign of his relinquishing his hold on family affairs. The acquisition of Bender's old home and the growth of the restaurant had given Sep an added interest in life. It was typical of his generosity, said his neighbours, that he had given Edward the house which had been Bender's when the boy attained the age of twenty-one. The restaurant, on the ground floor, would be Robert's in time, and the more shrewd of Caxley's citizens wondered why Sep could not foresee that there might be friction between Edward and his young uncle in the years to come.

But on this bright May morning all was well in Edward's world. It had needed courage to tell his two women-folk that he proposed to set up his own establishment, and even now, when he looked back on the scene at Rose Lodge, Edward winced.

15 The Market Square, still generally known in Caxley as 'North's', had fallen empty at Michaelmas 1938. The Parker family, who had been tenants for several years, had prospered, and bought a house in the village of Beech Green a few miles away. The property had become Edward's that same year on his twenty-first birthday. It was the most splendid present imaginable, for the boy had loved the house as long as he could remember. The idea of living there one day had been with him for many years, a secret joyous hope which he fully intended to turn into reality.

'It's a big responsibility for a young man in your position,' Grandma North quavered, when the old home was first made over to him. 'I know your Grandpa Howard has arranged for a sum of money to keep the place in repair, but what happens when he's gone? You may have a wife and family to keep by then.'

'We'll all live there,' cried Edward cheerfully, 'and you shall come and tell us how badly we keep it, compared with your days.'

'Well, you may laugh about it now, my boy,' said the old lady, a little querulously, 'but I know what a big place that is to keep going. The stairs alone are a morning's work, and no one ever managed to keep that back attic free from damp. Your Grandpa Howard's never lived there as I have. He's no notion of what it means in upkeep.'

Hilda North had never liked Septimus Howard. She had watched him rise as her own husband had steadily declined. Old age did not mellow her feelings towards this neighbour of a lifetime, and the marriage of her darling son Bertie to Kathy Howard and the earlier marriage of her daughter Winnie to Leslie, Edward's ne'er-do-well father, did nothing to allay the acrimony which she felt towards the Howard family.

'Thank God,' she said often to Edward, 'that you take after the North side of the family, despite your name. Your dear mother's been both father and mother to you. Really, I sometimes think it was a blessing your father left her. She's better without him.'

Edward was wise enough to keep a silent tongue when the old lady ran on in this vein. He knew quite well that there was a strong streak of the Howards in his make-up. He hoped, in all humility, that he had something of Sep Howard's strength of character. He was beginning to guess, with some astonishment, that he might possess some of his erring father's attraction for the opposite sex.

He often wondered about his father. It was impossible to get a clear picture of him from either side of the family, and his

15

own memories were hazy. Leslie Howard had decamped with an earlier love when Edward was four and the second child, Joan, only a few months old. As far as was known, he flourished, as the wicked so often do, in a Devonshire town. He had never been seen in Caxley again.

'Too ashamed, let's hope!' said Edward's grandmother North tartly, but Edward sometimes wondered. What was the result of that flight from the family? He had never heard his father's side of the affair. It was as tantalising as a tale half-read. Would he ever know the end of the story?

Edward had dropped the bombshell on a mellow September evening, a week or two before Michaelmas Day, when the Parkers were to vacate his newly acquired property. The two women were sitting in the evening sunshine admiring the brave show of scarlet dahlias. Around them, the gnats hummed. Above them, on the telephone wires, were ranged two or three dozen swallows like notes on staves of music. Soon they would be off to find stronger sunshine.

It was too bad to shatter such tranquillity, thought Edward, pacing restlessly about the garden, but it had to be done. He spoke as gently as his taut nerves allowed.

'Mother! Grandma!' He stopped before the two placid figures. Sun-steeped, vague and sleepy, they gazed at him with mild expectancy. Edward's heart smote him, but he took the plunge.

'Don't let this be too much of a shock, but I'm thinking about living in the market square myself when the Parkers leave.'

His mother's pretty mouth dropped open. His grandmother did not appear to have heard him. He raised his voice slightly.

'At the old house, Grandma dear. I want to move in at Michaelmas.'

'I heard you,' said the old lady shortly.

'But why, Edward? Why?' quavered his mother. 'Aren't you happy here?'

To Edward's alarm he saw tears welling in his mother's blue eyes. Just as he thought, there was going to be the devil of a scene. No help for it then, but to soldier on. He sat down on the iron arm of the curly garden seat upon which the two were reclining, and put a reassuring arm about his mother's shoulders.

'Of course I'm happy here—' he began.

'Then say no more,' broke in his mother swiftly. 'What should we do without a man in the house? We're so nicely settled, Edward, don't go upsetting things.'

'What's put this in your head?' queried his grandmother. 'Getting married, are you?'

'You know I'm not,' muttered Edward, rising from his perch and resuming his prowlings. 'It's simply that the house is now mine, it's empty, and I want to live there.'

'But it will be far too big for you alone, Edward,' protested his mother. 'And far too expensive.'

'I've worked it all out and I can manage quite well. I don't intend to use all the house, simply the top floor. The rest can be let, and bring me in a regular income.'

'Well, I must say,' cried his mother reproachfully, 'you seem to have been planning this move for some time! I can't tell you what a shock it is! I'd no idea you felt like this about things. What about poor Grandma? How do you think she is going to like it when there are only women left alone to cope with everything here?'

Winnie produced a handkerchief and mopped her eyes. Her mother, made of sterner stuff, sniffed militantly and Edward prepared to hear the old lady's vituperation in support of her daughter. What a hornet's nest he had disturbed, to be sure! But a surprise was in store.

'Let him go!' snapped old Mrs North testily. 'If he wants to go and ruin himself in that damp old shop by the river, then let him, silly young fool! I've lived alone before, and I won't be beholden to my grandchildren. He doesn't know when he's well off. Let him try managing that great place for a bit! He'll soon learn. And for pity's sake, Winnie, stop snivelling. Any-one'd think he was off to Australia the way you're carrying on!'

It had been too much to expect an ally at Rose Lodge, but the old lady's impatient dismissal of the affair greatly helped Edward. After a few uncomfortable days, whilst Edward tried to avoid his mother's martyred gaze and the sound of inter-mittent argument about the subject between the two women, he managed to make them see that he was adamant in his decision.

'Dash it all, I'm less than a mile away. I shall be in and out of Rose Lodge until you'll probably get fed up with me. I can do any odd jobs, and Tom comes twice a week for the garden. He's promised me to keep an eye on things. And you'll see Joan as regularly as you always do.'

Joan, Edward's sister, now eighteen, was in London, training to teach young children. Her vacations were lengthy and just occasionally she managed to get home on a Sunday during term-time. Edward had written to her telling of his plans and had received enthusiastic support. There was an unusually strong bond of affection between the brother and sister, forged in part by the absence of a father. Certainly, during the stormy period which preceded Edward's move, he was doubly grateful for Joan's encouragement.

As soon as the Parkers had gone to their new home, Edward put his plans into action. He decided to make the attic floor into his own domain, and the four rooms became a bedroom and sitting-room, both overlooking the market square and facing south, and a kitchen and bathroom at the back. He had papered and painted the rooms himself, and although the paper was askew in places and a suspicion of rust was already becoming apparent on the bathroom pipes, the whole effect was fresh and light.

Surveying his handiwork from the bath Edward felt a glow of pride. This was all his own. At times he could scarcely believe his good luck. The spacious rooms below were already occupied by a young bank clerk who had been at Caxley Grammar School with Edward some years before. He and his wife seemed careful tenants, likely to remain there for some time. Their first child was due in the autumn.

The future looked pretty bright, decided Edward, reviewing the situation. He enjoyed his work as an agricultural engineer at the county town some fifteen miles away, and promotion seemed likely before long. The family appeared to have come round completely to the idea of his living apart and no one could possibly realise how exciting he found his newly-won independence.

And then there was his flying. He had joined the R.A.F.V.R. when he was eighteen and had first flown solo on a bright spring day over two years ago. It was the culmination of an ambition which had grown steadily in fervour since he was ten. Now most weekends were spent at the aerodrome west of Caxley and his yearly holiday was earmarked for annual training. He liked the men he met there, their cheerful company and their predictable jokes, but better still he liked the machines with their fascinatingly complicated engines and their breath-takingly flimsy superstructure.

In a few hours he would be in the air again, he thought joyfully, looking down on the patchwork of brown and green fields far below. For this was one of the blessed Sundays when he set off early in his two-seater Morris in his carefully casual new sports jacket and a silk scarf knotted about his neck in place of the workaday tie.

He stood up in the bath and began to towel himself vigorously. A pigeon cooed on the gutter above the steamy window. Edward could see the curve of its grey breast against the sky.

'Two rashers and two eggs,' called Edward to the bird, above the gurgle of the bath water swirling down the waste pipe, 'and then I'm off!'

A thought struck him. The car's spare tyre was at Uncle Bertie's garage. He must remember to pick it up on his way. The possibility of a puncture somewhere on Salisbury Plain, even on a fine May morning such as this, was not to be borne, especially on a day dedicated to flying.

He shrugged himself into his shabby camel-hair dressing-gown and went, whistling, in search of the frying-pan.

2

The Shadow of War

EDWARD's Uncle Bertie was his mother's brother and now the head of the North family. He lived in a four-square red-brick house some yards from the busy High Street of Caxley where his motor business flourished.

One approached Bertie's house by way of a narrow lane. It started as a paved alley between two fine old Georgian buildings which fronted the pavements, but gradually widened into a gravelled track which led eventually to the tow path by the river Cax. Edward always enjoyed the sudden change from the noise of the street as he turned into this quiet backwater.

As he guessed, Bertie was already at work in the garden. Oil can in hand, he was bending over the mower when his nephew arrived. He straightened up and limped purposefully towards him, waving the oil can cheerfully. For a man who had lost one foot in the war, thought Edward, he moved with remarkable agility.

'You want your spare wheel,' said Bertie. 'I'll give you the garage key and you can help yourself.'

They moved towards the house, but Bertie checked suddenly to point out a thriving rose which was growing against the wall.

'Look at that, my boy! I planted it when your Aunt Kathy and I married. Just look at the growth it's made in these few years!'

Edward looked obediently, but he was already impatient to

be off to his flying. Catching sight of the expression on his handsome nephew's dark young face, Bertie threw back his head and laughed.

'You're no gardener, Edward! I forgot. Too bad to hold you up. Come and say ''Hello'' to the family before you set off.'

His Aunt Kathy was beating eggs in a big yellow basin. Her dark hair was tucked into a band round her head so that she looked as if she were wearing a coronet. How pretty she was, thought Edward, as slim and brown as a gipsy! No wonder Uncle Bertie had waited patiently for her all those years. He remembered Grandma North's tart comments to his mother on the marriage.

'I should've thought Bertie would have had more sense than to marry into the Howard family. Look what it brought you – nothing but unhappiness! And a widow too. Those two children will never take to a stepfather – even one as doting as dear Bertie. I can see nothing but misery ahead for that poor boy!'

' ''That poor boy'' is nearly forty,' his mother had replied with considerable vigour, 'and he's loved her all his life. Long faces and sharp tongues won't harm that marriage, you'll see.'

And all Caxley had seen. Bertie and Kathy, with her son and daughter by her first husband, were living proof of mature happiness, and when a son was born a year or so later, the little town rejoiced with them. Even Grandma North agreed grudgingly that it was all running along extraordinarily smoothly and put it down entirely to Bertie's exceptionally sweet North disposition.

'Where are the children?' asked Edward.

'Fishing,' replied Kathy, smiling. 'Unless you mean Andrew.

He's asleep, I hope. He woke us at four this morning with train noises – shunting mostly. It makes an awful din.'

'That boy wants to look forward, not backwards,' observed Edward. 'He wants to get his mind on aeroplanes.'

'I think one air fanatic in the family is enough,' commented Bertie, handing over the key to the garage. 'Off you go. Have a good day.'

And Edward departed on the first stage of his journey westward.

'It would never surprise me,' said Bertie to his wife, when Edward had gone, 'to hear that Edward had decided to join the R.A.F. His heart's in aeroplanes, not tractors and binders.'

'But what about our business?' queried Kathy. 'I thought you'd planned for him to become a partner?'

'I shan't press the boy. We've two of our own to follow on if they want to.'

'But *flying*,' protested Kathy, sifting flour energetically into the beaten eggs. 'It's so dangerous, Bertie. Edward might be killed!'

'He might indeed,' observed Bertie soberly. And thousands more like him, he thought privately. He watched his pretty wife at her work, and thought, not for the first time, how much there was which he could not discuss with her. Did she ever, for one fleeting moment, face the fact that war was looming closer and closer? This uneasy peace which Chamberlain had procured at Munich could not last long. There was menace on every side. It must be met soon. Bertie knew in his bones that it was inevitable.

'What a long face!' laughed Kathy, suddenly looking up from her cooking. 'You look as though you'd lost a penny and found a halfpenny.'

She crossed the kitchen towards the oven, shooing him out of the way as if he were one of the children.

'It's time this sponge was in,' she cried. 'Don't forget Mum and Dad are coming to tea this afternoon. You'd better get on in the garden while the sun's out.'

She paused briefly by the window to gaze at the shining morning.

'Isn't it lovely, Bertie? When it's like this I can't believe it will ever be any different – just sunshine all the time. Do you feel that way too, Bertie?'

'I don't think I'm quite such an incurable optimist,' answered Bertie, lightly. 'More's the pity maybe.'

He made his way back to the mower, his thoughts still with him. The grass was still too wet to cut, he decided. He would take a stroll along the towpath and watch the river flowing gently eastward beneath the cloudless sky. There was something very comforting about flowing water when one's spirits were troubled.

He turned left outside his garden gate, his back to the town, and limped steadily towards the tunnel of green shade made by a dozen or so massive chestnut trees, now lit with hundreds of flower-candles, which lined the banks some quarter of a mile away. The sunshine was warm upon his back, and broke into a thousand fragments upon the surface of the running water, dazzling to the eye. Just before the dark cavern formed by the chestnut trees, the river was shallow, split by a long narrow island, the haven of moorhen and coot.

Here Bertie paused to rest his leg and to enjoy the sparkle of the fretted water and the rustling of the willow leaves on the islet. The shallows here were spangled with the white flowers of duckweed, their starry fragility all the more evident by contrast with a black dabchick who searched busily for food among them, undisturbed by Bertie's presence.

The mud at the side of the water glistened like brown satin and gave forth that peculiarly poignant river-smell which is never forgotten. A bee flew close to Bertie's ear and plopped down on the mud, edging its way to the brink of the water to drink. A water-vole, sunning itself nearby, took to the stream, and making for the safety of the island left an echelon of ripples behind its small furry head.

The change in temperature beneath the great chestnut trees was amazing. Here the air struck cold upon Bertie's damp forehead. The path was dark, the stones treacherously slimy and green with moss. There was something dark and secret about this part of the Cax. No wonder that the children loved to explore its banks at this spot! It was the perfect setting for adventure. To look back through the tunnel to the bright world which he had just traversed was an eerie experience. There it was all light, gaiety and warmth – a Kathy's world, he thought suddenly – where no terrors were permitted.

But here there was chill in the air, foreboding, and a sense of doom. He put a hand upon the rough bark of a massive trunk beside him and shuddered at its implacable coldness. Was this his world, at the moment, hostile, menacing, full of unaccountable fears?

He was getting fanciful, he told himself, retracing his steps. It was good to get back into the sunshine, among the darting birds and the shimmering insects which played above the kindly Cax. He would put his morbid thoughts behind him and return to the pleasures of the moment. There was the lawn to be cut and the dead daffodils to be tied up. He quickened his pace, advancing into the sunshine.

In the market square the bells of St Peter's called the citizens of Caxley to Matins. Under the approving eyes of the bronze Queen Victoria whose statue dominated the market place, a trickle of men, women and children made their way from the dazzling heat into the cool nave of the old church. The children looked back reluctantly as they mounted the steps. A whole hour of inaction, clad in white socks, tight Sunday clothes, and only the hat elastic wearing a pink groove under one's chin to provide entertainment and furtive nourishment, loomed ahead. What a wicked waste of fresh air and sunshine!

Septimus Howard and his wife Edna crossed the square from his bakery as the bells clamoured above them, but they were making their way to the chapel in the High Street where Sep and his forbears had worshipped regularly for many years.

Automatically, he glanced across at Howard's Restaurant which occupied the entire ground floor beneath Edward's abode. The linen blinds were pulled down, the CLOSED card hung neatly in the door. His son Robert had done his work properly and left all ship-shape for the weekend. It was to be hoped, thought Sep, that he would be in chapel this morning. He was far too lax, in Sep's opinion, in his chapel-going. It set a poor example to the work people.

Edward's presence he could not hope to expect, for he and

his sister Joan were church-goers, taking after the North side of the family. Not that they made many attendances, as Sep was well aware. He sympathised with Edward's passion for flying, but would have liked to see it indulged after he had done his duty to his Maker.

The congregation was sparse. No doubt many were gardening or had taken advantage of the warmth to drive with their families for a day at the sea. It was understandable, Sep mused, but indicative of the general slackening of discipline. Or was it perhaps an unconscious desire to snatch at happiness while it was still there? After the grim aftermath of the war, and the grimmer times of the early thirties, the present conditions seemed sweet. Who could blame people for living for the present?

Beside him Edna stirred on the hard seat. Her dark hair, scarcely touched with grey, despite her seventy years, curled against her cheek beneath a yellow straw hat nodding with silk roses and a golden haze of veiling. To Sep's eye it was not really suitable headgear for the Sabbath, but it was impossible to curb Edna's exuberance when it came to clothes, and he readily admitted that it set off her undimmed beauty. He never ceased to wonder at the good fortune which had brought into his own quiet life this gay creature, whose presence gave him such comfort.

Now the minister was praying for peace in their time. Sep, remembering with infinite sadness the loss of his first-born Jim in the last war, prayed with fervent sincerity. What would happen to the Howards if war came again, as he feared it must? Robert, in his thirties, would go. Edward, no doubt, would be called up at once to the Royal Air Force. Leslie, his absent son whom he had not seen since he left Caxley and his wife Winnie years earlier, would be too old to be needed.

And he himself, at seventy-three? Thank God, he was still fit and active. He could continue to carry on his business and the restaurant too, and he would find time to work, as he had done earlier, for the Red Cross.

What dreadful thoughts for a bright May morning! Sep looked at the sunshine spilling lozenges of bright colour through the narrow windows across the floor of the chapel, and squared his shoulders.

He must trust in God. He was good and merciful. A way must surely be found for peace between nations. That man of wickedness, Adolf Hitler, would be put down in God's good time. He had reached the limit of his powers.

He followed Edna's nodding roses out into the sunny street. Someone passed with an armful of lilac, and its fragrance seemed the essence of early summer. Opposite, at the end of one of the roads leading to the Cax, he could see a magnificent copper beech tree, its young thin leaves making a haze of pink against the brilliant sky.

It was a wonderful day. It was a wonderful world. Surely, for men of faith, all would be well, thought Sep, retracing his steps to the market square.

But despite the warmth around him, there was a little chill in the old man's heart, as though the shadow of things to come had began to fall across a fine Sunday in May in the year 1939.

3

Evacuees in Caxley

As THE SUMMER advanced, so did the menacing shadow of war. It was plain that Germany intended to subdue Poland, and Caxley people, in common with the rest of Britain, welcomed the Prime Minister's guarantee that Britain would stand by the threatened country. The memory of Czechoslovakia's fate still aroused shame.

'Hitler's for it if he tries that game again with Poland,' said one worthy to another in the market square.

'If we gets the Russians on our side,' observed his crony, 'he don't stand a chance.'

There was a growing unity of purpose in the country. The ties with France, so vividly remembered by the older generation who had fought in the Great War, were being strengthened daily. If only the Government could come to favourable terms with Russia, then surely this tripartite alliance could settle Hitler's ambitions, and curb his alarming progress in Europe.

Meanwhile, plans went ahead for the evacuation of children, the issue of gas masks, the digging of shelters from air attacks, and all the civilian defence precautions which, if not particularly reassuring, kept people busy and certainly hardened their resolve to show Hitler that they meant business.

The three generations in the Howard and North families faced the threat of war typically. Septimus Howard, who had been in his fifties during the Great War of 1914–18, was sad but resolute.

'It's a relief,' he said, voicing the sentiments of all who heard him, 'to know where we stand, and to know that we are acting in the right way. That poor man Chamberlain has been sorely hoodwinked. He's not alone. There are mighty few people today who will believe that evil is still abroad and active. But now his eyes are opened, and he can see Hitler for what he is – a liar, and worse still, a madman.'

Bertie North, who had fought in France as a young man and had lost a foot as a result, knew that the war ahead would involve his family in Caxley as completely as it would engage the armed men. This, to him, was the real horror, and the thought of a gas attack, which seemed highly probable, filled him with fury and nausea. Part of him longed to send Kathy and the three children overseas to comparative safety, but he could not ignore that inward voice which told him that this would be the coward's way. Not that Kathy would go anyway – she had made that plain from the start. Where Bertie was, there the family would be, she maintained stoutly, and nothing would shake her.

Only two things gave Bertie any comfort in this dark time. First, he would return to the army, despite his one foot.

'Must be masses of paper work to do,' he told Sep. 'I can do that if they won't let me do anything more martial, and free another chap.'

The second thing was the attitude of mind, in which the young men most involved faced the situation. Bertie remembered with bitter pain the heroic dedication with which his own generation had entered the war. High ideals, noble sacrifices, chivalry, honour and patriotism had been the words – and not only the words – which sent a gallant and gay generation into battle. The awful aftermath had been doubly poignant.

Today there was as much courage and as much resolution. But the young men were not blinded by shining ideals. This would be a grim battle, probably a long one. There was no insouciant cry of 'Over by Christmas', as there had been in 1914. They were of a generation which knew that it was fighting for survival, and one which knew too that in modern warfare there is no real victor. Whatever the outcome it would be a long road to recovery when the war itself was past.

Nevertheless, for Edward and his friends, hearts beat a little faster as action appeared imminent. What if Hitler had annexed an alarming amount of Europe? The Low Countries and France would resist to a man, and the English Channel presented almost as great an obstacle to an invader today as it did to Napoleon. This year had given England time to get ahead with preparations. The uneasy peace, bought by Mr Chamberlain at Munich a year earlier, may have been a bad thing, but at least it had provided a breathing space.

'Thank God I'm trained for something!' cried Edward to his mother. 'Think of all those poor devils who will be shunted into the army and sent foot-slogging all over Europe! At least I shall have some idea of what I'm to do.'

He spent as much time training now as he could possibly manage. He had a purpose. It was a sober one, but it gave him inward courage. Whatever happened, he intended to be as ready and fit as youth, good health and steady application to his flying would allow.

Edward, most certainly, was the happiest man in the family despite the fact that he was the most vulnerable.

During the last week of August it became known that all hope of an alliance with Russia had gone. Triumphantly the Nazis announced a pact with the Soviet Union. Things looked black indeed for England and her allies, but assurances went out again. Whatever happened, Britain would stand by her obligations to Poland. After a period of anxiety over Russia's negotiations, it was good to know the truth.

On August 24th the Emergency Powers Bill was passed, together with various formalities for calling up the armed forces. Edward's spirits rose when he heard the news at six o'clock. How soon, he wondered, before he set off?

It was a few days later that the House of Commons met again. The question facing the country, said one speaker, was: 'Shall one man or one country be allowed to dominate Europe?' To that question there could be only one answer.

People in Caxley now prepared to receive evacuees from London and another nearby vulnerable town into their midst. No one could pretend that this move was whole-heartedly welcome. The genuine desire to help people in danger and to afford them a port in a storm, was tempered with doubts. Would strangers fit into the home? Would they be content? Would they be co-operative?

Sep and Edna had offered to take in six boys of school age. If they could have squeezed in more they would have done. Frankly, Edna welcomed the idea of children in the house again. The thought that they might be unruly, disobedient or difficult to handle, simply did not enter her head or Sep's.

'It is the least we can do,' said Sep gravely. 'How should we feel if we had ever had to send our children to strangers?'

Bertie and Kathy expected a mother and baby to be billeted with them in the house by the river. The fate of Edward's flat was undecided at the moment, and the future of Rose Lodge hung in the balance. There was talk of its being requisitioned as a nurses' hostel, in which case Winnie and her mother might move back to Edward's new domain in the market square.

'Proper ol' muddle, ennit?' observed the dustman to Edward. 'Still, we've got to show that Hitler.' He sighed gustily.

'Wicked ol' rat,' continued the dustman, 'getting 'is planes filled up with gas bombs, no doubt. You see, that's what'll 'appen first go off. You wants to keep your gas mask 'andy as soon as the balloon goes up. Can't think what them Germans were playing at ever to vote 'im in.'

He replaced the dustbin lid with a resounding clang.

'Ah well,' he said indulgently, 'they're easy taken in – foreigners!'

And with true British superiority he mounted the rear step of the dust lorry and rode away.

It was on Friday, September 1st that evacuation began and Caxley prepared for the invasion. Beds were aired, toys brought down from attics, welcoming nosegays lodged on bedroom mantelpieces and pies and cakes baked for the doubtless starving visitors.

'Isn't it odd,' remarked Joan Howard to her mother, as she staggered from the doorstep with a double supply of milk, 'how we expect evacuees to be extra cold and extra hungry.

We've put twice as many blankets on their beds as ours, and we've got in enough food to feed an army.'

'I know,' agreed Winnie. 'It's on a par with woollies and shoes. Have you noticed how everyone is buying one or two stout pairs of walking shoes and knitting thick sweaters like mad? I suppose we subconsciously think we'll be marching away westward when war comes, with only a good thick sweater to keep out the cold when we're asleep under a hedge at night.'

'Very sensible,' approved old Mrs North, who was busy repairing a dilapidated golliwog which had once been Joan's. 'I can't think why you two don't take my advice and stock up with Chilprufe underclothes. You'll regret it this time next year. Why, I remember asking Grandpa North for five pounds when war broke out in 1914, and I laid it out on vests, combinations, stockings, tea towels and pillow slips – and never ceased to be thankful!'

Joan laughed. Despite the horrors which must surely lie ahead, life was very good at the moment. She had just obtained a teaching post at an infants' school in the town and was glad to be living at home to keep an eye on her mother and grandmother. As soon as things were more settled, however, she secretly hoped to join the W.A.A.F. or the A.T.S. Who knows? She might be posted somewhere near Edward.

It was not yet known if Rose Lodge would be wanted to house an influx of nurses. Meanwhile, the three women had prepared two bedrooms for their evacuees.

Winnie and Joan left the house in charge of old Mrs North and made their way towards the station. The local Reception Officer was in charge there, assisted by a dozen or so local teachers. Winnie and her daughter were bound for a school which stood nearby. Here the children would come with their teachers to collect their rations for forty-eight hours and to rest before setting off for their new homes. Winnie was attached to the Women's Voluntary Service Corps and as Joan's school was closed for the time being she had offered to go and help.

A train had just arrived at the station, and the children were being marshalled into some semblance of order by harassed teachers. The children looked pathetic, Joan thought, clutching bundles and cases, and each wearing a label. A gas mask, in a neat cardboard box, bounced on every back or front, and one's first impression was of a band of refugees, pale and shabby.

But, on looking more closely, Joan noticed the cheeks which bulged with sweets, the occasional smile which lightened a tired face and the efficient mothering by little girls of children smaller than themselves. Given a good night's rest, Joan decided, these young ones would turn out to be as cheerful and resilient a lot as she had ever met during her training in London.

Inside the school hall an army of helpers coped with earlier arrivals. To Joan's secret delight, and her mother's obvious consternation, she saw that Miss Mobbs was in charge. This formidable individual had once been a hospital sister in the Midlands but retired to Caxley to look after a bachelor brother some years before.

'Poor man,' Caxley said. 'Heaven knows what he's done to deserve it! There's no peace now for him.'

But running a home and cowing a brother were not enough for Miss Mobbs. Within a few weeks she was a driving force in several local organisations, and the scourge of those who preferred a quiet life.

At the moment she was in her element. Clad in nurse's costume, her fourteen-stone figure dominated the room as she swept from table to table and queue to queue, rallying her forces.

'That's the way, kiddies,' she boomed. 'Hurry along. Put your tins in your carrier bags and don't keep the ladies waiting!'

'Old boss-pot,' muttered one eight-year-old to her companion, much to Joan's joy. ''Ope 'Itler gets 'er.'

Miss Mobbs bore down upon Winnie.

'We've been looking for you, Mrs Howard. This way. A tin of meat for every child and your daughter can do the packets of sugar.'

Joan observed, with mingled annoyance and amusement, that her mother looked as flustered and apologetic as any little probationer nurse and then remembered that, of course, years ago her mother really had been one. Obviously the voice of authority still twanged long-silent chords.

'Better late than never,' remarked Miss Mobbs with false heartiness. But her strongly disapproving countenance made it quite apparent that the Howards were in disgrace.

Glasses flashing, she sailed briskly across the room to chivvy two exhausted teachers into line, leaving Joan wondering how many more women were adding thus odiously to the horrors of warfare.

She and her mother worked steadily from ten until four, handing out rations to schoolchildren and their teachers and to mothers with babies. A brief lull midday enabled them to sip a cup of very unpleasant coffee and to eat a thinly spread fish-paste sandwich. Joan, whose youthful appetite was lusty, thought wistfully of the toothsome little chicken casserole her mother had left in the oven for Grandma North, and was unwise enough to mention it in Miss Mobbs' hearing.

'It won't hurt some of us to tighten our belts,' claimed that redoubtable lady, clapping a large hand over her own stiff leather one. Joan noticed, uncharitably, that it was fastened at the last hole already.

'We shan't beat Hitler without a few sacrifices,' she continued, putting three spoonsful of sugar into her coffee, 'and we must be glad of this chance of doing our bit.'

Really, thought Joan, speechless with nausea, it was surprising that Miss Mobbs had not been lynched, and could only suppose that the preoccupation of those present, and perhaps a more tolerant attitude towards this ghastly specimen than her own, accounted for Miss Mobbs' preservation.

At four o'clock they returned to Rose Lodge to find that their own evacuees had arrived and were already unpacking. Two women teachers, one a middle-aged widow, and the other a girl not much older than Joan, were sharing Edward's former room, and a young mother with a toddler and a six-weeks-old baby occupied the larger bedroom at the back of the house which had been Joan's until recently.

Grandmother North, trim and neat, her silver hair carefully waved and her gold locket pinned upon her dark silk blouse, was preparing tea. She looked as serene and competent as if she were entertaining one or two of her old Caxley friends. Only the flush upon her cheeks gave any hint of her excitement at this invasion.

'Where are we having it?' asked Joan, lifting the tray.

'In the drawing-room, of course,' responded her grand-mother. 'Where else?'

'I thought – with so many of us,' faltered Joan, 'that we might have it here, or set it in the dining-room.'

'Just because we're about to go to war,' said Grandma North with hauteur, 'it doesn't follow that we have to lower our standards.'

She poured boiling water into the silver tea pot, and Joan could not help remembering the advertisement which she had read in *The Caxley Chronicle* that morning. Side by side with injunctions to do without, and to tackle one's own repairs in order to leave men free for war work, was the usual story from a local employment agency.

'Patronised by the Nobility and Gentry,' ran the heading, followed by:

'Titled lady requires reliable butler and housekeeper. 4 in family. 3 resident staff.'

There was a touch of this divine lunacy about her grand-mother, thought Joan with amusement, and gave her a quick peck of appreciation.

'Mind my hair, dear,' said Mrs North automatically, and picking up the teapot she advanced to meet her guests.

'We're going to be a pretty rum household,' was Joan's private and unspoken comment as she surveyed the party when they were gathered together. Grandma North sat very upright behind the tea tray. Her mother, plump and kindly, carried food to the visitors, while she herself did her best to put the young mother at her ease and to cope with Bobby's insatiable demands for attention. This fat two-year-old was going to cause more damage at Rose Lodge than the rest of them put together, Joan surmised.

Already he had wiped a wet chocolate biscuit along the cream chintz of the armchair, and tipped a generous dollop of milk into his mother's lap, his own shoes and Joan's. Now he was busy hammering bread and butter into the carpet with a small, greasy and powerful fist. His mother made pathetic and ineffectual attempts to control him.

'Oh, you are a naughty boy, Bobby! Look at the lady's floor! Give over now!'

'Please don't worry,' said Grandma North, a shade frostily. 'We can easily clean it up later.'

Joan felt sorry for the young mother. Exhausted with travelling, parted from a husband who had rejoined his ship the day before, and wholly overwhelmed by all that had befallen her, she seemed near to tears. As soon as was decently possible, she hurried Bobby upstairs to bed and made her escape.

Mrs Forbes, the older teacher, seemed a sensible pleasant person, though from the glint in her eye as she surveyed Bobby's tea-time activities, it was plain that she would have made use of a sharp slap or two to restrain that young gentleman. Her companion, Maisie Hunter, was a fresh-faced curly-haired individual whose appetite, Joan noticed, was as healthy as her own.

How would they all shake down together, she wondered, six women, and two babies – well, one baby and a two-year-old fiend might be a more precise definition – under the roof of Rose Lodge? Time alone would tell.

4

War Breaks Out

BY SUNDAY MORNING, the visitors at Rose Lodge appeared to have settled down. This was by no means general in Caxley. Already, much to the billeting authorities' dismay, some mothers and children were making their way back to the danger zone in preference to the dullness of country living. Others were making plans to be fetched back to civilisation during the week. Their hosts were torn between relief and the guilty feeling that they had failed in their allotted task of welcoming those in need.

The early news on the wireless said that the Prime Minister would speak at eleven-fifteen, and Mrs North invited the household to assemble in the drawing-room.

'I suppose this is it,' said Joan.

'And about time too,' rapped out the old lady. 'All this shilly-shallying!'

She, with Winnie and Joan were going to lunch at Bertie's. The parents of the young mother, Nora Baker, were coming to spend the day, and Mrs Forbes' son was paying a last visit before setting off to an army camp in the north.

'Let them have the house to themselves for the day,' Bertie said, 'and come and see us.'

And so it had been arranged.

Just before the broadcast, the inhabitants of Rose Lodge settled themselves in the drawing-room. Bobby, mercifully, had been put into his cot for his morning sleep, but the baby, freshly-bathed and fed, kicked happily on the floor enjoying the admiration of so many women.

By now it was known that an ultimatum had been handed to Germany to expire at 11 a.m. There was a feeling of awful solemnity when finally the Prime Minister's voice echoed through the room. There had been no reply to the ultimatum, he told his anxious listeners, and in consequence we were already at war.

Joan felt a cold shiver run down her back. She shot a glance at the older women around her. Their faces were grave and intent. Only Nora Baker and her baby seemed unaffected by the terrible words. The baby gazed with blue, unfocused eyes at the ceiling, and its mother nodded and smiled gently.

'It is the evil things we shall be fighting against,' said Mr Chamberlain, 'brute force, bad faith, injustice, oppression and persecution'.

Old Mrs North nodded emphatically. A little nerve twitched at the corner of her mouth, but otherwise she looked calm and approving.

The speech ended and she turned off the set.

'Thank goodness, that poor man has done the right thing at last,' she said.

'Well, we know where we are,' agreed Mrs Forbes.

She had hardly finished speaking when the sound of wailing came from the distance, to be followed, seconds later, with a similar sound, five times as loud, as the air-raid siren at the Fire Station sent out its spine-chilling alarm.

'It *can't* be an air raid,' whispered Winnie. They all gazed at each other in incredulous perplexity.

'Trust the Germans,' said Mrs North briskly. 'Too efficient by half. And where did I leave my gas mask?'

'Gas!' gasped little Mrs Baker, snatching up the baby. She had become a greenish colour, and the child's pink face close to hers made her appear more terror-stricken than ever.

'I'll go and get the gas-masks,' said Joan, and began methodically to shut the windows. How idiotic and unreal it all seemed, she thought, suddenly calm.

'I must get Bobby,' cried the young mother. 'Oh, my Gawd, who'd think we'd get gassed so soon?'

'I'll fetch him,' said Winnie. She and Joan ran upstairs to collect their gas masks, a bottle of brandy and – no one quite knew why – a rug and a box of barley sugar. Meanwhile the two teachers ran round the house closing windows and looking anxiously up into the sky for enemy invaders.

They were hardly back in the drawing-room before the sirens sounded again, but this time on one long sustained note which, they were to learn, heralded safety.

'That's the "All Clear",' cried Joan. 'What can have happened?'

'Very confusing,' said her grandmother severely. 'It was far better arranged in our war, with the Boy Scouts blowing bugles.'

'No doubt someone pressed the wrong button,' said Winnie. 'What a fright to give us all!'

Mrs Baker, her baby clutched to her bosom and a very disgruntled and sleepy Bobby clinging to her skirt, had tears running down her face. The others did their best to comfort her, and Joan insisted on administering a dose of brandy. It seemed a pity to have brought it all the way downstairs, she thought, and to take it back again unopened.

'D'you think it's safe to put them upstairs to sleep?' asked Mrs Baker pathetically.

'Perfectly,' said old Mrs North. 'Take my word for it, that stupid fellow Taggerty's at the bottom of this. Fancy putting him in charge at the A.R.P. place! If he's anything like that foolish cousin of his we had in the shop, he'll lose his head on every possible occasion. I hope he gets thoroughly reprimanded.'

'I don't think Taggerty has anything to do with it,' began Winnie. But her mother was already across the hall and beginning to mount the stairs.

'We must hurry,' she was saying. 'Bertie asked us there for twelve and we musn't keep the dear boy waiting.'

If they had just ejected a troublesome wasp from the drawing-room she could not have been less concerned, thought Joan in admiration, following her small, upright figure aloft.

To Joan and Winnie's delight, Edward was at Bertie's.

'We tried to ring you last night,' cried his mother, 'but there was no reply. How did you get on?'

'Don't talk about it,' said Edward, throwing up his hands despairingly. 'I trotted along to report at the town centre and I'm on *indefinite leave*, if you please! *Indefinite leave*'!

'What exactly does that mean, dear?' asked Winnie anxiously.

'It means that I go back to work as usual, and sit on my bum waiting to be called up.'

'Language, Edward, language!' interjected his grandmother severely. 'There's no need to be vulgar just because you're disappointed.'

'No uniform?' said Joan.

'Only when I report each week,' said Edward. 'It seems the

43

training units are bunged up at present. I suppose our turn'll come, but it's the hell of a nuisance, this hanging about.'

'At least you know what you will be doing when you do get started,' comforted Bertie. 'How are your evacuees, mamma?'

'Very pleasant people,' said the old lady firmly. 'And yours?'

'Gone home,' said Kathy entering. 'Took one look at the bedroom and said it wasn't what they were used to.'

'Now, I wonder how you take that?' queried Joan.

'With a sigh of relief,' said Bertie, taking up the carving knife. 'She was quite the ugliest woman I've ever clapped eyes on, and the babies were something fearful. Enough to give us all night terrors.'

'Now, Bertie!' said his mother reprovingly. 'Don't exaggerate!'

'The trouble is,' said Edward, looking at his Aunt Kathy, 'your standards are too high. You don't know when you're well off.'

Bertie made no reply. But he smiled as he tackled the joint.

During the next few weeks, Caxley folk and their visitors did their best to shake down together, while the seasonal work went on in the mellow September sunshine. The harvest was gathered in, corn stacked, apples picked. In the kitchens frugal housewives made stores of jam and preserves, bottled their fruit and tomatoes and put eggs to keep in great buckets of isinglass.

Those who remembered the food shortages of the earlier war told gruesome tales to younger women.

'And I had to feed my family on puddings made of chicken maize on more than one occasion,' said one elderly evacuee.

'And not a spoonful of sugar to be had. You stock up with all you can. Rationing'll be tighter still this time.'

There was general dismay among farmers who had lost land to the defence departments. 'Where corn used to grow for hundreds of years,' *The Caxley Chronicle* reported one as saying, 'camps are now sprouting in profusion. Thousands of acres of good farmland have been sterilised for artillery ranges, exercise grounds for tanks, barracks and aerodromes.'

Edward, reading this at his solitary breakfast table snorted impatiently. They'd got to train *somewhere*, hadn't they? Oh, if only he could get started!

He flipped over the page.

'Petrol rationing hits delivery vans,' he read. 'Old cycles being brought out again.'

His eye caught a more bizarre morsel of wartime news.

'New Forest ponies may be painted with white stripes to make them more visible to motorists in the black-out.'

Edward laughed aloud.

'Good old *Caxley Chronicle*! And what's on at the flicks this week?'

Will Hay in *Ask a Policeman* and Jessie Matthews in *Climbing High*, he read with approval. Below the announcement was a new wartime column headed 'Your Garden and Allotment in Wartime.'

'Thank God I'm spared that,' exclaimed Edward, throwing the paper into a chair. But the caption had reminded him that he had promised his Uncle Robert, who so lovingly tended the garden of their shared premises, that he would give him a lift this morning on his way to work.

*   *   *

Edward's Uncle Robert was the youngest of Sep Howard's children and only eleven years older than Edward. He felt towards this youthful uncle rather as he did towards the youngest child of Bender and Hilda North, his attractive aunt Mary, who was much the same age as Robert. They seemed more like an older brother and sister than members of an earlier generation.

Aunt Mary he saw seldom these days, which was a pity. She was a moderately successful actress, better endowed with dazzling good looks than brain, but hard-working and with the good health and even temper which all three North children enjoyed.

'A messy sort of life,' Grandpa Sep Howard had commented once. 'I'm glad no child of mine wanted to take it up.' To Sep, staunch chapel-goer, there was still something of the scarlet woman about an actress.

Robert, of course, Edward saw almost daily. He did part of the supervision of Howard's bakery at the corner of the market square, but spent the major part of his time in running the restaurant on the ground floor below Edward's establishment.

Howard's Restaurant had flourished from the first and had now been in existence for about eight years. Sep's dream of little white tables and chairs set out on the lawn at the back of the property had come true. The garden, which had been Bender North's joy, remained as trim and gay as ever and added considerably to Caxley's attractions in the summer.

'I suppose you won't be running this little bus much longer,' observed Robert as they sped along.

'I've just enough petrol to keep her going for about a fortnight. With any luck I'll be posted by then.'

Robert was silent. Edward would dearly have liked to know

Robert's feelings about the war, but he did not like to ask. No doubt Robert's job would be considered as a highly necessary one and he would be more advantageously employed there than in some humdrum post in one of the services. Nevertheless, Edward had not heard him mention volunteering or offering his services in any more martial capacity, despite the fact that he was only in his early thirties. In some ways, Edward mused, Robert was a rum fish.

Take this stupid business of his tenants, the couple who lived below his own flat and above Robert's restaurant, thought Edward. They were quiet people, taking care to be unobtrusive, but Robert had complained bitterly to Edward that the ceiling of the café was flaking and that this was due to the 'banging about upstairs'.

'And they had the cheek to say that the cooking smells from my restaurant went up into their sitting room,' asserted Robert.

'Daresay they do, too,' said Edward equably. 'There's a pretty high stink of frying sometimes. I can even get a whiff on the floor above them.'

Robert's face had darkened.

'Well, you knew what to expect when you came to live over a restaurant,' he said shortly. 'The old man was a fool ever to think that the property could be divided. The floors above my bit should have been kept for storing things.'

Edward had been amazed at the depth of feeling with which Robert spoke. For the first time in his carefree life, Edward realised that he was encountering jealousy, and a very unpleasant sight it was. Luckily, he had inherited a goodly portion of the Norths' equanimity and could reply evenly. But the barb stuck, nevertheless.

47

He dropped Robert now at his wholesaler's and drove on to the office. If only his posting would come through! There was no interest in his work during these tedious waiting days, and he was getting thoroughly tired of Caxley too, as it was at present. He was fed up with hearing petty tales about evacuees' head-lice and wet beds; and fed-up too with the pomposity of some of the Caxleyites in positions of wartime authority. Somehow, in these last few weeks Caxley had become insupportable. He felt like a caged bird, frantic to try his wings, in more ways than one.

Ah well, sighed Edward philosophically as he turned into the yard at the side of the office, it couldn't be long now. Meanwhile, Will Hay and Jessie Matthews were on at the flicks. He would ask that nice little teacher, Maisie Something-or-other at Rose Lodge, to accompany him. At least it was a new face in dull old Caxley.

Edward was not alone in his frustration. This was the beginning of a period which later became known as 'the phoney war', when the Allied forces and those of the Germans faced each other in their fortresses and nothing seemed to happen.

The Caxley Chronicle echoed the general unease. 'Don't eat these berries!' said one heading. Foster parents should make sure that their charges knew what deadly nightshade looked like. Could they distinguish between mushrooms and toadstools?

The Post Office issued a tart announcement pointing out that it had a much depleted staff and far more work than usual.

Someone wrote to say that country people were being exploited. Why should a farm labourer, with about thirty shillings a week left after paying his insurance, feed the parents of his two evacuees when they spent Sundays with them? And who was expected to pay for the new mattress that was needed? There was no doubt about it – the heroic spirit in which the nation had faced the outbreak of war was fast evaporating, in this anti-climax of domestic chaos and interminable waiting.

'If anyone else tells me to Stand By or to Remain Alert,' said Bertie dangerously, 'I shall not answer for the consequences.'

'It's better than being told We're All In It Together,' consoled Kathy.

Joan, meanwhile, had started her new job, for the schools had reopened. A London school's nursery unit had been attached to the combined infants' school and this was housed in the Friends' Meeting House, a pleasant red-brick building perched on a little grassy knoll on the northern outskirts of Caxley. A Viennese teacher, who had escaped a few months before Austria was overrun by the Nazis, was in charge, and Joan was her willing assistant.

She loved the chattering children in their blue and white checked overalls. The day seemed one mad rush from crisis to crisis. There was milk to be administered, potties to empty, dozens of small hands and faces to wash, tears to be quenched, passions to be calmed and a hundred activities to take part in.

She loved too, the atmosphere of the old premises. It was an agreeably proportioned building with high arched windows along each side. Round the walls were dozens of large wooden hat pegs used by Quakers of past generations. The floor was of scrubbed boards, charming to look at but dangerously splintery for young hands and knees.

Outside was a grassy plot. In one half stood a dozen or so small headstones over the graves of good men and women now departed. There was something very engaging, Joan thought, to see the babies tumbling about on the grass, and supporting themselves by the little headstones. Here the living and the dead met companionably in the autumn sunlight, and the war seemed very far away indeed.

A steep flight of stone steps led from the road to the top of the grassy mound upon which the meeting house stood. An old iron lamp, on an arched bracket, hung above the steps, and Joan often thought what a pleasant picture the children made as they swarmed up the steps beneath its graceful curve, clad in their blue and white.

Her mother came on two afternoons a week to help with the children. Three afternoons were spent at the hospital, for Winnie did not want to tie herself to a regular full-time job, but preferred to do voluntary service when and where she could. There was her mother to consider and the evacuees. Winnie determined to keep Rose Lodge running as smoothly as she could, and only prayed that the proposal that it should be turned into a nurses' hostel would be quietly forgotten.

She found the small children amusing but thoroughly exhausting. The nursing afternoons were far less wearing.

She said as much to Joan as they walked home together one afternoon, scuffling the fallen leaves which were beginning to dapple the footpath with red and gold.

'I suppose it's because I was trained to nurse,' she remarked.

'Rather you than me,' responded Joan. 'It's bad enough mopping up a grazed knee. Anything worse would floor me completely.'

They turned into the drive of Rose Lodge and saw old Mrs North at the open front door. She was smiling.

'You've just missed Edward on the telephone. He's as pleased as a dog with two tails. He's posted at last to – now, what was it? – a flying training school in Gloucestershire.'

'Well,' said Joan thankfully, 'there's one happy fellow in Caxley tonight!'

5

Grim News

EDWARD ARRIVED at the flying training school on a dispiritingly bleak October afternoon. The aerodrome lay on a windswept upland, not unlike his own downland country. In the distance, against the pewter-grey sky, a line of woods appeared like a navy-blue smudge on the horizon; but for mile upon mile the broad fields spread on every side, some a faded green, some ashen with bleached stubble and some newly-furrowed with recent ploughing.

Edward surveyed the landscape from a window by his bed. His sleeping quarters were grimly austere. A long army hut, with about ten iron beds on each side, was now his bedroom. A locker stood by each bed, and the grey blankets which served as coverlets did nothing to enliven the general gloom.

But at any rate, thought Edward hopefully, he had a window by his allotted place and the hut was warm.

There was an old man working some twenty yards from the window where a shallow ditch skirted a corner of the aerodrome. A row of pollarded willows marked the line of the waterway, and the old man was engaged in slashing back the long straight boughs. His coat was grey and faded in patches, his face lined and thin. He wore no hat, and as he lunged with the bill-hook, his sparse grey hair rose and fell in the wind. It reminded Edward of the grey wool which catches on barbed wire, fluttering night and day throughout the changing seasons.

He seemed to be part of the bleached and colourless background – as gnarled and knotty as the willow boles among which he worked, as dry and wispy as the dead grass which rustled against his muddy rubber boots. But there was an intensity of purpose in his rhythmic slashing which reminded Edward, with a sudden pang, of his grandfather Sep Howard, so far away.

He turned abruptly from the window, straightened his tunic, and set off through the wind to the sergeants' mess.

He entered a large room furnished with plenty of small tables, armchairs, magazines and a bar. The aerodrome was one of the many built during the thirties, and still had, at the outbreak of war, its initial spruceness and comfort.

Edward fetched himself some tea, bought some cigarettes, and made his way towards a chair strategically placed by a bronze radiator. He intended to start the crossword puzzle in the newspaper which was tucked securely under his elbow. There were only five or six other men in the mess, none of whom he knew. But he had scarcely drunk half his tea and pencilled in three words of the puzzle before he was accosted by a newcomer.

'So you're here too?' cried his fellow sergeant pilot. Edward's heart sank.

There was nothing, he supposed, violently wrong with Dickie Bridges, but he was such a confoundedly noisy ass. He had met him first during voluntary training and found him pleasant enough company on his own, but unbearably boastful and excitable when a few of his contemporaries appeared.

When parties began to get out of hand you could bet your boots that Dickie Bridges would be among the first to sling a glass across the room with a carefree whoop. He was, in peacetime, an articled clerk with a firm of solicitors in Edward's county town. Rumour had it that their office was dark and musty, the partners, who still wore wing collars and cravats, were approaching eighty, one was almost blind and the other deaf. However, as they saw their clients together, one was able to hear them and the other to see them, and the office continued to function in a delightfully Dickensian muddle. Edward could only suppose that with such a restricting background it was natural that Dickie should effervesce when he escaped.

Edward made welcoming noises and made room on the table for Dickie's tea cup. Typical of life, he commented to himself, that of all the chaps he knew in the Volunteer Reserve, it should be old Dickie who turned up! Nevertheless, it was good to see a familiar face in these strange surroundings and he settled back to hear the news.

'Know this part of the world?' asked Dickie, tapping one of Edward's cigarettes on the table top.

'No. First time here.'

'Couple of decent little pubs within three miles,' Dickie assured him. 'But twenty-odd miles to any bright lights – not that we'll see much of those with the blackout, and I hear we're kept down to it pretty well here.'

'Better than kicking about at home,' said Edward. 'I would have been round the bend in another fortnight.'

'Me too,' agreed Dickie.

Edward remembered the two old partners in Dickie's professional life and enquired after them.

'They've both offered their military services,' chuckled Dickie, 'but have been asked to stand by for a bit. If they can't get into the front line they have hopes of being able to man a barrage balloon in the local park. Even the blind one says he can see *that*!'

Edward, amused, suddenly felt a lift of spirits. Could Hitler ever hope to win against such delicious and lunatic determination? He found himself warming towards Dickie, and agreeing to try one of the two decent little pubs the next evening.

Back at Caxley the winter winds were beginning to whistle about the market square, and people were looking forward to their first wartime Christmas with some misgiving. The news was not good. A number of merchant ships had been sunk and it was clear that Hitler intended to try to cut the nation's lifelines with his U-boats.

Cruisers, battleships and destroyers had all been recent casualties, and there seemed to be no more encouraging news from the B.E.F. in France.

The evacuees were flocking back to their homes and the people of Caxley folded sheets and took down beds wondering the while how soon they would be needed again. Petrol rationing, food rationing and the vexatious blackout aggravated the misery of 'the phoney war'. In particular, men like Bertie, who had served in the First World War and were anxious to serve in the present conflict, could get no satisfaction about their future plans.

Sep Howard had added worries. His supplies were cut down drastically, and some of his finest ingredients, such as preserved fruit and nuts, were now impossible to obtain. It grieved Sep to use inferior material, but it was plain that there was no alternative. 'Quality,' or 'carriage trade,' as he still thought of it, had virtually gone, although basic fare such as bread and buns had increased in volume because of the evacuees in Caxley. His workers were reduced in numbers, and petrol rationing severely hampered deliveries.

But business worries were not all. His wife Edna was far from well and refused to see a doctor. Since the outbreak of war she had served in the shop, looked after the six evacuee boys, and run her home with practically no help. She attacked everything with gay gusto and made light of the giddiness which attacked her more and more frequently.

"Tis nothing,' she assured the anxious Sep. 'Indigestion probably. Nothing that a cup of herb tea won't cure.'

The very suggestion of a doctor's visit put her into a panic.

'He'll have me in hospital in two shakes, and I'd die there! Don't you dare fetch a doctor to me, Sep.'

It was as though, with advancing age, she was returning to the gipsy suspicions and distrust of her forbears. She had always loved to be outside, and now, even on the coldest night, would lie beneath a wide-open window with the wind blowing in upon her. Sep could do nothing with the wilful woman whom he adored, but watch over her with growing anxiety.

One Sunday evening they returned from chapel as the full moon rose. In the darkened town its silvery light was more welcome than ever, and Edna stopped to gaze at its beauty behind the pattern of interlaced branches. She was like a child still, thought Sep, watching her wide dark eyes.

'It makes me feel excited,' whispered Edna. 'It always has done, ever since I was little.'

She put her hand through Sep's arm and they paced homeward companionably, Edna's eyes upon the moon.

It was so bright that night that Sep was unable to sleep. Beside him Edna's dark hair stirred in the breeze from the window. Her breathing was light and even. A finger of moonlight glimmered on the brass handles of the oak chest of drawers which had stood in the same position for all their married life. Upon it stood their wedding photograph, Edna small and enchantingly gay, Sep pale and very solemn. The glass gleamed in the silvery light.

It was very quiet. Only the bare branches stirred outside the window, and very faintly, with an ear long attuned to its murmur, Sep could distinguish the distant rippling of the Cax.

An owl screeched and at that moment Edna awoke. She sat up, looking like a startled child in her little white nightgown, and began to cough. Sep raised himself.

'It hurts,' she gasped, turning towards him, her face puckered with astonishment. Sep put his arms round her thin shoulders. She seemed as light-boned as a bird.

She turned her head to look at the great glowing face of the moon shining full and strong at the open window. Sighing, she fell softly back against Sep's shoulder, her cloud of dark hair brushing his mouth. A shudder shook her body and her breath escaped with a queer bubbling sound.

In the cold moonlit silence of the bedroom, Sep knew with awful certainty that he held in his arms the dead body of his wife.

*   *   *

In the months that followed Sep drifted about his affairs like a small pale ghost. He attended to the shop, the restaurant, his chapel matters and council affairs with the same grave courtesy which was customary, but the spirit seemed to have gone from him, and people told each other that Sep had only half his mind on things these days. He was the object of sincere sympathy. Edna Howard had not been universally liked – she was too wild a bird to be accepted in the Caxley hen-runs – but the marriage had been a happy one, and it was sad to see Sep so bereft.

Kathy was the one who gave him most comfort. If only Jim had been alive, Sep thought to himself! But Jim, his firstborn, lay somewhere in Ypres, and Leslie, his second son, was also lost to him. They had not met since Leslie left Winnie and went to live in the south-west with the woman of his choice.

Sep would have been desolate indeed without Kathy and Bertie's company. He spent most of his evenings there when the shop was closed, sitting quietly in a corner taking comfort from the children and the benison of a happy home. But he refused to sleep there, despite pressing invitations. Always he returned through the dark streets to the market square, passing the bronze statue of good Queen Victoria, before mounting the stairs to his lonely bedroom.

As the days grew longer the news became more and more sombre. The invasion of neutral Norway in April 1940 angered Caxley and the rest of the country. The costly attempts to recapture Narvik from the enemy, in the weeks that followed, brought outspoken criticism of Mr Chamberlain's leadership. Events were moving with such savagery and speed that it was clear that the time had arrived for a coalition government, and on May 10 Mr Churchill became Prime Minister.

Earlier, on the same day, Hitler invaded Holland. The news was black indeed. Before long it was known that a large part of the British Army had retreated to Dunkirk. The question 'How long can France hold out?' was on everyone's lips.

'They'll never give in,' declared Bertie to Sep, one glorious June evening in his garden. 'I've seen the French in action. They'll fight like tigers.'

The roses were already looking lovely. It was going to be a long hot summer, said the weatherwise of Caxley, and they were to be proved right. It did not seem possible, as the two men paced the grass, that across a narrow strip of water a powerful enemy waited to invade their land.

'They'll never get here,' said Bertie robustly. 'Napoleon was beaten by the Channel and so will Hitler be. The Navy will see to that.'

'At times I half-hope they will get here,' said Sep with a flash of spirit. 'There will be a warm welcome! I've never known people so spoiling for an encounter.'

Bertie was enrolled as a Local Defence Volunteer, soon to be renamed the Home Guard, and enjoyed his activities. One day, he hoped, he would return to army duties, but meanwhile there was plenty to organise in the face of imminent invasion.

Edward, now commissioned, had been posted to a squadron of Bomber Command in the north of England and was engaged in night bombing. Dickie Bridges was one of his crew. His letters showed such elation of spirit that the family's fears for him were partly calmed. Edward, it was plain, was doing exactly what he wanted to do – he was flying, he was in the thick of things, he was at the peak of his powers and deeply happy. The mention of a girl called Angela became more frequent. She was a Waaf on the same station and Winnie surmised that much of Edward's happiness came from her propinquity.

On a glorious hot June day, while haymaking was in full spate in the fields around Caxley and children refreshed themselves by splashing in the river Cax, the black news came over the radio that France had fallen. Joan Howard heard it in a little paper shop near the nursery school at dinner time. The old man who kept the shop beckoned her to the other side of the counter, and she stood, holding aside a hideous bead curtain which screened the tiny living-room from the shop, listening to the unbelievable news. She grew colder and colder. What would happen now?

The old man switched off the set when the announcement was over and turned to face her. To Joan's amazement his expression was buoyant.

'Now we're on our own,' he exclaimed with intense satisfaction. 'Never trusted them froggies for all old Winston said. We're better off without 'em, my dear. What was you asking for? *The Caxley Chronicle?* Thank you, dear. That's threepence. And now I'm off to get me Dad's old shot-gun polished up!'

She returned up the steep hill to the nursery school with the dreadful news. Miss Schmidt, the Viennese warden, always so gay and elegant, seemed to crumple into a frail old lady when Joan told her what she had heard.

'He is unbeatable,' she cried, and covered her face with her hands. Joan remembered the man in the paper shop and felt courage welling up in her.

'Rubbish!' she said stoutly. 'He's got us to reckon with. We'll never give in!'

'That is what my people said,' Miss Schmidt murmured, 'and the Poles and the Dutch. All of us – and now the French. The devil himself is with that man. He will rule the world.'

'You must not think that!' cried Joan. 'You know what the Prime Minister has said: "We'll fight on for years, if necessary alone," and it's true! We've all the Empire behind us. We can't lose, we can't!'

A child came up at this moment clamouring urgently for attention, and Miss Schmidt wiped away her tears and returned to her duties. But Joan could see that she could not believe that there was any hope for this small island where she had found brief refuge.

As for Joan herself, in some strange way her spirits grew more buoyant as the day wore on. Walking home that afternoon, through the brilliant sunshine, the confident words of the old man echoed in her ears: 'Now we're on our own. Better off without 'em, my dear!' They were as exhilarating as a marching song.

All Caxley seemed to share her mood, she discovered during the next few days. There was a fierce joy in the air, the relish of a fight.

'I'm sharpening up my filleting knife,' said Bill Petty at the fish stall in the market. The son of fat Mrs Petty, now dead, who had served there for years, Bill was a cripple who could never hope to see active service. His gaiety was infectious.

'I'll crown that Hitler with a jerry!' cried his neighbour at the crockery stall. 'Very suitable, don't you think?'

The spirit of Caxley was typical of the whole nation, roused, alert and ready to fight. As Doctor Johnson said: 'When a man knows he is going to be hanged in a fortnight, it concentrates his mind wonderfully.' Caxley concentrated to the full. Feverishly, defence plans went forward, old weapons were unearthed from cupboards and attics, and everyone intended to make it a fight to the finish.

'The Pry Minister,' said the B.B.C. announcer, 'will speak to the nation at hah-past nine tonight.' And the nation, listening, rejoiced to hear that brave belligerent voice saying: 'What has happened in France makes no difference to our actions and purpose. We have become the sole champions now in arms to defend the world cause. We shall fight on unconquerable until the curse of Hitler is lifted from the brows of mankind. We are sure that in the end all will come right.'

And somehow, despite the disaster of Dunkirk, the shortage of weapons, and the acknowledged might of the enemy, the people felt sure that all would come right.

It was two days later that a letter arrived at Rose Lodge from Edward. It was short and to the point.

'Angela and I have just got engaged. So happy. Will bring her down to see you next weekend.
Love to you all,
Edward.'

6

Edward in Love

SHE WOULD never do, thought Winnie, gazing at Angela.
She would never do at all. And yet, what was to be done
about it? There was Edward, his dark eyes – so like his
father's – fixed upon the girl, and his face wearing the expression
which her mother so aptly described as 'the-cat's-got-at-
the cream.'

The memory of her own disastrous infatuation rushed at her
from across the years. Was Edward about to make such an error
of judgment? Or was she herself over-sensitive to the circumstances?

She tried to rationalise her feelings as she poured tea in the
drawing-room at Rose Lodge. After all, she did not really
know the girl. She must have faith in Edward's judgment. He
was twenty-three, quite old enough to know his own mind. He
was certainly very much in love, by the look of things.
But – was she?

It was impossible to tell from Angela's cool, polite de-
meanour. She was small and very fair, with the neat good looks
which would remain unchanged for many years. Just so had
Winnie's mother been, trim and upright, and only recently
had come the grey hair and wrinkles of old age to mar the
picture. Old Mrs North's sharp blue eyes were now assessing
the girl before them and Winnie wondered what she would
have to say when at last they were free to speak together.

She did not have long to wait. Edward took Angela to meet Bertie and Kathy and to show her something of Caxley. Winnie and her mother washed up the rarely-used fragile best china while their tongues wagged. Old Mrs North was surprisingly dispassionate. She loved Edward dearly and Winnie quite expected fierce criticism of his choice.

'Seems a ladylike sort of gal,' declared the old lady, dexterously exploring the inside of the teapot with the linen towel. 'And got her head screwed on, I don't doubt.'

'That's what worries me a bit,' confessed Winnie. 'Do you think she's in love with him? I think Edward's rather romantic, for all his shyness.'

'Hardly surprising,' commented her mother dryly. 'And I'd sooner see the girl level-headed about this business than getting foolishly infatuated. Let's face it, Winnie – we've seen what happens in that sort of situation in our own family.'

Winnie flushed. It was all so true, and yet, despite the wisdom of her mother's words, the nagging doubt remained. Was this girl the sort who could make Edward happy? She could only hope so.

They were married in August in a little grey church in the village by the aerodrome. Winnie and Joan had a nightmarish railway journey involving many changes and delays. They were the only representatives of Edward's family, for Bertie was now back in the army, blissfully happy in charge of fleets of army lorries at a maintenance unit. Kathy could not leave her family, and Sep and Robert were inextricably tied up with their business commitments.

Angela's mother was there. Her husband had left her some years before, but she was in the company of a prosperous-looking sixty-year-old who was introduced as 'a very dear friend'. Winnie disliked both on sight. Angela's mother was an older edition of the daughter, taut of figure, well-dressed, with curls of unnaturally bright gold escaping from the smart forward-tilting hat. Her fashionable shoes, with their thick cork soles and heels, made Winnie's plain court shoes look very provincial. She sported a marcasite brooch in the shape of a basket of flowers on the lapel of her grey flannel suit, and spoke to Joan and Winnie in a faintly patronising way which they both found intolerable.

She had travelled from Pinner in the friend's car, and Winnie would dearly have loved to enquire about the source of the petrol for this journey, but common decency forbade it.

The service was simple, the wedding breakfast at the local public house was informal, and the pair left for a two-day honeymoon somewhere in the Yorkshire dales. On their return the bridegroom would continue his bombing of Wilhelmshaven, Kiel or Bremen. How idiotic and unreal it all seemed, thought Winnie, making her way back to the station. The only real crumb of comfort was the memory of Edward's face, alight with happiness.

The golden summer wore on, and the blue skies above Caxley and the southern counties were criss-crossed with trails and spirals of silver vapour as the Battle of Britain raged in the air above the island. This was truly a battle for life and freedom as opposed to death and slavery at the hands of the Nazis.

Across the channel the enemy amassed his armies of invasion, and by night and day sent waves of bombers to attack London and the south-east. The achievements of the R.A.F. gave the nation unparalleled hope of ultimate victory – long though it might be in coming.

The raids now began in earnest. The phoney war was at an end and the evacuees again began to stream from the stricken towns. Many of them spent the rest of the war away from their own homes. Many had no homes to return to. Many adopted the town of their refuge, grew up, married and became happy countrymen for the rest of their lives.

Sep's six boys had been found new billets when Edna died. Now he was anxious to have at least two back with him, despite the fact that his household help was sketchy. It was old Mrs North who thought of Miss Taggerty as housekeeper.

Miss Taggerty, almost as old as Sep, had once been in charge of Bender North's kitchenware department. She retired to look after an exasperating old father who was bed-ridden when being watched and remarkably spry on his pins when not, and who lived until the age of ninety-seven in a state of ever-growing demand. On his death, his cottage was due for demolition and poor, plain Miss Taggerty was to be made homeless.

The family had been anxious about Sep for sometime. Joan very often called in to see her grandfather on the way home from school. He was touchingly grateful for her visits and Joan grew to love him, during this summer, more deeply than ever before. Bit by bit she began to realise how much Edna had meant to this lonely old man.

They sat together one hot afternoon in the little yard by the bakehouse, and Sep spoke of his lost wife. On the grey cobbles, near their outstretched legs, a beautiful peacock butterfly settled, opening and closing its bright powdery wings in the sunshine.

'Edna was like that,' said Sep in a low voice, almost as if he spoke to himself. 'As bright and lovely. I never cease to wonder that she settled with me – someone as humdrum and grey as that old cobblestone there. She could have had anyone in the world, she was so gay and pretty. I'd nothing to give her.'

'Perhaps,' said Joan, 'she liked to be near something solid and enduring, just as that butterfly does. If you are fragile and volatile then you are attracted to something stable. Surely that's why you and Grandma were so happy. You gave each other what the other lacked.'

'Maybe, maybe!' agreed Sep absently. There was a little pause and then he turned to look at his grandchild.

'You're a wise girl,' he said. 'Stay wise. Particularly when you fall in love, Joan. You need to consult your head as well as your heart when you start to think of marrying – and so many people will give you advice. Listen to them, but let your own heart and head give you the final answer.'

'I will,' promised Joan.

Later she was to remember this conversation. And Sep, with infinite sadness, was to remember it too.

Meanwhile, it was arranged for Miss Taggerty to take up her abode at Sep's house. The family was relieved to think that Sep would be properly looked after at last. With winter approaching, such things as well-aired sheets, good fires and a hot steak and kidney pudding made from rationed meat now and again, were matters of some domestic importance. With Miss

Taggerty in the market square house the two evacuee boys could return, and Sep would be glad to feel that he was doing his war-time bit as well as having the pleasure of young company. As for Miss Taggerty, her cup of happiness was full. Used to a life of service, a gentle master such as Sep was a god indeed after the Moloch of her late father.

The winter of 1940 was indeed a bitter one. The war grew fiercer. Britain stood alone, at bay, the hope of the conquered nations and the inspiration of those who would later join in the struggle. The weather was unduly cold, fuel was short and food too. In Caxley, as elsewhere, this Christmas promised to be a bleak one.

But December brought one great glow of hope. The Lend-Lease Bill was prepared for submission to the United States' Congress. It meant that Britain could shape long-term plans of defence and attack with all the mighty resources of America behind her. It was a heart-warming thought in a chilly world.

Rose Lodge was to be the rendezvous for as many members of the Howard and North families as could manage it that Christmas. It looked as though it might be the last time that they would meet there, for, with the renewal of fighting, the question of turning the house into a nurses' hostel once again cropped up. This time it seemed most probable that it would be needed early in the New Year, and Winnie and her mother planned to move into the top floor of their old home, now Edward's, in the market square, for the duration of the war. At the moment, Robert was being allowed to use the flat as storage space. The thought of moving out his supplies was something of a headache but, as Sep pointed out rather sternly, it must be done.

Edward and Angela arrived late on Christmas Eve. He had

three days' leave and they had been lucky enough to get a lift down in a brother officer's car, three jammed in the back and three in the front. They were to return in the same fashion on Boxing Night.

They were in great good spirits when they burst in at the door. It was almost midnight but old Mrs North insisted on waiting up and the two women had a tray of food ready by the fire.

'If only I had a lemon,' cried Winnie, pouring out gin and tonic for the pair, 'I think I miss lemons and oranges more than anything else. And Edward always says gin and tonic without lemon is like a currant bun with no currants!'

'Not these days, mum,' said Edward stoutly. 'Gin alone, tonic alone would be marvellous. To have the two together in one glass in war-time is absolutely perfect.'

'And how do you find domestic life?' Winnie asked her daughter-in-law.

'Wonderful, after those awful days in the W.A.A.F.', said Angela. 'I potter about in my own time, and it's lovely to compare notes with the other girls who pop in sometimes when they're off-duty.'

She went on to describe the two rooms in which she and Edward now lived in the village near the aerodrome. Life in the services had obviously never appealed to Angela and her present circumstances, though cramped and somewhat lonely, were infinitely preferable.

'If only Edward hadn't to go on those ghastly raids,' claimed his wife. 'I stay up all night sometimes, too worried to go to bed. Luckily, there's a phone in the house, and I ring up the mess every so often to see if he's back.'

'You'd do better to go straight to bed with some hot milk,' observed Winnie. 'It would be better for you and far better for Edward too, to know that you were being sensible. It only adds to his worries if he thinks you are miserable.'

'I'm surprised you are allowed to ring up,' said Mrs North.

'Oh, they don't exactly *like* it,' said Angela, 'but what do they expect?'

Edward changed the subject abruptly. He had tried to argue with Angela before on much the same lines, and with as little effect.

'Shall we see all the family tomorrow?'

'Bertie and Kathy and the children are coming to tea. They're bringing your grandfather too. He misses grandma, particularly at Christmas, and they will all be together for Christmas dinner at Bertie's.'

'And there's just a chance,' added his grandmother North, 'that Aunt Mary may look in. She starts in pantomime one day this week, and may be able to come over for the day.'

Edward stretched himself luxuriously.

'It's wonderful to be back,' he said contentedly. 'Nowhere like Caxley. I can't wait for this bloody war to be over to get back again.'

'Language, dear!' rebuked his grandmother automatically, rising to go up to bed.

Before one o'clock on Christmas morning all the inhabitants of Rose Lodge were asleep.

All but one.

Edward lay on his back, his hands clasped behind his head,

staring at the ceiling. Beside him Angela slept peacefully. He was having one of his 'black half-hours' as he secretly called them. What hopes had he of survival? What slender chances of returning to Caxley to live? Losses in Bomber Command were pretty hair-raising, and likely to become worse. He could view the thing fairly dispassionately for himself, although the thought of death at twenty-four was not what he looked for. But for Angela? How would she fare if anything happened to him? Thank God there were no babies on the way at the moment. He'd seen too many widows with young children recently to embark lightly on a family of his own.

The memory of his last raid on Kiel came back to him with sickening clarity. They had encountered heavy anti-aircraft fire as they approached their target and the Wellington had been hit. Luckily not much damage was done. They dropped their load and Edward wheeled for home. But several jagged pieces of metal, razor-sharp, had flown across the aircraft from one side to the other, and Dickie Bridges was appallingly cut across the face and neck.

One of the crew had been a first-year medical student when he joined up, and tied swabs across a spouting artery and staunched the blood as best he could. Nevertheless, Dickie grew greyer and greyer as the Wellington sped back to base and it was obvious that something was hideously wrong with his breathing. Some obstruction in the throat caused him to gasp with a whistling sound which Edward felt he would remember until his dying day.

As they circled the aerodrome he was relieved to see the ambulance – known, grimly, as 'the blood cart' – waiting by the runway. Sick and scared, Edward touched down as gently as he could and watched Dickie carried into the ambulance. He knew, with awful certainty, that he would never see him alive again.

Dickie Bridges died as they were getting him ready for a blood transfusion, and next day Edward sat down with a heavy heart and wrote to his crippled mother. He had been her only child.

Damn all wars! thought Edward turning over violently in bed. If only he could be living in the market square, sharing his flat with Angela, starting a family, flying when he wanted to, pottering about with his friends and family in Caxley – what a blissful existence it would be!

And here he was, on Christmas morning too, full of rebellion when he should be thinking of peace and goodwill to all men. Somehow it hardly fitted in with total war, Edward decided sardonically.

He thought of all the other Christmas mornings he had spent under this roof, a pillowcase waiting at the end of the bed, fat with knobbly parcels and all the joy of Christmas Day spread out before him. They had been grand times.

Would this be the last Christmas for him? He put the cold thought from him resolutely. His luck had held so far. It would continue. It was best to live from day to day, 'soldiering on', as they said. Enough that it was Christmas time, he was in Caxley, and with Angela!

He pitched suddenly into sleep as if he were a pebble thrown into a deep pond. Outside, in the silent night, a thousand stars twinkled above the frost-rimed roofs of the little town of Caxley.

7

The Market Square Again

THE NEW YEAR of 1941 arrived, and the people of Caxley, in company with the rest of the beleaguered British, took stock and found some comfort. The year which had passed gave reason for hope. Britain had held her own. Across the Atlantic the United States was arming fast and sending weapons in a steady stream to the Allied forces.

Even more cheering was the immediate news from Bardia in North Africa where the Australians were collecting twenty thousand Italian prisoners after one of the decisive battles in the heartening campaign which was to become known as the Desert Victory.

'The longer we hangs on the more chance we has of licking 'em!' pronounced an old farmer, knocking out his cherrywood pipe on the plinth of Queen Victoria's statue in the market square. He bent painfully and retrieved the small ball of spent tobacco which lay on the cobbles, picked one or two minute strands from it and replaced them carefully in his pipe.

'Not that we've got cause to get *careless*, mark you,' he added severely to his companion, who was watching the stubby finger ramming home the treasure trove. 'We've got to harbour our resources like Winston said – like what I'm doin' now – and then be ready to give them Germans what for whenever we gets the chance.'

And this, in essence, was echoed by the whole nation.

'Hanging on,' was the main thing, people told each other, and putting up with short commons as cheerfully as possible. It was not easy. As the months went by, 'making-do-and-mending' became more and more depressing, and sometimes well-nigh impossible. Another irritating feature of war-time life was the unbearable attitude of some of those in posts of officialdom.

It was Edward who noticed this particularly on one of his rare leaves in Caxley. It occurred one Saturday afternoon when the banks were closed and he needed some ready money. Luckily, he had his Post Office savings book with him and thrust his way boisterously through the swing doors, book in hand. Behind the counter stood a red-haired girl whose protruding teeth rivalled Miss Taggerty's.

Edward remembered her perfectly. They had attended the same school as small children and he had played a golliwog to her fairy doll in the Christmas concert one year. On this occasion, however, she ignored his gay greeting, and thrust a withdrawal form disdainfully below the grille, her face impassive. Edward scribbled diligently and pushed it back with his book, whereupon the girl turned back the pages importantly in order to scrutinize the signature in the front and compare it with that on the form. For Edward, impatient to be away, it was too much.

'Come off it, Foof-teeth!' he burst out in exasperation, using the nickname of their schooldays. And only then did she melt enough to give him a still-frosty smile with the three pound notes.

There were equally trying people in Caxley, and elsewhere, who attained positions of petty importance and drove their neighbours to distraction: air raid wardens who seemed to relish every inadvertent chink of light in the black-out curtains, shop assistants rejoicing in the shortage of custard-powder, bus conductors harrying sodden queues, all added their pin-pricks to the difficulties of everyday living, and these people little knew that such irritating officiousness would be remembered by their fellow-citizens for many years to come, just as the many little kindnesses, also occurring daily, held their place as indelibly in their neighbours' memories. Friends, and enemies, were made for life during war-time.

Howard's Restaurant continued to flourish despite shortages of good quality food stuffs which wrung Sep's heart. Robert failed his medical examination when his call-up occurred. Defective eyesight and some chest weakness sent him back to running the restaurant. Secretly, he was relieved. He had dreaded the discipline and the regulations almost more than the dangers of active service. He was content to plough along his familiar furrow, fraught though it was with snags and pitfalls, and asked only to be left in peace. He said little to his father about his feelings, but Sep was too wise not to know what went on in his son's head.

The boy was a disappointment to him, Sep admitted to himself. Sometimes he wondered why his three sons had brought so much unhappiness in their wake. Jim's death in the First World War had taken his favourite from him. Leslie, the gay lady-killer, had betrayed his trust and vanished westward to live with someone whom Sep still thought of as 'a wanton woman', despite her subsequent marriage to his son.

And now, Robert. Without wife or child, curiously secretive and timid, lacking all forms of courage, it seemed, he appeared to Sep a purely negative character. He ran the restaurant ably, to be sure, but he lacked friends and had no other interests in the town. Perhaps, if marriage claimed him one day, he would come to life. As it was he continued his way, primly and circumspectly, a spinsterish sort of fellow, with a streak of petty spite to which Sep was not blind.

His greatest comfort now was Kathy. He saw more of her now than ever, for Bertie was away in the army, and she and the children were almost daily visitors to the house in the market square. She grew more like her dear mother, thought Sep, with every year that passed. She had the same imperishable beauty, the flashing dark eyes, the grace of movement and dazzling smile which would remain with her throughout her life.

Yes, he was lucky to have such a daughter – and such wonderful grandchildren! He loved them all, but knew in his secret heart that it was Edward who held pride of place. There was something of Leslie – the *best* of Leslie, he liked to think – something of the Norths, and a strong dash of himself in this beloved grandson. He longed to see children of Edward's before he grew too old to enjoy their company. Did his wife, that beautiful but rather distant Angela, really know what a fine man she had picked? Sometimes Sep had his doubts, but times were difficult for everyone, and for newly-weds in particular. With the coming of peace would come the joy of a family, Sep felt sure.

And for Joan too, he hoped. She was a North, despite her name, if ever there was one, and the Norths were made for domesticity. There flashed into the old man's mind a picture of his dead friend Bender North, sitting at ease in his Edwardian drawing-room, above the shop which was now Howard's

Restaurant. He saw him now, contented and prosperous, surveying the red-plush furniture, the gleaming sideboard decked with silver, smoking his Turk's-head pipe, at peace with the world. Just as contentedly had Bertie settled down with Kathy. He prayed that Joan, in her turn, might find as felicitous a future in a happy marriage. It was good, when one grew old, to see the younger generations arranging their affairs, and planning a world which surely would be better than that in which Sep had grown up.

Joan was indeed planning her future, unknown to her family. She was still absorbed in her work at the nursery school and as the months of war crept by it became apparent that the chances of joining the W.A.A.F. became slighter.

For one thing, the numbers at the school increased rapidly. As local factories stepped-up their output more young women were needed, and their children were left in the care of the school. And then the Viennese warden was asked to take over the job of organising nursery work for the whole county, and Joan, trembling a little at such sudden responsibility, was put in charge.

She need not have worried. Despite her youth, she was well-trained, and had had varied experience. Allied to this, her equable North temperament and her genuine affection for the children, made her ideally suited to the post. Two women had been added to the staff, one of them being Maisie Hunter who had arrived at the beginning of the war as an evacuee at Rose Lodge and who had remained in the neighbourhood. She was a tower of strength to Joan. The second teacher was a wispy young girl straight from college, anxious to do the right thing, and still with the words of her child-psychology lecturer ringing in her ears. Joan could only hope that face-to-face encounters with healthy three-year-olds would in time bring her down to earth a little, and give her confidence.

All this made Joan realise that her duty really lay with these young children and the job with which she had been landed. In some ways she regretted it. Her dream of being posted somewhere near Edward, perhaps even learning to fly one day, was doomed to fade. Nevertheless, this job was one equally valuable, and one which she knew she could tackle. It meant too that she could keep an eye on her mother and grandmother. Winnie was more active than ever, it seemed, but there were times when old Mrs North looked suddenly frail, and her memory, until now so acute, was often at fault. The oven would be left on, telephone messages were forgotten, spectacles and bags mislaid a dozen times a day and, worse still, the autocratic old lady would never admit that any of these little mishaps were her own fault. Physically, she was as active as ever, mounting the steep stairs to the flat in the market square as lightly as she had done when she lived there as mistress of the house so many years before.

All three women found the quarters somewhat cramped after Rose Lodge, but they all enjoyed living again in the heart of Caxley, close to their neighbours, and with the weekly market to enliven the scene each Thursday. They were handy too for the shops and for Sep's restaurant down below where they frequently called for a meal.

They found too that they were admirably placed to receive visits from their family and friends. Buses were few and far between, but the market square was a main shopping point, and friends and relations from the villages could call easily. Old Mrs North's sister, Ethel Miller, whose husband farmed at Beech Green, frequently came to see them bearing farm eggs, butter, and an occasional chicken or duck – treasures indeed in wartime.

It was her Aunt Ethel who first introduced Michael to Joan. He was one of three junior army officers billeted at the farm, and Joan had heard a little about them all. They seemed to be a cheerful high-spirited trio and her aunt was devoted to them – indeed, so fulsome was she in her praise, that Joan had tended to think that their charms must be considerably overrated.

'Michael is picking me up at six o'clock,' said Aunt Ethel, glancing at the timepiece on the mantelpiece. She had been ensconced on the sofa when Joan came in from school at tea-time.

'He's had to collect some equipment from the station in the truck,' she explained, 'and offered me a lift.'

At ten past six they heard the sound of footsteps pounding up the stairs and Joan opened the door to admit the young man. He was full of apologies for being late, but he did not look particularly downcast, Joan observed. Aunt Ethel, anxious to get back to the family and the farm, made hurried farewells, and the two vanished after a few brief civilities. Joan, in spite of herself, was most impressed with the stranger.

He was exceptionally tall, a few inches over six feet, slender and dark. He had grey bright eyes with thick black lashes, and his face was lantern-jawed and pale. He was an Irishman, Joan knew, and he looked it. In the few words which he had spoken, Joan had recognised the soft brogue and the intonation full of

Irish charm. A heart-breaker, if ever there was one, commented Joan amusedly to herself!

They did not meet again for some time, but one Saturday early in October, Joan offered to take some wool to the farm for her aunt.

'It will do me good to get some exercise,' she said, trundling out her bicycle from the shed where Bender had once kept mangles and dustbins, buckets and baths, in the old days.

It was a still misty day. Cobwebs were slung along the hedges like miniature hammocks. Droplets hung on the ends of wet twigs. There was a smell of autumn in the air, a poignant mixture of dead leaves, damp earth and the whiff of a distant bonfire.

Halfway to Beech Green a sharp hill caused Joan to dismount. She stood still for a moment to get back her breath. Above her a massive oak tree spread gnarled wet arms. Looking up into its intricacies of pattern against the soft pale sky she noticed dozens of cobwebs draped like scraps of grey chiffon between the rough bark of the sturdy trunk and the branches. Far away, hidden in the mist, a train hooted. Near at hand, a blackbird scrabbled among papery brown leaves beneath the hedge. Otherwise silence enveloped the girl and she realised, with a shock, how seldom these days she enjoyed complete solitude.

What a long time it was too, she thought, since she had consciously observed such everyday natural miracles as the cobwebs and the blackbird's liquid eye! Engrossed with the children and their mothers, walking to and from the nursery school along the pavements of Caxley, restricted by war from much outside activity, she had quite forgotten the pleasure which flowers and trees, birds and animals had subconsciously supplied. She free-wheeled down the long hill to the farm, exhilarated by her unaccustomed outing.

Her aunt was busy making a new chicken run and, with a quickening of the heart, Joan saw that Michael was wielding the mallet which drove in the stakes.

'You dear girl,' exclaimed Aunt Ethel, proffering a cold damp cheek to be kissed, while her fingers ripped open the package. 'Four whole ounces! I can't believe it! Now I shall be able to knit Jesse a good thick pair of winter socks. How on earth did Hilda manage it?'

'Sheer favouritism,' replied Joan. 'It was under-the-counter stuff, and passed over with much secrecy, I understand. They only had two pounds of wool altogether, grandma said, and you had to be a real old blue-blooded Caxleyite to nobble an ounce or two.'

Michael laughed at this, and Joan found him more attractive than ever.

'Now hold the end of this wire,' directed Aunt Ethel, returning to the business in hand, 'and we'll be done in no time. Then you must stop and have lunch. It's rabbit casserole with lots of carrots.'

'S'posed to keep off night-blindness, whatever that is,' said Michael jerkily, between powerful blows with the mallet.

When the job was done and the excellent rabbit demolished, Michael and Joan sat in the warm farm kitchen and talked. Uncle Jesse was in the yard attempting to repair a wiring fault in his ancient Ford, while Aunt Ethel had gone upstairs 'to sort the laundry', she explained, although Joan knew very well that she was having the nap which she refused to admit she took every afternoon.

Michael talked easily. He told her about his home in Dublin
and his family there.

'My old man keeps a hotel. Nothing in the five-star range,
you know. Just a little place where the commercials stay over-
night – but we've a quiet decent little house there and a grand
garden.'

He had two sisters and a brother, he told her. His mother
was an invalid, and he wanted to get back soon to see her.

'And what do you do,' asked Joan, 'when you're not in the
Army?'

'I'm not too sure,' answered Michael. 'You see, I'd just got
my degree at Trinity College when war broke out. Maybe I'll
teach. I read modern languages. Oh, there now, I can't tell you
what I'll do, and that's the truth!'

Joan was intrigued with the way the last word came out as
'troot'. Despite his vagueness about the future, it was apparent
that he intended to do something worthwhile. She told him a
little about her own work and he seemed deeply interested.

'You're lucky,' he said. 'You know where you're going.
Maybe I'll know too before long, but let's get the war over
first, I think. Somehow, it's difficult to make plans when you
may be blown to smithereens tomorrow.'

He spoke cheerfully, his wide smile making a joke of the
grim words.

'I wish I could see you home,' he said when at last Joan rose
to go. 'But I'm on duty in half an hour. Can I ring you one day
soon? Are you ever free?'

'I'm completely free,' Joan said.

'Good!' replied the young man with evident satisfaction.

They walked together to the front door of the farmhouse.

Joan's dilapidated bicycle stood propped against the massive door-scraper which had served generations of muddy-booted Millers.

Across the lawn a copper beech tree stood against the grey-fawn sky, like some old sepia photograph, framed in the oblong of the doorway.

'It's a grand country,' said Michael softly.

'Lovelier than Ireland?'

'Ah, I'm not saying that! Have you never been?'

'Never.'

'You must go one day when the war's over. I'll look forward to showing it to you.'

'That would be lovely,' said Joan, primly polite. She mounted the bicycle and smiled her farewells. He saluted very smartly, eyes twinkling, and watched her ride away.

She reported on her visit to her mother and grandmother as they sat by the fire that evening, saying little about Michael. She was more deeply attracted than she cared to admit, and felt that she could not face any family probings.

Old Mrs North's sharp eye, however, missed nothing.

'An attractive young man, that Michael,' she said, briskly tugging at her embroidery needle. 'Even if he is Irish.'

Joan smiled.

'Pity he's a Roman Catholic,' continued the old lady. 'Off to seven o'clock mass as regular as clockwork, Ethel says. But there,' she added indulgently, 'I expect it keeps him out of mischief.'

Joan nodded. But her smile had gone.

8

The Invasion

EDWARD HAD been posted yet again. This time it was to a station in Wales where he would be a staff pilot, instructing others in the art of flying bombers. This was a rest period, for six months or possibly longer, between operational tours.

Angela was more than usually disgruntled at the move. She insisted on accompanying her husband wherever he might be, and was beginning to get heartily sick of other people's houses and unending domestic problems. As the war dragged on, she became steadily more discontented with her lot, and Edward was sincerely sorry for her. He knew how long the days were, cooped in two rooms, in someone else's home. He realised, only too well, the anxiety she suffered when he was on operations. And he was beginning to see that Angela had very few inner resources to give her refreshment and strength to combat her tedium.

She seemed to spend most of her time in the company of other young wives as bored as she was herself. They met for innumerable coffee parties and games of bridge. Edward had suggested more fruitful ways of spending the time. There was plenty of voluntary work to be done, helping in hospitals, schools, A.R.P. centres and so on but Angela's answer had been disturbing and illuminating.

'I married you to get out of the W.A.A.F. Why the devil should I put my head into another noose?'

It was not very reassuring to a newly-married man, and as the months lengthened into years Edward began to realise that Angela had meant every word of that remark. Perhaps they should have started a family, foolhardy though it seemed. Would things have been more satisfactory? He doubted it. Edward was too wise to pin his hopes on motherhood as a panacea to all marital ills, and he had observed other young couples' problems with babies in wartime. It was difficult enough to obtain accommodation without children. Those who had them were definitely at a disadvantage.

No, thought Edward, they had been right to wait. But would the time ever come when they both looked forward to children? With a heavy heart, he began to face the fact that Angela might have waited too long.

It was at the end of May when Edward and Angela made their next visit to Caxley.

'No family yet then?' Mrs North greeted them, with devastating directness. 'Why's that?'

Angela pointedly ignored the question. Edward laughed, hugged his diminutive grandmother and pointed out of the window to the market square.

'That partly,' he replied.

A steady flow of army transport was travelling across the square heading south to the ports. Lorries, armoured cars and tanks had been pouring through Caxley for days now, and the thunder of their passage shook the old house and caused head-aches among the inhabitants.

But there was no heart-ache. This, they knew, was the start

of a great invasion – an invasion in reverse. The time had come when this mighty allied force could cross the Channel and begin the task of liberating oppressed Europe. Who would have thought it? they bellowed to each other, against the din. Four years ago it was the British Isles which awaited invasion! The tables were turned indeed.

Edward was now stationed within eighty miles of Caxley and was back on operational duty. He had no doubt that he would be busy bombing supply bases and cutting the communications of the retreating enemy. He should see plenty of activity, he told himself. It would be good to support an attacking army in Europe.

'Make no mistake,' he told his family, 'we're on the last lap now. Then back to Caxley and peace-time!'

That afternoon, while Angela was at the hairdresser's, he walked through the throbbing town to see Bertie who was also on brief leave. He found him pushing the lawn mower, his fair hair turning more and more ashen as the grey hairs increased, but still lissom in figure and with the same gentle good looks.

They greeted each other warmly.

'Kathy's out on some W.V.S. ploy,' said Bertie, 'and the children are still at school. Come and have a look at the river. It's quieter there than anywhere else in Caxley at the moment. But, by God, what a welcome sound, Edward, eh? Great days before us, my boy!'

It was indeed peaceful by the Cax. The shining water slipped along reflecting the blue and white sky. Here and there it was spangled with tiny white flowers which drifted gently to and fro with the current. On the tow path, across the river, a cyclist pedalled slowly by, and his reflection, upside down, kept pace with him swiftly and silently. The moment was timeless and unforgettable.

'Tell me,' said Bertie, 'has Joan said anything to you about Michael?'

'Not much,' replied Edward, startled from his reverie by something in his uncle's tone. 'Why, what's up?'

'They're very much in love,' said Bertie slowly. 'And to my mind would make a very good pair. He's a Catholic, of course, but it doesn't worry me. I wondered if it would complicate matters with the family.'

'Grandfather'd hate it,' admitted Edward bluntly. 'And probably Grandma North. I can't see anyone else losing much sleep over it. Surely, it's their affair.'

'I agree,' said Bertie. They paced the path slowly. Edward noticed that Bertie's limp was more accentuated these days and remembered, with a slight shock, that his uncle must now be over fifty.

'After all,' continued Edward ruminatively, 'you can't call the Norths a deeply religious family – and Joan and I, for all we're called Howard, take after the Norths in that way. I can't truthfully say I'm a believer, you know. There's too much to accept in church teaching – I boggle at a lot of it. But for those who really are believers, well, it's probably better to go the whole hog and be a Catholic. You know where you are, don't you?'

'Meaning what?' asked Bertie, smiling at Edward's honest, if inelegant, reasoning.

'Well, if Joan is as luke-warm as I am, and yet she recognises that Michael has something in his faith which means something to him, then she may be willing for the children to be brought up in the same way. I just don't know. I've never talked of such things with her.'

They turned in their tracks and made their way slowly back. A kingfisher, a vivid arrow of blue and black, streaked across the water and vanished into the tunnel made by the thick-growing chestnut trees.

'Lucky omen!' commented Bertie.

'In love or war?' asked Edward, gazing after it.

'Both, I predict,' said Bertie confidently, limping purposefully homeward.

It was at the end of that same week that Michael and Joan mounted the stairs to the flat and told Winnie and her mother that they were engaged.

Edward and Bertie were back on duty, Michael was moving to the coast the next day with his unit. The young couple did not blind themselves to the risks of the next few days. The casualties would be heavy, and it was likely that the army would bear the brunt of the attack. But nothing could dim their happiness, and Winnie and old Mrs North were glad to give them their blessing.

When at last Michael had gone and Joan returned, pink and a little damp-eyed from making her farewells, Mrs North spoke briskly the thoughts which were shared, but would have been left unuttered, by Winnie.

'Well, dear, I'm very happy for you. I've always liked Michael, as you know, and as long as you face the fact that there will be a new baby every twelve months or so, I'm sure it will work out well. You'll stay C. of E. I suppose?'

'No, grandma,' replied Joan composedly. 'I shall become a Roman Catholic, like all those babies-to-be.'

'Pity!' said the old lady. 'Well, you know your own business best, I suppose. Sleep well, and remember to take that ring off whenever you put your hands in water. Goodnight, dears.'

She put up her soft papery cheek to be kissed as usual, and went off to bed.

Winnie looked at her daughter. She looked tired out. Who wouldn't, thought Winnie, with all she had been through, and with Michael off to battle at first light? And yet there was a calmness about her which seemed unshakeable. Just so had she herself been when breaking the news of her engagement to Joan's father. Please, she prayed suddenly, let her marriage be happier than mine! And happier than Edward's! It was the first time, she realised suddenly, that she had admitted to herself that Edward's marriage was heading for the rocks. Were they all to be doomed to unhappiness with their partners?

She put the dark fear from her and kissed her daughter affectionately.

'Bed, my love,' she said.

It was Sep, of course, who felt it most. Joan told him the news herself the next day. She found him pottering about in his bakehouse, stacking tins and wiping the already spotless shelves.

She thought how little the place had changed since she was a child. The same great scrubbed table stood squarely in the middle of the red-tiled floor. The same comfortable warmth embraced one, and the same wholesome smell of flour and newly-baked bread pervaded the huge building. And Sep too, at first sight, seemed as little changed. Small, neat, quiet and deft in his movements, his grey hair was as thick as ever, his eyes as kindly as Joan always remembered them.

'Sit 'ee down, sit 'ee down,' cried Sep welcomingly, pulling forward a tall wooden stool. 'And what brings you here, my dear?'

Joan told him, twisting Michael's beautiful sapphire ring about her finger as she spoke. Sep heard her in silence to the end.

'I know you can't approve wholeheartedly, Grandpa,' said Joan, looking up at his grave face, 'but don't let it come between us, please.'

Sep sighed.

'Nothing can,' he said gently. 'You are part of my family, and a very dear part, as you know. And you're a wise child, I've always said so. Do you remember how you comforted me when your dear grandmother died?'

'You asked me then to choose wisely when I got married,' nodded Joan. 'I remember it very well. Do you think that I've chosen unwisely after all?'

'You have chosen a good man; I have no doubt of that,' replied Sep. 'But I cannot be happy to see you embracing his faith. You know my feelings on the subject. It is a religion which I find absolutely abhorrent, battening on the poor and ignorant, and assuming in its arrogance that all other believers are heretics.'

'Michael would tell you that it is the one gleam of hope in the lives of many of those poor and ignorant people,' replied Joan.

'Naturally he would,' responded Sep shortly. 'He is a devout Catholic. He believes what he is told to believe.'

He turned away and stood, framed in the doorway, looking with unseeing eyes at the cobbled yard behind the bakehouse. The clock on the wall gave out its measured tick. Something in one of the ovens hissed quietly. To Joan the silence seemed ominous. Her grandfather wheeled round and came back to where she sat, perched high on the wooden stool.

'We'll say no more. There must be no quarrels between us two. You will do whatever you think is right, I know, without being swayed by people round you. But think, my dear, I beg of you. Think, and pray. There are your children to consider.'

'I have thought,' replied Joan soberly.

'And whatever your decision,' continued Sep, as though he had not heard her interjection, 'we shall remain as we've always been. I want you to feel that you can come to me at any time. Don't let anything – ever – come between us, Joan.'

She rose from the stool and bent to kiss the little man's forehead.

'Nothing can,' she assured him. 'Nothing, grandpa.'

But as she crossed the market square, and paused by Queen Victoria's statue to let the war-time traffic thunder by, her heart was torn by the remembrance of Sep's small kind face, suddenly shrivelled and old. That she, who loved him so dearly, could have wrought such a change, was almost more than she could bear.

On the night of June 5 in that summer of 1944 a great armada sailed from the English ports along the channels already swept clear of mines. By dawn the next day the ships stood ready off the Normandy coast for the biggest amphibious operation of the war – the invasion of Europe.

Edward was engaged in attacking enemy coast-defence guns, flying a heavy bomber. As the first light crept across the sky, the amazing scene was revealed to him as he flew back to base. The line upon line of ships, great and small, might have been drawn up ready for a review. A surge of pride swept him as he looked from above. The fleet in all its wartime strength was an exhilarating sight. Edward, for one, had not the faintest doubt in his mind that by the end of this vital day victory would be within sight.

Excitement ran high in the country. News had just been received of the liberation of Rome under General Alexander's command, but people were agog to know what was going on across the strip of water which had so long kept their island inviolate.

At midday the Prime Minister gave welcome news to the House of Commons. 'An immense armada of upwards of four thousand ships, together with several thousand smaller craft, crossed the Channel,' he told them and went on to say that reports coming in showed that everything was proceeding according to plan. 'And what a plan!' he added.

It was the success of this vast enterprise, on sea and land simultaneously, which gripped the imagination of the country. Napoleon had been daunted by the Channel. Hitler, for all his threats, had been unable to cross it. The success of the allied British and American armies in this colossal undertaking was therefore doubly exciting.

The inhabitants of Caxley kept their radio sets switched on, eager to hear every scrap of news which came through. Joan longed to know where Michael was and how he was faring. There must have been heavy casualties, she knew, and the suspense was agonising.

The Norths and Howards knew where their other fighting men were. Bertie was stationed not far from Poole, and Edward was based in Kent. They did not expect to hear or see much of the pair of them in these exciting times, but the fortunes of Michael, now somewhere in the thick of things in Normandy were the focus of their thoughts.

As the days went by they grieved for Joan watching anxiously for the postman's visits. There was sobering news during the next week, about stubborn enemy resistance at the town of Caen. It was apparent that failure to capture this key-point would mean that a large force of allied troops would be needed there for some time. Could the enemy make a come-back?

One sunny morning the longed-for letter arrived and Joan tore it open in the privacy of her bedroom. She read it swiftly.

'My darling Joan,

All's well here. Tough going, but not a scratch, and a grand set of chaps. We are constantly on the move – but in the right direction, Berlin-wards. The people here are being wonderful to us.

I can't wait to get home again. Look after yourself. I'll write again as soon as I get a chance.

All my love,

Michael'

Joan sat down hard on the side of the bed and began to cry. There was a tap at the door and her grandmother looked in.

93

Tears were rolling steadily down the girl's cheeks, splashing upon the letter in her hands.

A chill foreboding gripped the old lady. In a flash she remembered the dreadful day during the First World War when she had heard the news that Bertie was seriously wounded in hospital. The memory of that nightmare drive to see him was as fresh in her mind as if it had happened yesterday.

She advanced towards her granddaughter, arms outstretched to comfort.

'Oh, Joan,' she whispered. 'Bad news then?'

The girl, sniffing in the most unladylike way, held out the letter.

'No, grandma,' she quavered. 'It's good news. He's safe.'

And she wept afresh.

9

Edward and Angela

IT WAS the beginning of the end of the war, and everyone
knew it. Perhaps this was the most hopeful moment of the
long conflict. The free world still survived. Within a year
Europe would be liberated, and two or three months later,
hostilities would cease in the Far East. Meanwhile, a world
which knew nothing yet of Belsen and Hiroshima, rejoiced in
the victory which was bound to come.

It was the beginning of the end too, Edward realised, of his
marriage. Things had gone from bad to worse. No longer
could he blind himself with excuses for Angela's estrangement.
Indifference had led to recriminations, petty squabbles, and now
to an implacable malice on his wife's part. Edward, shaken to
the core, had no idea how to cope with the situation now that
things had become so bleakly impossible.

Any gesture of affection, any attempt on his part to heal the
breach was savagely rebuffed. Anything sterner was greeted
with hysterical scorn. If he was silent he was accused of sulking,
if he spoke he was told he was a bore.

It was about this time that an old admirer of Angela's
appeared. She and Edward had been invited to a party at a
friend's house. There was very little social life in the small
Kentish town where they were then living, and Angela
accepted eagerly. Edward preferred to be at home on the rare
occasions when that was possible. He dreaded too the eyes

which watched them, and knew that the break-up of their marriage was becoming all too apparent. But he went with good grace and secretly hoped that they would be able to get away fairly early.

It was a decorous, almost stuffy, affair. About twenty people, the local doctor and his wife, a schoolmaster, a few elderly worthies as well as one or two service couples, stood about the poorly-heated drawing-room and made falsely animated conversation. Their hostess was a large kind-hearted lady swathed in black crêpe caught on the hip with a black satin bow. She was afflicted with deafness but courageously carried on loud conversations with every guest in turn. As the rest of the company raised their voices in order to make themselves heard, the din was overwhelming. Edward, overwrought and touchy, suddenly had a vision of the leafy tunnel of chestnut trees which arched above the Cax, and longed with all his soul to be there with only the whisper of the water in his ears.

As it was, he stood holding his weak whisky and water, his eyes smarting with smoke and his face frozen in a stiff mask of polite enjoyment. The doctor's wife was telling him a long and involved story about a daughter in Nairobi, of which Edward heard about one word in ten. Across the room he could see Angela, unusually gay, talking to an army officer whom he had not seen before.

They certainly seemed to enjoy each other's company, thought Edward, with a pang of envy. How pretty Angela was tonight! If only she would look at him like that – so happily and easily! The tale of the Nairobi daughter wound on interminably, and just as Edward was wondering how on earth he could extricate himself, he saw Angela's companion look across, touch Angela's arm, and together they began to make their way towards him.

At the same moment the doctor's wife was claimed by a faded little woman in a droopy-hemmed stockinette frock. They pecked each other's cheeks and squawked ecstatically. Thankfully, Edward moved towards his wife.

'Can you believe it?' cried Angela, 'I've found Billy again, after all these years! Billy Sylvester, my husband.'

'How d'you do?' said the men together.

'Billy has digs at the doctor's,' Angela prattled on excitedly. Edward wondered if he had heard all about the daughter in Nairobi, and felt a wave of sympathy towards the newcomer.

'We used to belong to the same sports club years ago,' continued Angela, 'before Bill went into the army. Heavens, what a lot of news we've got to exchange!'

'Mine's pretty dull,' said Billy with a smile. He began to talk to Edward, as the daughter of the house moved across to replenish their glasses. He had been in the town now for about a month, it transpired, and was in charge of stores at his camp.

'Any chance of going overseas?' asked Edward.

'Not very likely,' replied Billy, 'I'm getting a bit long in the tooth, and my next move will be either up north or west, as far as I can gather.'

Edward watched him with interest, as they sipped amidst the din. He was probably nearing forty, squarely built, with a large rather heavy face, and plenty of sleek black hair. He spoke with a pleasing Yorkshire accent, and gave the impression of being a sound business man, which was indeed the case. He did not appear to be the sort of man who would flutter female hearts, but Angela's blue eyes were fixed upon him in such a challenging manner, that Edward wondered what lay hidden from him in the past. Probably nothing more serious than a schoolgirl's crush on the star tennis player at the club, he decided. Or, even more likely, yet another gambit to annoy an unwanted husband. He was getting weary of such pinpricks, he had to admit.

Nevertheless, he liked the fellow. He liked his air of unpretentious solidity, the fact that his deep voice could be heard clearly amidst the clamour around them, and the way in which he seemed oblivious of Angela's advances.

After some time, Edward saw one of his friends across the room. He was newly-married and his young shy wife was looking well out of her depth.

'Let's go and have a word with Tommy,' said Edward to Angela.

'You go,' she responded. 'I'll stay with Bill.'

And stay she did, much to the interest of the company, for the rest of the evening.

Edward saw very little of Billy Sylvester after that. Occasionally, they came across each other in the town, and on one bitterly cold morning they collided in the doorway of 'The Goat and Compasses'. Angela, Edward knew, had seen something of him, but he had no idea how often they met. Angela spoke less and less, but she had let out that Billy had parted from his wife before the war, and that he had two boys away at boarding school.

Air attacks in support of the allied forces were being intensified and Edward was glad to have so much to occupy him. He had been promoted again, and was beginning to wonder if he would stay in the Air Force after the war. In some ways he wanted to. On the other hand the restrictions of service life, which he had endured cheerfully enough in war-time, he knew would prove irksome, and certainly Angela would be against the idea. He was beginning to long for roots, a home, a family, something to see growing. In his more sanguine moments he saw Angela in the Caxley flat, refurbishing it with him, starting life afresh. Or perhaps buying a cottage near the town, on the hilly slopes towards Beech Green, say, or in the pleasant southern outskirts of Caxley near the village of Bent? And then the cold truth would press in upon him. In his heart of hearts he knew that there could never be a future with Angela. She had already left him. The outlook was desolate. Meanwhile, one must live from day to day, and let the future take care of itself.

He returned home one wet February afternoon to find the flat empty. This did not perturb him, as Angela was often out. He threw himself into an armchair and began to read the newspaper. Suddenly he was conscious of something unusual. There was no companionable ticking from Angela's little clock on the mantelpiece. It had vanished. No doubt it had gone to be repaired, thought Edward, turning a page. He looked at his watch. It had stopped. Throwing down the paper, he went into the bedroom to see the time by the bedside alarm clock. The door of the clothes cupboard stood open and there were gaps where Angela's frocks and coats had hung.

Propped against the table lamp was a letter. Edward felt suddenly sick. It had come at last. His hands trembled as he tore it open.

'Dear Edward,

Billy and I have gone away together. Don't try to follow us. Nothing you can do or say will ever bring me back. I don't suppose you'll miss me anyway.

Angela'

At least, thought Edward irrelevantly, she was honest enough not to add 'Love'. What was to be done? He thrust the letter into his pocket and paced up and down the bedroom. He must go after her, despite her message. She was his wife. She must be made to return.

He stopped short and gazed out into the dripping garden. The tree trunks glistened with rain. Drops pattered on the speckled leaves of a laurel bush, and a thrush shook its feathers below.

Why must she be made to return? He was thinking as Sep might think, he suddenly realised. Angela was not a chattel. She spoke the plain truth in her letter. She would never return. And what sort of life could they hope to live if he insisted on it? It was best to face it. It was the end.

The thrush pounced suddenly and pulled out a worm from the soil. It struggled gamely, stretched into a taut pink rubbery line. The thrush tugged resolutely. Poor devil, thought Edward, watching the drama with heightened sensibilities. He knew how the worm felt – caught, and about to be finished. The bird gave a final heave. The worm thrashed for a moment on the surface and was systematically jabbed to death by the ruthless beak above. Just so, thought Edward, have I been wounded, and just so, watching the thrush gobble down its meal, have I been wiped out. He watched the thrush running delicately across the wet grass, its head cocked sideways, searching for another victim.

He threw himself upon the bed and buried his face in the coverlet. There was a faint scent of the perfume which Angela used and his stomach was twisted with sudden pain. One's body, it seemed, lagged behind one's mind when it came to parting. This was the betrayer – one's weak flesh. A drink was what he needed, but he felt unable to move, drained of all strength, a frail shell shaken with nausea.

Suddenly, as though he had been hit on the back of the head, he fell asleep. When he awoke, hours later, it was dark, and he was shivering with the cold. His head was curiously heavy, as though he were suffering from a hangover, but he knew, the moment that he awoke, what had caused this collapse. Angela had gone.

The world would never be quite as warm and fair, ever again.

Meanwhile, in Caxley, Joan was receiving instruction from the local Roman Catholic priest, much to her own satisfaction and to her grandfather's secret sorrow.

The wedding was planned for the end of April, when Michael expected leave, and would take place in the small shabby Catholic church at the northern end of Caxley.

Old Mrs North made no secret of her disappointment.

'I've always hoped for a family wedding at St Peter's,' she said regretfully to Joan. 'Your dear mother would have made a lovely bride. I so often planned it. The nave is particularly suitable for a wedding. I hoped Winnie would have a train.

Nothing more dignified – in good lace, of course. And the flowers! They always look so beautiful at the entrance to the chancel. Lady Hurley's daughter looked a picture flanked by arum lilies and yellow roses! D'you remember, Winnie dear? It must have been in 1929. I suppose there's no hope of you changing your mind, dear, and having the wedding at dear old St Peter's?'

'None at all,' smiled Joan. 'Of course, if I'd met Michael four or five hundred years ago we should have been married in St Peter's. But thanks to Henry the Eighth I must make do with the present arrangements.'

'Now, that's a funny thing,' confessed her grandmother. 'It never occurred to me that St Peter's was once Roman Catholic! It really gives one quite a turn, doesn't it?'

Preparations went on steadily. Joan got together a sizeable quantity of linen and household goods. Kind friends and relatives parted with precious clothing coupons and she was able to buy a modest trousseau. Sep made the most elegant wedding cake consistent with war-time restrictions and embellished it, touchingly, with the decorations from his own wedding cake which Edna had treasured.

He had given Joan a generous dowry.

'You will want a house of your own one day,' he told her. 'This will be a start. I hope it won't be far from Caxley, my dear, but I suppose it depends on Michael. But I hope it won't be in Ireland. Too far for an old man like me to visit you.'

Joan could not say. Somehow she thought that Ireland would be her home in the future. As Sep said, it all depended on Michael.

One thing grieved her, in the midst of her hopeful preparations. Sep would be present at the reception, but he could not face the ceremony in the Catholic church. His staunch chapel principles would not allow him to put a foot over the threshold.

In the midst of the bustle came Edward's catastrophic news. Joan, herself so happy, was shocked and bewildered. The bond between Edward and herself was a strong one, doubly so perhaps, because they had been brought up without a father. She had never shared her mother's and grandmother's misgivings about Angela, for somehow she had felt sure that anyone must be happy with Edward, so cheerful, so dependable as he was. This blow made her suddenly unsure of her judgment. Loyalty to her brother made her put the blame squarely on Angela's shoulders. On the other hand, a small doubting voice reminded her of the old saw that it takes two to make a marriage.

Had Edward been at fault? Or was this tragedy just another side-effect of war? She prayed that she and Michael would be more fortunate.

Her mother took the news soberly and philosophically. She had known from the first that Angela would never do. Much as she grieved for Edward, it was better that they should part now, and she thanked Heaven that no children were involved in the parting.

It was old Mrs North, strangely enough, who seemed most upset. Normally, her tart good sense strengthened the family in times of crisis. This time she seemed suddenly old – unable to bear any more blows. The truth was that the ancient wound caused by Winnie's unhappy marriage to Leslie Howard, was opened again. With the controversial marriage of Joan imminent, the old lady's spirits drooped at this fresh assault.

Edward was very dear to her. He could do no wrong. In her eyes, Angela was a thoroughly wicked woman, and Edward was well rid of her. But would any of her family find married happiness? Would poor Joan? Sometimes she began to doubt it, and looked back upon her own long years with Bender as something rare and strange.

Edward was at the wedding to give the bride away. He looked thinner and older, and to Joan's way of thinking, handsomer than ever. He refused to speak of his own affairs, and set himself out to make Joan's wedding day the happiest one of her life.

With the exception of Sep and Robert the rest of Joan's relations were there with Kathy's auburn-haired daughter as bridesmaid, and Bertie and Kathy's small son as an inattentive page. Michael's mother was too ill to travel and his father too was absent, but a sister and brother, with the same devastating Irish good looks as the bridegroom, were present, and impressed old Mrs North very much by their piety in church.

'I must say,' she said to Winnie, in tones far too audible for her daughter's comfort, 'the Catholics do know how to behave in church. Not afraid to bend the knee when called for!'

Winnie was glad that something pleased the old lady, for she knew that she found the small church woefully lacking in amenities compared with Caxley's noble parish church built and made beautiful with the proceeds of the wool trade, so many centuries earlier.

There were few Roman Catholics in Caxley. One or two families from the marsh, descended from Irish labourers who had built the local railway line, attended the church. Two ancient landed families came in each Sunday from the countryside south of the town, but there was little money to make the church beautiful. To old Mrs North the depressing green paint, the dingy pews and, above all, the crucified figure of Christ stretched bleeding high above the nave, was wholly distasteful. A church, she thought, should be a dignified and beautiful place, a true house of God, and a proper setting for the three great dramas of one's life, one's christening, one's marriage and one's funeral. This poor substitute was just not good enough, she decided firmly, as they waited for the bride.

Her eyes rested meditatively upon the bridegroom and his brother, and her heart, old but still susceptible, warmed suddenly. No doubt about it, they were a fine-looking family. One could quite see the attraction.

There was a flurry at the end of the church and the bride came slowly down the aisle on her brother's arm. Old Mrs North struggled to her feet, and looking at her granddaughter's radiant face, forgot her fears. If she knew anything about anything, this was one marriage in the Howard family which would turn out well!

10

Victory

THE HONEYMOON was spent at Burford and the sun shone
for them. The old town had never looked lovelier, Joan
thought, for she had visited it often before the war. This
was Michael's first glimpse of the Cotswolds. He could not
have seen Burford at a better time. The trees lining the steep
High Street were in young leaf. The cottage gardens nodded
with daffodils, and aubretia and arabis hung their bright
carpets over the grey stone walls.

As May broke, they returned to Caxley and to neglected
news of the world of war. Much had happened. A photograph
of the ghastly end of Mussolini and his mistress, Signorina
Petacci, shocked them as it had shocked the world. And now,
the suicide of Hitler was announced. On the last day of April,
as Joan and Michael had wandered along the river bank at
Burford, Hitler and his newly-married wife, Eva Braun had
done themselves to death, with pistol and poison.

A week later came the unconditional surrender of the
enemy. By that time, Michael was back with his regiment, and
Joan watched the celebrations of victory with her family in
the market square.

The cross of St George fluttered on the flag pole of St Peter's,
close by the flapping Union Jack at the Town Hall. The Corn
Exchange was draped with bunting and some irreverent
reveller had propped a flag in Queen Victoria's hand. The

public houses were busy, sounds of singing were abroad and everywhere people stopped to congratulate each other and share their relief.

But there was still the knowledge that the war was not completely finished, and Joan listened with her family to the voice of Churchill giving the nation grave thoughts in the midst of rejoicing.

'I wish,' he said, 'I could tell you tonight that all our toils and troubles were over. But, on the contrary, I must warn you that there is still a lot to do, and that you must be prepared for further efforts of mind and body.' He went on to point out that 'beyond all lurks Japan, harassed and failing, but still a people of a hundred millions, for whose warriors death has few terrors.'

He was listened to with attention; but the moment was too happy to darken with sober warnings. For most of his hearers one splendid fact dazzled them. Victory in Europe was accomplished. Victory in the rest of the world must follow soon. And then, after six bloody years, they would have peace at last.

In the months that followed, old Mrs North spoke joyfully of returning to Rose Lodge. Winnie had her doubts about the wisdom of this step. Now that there were only the two of them to consider, the house seemed over-large, and they must face the problem of little or no help in running it. Mrs North refused to be persuaded.

'I absolutely set my face against finding another place,' she declared flatly. 'Rose Lodge is my home, bought for me by your dear father. The nurses are moving out in a month or two. There's no reason at all why we shouldn't get out the old furniture from store and move in right away. Besides, Edward will want this flat again the minute he's demobbed. We must leave everything ready for him.'

Winnie was wise enough to drop the subject for the time being, but returned to the attack whenever she had a chance. It was no use. The old lady was unshakeable in her determination.

'Go back,' Bertie advised his sister. 'Dash it all, she's getting on for eighty! She may well as enjoy her own for the rest of her time. Rose Lodge was all she ever wanted when she lived in the market place, and she's had to do without it for years.'

'I suppose we must,' sighed Winnie. 'But I shall shut off some of the rooms. It's a house that eats fuel, as you know, and I really don't think I can cope with the cleaning single-handed.'

'We're all getting old,' agreed Bertie cheerfully. 'But I bet mamma will be in and out of the locked rooms smartly enough with a duster.'

Soon after this Edward had a few days' leave, and within twenty-four hours was thanking his stars that his stay would be a short one. If anyone had ever told him that Caxley would pall, he would have denied it stoutly. But it was so.

He knew that he was under strain. He knew that Angela's desertion was a greater shock than he cared to admit. He was torn with remorse, with guilt, with what he might have left undone. He had thrown himself, with even more concentration, into his flying duties and now lived on the station, hoping, in part, to forget his trouble. All this added to the tension.

Perhaps he had relied too much on the healing powers of his native town. Perhaps, after all, he had outgrown the childhood instinct to return home when hurt. Perhaps the people of Caxley, his own family included, were as spent as he was after six years of lean times and anxiety. Whatever the causes, the results for Edward were plain. He could not return to Caxley to live, as things were.

His womenfolk said very little to him, but there was a false brightness in their tones when they did, and a sad brooding look of inner pain when they watched him. Edward found both unendurable. Bertie was the only person he could talk to, and to him he unburdened his heart.

'I just can't face it,' he said savagely, kicking the gravel on Bertie's garden path. 'Anyone'd think I was suddenly an idiot. They talk to me as though I'm a child who is ill. And then I snap at them, and feel an utter heel. God, what's going to be the end of it?'

'It's the hardest thing in the world,' observed Bertie, 'to accept pity gracefully. It's easy enough to give it.'

'It isn't only pity,' retorted Edward. 'There were two old cats whispering behind their hands in the restaurant, and I've had one or two pretty unpleasant remarks chucked at me. The top and bottom of it is that Caxley's little and mean, and I never saw it before. I feel stifled here – as though everyone has known and watched the Howards for generations. We're simply actors to them – people to look at, people to feed their own cheap desire for a bit of drama.'

'If you haven't realised that until now,' said Bertie calmly, 'you're a good deal more naïve than I thought. We all have to take our turn at being a nine days' wonder. It's yours now, and damned unpleasant too – but you'll be forgotten by next week when someone else crops up for the place in the limelight.'

'You're right,' agreed Edward bitterly. 'But it makes a difference to me for good, even if other people forget in a day or two. In any case I shall get a job elsewhere for a year or two, and then see how I feel about Caxley. What is there to bring me back?'

'Nothing,' said Bertie. 'Except us. I'm not trying to wring your withers and all that – but when this has blown over, I hope you'll want to come back to the family again.'

'Maybe I will. Maybe I won't. All I need now is to thrash about a bit and see other places and find a useful job. One thing, I'm alone now, and I'll take good care I stay that way. I've had enough of women's ways to last me a lifetime.'

Bertie observed his nephew's devastating, if sulky, good looks with a quizzical eye, but forbore to comment on his last remark.

'There's a chap in the mess at the moment,' continued Edward, 'whose father runs a factory for making plastic things – a sort of progression from perspex and that type of thing. He says there should be a great future in plastic materials. Might even make them strong enough for use in buildings and ships and so on.'

'Would you want to go in for that sort of thing?'

'I'm interested,' nodded Edward. 'Jim took me to meet the old boy a few weeks ago. I liked him. He's got ideas and he works hard. I know he wants to build up the works as soon as he can. If he offered me a job, I think I'd take it.'

'Where would it be?'

'Near Ruislip. I'd rather like to be near London, too.'

'It sounds a good idea,' agreed Bertie, glad to see that his companion could still be kindled into life. 'I hope it comes off.'

They wandered through the garden gate to the tow path. The Cax reflected the blue and white sky above it. In the distance a fisherman sat immobile upon the opposite bank. Edward looked upon the tranquil scene with dislike, and skimmed a pebble viciously across the surface of the water towards the town.

'And at least I'd get away from here,' was his final comment.

The Cax flowed on placidly. It had seen centuries of men's tantrums. One more made very little difference.

That evening the occupants of the flat above Howard's Restaurant descended for their dinner. They did this occasionally when the restaurant was shut, and Robert was agreeable. He waited on them himself and joined the family party at coffee afterwards.

Sep came across and Bertie too was present. It was a cheerful gathering. Although the curtains were drawn across the windows looking on to the market place, those at the back of the building remained pulled back, and the sky still glowed with the remains of a fine July sunset. The little white tables and chairs, set out upon the grassy lawn sloping down gently to the Cax, glimmered in the twilight. It was comfortably familiar to Edward, and even his frayed nerves were soothed by the view which had remained the same now for years.

It was Joan who brought up the subject of Edward's return to the flat.

'How soon, do you think,' she asked, 'before you can come home again?'

Better now than later, decided Edward.

'I don't think that I shall come back to Caxley for a while,' he answered deliberately.

'Why ever not?' exclaimed old Mrs North. 'It's your home, isn't it?'

Edward drew a crescent very carefully on the white table-cloth with the edge of a spoon, and was silent.

'Edward's quite old enough to do as he pleases, mamma,' said Bertie quietly.

'I hope you will come back, dear boy,' said Sep, putting a frail old hand on his grandson's sleeve.

'One day, perhaps,' said Edward, putting his own hand upon his grandfather's. 'But I want to have a spell elsewhere. You understand?'

'I understand,' said the old man gravely. 'You know what is best for you.'

'There's no need to feel that you are pushing us out,' began his mother, not quite understanding the situation. 'You know that we shall go back to Rose Lodge very soon.'

'Yes, dear, I do know that,' replied Edward, as patiently as he could. He drew a circle round the crescent, turning the whole into a plump face with a large mouth. He became conscious of Robert's eyes fixed upon him, and put down the spoon hastily, like a child caught out in some misdemeanour. But it was not the mutilation of the white starched surface which gave Robert that intent look, as Edward was soon to discover.

It was now almost dark and Sep rose to go, pleading a slight headache.

'I shall see you again before you leave,' he said to Edward, turning at the door. Edward watched him cross the market square, his heart full of affection for the small figure treading its familiar way homeward.

The ladies too had decided to retire. Goodnights were said, and Bertie, Edward and Robert were alone at the table. Robert carefully refilled the three coffee cups. His face was thoughtful.

'Have you any idea,' he asked 'when you'll come back to Caxley?'

'None,' said Edward shortly. 'At the moment I feel as though I want to turn my back on it for good.'

A sudden glint came into Robert's eyes. It was not unnoticed by the watchful Bertie.

'In that case,' said Robert swiftly, 'you won't want the rooms upstairs. Would you think of letting me have them? I would give you a good price to buy the whole of this property outright.'

Edward looked at Robert in astonishment. His Uncle Bertie's face had grown pink with concern.

'Thanks for the offer,' said Edward shortly, 'but I wouldn't do anything to upset Grandpa Howard. And in any case, I don't intend to part with the property.'

'You've no business to make such a suggestion,' exclaimed Bertie. His blue eyes flashed with unaccustomed fire. Edward had never seen his uncle so angry, and a very intimidating sight he found it.

'If he doesn't want it, why hang on to it?' demanded Robert. A little nerve twitched at the corner of his mouth, and he glared across the table at his brother-in-law.

'He may want it one day,' pointed out Bertie, 'as well you know. It is unfair to take advantage of the boy at a time like this. More than unfair – it's outrageous!'

'He's being nothing more nor less than a dog in the manger,' retorted Robert heatedly. 'He doesn't want it, but he'll dam' well see I don't have it! Why on earth the old man ever made such a barmy arrangement I shall never know! I'm his son, aren't I? How does he expect me to run this place with no storage rooms above it? The old fool gets nearer his dotage daily – and others profit by it!'

Edward, who had grown tired of listening to the two men arguing his affairs as though he were not present, felt that he could stand no more.

'Oh, shut up, both of you,' he cried. 'We'll keep Grandpa out of this, if you don't mind. And forget the whole thing. You can take it from me, Robert, the house remains mine as he intended, whether I live here or not, and you must like it or lump it.'

He rose from the table, looking suddenly intensely weary.

'I'm off to bed. See you in the morning. Goodnight!'

'I'm off too,' said Bertie grimly. He limped towards the door of the restaurant as Edward began to mount the stairs to his own apartment.

He heard the door crash behind his uncle, and then two sounds, like pistol shots, as Robert viciously slammed the bolts home.

The sooner I get out of this, the better, determined Edward, taking the last flight of stairs two at a time.

The next morning he made his round of farewells cheerfully. Robert seemed to have forgotten the previous evening's unpleasantness and wished him well. Sep's handshake was as loving as ever. He called last of all on Bertie.

'I'm sorry I lost my temper last night,' Bertie greeted him.

'I hate to say this, Edward, but you must be wary of Robert. He's a man with a grievance, and to my mind he gets odder as the years go by.'

'I'll watch out,' smiled Edward, making light of it.

'He's let this separation of the house and the restaurant become an obsession,' continued Bertie, 'and he's decidedly unbalanced when the subject crops up. Hang on to your own, my boy. It would break Sep's heart if he thought you'd broken with Caxley for good.'

'I know that,' said Edward quietly.

They parted amicably, glad to know each other's feelings, and Edward made his way up Caxley High Street noticing the placards on the buildings and in shop windows exhorting the good people of Caxley to support rival candidates in the coming election. Not that there would be much of a fight in this secure Conservative seat, thought Edward. The outcome was a foregone conclusion. And so, he felt sure, was the return of the Conservative party to power. The hero of the hour was Winston Churchill. It was unthinkable that he should not lead the nation in peacetime, and as bravely as he had in these last five years of grim warfare.

He was right about Caxley's decision. The Conservative candidate was returned, but by a majority so small that his supporters were considerably shaken. When at last the nation's wishes were made known, and the Socialists were returned with a large majority, Edward was flabbergasted and disgusted, and said so in the mess.

Back in Caxley old Mrs North summed up the feelings of many of her compatriots, as she studied the newspaper on the morning of July 27.

'To think that dear Mr Churchill has got to go after all he's done for the nation! The ungrateful lot! I'm thoroughly ashamed of them. The poor man will take this very hard, and you can't wonder at it, can you? I shall sit straight down, Winnie dear, and write to him.'

And, with back straight as a ramrod and blue eyes afire, she did.

The end of the conflict was now very close. Millions of leaflets demanding surrender were showered on the inhabitants of Japan. The last warning of 'complete and utter destruction' was given on August 5. On the following day the first atomic bomb was cast upon Hiroshima, and on August 9 a second one was dropped on the city of Nagasaki. Within a week the terms set out by the Allied Governments were accepted, and the new Prime Minister, Mr Attlee, broadcast the news at midnight.

Overwhelming relief was, of course, the first reaction. There were still a few places in the Far East where fighting continued, but virtually this was the end of the war. Soon the men would be back, and life would return to normal.

Sep surveyed the happy crowds from his bedroom window, and thought of that other victory, nearly thirty years earlier, when the flags had fluttered and the people of Caxley had greeted peace with a frenzy of rejoicing. Today there was less madness, less hysteria. It had been a long bitter struggle, and there had been many casualties, but the numbers had been less than in that earlier cruel war.

He remembered how he had stood grieving for his dead son amidst his neighbours' cheers. Thank God that his family had been spared this time! He looked down upon the bronze crown of Queen Victoria below him, and wondered inconsequently what she would make of a victory finally won by an atomic bomb. The descriptions of its ghastly power had affected Sep deeply. Now that such forces were known to the world, what did the future hold for mankind? What if such a weapon fell into the hands of a maniac like Hitler? Would the world ever be safe again?

Four young men, aflame with bonhomie and beer, had caught each other by the coat tails and were stamping round Queen Victoria's plinth shouting rhythmically 'Victory for us! Victory for us! Victory for us!' to the delight of the crowd.

Sep turned sadly from the window. Victory indeed, but at what a price, mourned the old man, at what a price!

PART TWO

1945—1950

11

Edward Starts Afresh

T HE RETURN to Rose Lodge was accompanied by the usual frustrations and set-backs. The decorators waited for the plasterers' work to be completed. The electricians waited for the plumbers to finish their part. A chimney was faulty. Damp patches had appeared mysteriously on the landing ceiling. The paintwork inside and out showed the neglect of six years of war and hard wear.

At times Winnie wished that she had stuck to her guns and refused point blank to return. But her mother's joy was not a whit dampened by the delays, and she threw herself with zest into the job of choosing wallpaper and curtaining from the meagre stocks available. Tirelessly she searched the shops for all the odds and ends needed to refurbish her home. One morning she would be matching fringe for the curtains, or gimp for a newly upholstered chair; on the next she would be comparing prices of coke and anthracite for the kitchen boiler. She was just as busy and excited as she had been years ago, Winnie recalled, when the family moved to Rose Lodge for the first time. Bertie had been quite right. Rose Lodge meant everything to their mother, and it was obviously best that she should spend the rest of her days there.

They moved from the market square on a blustery November day. Ragged low clouds raced across the sky. The Caxley folk, cowering beneath shuddering umbrellas, battled against the wind that buffeted them. Vicious showers of rain slanted across the streets, and the removal men dripped rivulets from their shiny macintoshes as they heaved the furniture down the stairs and into the van.

But, by the evening, Winnie and her mother sat exhausted but triumphant one on each side of the familiar drawing-room hearth.

'Home, at last,' sighed the old lady happily, looking about her. It was still far from perfect. The curtains hung stiffly, the carpet had some extraordinary billows in it, the removal men had scraped the paint by the door and chipped a corner of the china cabinet, but she was content.

'And to think,' she continued, 'that Edward will be demobilised in a few weeks' time, and dear Bertie, and perhaps Michael, and we can all have a proper family Christmas here together. The first peacetime Christmas!'

'I wonder how Joan's managing,' answered Winnie, still bemused from the day's happenings. 'I hope she won't feel lonely.'

'Lonely?' echoed her mother, 'In the market place? Take my word for it, she's as right as ninepence with the flat to play with and her own nice new things to arrange. She'll thoroughly enjoy having a place of her own.'

'You're probably right, mamma,' said Winnie. 'Early bed for us tonight. There are muscles aching in my back and arms which I never knew I had before.'

By ten o'clock Rose Lodge was in darkness and its two occupants slept the sleep of the happy and the exhausted.

*　　*　　*

It was Joan who had written to Edward to ask if she and Michael might have the flat temporarily, and he was delighted to think of it being of use to the young couple. He had been offered a good post in the plastics firm, as he had hoped, and was already looking forward to finding a flat or a house somewhere near London and the job.

This suited Joan and Michael admirably. It was plain that the nursery school would close now that the war was over, despite the recommendations of the Education Act of 1944. Joan grieved at the thought, but numbers were dwindling steadily, as the men came back, and the evacuees moved away from Caxley. By Easter the school would be no more, and the Quaker meeting house which had echoed to the cries and mirth of the babies, tumbling about the scrubbed floor in their blue-checked overalls, would once more be silent and empty, but for the decorous meetings of the children's war-time hosts, the Friends.

She was glad, though, that she had a job to do, for it transpired that Michael's demobilisation would be deferred. He was now in Berlin, and his fluency in German was of great use. He had been given further promotion and asked to stay on until the spring, but he had Christmas leave and the two spent a wonderful week arranging their wedding presents and buying furniture for the future.

'None of this blasted utility stuff,' declared Michael flatly. 'I'm sick of that sign anyway. We'll pick up second-hand pieces as we go – things we shall always like.' And so they went to two sales, and haunted the furniture shops in Caxley High Street which offered the old with the new.

Christmas Day was spent at Rose Lodge to please Mrs North.

Edward and Bertie, recently demobilised, were in high spirits. All the conversation was of the future and Winnie, surveying the Norths and Howards filling the great drawing-room, thought how right it was that it should be so. The immediate past was bleak and tragic; and, for her particularly, earlier years in this house held sad memories. She remembered arriving with Joan as a baby and Edward as a toddler to find her mother dressing the Christmas tree in just the same place as the present one. Leslie had left her, and the long lonely years had just begun. She often wondered what had become of him – the handsome charmer whose son was so shatteringly like him in looks – but hoped never to see him again. He had hurt her too cruelly.

One evening before Michael returned to Germany, Joan and he talked over their plans for the future. At one time he had thought of following up his Dublin degree with a year's training for his teacher's diploma, but now he had his doubts about this course.

'I don't think I could face sitting at a desk and poring over books again. The war's unsettled me – I want to start doing something more practical. I've talked to other fellows who broke their university course, or who had just finished, like me, and there are mighty few who have got the guts to return to the academic grind again. Somehow one's brain gets jerked out of the learning groove. I know for a fact mine has.'

He faced Joan with a smile.

'Besides,' he continued, 'I've a wife and a future family to support now. I must earn some money to keep the home together. We shan't want to stay in Caxley all our lives, you know, and we shall have to buy a house before long.'

'But what do you want to do?' asked his wife earnestly. 'I

do understand about not wanting to go back to school, I couldn't face it myself. But what else have you thought of? It seems a pity not to use your languages.'

'I wouldn't mind doing the same sort of thing that my father does – hotel work. Here or abroad. I'm easy. And perhaps, one day, owning our own hotel. Or a chain of them.'

His eyes were sparkling. He spoke lightly, but Joan could see that there was an element of serious purpose behind the words.

'Or I could stay in the army. That's been put to me. What do you feel about that, my sweet?'

'Horrible,' said Joan flatly. 'I've had enough of the army; and the idea of moving from one army camp to another doesn't appeal to me one little bit. And you know how *backward* army children are, poor dears, shunted from pillar to post and just getting the hang of one reading method when they're faced with an entirely different one.'

Michael laughed at this practical teacher's approach.

'I can't say I'm keen to stay myself,' he agreed. 'Six years is enough for me. We'd be better off, of course, but is it worth it?'

'Never,' declared Joan stoutly. 'Let's be poor and lead our own lives.'

And with that brave dictum they shelved the future for the remainder of his leave.

Meanwhile, Edward had been finding out just how difficult it was to get somewhere to live near London. He tried two sets of digs whilst he was flat hunting and swore that he would never entertain the thought of lodgings again. The only possible hotel within striking distance of the factory was expensive, noisy, and decidedly seedy.

It was Jim, the son of his employer, who saved him at last.

'I've got a house,' he cried triumphantly one morning, bursting into the office which he shared with Edward. 'It's scruffy, it's jerry-built, but it's got three bedrooms and a garden. Eileen is off her head with delight. Now the boy can have a bedroom of his own, and the baby too when it arrives.'

Edward congratulated him warmly. Then a thought struck him.

'And what about the flat?'

'A queue for that as long as your arm,' began Jim. He stopped pacing the floor and looked suddenly at his colleague. 'Want it?' he asked, 'because if you do, it could be yours. The others can wait. I'll have a word with the old man.'

After a little negotiation, it was arranged, and Edward moved in one blue and white March day. A speculative builder, an old school friend of Edward's employer, had acquired the site a few years before the war, and had erected two pairs of presumably semi-detached houses, well-placed in one large garden. Each house was divided into two self-contained flats, so that there were eight households all told in about an acre of ground.

The plot was situated at the side of an old tree-lined lane and was not far from a golf course. A cluster of fir trees and a mature high hedge screened the flats from the view of passers by. The ground-floor tenants agreed to keep the front part of the garden in order, the upstairs tenants the back.

The rent was pretty steep, Edward privately considered, by Caxley standards, but he liked the flat and its secluded position and would have paid even more for the chance of escaping from digs and hotels. He surveyed his new domain thankfully. He had a sitting-room, one bedroom, a kitchen, a bathroom and a gloriously large cupboard for trunks, tennis racquets, picnic baskets and all the other awkward objects which need to be housed. He was well content.

He saw little of his neighbours in the first few weeks, and learned more about them from Jim than from this own brief encounters. His own flat was on the ground floor, and immediately beside him lived a middle-aged couple, distantly related to the owner, and now retired. Edward liked the look of them. The wife had wished him 'Good morning' in a brisk Scots brogue and her husband reminded him slightly of his grandfather, Bender North.

Above them lived a sensible-looking woman, a little older than Edward himself, who mounted a spruce bicycle each morning and pedalled energetically away. Edward had decided that she was an efficient secretary in one of the nearby factories, but Jim told him otherwise.

'Headmistress of an infants' school,' he informed him. 'Miss Hedges – a nice old bird. She was awfully kind to Eileen when she was having our first. And the two above you are secretaries, or so they say. I'd put them as shorthand-typists myself, but no doubt they'll rise in the scale before very long. Flighty, but harmless, you'll find.'

'And decorative,' added Edward. 'And much addicted to bathing. One at night and one in the morning, I've worked out. There's a cascade by my ear soon after eleven and another just after seven each morning, down the waste pipe.'

'Come to think of it,' said Jim, 'I believe you're right. Trust a countryman to find out all the details of his neighbours' affairs! It had never occurred to me, I must admit.'

'It's a pity my grandmother can't spend an afternoon there,' replied Edward. 'She'd have the life history of every one of us at her finger tips before the sun set! Now, Jim let's get down to work.'

The first Caxley visitors to the flat were his Uncle Bertie and Aunt Kathy, on their way to meet friends in London.

'You look so happy!' exclaimed his aunt, kissing him. She stood back and surveyed him with her sparkling dark eyes. 'And so smart!' she added.

'My demob suit,' said Edward, with a grimace. 'And tie, too.'

'Well, at least the tie's wearable,' observed Bertie. 'At the end of my war, I was offered the choice of a hideous tie or "a very nice neckerchief." How d'you like that?'

Edward pressed them for all the Caxley news. Bertie noticed that he was eager for every detail of the family. How soon, he wondered, before he would return? Certainly, he had visited Rose Lodge on several occasions, and his present home was conveniently near Western Avenue for him to make his way to Caxley within a short time. At the moment, however, it looked as though Edward was comfortably settled. His decree nisi was already through; before the end of the year he should be free, but as things were, it seemed pretty plain that his nephew was happy to return to a bachelor's existence.

The greatest piece of news they had to offer was that Joan was expecting a child in the late summer, and that Michael, now demobilised, had decided to learn more about the catering trade by working for a time in Howard's Restaurant. Sep had suggested this move, and although Michael realised that there might be difficulties, he was glad to accept the work as a temporary measure, until the baby arrived.

'And how has Robert taken it?' asked Edward, after expressing his delight at the prospect of becoming an uncle.

'Fairly quietly, so far. I don't think it would be very satisfactory permanently though. His temper is getting more and more unpredictable. Two waitresses have left in the last month. It's my belief he's ill, but he flatly refuses to see the doctor.'

'He's a queer customer,' agreed Edward, 'but times are difficult. He must have a devil of a job getting supplies. Food seems to be shorter now than during the war – unless it's because I'm a stranger here and don't get anything tucked away under the counter for me. I'd starve if it weren't for the works' canteen midday, and some of the stuff they dish up there is enough to make you shudder.'

'Father says that people mind most about bread rationing,' said Kathy. "Never had it in our lives before," they say, really shocked, you know. And poor dear, he *will* get all these wretched bits of paper, bread units, *absolutely* right. You know what a stickler he is. I was in the shop the other day helping him. People leave their pages with him and then have a regular order for a cake, using so many each week. It makes an enormous amount of book work for the poor old darling. Sometimes I try to persuade him to give up. He's practically eighty, after all.'

'He won't,' commented Bertie, 'he'll die in harness, and like it that way. And Robert's more of a liability than a help at the moment. He resents the fact that Sep didn't hand over the business to him outright, when he gave you the house. It's beginning to become more of an obsession than ever, I'm afraid.'

'He was always dam' awkward about that,' said Edward shortly. 'Good heavens! Surely Grandpa can do as he likes with his own? If there's anything I detest it's this waiting for other men's shoes – like a vulture.'

'Vultures don't wear shoes,' pointed out Kathy, surveying her own neat pair. 'And whatever it is that screws up our poor Robert it makes things downright unpleasant for us all, particularly Father.'

'And Michael and Joan?'

'Michael's such a good-tempered fellow,' said Bertie, 'that he'll stand a lot. And Joan's at the blissfully broody stage just now. I caught her winding wool with Maisie Hunter the other evening with a positively maudlin expression on her face.'

'Maisie Hunter?' echoed Edward. 'I thought she'd got married.'

'Her husband-to-be crashed on landing at Brize Norton, about six weeks before the war ended.'

'I never heard that,' Edward said slowly. 'Poor Maisie.'

Bertie glanced at his watch and rose to go.

'Come along, my dear,' he said, hauling Kathy to her feet. 'We shall meet all the home-going traffic, if we don't look out.'

Edward accompanied them to the gate and waved goodbye as the car rounded the bend in the lane. It was strange, he thought, how little he envied them returning to Caxley. It was another world, and one which held no attraction for him. Much as he loved his family, he was glad that he was free of the tensions and squabbles in which they seemed now involved.

He bent down to pull a few weeds from the garden bed

which bordered the path, musing the while on his change of outlook. He revelled in his present anonymous role. It was wonderful to know that one's neighbours took so little interest in one's affairs. It was refreshing to be able to shut the door and be absolutely unmolested in the flat, to eat alone, to sleep alone, and to be happy or sad as the spirit moved one, without involving other people's feelings. It was purely selfish, of course, he knew that, but it was exactly what he needed.

He straightened his aching back and looked aloft. An aeroplane had taken off from nearby Northolt aerodrome and he felt the old rush of pleasure in its soaring power. And yet, here again, there was a difference. He felt not the slightest desire to fly now. Would the longing ever return? Or would this numb apathy which affected him remain always with him, dulling pleasure and nullifying pain?

It was useless to try to answer these questions. He must be thankful for the interest of the new job, and for this present quietness in which to lick his wounds. Perhaps happiness and warmth, ambition and purpose, would return to him one day. Meanwhile, he must try and believe all the tiresome people who kept reminding him that 'Time was the Great Healer'.

Perhaps, they might, just possibly, be right.

12

A Family Tragedy

As THE summer advanced, affairs in the market place went from bad to worse. The aftermath of the war – general fatigue – was felt everywhere. Food was not the only thing in short supply. Men returning from active service found it desperately hard to find somewhere to live. Women, longing for new clothes, for colour, for gaiety, still had to give coupons for garments and for material for making them, as well as for all the soft furnishings needed. 'Makes you wonder who won the war!' observed someone bitterly, watching Sep clip out the precious snippets of paper entitling her to three loaves, and the feeling was everywhere.

Sep, hard-pressed with work and smaller than ever in old age, maintained his high standards of service steadily. But he was a worried man. The shop was doing as well as ever, but the returns from the restaurant showed a slight decline as the weeks went by, and Sep knew quite well that Robert was at fault. It was becoming more and more difficult to keep staff. Robert was short with the waitresses in front of customers, and impatient and sarcastic with the kitchen staff. How long, wondered Sep, before Michael, who was working so wonderfully well, found conditions unendurable?

He made up his mind to take Robert aside privately and have a talk with him. The fellow was touchy and might sulk, as he had so often done as a boy, but at the rate he was going on

Howard's Restaurant would soon be in Queer Street. Sep did not relish the task, but he had never shirked his duty in his life, and it was plain that this unpleasant encounter must take place.

He crossed the square from the shop as the Town Hall clock struck eight. The restaurant was closed, the staff had gone and Robert was alone in the kitchen reading *The Caxley Chronicle*. Sep sat down opposite him.

'My boy, I'll come straight to the point. Business is slipping, as you know. Any particular reason?'

'Only that I'm expected to run this place with a set of fools,' muttered Robert, scowling at his clenched hands on the table top.

'I'm worried more about you than the business,' said Sep gently. 'You've been over-doing it. Why not take a holiday? We could manage, you know, for a week, say.'

Robert jumped to his feet, his face flushing.

'And let Michael worm his way in? Is that what you want? It's to be Edward all over again, I can see. What's wrong with me – your own son – that you should slight me all the time?'

'My boy—' began Sep, protesting, but he was overwhelmed by Robert's passionate outburst.

'What chance have I ever had? Edward has the house given him at twenty-one. The house that should have been mine anyway. Do I get given anything? Oh no! I can wait – wait till I'm old and useless, with nothing to call my own.'

His face was dark and congested, the words spluttered from his mouth. To Sep's horror he saw tears welling in his son's eyes and trickling down his cheeks. The pent-up resentment of years was bursting forth and Sep could do nothing to quell the violence.

'I've never had a fair deal from the day I was born. Jim was a hero because he got himself killed. No one was ever allowed to mention Leslie, though he was the kindest of the lot to me, and I missed him more than any of you. Kath's been the spoilt baby all her life, and I've been general dog's body. Work's all I've ever had, with no time for anything else. The rest of the family have homes and children. I've been too busy for girls. Edward and Bertie and Michael came back from the war jingling with medals. What did I get for sticking here as a slavey? I'm despised, I tell you! Despised! Laughed at – by all Caxley—'

By now he was sobbing with self-pity, beating his palms against his forehead in a childish gesture which wrung his father's heart. Who would have dreamt that such hidden fires had smouldered for so long beneath that timid exterior? And what could be done to comfort him and to give him back pride in himself?

Sep let the storm subside a little before he spoke. His voice was gentle.

'I'm sorry that you should feel this way, my boy. You've let your mind dwell on all sorts of imagined slights. You were always as dear to me and your mother as the other children – more so, perhaps, as the youngest. No one blames you for not going to the war. You were rejected through no fault of your own. Everyone here knows that you've done your part by sticking to your job here.'

Robert's sobbing had ceased, but he scowled across the table mutinously.

'It's a lie! Everyone here hates me. People watch me wherever I go. They talk about me behind my back. I know, I tell you, I know! They say I couldn't get a girl if I tried. They say no one wants me. They say I'm under my dad's thumb – afraid to stand on my own feet – afraid to answer back! I'm a failure. That's what they say, watching and whispering about me, day in and day out!'

Sep stood up, small, straight and stern.

'Robert, you are over-wrought, and don't know what you are saying. But I won't hear you accusing innocent people of malice. All this is in your own mind. You must see this, surely?'

Robert approached his father. There was a strange light in his glittering eyes. He thrust his face very close to the old man's.

'My mind?' he echoed. 'Are you trying to say I'm out of my mind? I know well enough what people are saying about me. I hear them. But I hear other voices too – *private* voices that tell me I'm right, that the whisperers in Caxley will be confounded, and that the time will come when they have to give in and admit that Robert Howard was right all the time. They'll see me one day, the owner of this business here, the owner of the shop, the biggest man in the market square, the head of the Howard family!'

His voice had risen with excitement, his eyes were wild. From weeping self-pity he had swung in the space of minutes to a state of manic euphoria. He began to pace the floor, head up, nostrils flaring, as he gulped for breath.

'You'll be gone by then,' he cried triumphantly, 'and I'll see that Edward goes too. There will be one Howard only in charge. Just one. One to give orders. One to be the boss!'

'Robert!' thundered Sep, in the voice which he had used but rarely in his life. There was no response. Robert was in another world, oblivious of his father and his surroundings.

'They'll see,' he continued, pacing even more swiftly. 'My

time will come. My voices know. They tell me the truth. "The persecutors shall become the persecuted!" That's what my voices tell me.'

Sep walked round the table and confronted his son. He took hold of his elbows and looked steadily into that distorted face a little above his own.

'Robert,' he said clearly, as though to a distraught child. 'We are going home now, and you are going to bed.'

The young man's gaze began to soften. His eyes turned slowly towards his father's. He looked as though he were returning from a long, strange journey.

'Very well, father,' he said. The voice was exhausted, but held a certain odd pride, as though remnants of glimpsed grandeur still clung to him.

He watched his father lock up. Sep, white-faced and silent, walked beside his son across the market square, watching him anxiously.

Robert, head high, looked to left and right as he strode proudly over the cobbles. He might have been a king acknowledging the homage of his people, except that, to Sep's relief, the square was empty. When they reached their door Robert entered first, as of right, and swept regally up the stairs to his room, without a word.

When faithful old Miss Taggerty brought in Sep's bed-time milk, she found her master sitting pale and motionless.

'You don't look yourself, sir,' she said with concern. 'Shall I bring you anything? An aspirin, perhaps?'

'I'm all right. Just a little tired.'

'Shall I fetch Mr Robert?'

'No, no! Don't worry about me. I'm off to bed immediately.'

They wished each other goodnight. Sep watched the door close quietly behind the good-hearted creature, and resumed his ponderings.

What was to be done? Tonight had made plain something which he had long suspected. Robert's mind was giving way under inner torment. He was obsessed with a wrongful sense of grievance against himself, and worse still, a gnawing jealousy, aimed chiefly against Edward. These two evils had become his masters. These were 'the voices' which he claimed to hear, and which were driving him beyond the brink of sanity.

To Sep's generation, insanity in the family was something to be kept from the knowledge of outsiders. One pitied the afflicted, but one kept the matter as quiet as possible. So often, he knew from experience, attacks passed and, within a few months, rest and perhaps a change of scene, brought mental health again. It might be so with Robert.

He disliked the idea of calling in a doctor to the boy. Suppose that Robert were sent to a mental home? Would he ever come out again? Did doctors really know what went on in the human brain, and could they cure 'a mind diseased'? Wouldn't the mere fact of consulting a doctor upset his poor son's condition even more?

And yet the boy was in need of help, and he was the last person to be able to give it. How terrible it had been to hear that awful indictment of himself as a father! Was he really to blame? Had he loved him less? In all humility he felt that he could truthfully claim to have loved all his children equally – even Leslie, who had betrayed him.

And those fearful indications of a deluded mind – the assumption of omnipotence, of grandeur, to what might they lead? Would he become violent if he were ridiculed in one of these moods? Sep remembered the menacing glitter in his son's eyes, and trembled for him. What did the future hold for Robert?

He took his milk with him to the bedroom. The blinds were drawn against the familiar view of the market square and the indomitable figure of Queen Victoria. Miss Taggerty had turned the bedclothes back into a neat white triangle. Sep knelt beside the bed and prayed for guidance.

When he arose his mind was clear. He would sleep on this problem and see how things fared in the morning. There was no need to rush for help to the rest of the family. This was something to be borne alone if possible, so that Robert should be spared further indignities. He had suffered enough, thought Sep, torn with pity.

For a few weeks things went more smoothly. Robert never referred to that dreadful outburst. It was as though it had been wiped completely from his memory. For Sep, the incident was unforgettable, but he said nothing.

Nevertheless, it was obvious that the young man was in a precarious state of mind. Sep did what he could to relieve the pressure of work at the restaurant, and Michael's efforts ensured the smooth running of the place. His cheerfulness and good looks soon made him popular, which was good for trade but not, as Sep realised, for Robert's esteem.

Kathy, knowing that staff were hard to get at the restaurant offered to help whenever possible. She and Bertie realised that Robert was under strain, although they had no idea of the seriousness of his malaise.

'You'd be more use, my dear, in the shop,' said Sep. 'It would leave me free to go across to Robert's more often, and you know exactly where everything is at home.'

'I was brought up to it,' laughed Kathy. 'I'd enjoy it, you know, and now that the children are off my hands, it will give me an interest.'

Her presence was a great comfort to Sep, and meant that he could keep a discreet, if anxious, eye on affairs across the square.

During these uneasy weeks Joan's baby was born. It was a girl, and the family were all delighted. She was born in the nursing home to the north of Caxley, on the road to Beech Green and Fairacre, where so many other Caxley citizens had first seen the light. Michael was enormously pleased and visited his wife and daughter every evening.

Joan remained there for a fortnight. It was decided that she should go for a week or two to Rose Lodge to regain her strength, and submit to the welcome cossetings of her mother and grandmother. The house was certainly more convenient than the flat, and the baby would have the benefit of the garden air as well as the doting care of three women. She was to be christened Sarah.

'No hope of the poor little darling being christened at St Peter's, I suppose?' sighed Mrs North.

'You know there isn't,' replied Joan, smiling at her grandmother's naughtiness.

'I never seem to have any luck with family ceremonies,'

commented the old lady. She brightened as a thought crossed her mind. 'Perhaps Kathy's girl one day?'

Soon after Joan returned to the flat trouble began again. Robert's antagonism towards Michael was renewed in a hundred minor insults. Despite his easy-going disposition, Michael's Irish blood was roused.

'The fellow's off his rocker,' declared Michael roundly one evening in the privacy of the flat. 'He's beginning to talk as though he's the King of England. Sometimes I wonder if we should stay.'

Letters from his family in Dublin had also unsettled him. His father was in failing health and it was plain that he longed for his son to return to carry on the hotel, although he did not press the boy to come if his prospects were brighter in Caxley. Joan did not know how to advise her husband. She herself half-feared the uprooting and the break with the family, especially with a young child to consider. On the other hand it was right that Michael should obey his conscience, and she would do whatever he felt was best. Certainly, as things were, there was nothing but petty frustrations for Michael in his work, and he had obviously learned all that could be learned from the comparatively small Caxley restaurant. It was time he took on something bigger, giving him scope for his ability.

She told her problem to her old friend Maisie Hunter, who was to be godmother to Sarah. Her answer was straight-forward.

'Michael's trying to spare you. Tell him you'll be happy to go to Dublin, and then watch his face. I'm sure he wants to go back home, and he's bound to do well.'

She was right, and the couple had almost decided to break the news to Sep and Robert and to write to Michael's father, when two things happened to clinch the matter.

Joan had put her daughter to sleep in the pram in the little garden sloping down to the Cax, when Robert burst from the restaurant in a state of fury.

'I won't have that thing out here,' he said, kicking at a wheel. 'This is part of my restaurant, as you well know. You can clear off!'

'Robert!' protested Joan, much shocked. 'I've always used the garden. What on earth has come over you?'

Two or three curious customers, taking morning coffee, gazed with interest upon the scene from the restaurant windows. Joan was horribly aware of their presence, and took Robert's arm to lead him further away. He flung her from him with such violence that she fell across the pram. The child broke into crying, and Joan, now thoroughly alarmed, lifted her from the pram.

'You'll use the garden no more,' shouted Robert. 'You're trespassing on my property. And if you leave that contraption here I shall throw it in the river!'

At this moment, Michael arrived, and took in the situation at a glance.

'Take the baby upstairs,' he said quietly. 'I'll deal with this.'

He propelled the struggling and protesting Robert into the little office at the end of the restaurant and slammed the door, much to the disappointment of the interested customers. He thrust Robert into an arm chair, and turned to get him a drink from the cupboard. He was white with fury, and his hand shook as he poured out a stiff tot, but he was in command of himself and the situation. He was facing an ill man, and a dangerous one, he realised.

Robert leapt from the chair, as Michael put the glass on the desk, and tried to make for the door. Michael administered a hard slap to each cheek, as one would to an hysterical patient, and Robert slumped again into the chair.

'Drink this slowly,' commanded Michael, 'and wait here until I get back.'

He left the office, turned the key in the lock, and told good old John Bush who had been in Sep's employ for forty years, to take charge while he saw to his wife and let Sep know what was happening.

Later that evening, Sep, Bertie and Michael held counsel.

'We must get a doctor to see him,' said Bertie firmly. 'I'll ring Dr Rogers tonight.'

'I blame myself,' said Sep heavily. 'He has not been himself for months. We should have got help earlier. It must be done now. I fear for Joan and the child if he is going to get these attacks of violence.'

'I want them to go back to Rose Lodge, but Joan is very much against it,' said Michael. 'But it's going to be impossible to stay over the restaurant, if he doesn't change his ways.'

'Let's get the doctor's verdict before we do anything more,' said Bertie.

Dr Rogers said little when he had examined his patient, but his grave looks alarmed Sep.

'Will he get better?' he asked anxiously. 'He's such a young man – so many years before him. What do you think?'

Dr Rogers would not commit himself, but provided various bottles of pills and promised to visit frequently. Meanwhile, he asked the family to call him in immediately if the symptoms of excessive excitement occurred again.

A few days later a letter arrived from Ireland from Michael's invalid mother. His father was sinking. Could he return? And was there any hope of him taking over the hotel?

'This settles it,' said Joan, looking at Michael's worried face as he read the letter again.

'But what about Howard's Restaurant? How will Sep manage?'

'John Bush can run the place blindfold. And Aunt Kathy would help, I know. Go and tell Sep what has happened. Take the letter.'

She knew full well how Sep would react.

'Of course you must go, my boy. Your father comes first, and your mother needs your presence at a time like this. You've been of enormous help to us here, but it's right that you should start a life of your own.'

And so, within two days, Michael returned to Dublin, and Joan and the baby were to join him as soon as possible. It was Bertie who drove them to Holyhead to catch the boat to Dun Laoghaire. Saying farewell to the family had been ineffably sad.

'I'll be back soon for a holiday,' she told them all bravely. It was hardest to say good-bye to Sep and Grandma North. They looked so old, so shattered at the parting.

'You are doing the right thing,' Sep assured her firmly. 'I'm sure you have a wonderful future in Ireland.'

Her grandmother was less hopeful and inclined to be tearful.

'Such a *long* way off, and a very wild sort of people, I hear. The thought of all those poor babies of yours being brought up in such *strange* ways quite upsets me. Do boil all the water, dear, whatever you do.'

Joan promised, and kissed her, hardly knowing whether to laugh or cry. Funny, exasperating, old Grandma! How long before she saw her again?

Dr Rogers' treatment seemed to have only a small sedative effect on Robert, but Sep tried to assure himself that the cure was bound to take a long time, and that his son's youth and a lessening of his work would finally ensure his recovery.

Kathy insisted on taking over the financial affairs of the restaurant while John Bush coped with the practical side. She was as quick at figures as her mother, Edna Howard, had been, and soon proved a competent business woman.

It was quite apparent that Robert resented her intrusion into his affairs, and Kathy ignored the snubs and sarcastic comments which punctuated the day's work. Robert was sick. Soon he would be better, and he would be happy again, she thought.

She was totally unprepared, therefore, for a sudden attack of the mania which had so appalled Sep months before. It happened, luckily, soon after the restaurant had closed and Kathy was checking the money. Perhaps the clinking of the coins reminded him of the fact that the business was not his. Perhaps the sight of his sister, sitting in the chair which had always been his own, inflamed him. No one would ever know; but resentment flared again, his voice grew loud and strident as he screamed his hatred of his family and his intention to get rid of them.

'My voices told me,' he roared at the terrified Kathy. 'They told me I would triumph, and I shall! Michael and Joan have gone. Old Bush will go, and you will go! There will be no one left but me – the unbeatable – the true heir!'

His lips were flecked with saliva, his eyes demented, as he bore down upon her. Dropping the money on the floor, Kathy tore open the door, and fled across the square to find help, the jingle of the rolling coins ringing in her ears.

The next day an ambulance took Robert and his attendants to the county mental hospital some twenty miles away. Sep, shattered, sat trying to understand Dr Rogers' explanation of his son's illness. He heard but one phrase in four and many of those were inexplicable to him. 'A progressively worsening condition,' he understood painfully well, but such terms as 'manic depressive' and the seriousness of 'hearing voices', as symptoms, meant nothing to the desolate old man.

To Sep, who knew his Bible, 'the voices' were simply Robert's demons – the outcome of the twin evils of jealousy and self-pity. Robert had been weak. He had succumbed to the temptations of his demons. His madness was, in part, a punishment for flying in the face of Providence.

When the doctor had gone, Sep stood at the back window and looked upon the row of willows lining the bank of the Cax. Three sons had once been his, gay little boys who had tumbled about the yard and moulded pastry in the bakehouse in their small fat hands.

One was long dead, one long-estranged, and now the last of the three was mad. Sep's life had been long and hard, but that moment by the window was the most desolate and despairing he had ever known.

13

New Horizons

EDWARD HEARD the news about Robert in a letter from his mother. He was deeply shocked, and very anxious about the effect this blow might have on his grandfather. He was thankful to know that his Aunt Kathy and John Bush were coping so ably with the restaurant, and glad to give permission to the faithful old employee to use his flat on the top floor. It would be some relief for Sep to know that there was someone reliable living on the premises.

He telephoned to the mental hospital that morning to hear how Robert was, but learnt very little more than his mother's letter had told him. He had the chance, however, of talking to the doctor in charge of the case, and asked to be kept informed of his progress, explaining his own relationship and his desire to do anything to spare the patient's very old father.

As he replaced the receiver Edward noted, with a start of surprise, how anxious he was. Robert had never been very close to him. They were eleven years and a generation apart. By temperament they were opposed, and resentment, which had no place in Edward's life, ruled his young uncle's. But this was a blow at the whole family, and Edward's reaction had been swift and instinctive. It was all very well to decide to cut loose, he admitted somewhat wryly to himself, but the old tag about blood being thicker than water held good, as this shock had proved.

He resolved to go to Caxley at the weekend to see how things were for himself. Sep was pathetically delighted with the surprise visit, and Edward was glad to find that he was taking Robert's illness so bravely.

'I should have insisted on getting medical advice earlier,' he told Edward. 'Robert is certainly having proper treatment now, and perhaps a spell away from us all will quicken his recovery.'

They talked of many things. Edward had never known him quite so forthcoming about the business. Perhaps he realised that Edward himself was now a keen and purposeful business man. It certainly amazed the younger man to realise how profitable the old-established shop and the newer restaurant were, and what a grasp his grandfather had of every small detail in running them. Since Robert's departure, trade had improved. There were now no staff troubles with Kathy and John Bush in charge, and after a long day visiting his mother and grandmother, Bertie and Kathy, Edward drove back to London very much happier in mind.

His own business affairs he found engrossing. He was now a partner in the firm, responsible chiefly for production and design. At his suggestion they had expanded their range of plastic kitchen equipment and were now experimenting with domestic refrigerators and larger deep-freeze receptacles for shops. This venture was proving amazingly successful and Edward found himself more and more absorbed and excited by the firm's development. Suddenly, after the apathy which had gripped him, he had found some purpose in life. He discovered a latent flair for design, an appreciation of line and form put to practical use, which gave him much inward satisfaction. The costing of a project had always interested him. He was, after all, the grandson of Bender North and Sep Howard, both men of business. He enjoyed planning a new design and then juggling with its economic possibilities. It was a fusion of two ways of thought and a new challenge every time it was undertaken.

He paid one or two visits to the continent to compare methods of production. He visited firms in Brussels and Paris who were engaged in much the same work as his own, and returned full of ideas. Jim and his father recognised that Edward was the most able of the three for this part of the business. His gaiety and charm, fast returning under the stimulus of new work, helped him to easy friendship. He had the ability to select ideas which could be adapted to their own business, and the power to explain them on his return to his partners. With Edward's drive, the firm was advancing rapidly.

In the early summer of 1947 Edward set off for a fortnight's visit to two firms in Milan. There were plumes of lilac blowing in the suburban gardens as the train rumbled towards the coast, and the girls were out and about in their pretty summer frocks. Edward approved of this 'new look' which brought back full skirts, neat waists, and gave women back the attractive curves which had been lost in the square military styles of wartime fashion. It was good to see colour and life returning to war-scarred England, to watch new houses being built, and see fresh paint brightening the old ones. There was hope again in the air, and the breezy rollicking tunes of the new musical *Oklahoma* exactly caught the spirit of the times – the looking-ahead of a great people to a future full of promise.

From Milan he made the long train journey to Venice, there

to spend the last few days meeting an Italian industrial designer who lived there, and sight-seeing. From the moment that he emerged from the station into the pellucid brilliance of Venetian sunlight, he fell under the city's spell. The quality of the light, which revealed the details of brickwork and carving, exhilarated him. To take a gondola to one's hotel, instead of a prosaic bus or taxi, was wholly delightful. If only he could stay four months instead of four days!

His hotel was an agreeable one just off St Mark's Square. He looked from his window upon a gondola station. There were twenty or more black high-prowed beauties jostling together upon the water. Their owners were busy mopping and polishing, shouting, laughing and gesticulating. Edward liked their energy, their raffish good looks and the torrents of words of which he only understood one in ten.

Picturesque though the scene was he was to find that its position had its drawbacks. The noise went on until one or two in the morning and began again about six. Luckily, Edward, healthily tired with walking about this enchanted place, did not lose much sleep.

On the last morning he awoke with a start. He was in the grip of some inexplicable fear. He found himself bathed in perspiration and his mind was perturbed with thoughts of Robert. He tossed back the bed clothes and lay watching the trembling reflections of the sun on water flickering across the ceiling. Against this undulating background he could see the face of Robert – a sad, haunted face, infinitely moving.

Outside, the gondoliers exchanged voluble jests in the bright Italian sunshine. The waters of Venice lapped against the walls and slapped the bottoms of the gondolas rhythmically. An Italian tenor poured forth a cascade of music from someone's wireless set.

But Edward was oblivious of his surroundings. In that instant he was hundreds of miles away in the cool early dawn of an English market square. What was happening at home?

After breakfast he felt calmer. He packed his bags and paid his bill, glad to be occupied with small everyday matters and telling himself that he had simply suffered from a nightmare. But the nagging horror stayed with him throughout the long journey to England, and as soon as he arrived he rang his Uncle Bertie for news.

'Bad, I'm afraid,' said Bertie's voice, 'as you'll see when my letter arrives. Robert was found dead in the hospital grounds. They think he had a heart attack. We'll know more later.'

'When was this?' asked Edward.

Bertie told him. He must have died, thought Edward, as he had suspected, at the moment when he himself awoke so tormentedly in the hotel bedroom.

This uncanny experience had a lasting effect upon Edward's outlook. Hitherto impatient of anything occult, he, the least psychic of men, had discovered that not all occurrences could be rationally explained. It was to make him more sympathetic in the years to come and more humble in his approach to matters unseen.

Robert's tragic death had another effect on Edward's future. Unknown to him, Sep, when his first grief had passed, crossed the market square to enter the offices of Lovejoy and Lovejoy, his solicitors. There, the will which he had drafted so long ago was drastically revised, and when Sep returned to the bakery he was well content.

*   *   *

It was about this time that Edward heard that his ex-wife Angela had had a son by Billy Sylvester, her second husband. Edward was glad to hear the news. It should make Angela a happier person. Despite the misery which she had inflicted upon him, Edward felt no resentment. He soberly faced the fact that he could not exempt himself from blame. They had never had much in common, and it was largely physical attraction which had drawn them together. Now, with the baby to think of, she would have some interest in the future. Nevertheless, Edward felt a pang when he thought about the child. He might have had a son of his own if things had worked out.

But domesticity did not play much part in his present affairs, although he enjoyed running the little flat. He took most of his meals out, and he grew increasingly fond of London. His life-long love of the theatre could now be indulged, and by a lucky chance he was able to meet a number of theatrical people.

His Aunt Mary, younger sister of Bertie and his mother Winnie, and the acknowledged beauty of the family, had a small part in a well-written light comedy which had already run for eight months and looked as though it were settled in the West End for another two years. It was one of those inexplicable successes. No great names glittered in the cast, the play itself was not outstanding; but it was gay, the dialogue crisp, the settings and the costumes ravishing. It was just what theatre-goers seemed to want, and Aunt Mary hoped that they would continue to do so.

Edward took her out on several occasions after the show. He had always enjoyed her company, and found something exhilarating in the mixture of North common-sense, typified by his good-humoured Uncle Bertie, and the racy sophistication which her mode of life had added to it.

Two husbands, little-mourned, lay in Aunt Mary's past. Many good friends of both sexes enlivened her present. She often brought one or more to Edward's supper parties, and he grew very fond of this animated company of friends, admiring the outward nonchalance which masked the resilience and dedication necessary to survive the ruthless competition of the stage world. They had something in common with business men, Edward decided. They needed to be long-sighted, ambitious and capable of grasping opportunity when it came. And, when times were hard, they must show the world a brave face to inspire confidence.

He liked to take out one or two of the pretty girls occasionally. It was good to laugh again, to be amused and to amuse in turn. He began to realise how little feminine company he had enjoyed. The war, early marriage, and the restrictions put upon him whilst awaiting his divorce, had combined with his temporary inner weariness to make him solitary. But although he enjoyed their company, there was not one among them with whom he would like to spend the rest of his days. The fact that they were equally heart-whole rendered them the more attractive.

More disturbing were the attentions of one of the girls who shared the flat above his own. As time passed, they had become better acquainted. Edward had used their telephone one evening when his own was out of order. He had stayed to coffee. Some evenings later they came to have a drink. From these small beginnings, not greatly encouraged by Edward, who enjoyed his domestic privacy, came more frequent visits by the girls.

Susan was engaged to a monosyllabic mountain of muscle who played Rugby football regularly on Wednesdays and

Saturdays, and squash or badminton in between to keep him-self fit for his place in the front row of the forwards. It was Elizabeth who was the more persistent of the two. She was small and dark, with an engaging cackling laugh, and Edward enjoyed her occasional company.

It was Elizabeth who called from the window, when he was gardening, offering him a drink. It was she who took in the parcels and delivered them to Edward when he returned from the office. And when he took to his bed with a short sharp bout of influenza it was Elizabeth who offered to telephone for the doctor and brought aspirins and drinks.

Edward, engrossed in his expanding business and intrigued with Aunt Mary's friends, had little idea of Elizabeth's growing affection. She was ardently stage-struck, and when she knew that Edward sometimes met people connected with the theatre, she grew pink with excitement. Edward found her touchingly young and unsophisticated. He invited her to come with him one evening to Aunt Mary's play, and to meet her afterwards.

It was a warm spring evening with London at its most seductive. A lingering sunset turned the sky to amethyst and turquoise. The costers' barrows were bright with daffodils, tulips and the first mimosa. In the brilliant shop windows, Easter brides trailed satin and lace. Hats as frothy as whipped egg-white, or as colourful as a handful of spring flowers, attracted the bemused window-gazers.

The play seemed to improve as its run lengthened, Edward thought. Aunt Mary queened it as becomingly as ever in all three acts. She was at her most sparkling afterwards at supper and brought a famous couple with her to dazzle Edward's young friend.

Later, while Edward was dancing with the actress and her husband was at the other side of the room talking with a friend, she watched Elizabeth's fond gaze follow Edward's handsome figure round the floor. He certainly was a personable young man, thought Aunt Mary, with family pride. He would have had a fine stage presence if he had cared to take up the profession.

'How well Edward fits into this sort of life,' said Elizabeth sighing. 'You can see that he loves London, and people, and a gay time.'

Aunt Mary, whose bright blue eyes missed nothing, either around her or in the human heart, seized her opportunity.

'I don't think you know Edward very well. He seems happy enough in town at the moment, but his roots are elsewhere. He doesn't know it yet himself, but Caxley will pull him back again before long. Of that I'm positive.'

'How can you say that?' protested Elizabeth. She looked affronted and hurt. 'What would Edward find in a poky little country town?'

'Everything worthwhile,' replied Aunt Mary composedly. 'He's his two Caxley grandfathers rolled into one, with a strong dash of my darling brother Bertie thrown in. That mixture is going to make a Caxley patriarch one day out of our dashing young Edward!'

'I don't believe it,' replied Elizabeth.

'Wait another ten years or so and you'll see,' promised Aunt Mary. But she felt quite certain that the pretty young thing beside her would not be prepared to wait at all. The rôle of country mouse would never do for her.

And that, thought Aunt Mary in her wisdom, was exactly as it should be.

14

Interlude in Ireland

WHILE EDWARD enjoyed the spring in London, the good people of Caxley greeted the returning warmth just as heartily. At Rose Lodge, the clumps of daffodils and pheasant-eyed narcissi which Bender had planted, so long ago, were in splendid bloom. Bertie's garden, close by the Cax, was vivid with grape hyacinths and crocuses beneath the budding trees. Even Sep's small flagged yard, behind the bakehouse, sported a white-painted tub of early red tulips, put there by Kathy's hand.

Pale-pink sticks of rhubarb with yellow topknots, the first pullets' eggs and bunches of primroses graced the market stalls. People were buying bright packets of flower seeds and discussing the rival merits of early potatoes. Felt hats were brushed and put away on top shelves, and straw ones came forth refurbished with new ribbon and flowers.

In the wide fields around Caxley the farmers were busy drilling and planting. Dim lights shone from lonely shepherds' huts as lambing continued. Along the hedges the honeysuckle and hawthorn put out their rosettes and fans of green, among the tattered tassels of the hazel catkins, and hidden beneath, the blue and white violets gave out the exquisite scent of spring from among their heart-shaped leaves.

Bertie, driving his mother to Beech Green one spring afternoon to visit her sister Ethel Miller, noticed the encourag-

155

ing sights and sounds with a great sense of comfort. He always enjoyed being in this familiar countryside and remembered the long bicycle rides which he and the Howard brothers took when these same lanes were white with chalky dust and most of the traffic was horse-drawn.

It grieved him to see the new estates going up on the slopes flanking Caxley. People must be housed, but the gracelessness of the straight roads, the box-like structures packed too closely together, the narrow raw strips of gardens and the complete lack of privacy, saddened him. He would hate to have to live in a house like that, he thought, passing one garishly-painted one with a board outside saying: SHOW HOUSE, and he guessed that many future occupants would feel the same way, but be forced by circumstances to make the best of a bad job. It seemed to Bertie that for so little extra cost and care something lovely might have been built upon the fields he remembered, to give pleasure and pride to the dwellers there as well as to the town as a whole. As it was, this new development, in Bertie's opinion, was nothing but an eyesore and, as a block of houses embellished with moulded concrete weatherboarding came into view, he put his foot heavily on the accelerator to reach the sanctuary of leafy lanes beyond, unaltered since his boyhood.

It was good to arrive at the old farmhouse. Nothing seemed to have changed in the square panelled room which the Millers still called 'the parlour', and through the windows the copper beech, pink with young leaf, lifted its arms against the background of the mighty downs. Only such an observant eye as Bertie's would notice significant details of a fast-changing way of farming. Sacks of chemical fertiliser were stacked in a nearby barn. Strange new machinery had its place beside the old harvest binder which Bertie remembered his Uncle Jesse buying at a distant sale. Jesse's sons, it seemed, were abreast of modern methods.

The two old ladies gossiped of family affairs. There had been a letter that morning from Joan in Dublin.

'She's invited Edward to visit them later in the summer. That's the best of having a hotel, isn't it?'

'It could work both ways,' Bertie pointed out, amused at his mother's matter-of-fact approach. 'Suppose all your relations wanted to come for the summer. You wouldn't make much profit, would you?'

'Don't be tiresome, dear,' said his mother automatically, in the tone she had used ever since he could remember. Bertie smiled, and sampled his aunt's gingerbread in contented silence.

'Will he go?' asked Ethel. 'Who knows? He might meet a nice Irish girl.'

'Heaven forbid, Ethel! We've had quite enough mixed marriages in our family as it is!'

'They're not *all* Catholics over there,' said her sister with asperity. 'I know very well that quite a few of them are Christians.'

'You mean *Protestants*, surely, Aunt Ethel,' put in Bertie mildly. The old lady looked at him frostily and then transferred her gaze to her sister.

'That boy of yours, Hilda,' she observed severely, 'interrupts his elders and betters even more than he used to.'

'I'm so sorry,' said Bertie with due humility, and sat back with his gingerbread to play the rôle of listener only.

But, driving home again through the thickening twilight, Mrs North said:

'You musn't mind what Ethel says, dear.'

'I don't, mamma,' replied Bertie calmly.

'She's getting old, you know, and a little peculiar in her ways.'

Bertie was about to say that Ethel was some years younger than she was herself, but had the sense to hold his tongue.

'Fancy suggesting that Edward might marry an *Irish* girl!' There was an outraged air about this remark which amused Bertie. If Aunt Ethel had suggested that Edward was considering marriage with an aborigine, his mamma could not have sounded more affronted.

'Irish girls are quite famous for their charm and good looks,' said Bertie. 'But I don't think you need to worry about Edward. No doubt he can find a wife when he wants one.'

'If ever!' snapped old Mrs North shortly. Bridling, she turned to watch the hedges flying by, and spoke no more until Bertie deposited her again at Rose Lodge.

The invitation to Ireland pleased Edward mightily. He missed his sister Joan, for despite their promises to visit each other, various reasons had prevented them from meeting and it was now eighteen months since they had seen each other.

Business affairs would keep Edward ceaselessly engaged for the next two or three months, but he promised to cross to Ireland during the last week of August. It would be his first visit to a country which had always intrigued him. He hoped, if he could arrange matters satisfactorily at the factory, to go on from Dublin to see something of the west coast. He looked forward eagerly to the trip.

When the time came he set off in high spirits. He was to make the crossing from Holyhead to Dun Laoghaire, and as the train rattled across Wales, Edward thought how little he knew of the countries which marched with his own. The war had fettered him, and for the last few years London had claimed him, apart from the occasional business trip abroad. Catching glimpses of Welsh mountains, and tumbling rivers so different from the placid Cax of home, he made up his mind that he would explore Wales and Scotland before he grew much older.

He slept soundly during the night crossing, and awoke to find the mailboat rocking gently in the great harbour of Dun Laoghaire, or Kingstown, as the old people at home still called it. Beyond the massive curves of the granite breakwaters, the little town basked in the morning sunshine. Gulls screamed above the glittering water. A maid twirled a mop from a window of the Royal Marine Hotel. A train, with a plume of smoke, chugged along the coast to Dublin. Edward's first glimpse of Ireland did not disappoint him.

He breakfasted aboard before meeting Joan and Michael who had driven the seven miles from Dublin to meet him.

'You both look younger – and fatter!' cried Edward with delight.

'It's Irish air and Irish food,' replied Joan. 'You see! You'll be twice the man at the end of your holiday.'

There was so much news to exchange on the drive to Dublin that Edward scarcely noticed his surroundings; but the soft, warm Irish air on his cheeks was strange and delicious.

Michael's father had died recently but his mother still made her home with them. Edward found her a gentler edition of his grandmother North, with some deafness which rendered her endearingly vague. Sarah, not yet two years old, with red curls and a snub nose, flirted outrageously with her uncle from the instant they met. She was in the care of a good-looking young nursemaid whose broad Irish speech Edward found entirely incomprehensible. She was equally incapable of understanding Edward, and for the duration of his stay they relied on smiles, and occasional interpretation from the family, for communication.

The hotel was small, but well-placed in one of the quiet streets near Stephen's Green. Joan and Michael worked hard here and the business was thriving. Edward explored Dublin, mainly on his own, browsing at the bookstalls along the quays by the River Liffey, and admiring the hump-backed bridges which crossed its broad waters. Michael took time off from his duties to show him Trinity College, not far from the hotel, and Edward thought that the vast eighteenth-century library, its sombre beauty lit by slanting rays of sunlight, was one of the most impressive places he had ever seen.

On the third morning Joan received a letter which she read at the breakfast table with evident satisfaction.

'She can come. Isn't that good?' she said to her husband.

'Maisie Hunter,' she told Edward. 'She's staying with an aunt in Belfast and said she would come down if she could manage it. She's arriving tomorrow by train.'

Although Edward liked Maisie, he felt a slight pang of regret. He was so much enjoying his present circumstances in this new place and among the friendly people who always seemed to have time to stop and talk with a curious stranger. At the moment he was content to forget Caxley and all its inmates.

He chided himself for such selfishness and offered to meet Joan's friend at the station.

'Take the car,' said Michael. 'She's bound to have a mountain of luggage.'

But all Maisie carried were two neat matching cases when Edward first saw her, in the distance, stepping from the train. She was thinner than he remembered her, and her brown hair, which used to hang to her shoulders, was now short and softly curled. It suited her very well, thought Edward, hurrying to meet her. Her obvious surprise delighted him.

'I'd no idea you were here! What a nice surprise.'

Her smile was warm, lighting up her sun-tanned face and grey eyes. No one could call Maisie Hunter a beauty: her features were not regular enough for such a description, but her skin and hair were perfect, and she had a vivacity of expression, combined with a low and lovely voice, which made her most attractive. Edward was now whole-heartedly glad to see her again.

'I've had a standing invitation to visit Joan,' she explained, as they drove towards Stephen's Green, 'and this seemed the right time to come. My aunt has her son and daughter arriving for a week's stay. But I didn't realise that I was interrupting a family reunion.'

Edward assured her truthfully that they were all delighted that she had come, and constituted himself as guide on this her first visit to Dublin.

'A case of the blind leading the blind,' he added, drawing up outside the hotel. 'But it's amazing how ready people are to drop what they are doing and take you wherever you want to go. Time stands still over here. That's Ireland's attraction to me.'

'You know what they say? "God made all the time in the world, and left most of it in Ireland." Now, where's my god-daughter?'

The next two or three days passed pleasantly. Edward and Maisie discovered the varied delights of Phoenix Park, revelling in the long walks across the windy central plain, watching the fine racehorses exercise and the little boys flying their kites in the warm summer breezes.

It was Michael who suggested that they took his car and set off to explore the western part of Ireland.

'I've a good friend who has a little pub on the shores of Lough Corrib,' he told them. 'There's no such modern nonsenses as telephones there, but tell him I sent you. He'll find room for you, without doubt. and the views there will charm your hearts from your breasts.'

Michael, waxing lyrical in the Celtic fashion, always amused Edward. Ireland was the finest place in the world, Michael maintained, and it was a positive sin not to see as much of its glories as possible during Edward's short stay. Persuaded, the two set out in the borrowed car, promising to return in a few days.

Edward had envisaged hiring a car and making this journey on his own. He had secretly looked forward to this solitary trip, stopping when and where he liked, sight-seeing or not as the mood took him. But now that he had a companion he found that he was enjoying himself quite as much. They were easy together, sometimes talking animatedly, sharing memories of Caxley characters, or sometimes content to relax in silence and watch the rolling green fields of Ireland's central plain slide past.

The welcome at 'The Star' was as warm as Michael had promised. It was a small whitewashed pub, set on a little knoll above the dark waters which reflected it. The sun was setting when they arrived, and long shadows streaked the calm surface of the lake. Edward thought that he had never seen such tranquillity. His bedroom window looked across an expanse of grass, close-cropped by a dozen or so fine geese, to the lake. Here and there on the broad waters were islets, misty-blue against the darkening sky. Moored against the bank were three white skiffs, and Edward made up his mind to take one in the morning to explore those secret magical places fast slipping into the veils of twilight.

But now the welcome scent of fried bacon and eggs came drifting from below, and he hurried down, trying to dodge the low beams which threatened his head, to find Maisie and their waiting meal.

Their brief holiday passed blissfully. They explored Galway and made a trip to the Aran Islands in driving rain, and lost their hearts, just as Michael said they would, to the sad grey-green mountains and the silver beaches of Connemara. But it was the waters of Lough Corrib, lapping beneath their windows at night and supplying them with the most delicious trout and salmon of their lives, which had the strongest allure.

On their last day they took a picnic and set off in the boat to row across to one of the many islands. Maisie was taking a turn at the oars and Edward, eyes screwed up against the dazzling sunshine, watched her square brown hands tugging competently and thought how much he would miss her. He had been happier in her company than he would have thought possible. He tried to explain to himself why this should be. Of course they had known each other, off and on, for almost ten years, so that they had slipped into this unexpected companionship with perfect ease. And then there was no tiresome coquetry about the girl, no playing on her feminity. She had tackled the long walks, the stony mountain tracks, and the quagmires too, with enthusiasm and with no useless grieving over ruined shoes. He remembered an occasion when they descended a steep muddy lane beside a tiny farm, lured by the distant prospect far below of a shining beach. Out of the cottage had run a stout Irishwoman who threw up her hands in horror to see their struggles through the mud.

'Come away now,' she cried, 'and go down through our farm yard. You'll be destroyed that way!'

He laughed aloud at the memory.

'What now?' queried Maisie, resting on her oars. Bright drops slid down their length and plopped into the lake. He told her.

'Once when I was out with Philip,' she began animatedly, and then stopped. Edward watched her expression change swiftly from gaiety to sadness. This was the first time that she had mentioned her dead fiance's name. They had not talked of their past at all during these few lovely days.

She looked away across the lake and spoke in a low but steady voice, as though she had made up her mind to speak without restraint.

'Once when I was out with Philip,' she repeated, and continued with the anecdote. But Edward did not hear it. He was too engrossed with his own thoughts. From his own experience, he guessed that this moment was one of great advance for Maisie's progress towards full recovery from her grief. If Ireland had been able to thaw the ice which held her heart, then that alone would make this holiday unforgettable.

He became conscious that she was silent, and smiling at him.

'You haven't heard a word, have you?' she asked. 'Don't fib. I don't mind. D'you know that something wonderful has just happened to me?'

'Yes,' said Edward gently. 'I can guess.'

'I've never spoken about him. I couldn't. But somehow, here, with nothing but lake and sky, it seems easy. My family mind so much for me, I don't dare to talk of it. I can't face the emotion it brings forth.'

'I've had my share of that,' replied Edward. 'Someone – I think it was Uncle Bertie – told me once that it's the hardest thing in the world to receive pity. The damnable thing is that it takes so many forms – and all of them hell for the victim.'

He found himself telling the girl about his own family's attitude to his broken marriage, and the comfort he had found in his solitary life.

'We've been lucky in having that,' agreed Maisie. 'My Caxley flat has been a haven. I should have gone mad if I had been living at home. There's a lot to be said for a single existence. Wasn't it Katherine Mansfield who said that living alone had its compensations? And that if you found a hair in your honey it was a comfort to know it was your own?'

An oar slipped from its rowlock and the boat rocked.

'Here, let me row for a bit,' said Edward, restored to the present. They crept gingerly past each other exchanging places, and Edward pulled steadily towards the nearest island.

They picnicked on salmon and cucumber sandwiches and hard-boiled eggs, afterwards lying replete in the sun. A moor-hen piped from the reeds nearby. The sun was warm upon their closed eyes. A little breeze shivered upon the surface of the lake and ruffled their hair.

'Damn going back,' said Edward lazily. 'I could stay here for ever.'

'Me too,' said Maisie ungrammatically. 'I feel quite different. You've been a great help, letting me talk about Philip. It was a thousand pities we never married, in more ways than one. Somehow one tends to build up a sort of deity from the person one's lost, and I think that is wrong. If we'd had a few years of married ups and downs perhaps I should have been able to bear it more bravely.'

'In some ways,' said Edward, 'you miss them more.' He remembered, with sharp poignancy, the perfume which Angela had used and how terribly it had affected him after their parting.

He propped himself on one elbow and looked down upon his companion. She looked very young and vulnerable, a long grass clamped between her teeth, her eyes shut against the sunlight. She'd had a tough road to travel, just as he had. Fortunately, he was further along that stony track, and knew that, in the end, it grew easier. He tried to tell her this.

'It gets better, you know, as you go on. All that guff about Time, the Great Healer, which irritates one so when one's still raw – well, it's perfectly true. I've just got out of the let-me-lick-my-wounds-in-solitude state, which you're still in, and all the things which wise old people like Sep told me are coming true. Hope comes back, and purpose, and a desire to do some-thing worthwhile – and, best of all, the perfectly proper feeling that it is *right* to be happy, and not to feel guilty when cheerfulness breaks in.'

Maisie opened her grey eyes, threw aside the grass and smiled at him.

'Dear Edward,' she said, 'you are an enormous comfort.'

They returned reluctantly to Dublin. Edward was to go back the next day to England. Maisie was going to her aunt's for a little longer.

'When do you go back to Caxley?' asked Edward, through the car window as Michael prepared to drive him to the station.

'Term starts on September the twelfth,' said Maisie. 'A Thursday. I'll probably go back on Tuesday or Wednesday.'

'I shall be down on Friday evening for the weekend,' said Edward with decision. 'Keep it free. Promise?'

'Promise,' nodded Maisie, as the car drove away.

15

Edward and Maisie

URING THE golden autumn months that followed Edward's visit to Ireland, work at the factory quickened its pace. Edward was as enthusiastic and conscientious as ever, but it did not escape the eyes of his partners that all his weekends were now spent at Caxley.

Elizabeth, in the flat above, watched Edward's car roar away early on Saturday mornings, or sometimes on Friday evenings, when pressure of work allowed. Aunt Mary, it seemed, was right when she predicted that Caxley would pull her attractive nephew homeward. What was she like, Elizabeth wondered, this Caxley girl who had succeeded where she had failed?

Not that she cared very much, she told herself defiantly. There were just as good fish in the sea, and the thought of spending her life in a tin-pot little dump like Caxley appalled her.

If Edward wanted to bury himself alive in a place like that, then she was glad that nothing had come of their affair. It was only, she admitted wistfully, that he was so extraordinarily handsome, and made such a wonderful escort. Meanwhile, it was no good grieving over her losses. Sensibly, she turned her attention to the other young men in her life. They might not have quite the same high standard of good looks and general eligibility as dear, lost Edward, but they were certainly more attainable.

In Caxley, of course, the tongues wagged briskly. The Howards had provided gossip of one sort or another for generations. There was that deliciously spicy affair of Sep's wife Edna's, the Caxley folk reminded each other, when Dan Crockford painted her portrait and the shameless hussy had sat for it *unchaperoned*. True, she was fully dressed, they added, with some disappointment in their tones, but Sep had been very upset about it at the time. It had happened years ago, in the reign of King Edward the Seventh in fact, but was still fresh in the memories of many old stalwarts of the market square.

Sep's rise in fortune was remembered too, and the buying of Bender North's old property, but there were few who grudged Sep his success. He bore himself modestly and his high principles were respected. Besides, he had faced enough trouble in his life with the death of his first-born in the war, and the goings-on of his second son Leslie. It must be hard to banish one's child, as Sep had done. Did he ever regret it, they asked each other? And then this last tragedy of poor Robert's! What a burden Sep had carried to be sure!

But this latest tit-bit was a pleasant one. It was a pity, of course, that Maisie Hunter was not a true-bred Caxley girl, but only a war-time arrival. On the other hand, as one pointed out to her neighbour over the garden hedge, a bit of fresh blood worked wonders in these old inter-married families of Caxley. And say what you like, if Maisie Hunter had chosen to stay all these years in Caxley, it proved that she had good sense and that she was worthy to marry into their own circle. It was to be hoped, though, that the children would take after Edward for looks. Maisie Hunter was *healthy* enough, no doubt, but certainly no oil painting – too skinny by half.

Thus flowed the gossip, but one important point was over-looked by the interested bystanders. It was taken for granted that Maisie Hunter would accept such a fine suitor with alacrity. The truth was that Edward's ardent and straight-forward wooing was meeting with severe set-backs. Maisie was beset with doubts and fears which were as surprising to Edward as they were painful to the girl herself.

Was he truly in love with her, or simply ready for domesti-city? Was he prompted by pity for her circumstances? The questions beat round and round in her brain, and she could find no answer.

She wondered about her own response. In the solitude of the little flat which had become so dear to her, she weighed the pros and cons of the step before her, in a tumult of confusion. She was now twenty-nine, and Edward was two years older. There was a lot to give up if she married. She was at the peak of a career she enjoyed. The idea of financial dependence was a little daunting, and she would hate to leave Caxley. She was not at all sure that she wanted to embark on the troubled seas of motherhood as soon as she married, and yet it would be best for any children they might have to start a family before she and Edward were much older.

And then, to be a *second* wife was so much more difficult than to be a *first*. Marriage, for Edward, had been such an unhappy episode. Could she make him as happy as he deserved to be? Would he secretly compare her with his first wife? Would he find her equally disappointing and demanding? Wouldn't it be safer if they didn't marry after all, she wondered, in despair?

It had all been so much simpler when she had become

engaged to Philip. They had both been very young. Love, marriage, and children had seemed so simple and straightforward then. Now everything was beset with doubts and complications. Philip's death had shaken her world so deeply, that any decision was difficult to make. Edward's patience with her vacillations made her feel doubly guilty. It was not fair to subject him to such suspense, but she could not commit herself while she was so tormented.

Thus the autumn passed for Maisie in a strange blur of intense happiness and horrid indecision. Edward came to see her each weekend, and often she travelled to London to meet him after school. In his company she was at peace, but as soon as she returned to Caxley the nagging questions began again. The Howards and Norths were dismayed at the delay in Edward's plans. It was quite apparent that he was in love. What on earth could Maisie be thinking of to shilly-shally in this way? Wasn't their Edward good enough for her?

November fogs shrouded the market square. The Cax flowed sluggishly, reflecting sullen skies as grey as pewter. People hurried home to their firesides, looked out hot-water bottles, took to mufflers, complained of rheumatic twinges, and faced the long winter months with resignation. The gloom was pierced on November 14 that year by the news of the birth of a son to the Princess Elizabeth. The church bells rang in the market square, and from village towers and steeples in the countryside around. Their joyous clamour was in Maisie's ears as she pushed a letter to Joan into the pillar box at the corner of the market place.

It had taken her a long time to write, but even longer to

decide if it should be written at all. But it was done, and now relief flooded her. All the things which she had been unable to tell Edward, she had written to his sister, and she begged for advice as unbiased as possible in the circumstances. Maisie respected Joan's good sense. In these last few agitated weeks, she had longed to talk with her, to discuss her doubts with someone of her own sex, age and background.

She awaited the reply from Ireland with as much patience as she could muster. No doubt Joan would take as much time and trouble with her answer as she herself had taken in setting out her problems. As the days passed, she began to wonder if it had been kind to press Joan on the matter. After all, she was an exceptionally busy person, and young Sarah took much of her attention.

At last the letter came. Maisie sped to the door, her breakfast coffee untasted. It lay, a square white envelope with the Irish stamp, alone on the door mat. Trembling, Maisie bent to pick it up. It was thin and light. Obviously, whatever message Joan sent was going to prove terse and to the point. She tore it open. Joan's neat handwriting covered only one side of the paper.

'You darling ass,
    All your ifs and buts are on Edward's account, I notice. Let him shoulder his own worries, if he has any, which I doubt – and please say "Yes." Go ahead and just be happy, both of you.
                        All our love,
                            Joan'
P.S. Dr Kelly has just confirmed our hopes. Prepare for a christening next April.'

Suddenly, the bleak November morning seemed flooded with warmth and light. This was exactly the right sort of message to receive – straightforward, loving and wise. How terrible, Maisie realised, it would have been to receive a long screed putting points for and against the marriage – merely a prolongation of the dreary debate which had bedevilled her life lately. Joan had summed up the situation at once, had recognised the nervous tension which grew more intense as time passed and had made Maisie's decision impossible. In a few lines she had pointed out something simple and fundamental to which worry had blinded her friend. Edward knew what he was undertaking. Maisie recalled his saying one evening, with a wry smile: 'You might give me credit for some sense. I've thought about it too, you know.'

She folded the letter, put it in her handbag like a talisman, and set off, smiling, for school.

'No long engagements for us,' said Edward firmly next weekend. 'You might change your mind again, and that I couldn't face.'

They had spent the winter afternoon visiting the family to tell them of their engagement and their future plans.

At Rose Lodge it was Grandma North who received the news with the greatest display of excitement.

'At last, a wedding in St Peter's!' she exclaimed, clapping her thin papery old hands together. Edward shook his head.

'Afraid not. For one thing we neither of us want it. And I don't think our vicar would relish a divorced man at his altar.'

'Not a church wedding?' faltered the old lady. 'Oh, what a disappointment! Really, it does seem hard!'

She rallied a little, and her mouth took on the obstinate curve which Edward knew so well.

'I'll have a word with the vicar myself, dear boy. Bender and I worked for the church all our lives, and the least he can do is to put on a nice little wedding service for our grandson.' She spoke as if the vicar would be arranging a lantern lecture in the church hall – something innocuous and sociable – with coffee and Marie biscuits to follow.

Edward broke into laughter. His grandmother began to pout, and he crossed the room in three strides and kissed her heartily. Unwillingly, she began to smile, and Winnie, watching them both, thought how easily Edward managed the wilful old lady whose autocratic ways grew more pronounced and embarrassing as the years passed.

'No, no church this time, but a wonderful wedding party at Sep's. He's already planning the cake decorations, and we shall expect your prettiest bonnet on the day.'

Mrs North appeared mollified, and turned her attention to more practical matters concerning linen, silver and china. It was clear that she was going to be busily engaged in the wedding preparations from now on.

And this time, thought Winnie, her eyes upon Edward and Maisie, there is happiness ahead. For a fleeting moment she remembered her first encounter with Angela, and the dreadful premonition of disaster to come. Now, just as deeply, she felt that this time all would be well for them both.

Sep too, had shared the same feeling when he had held their hands that afternoon and congratulated them.

'Dear boy, dear boy!' he repeated, much moved. His welcome to Maisie was equally warm. He had known and liked her for many years now. She would make Edward a good wife.

He accompanied them down the stairs from his parlour above the shop and said good-bye to them in front of the bow windows which displayed the delicious products of his bakehouse at the back. When they were out of sight, he glanced across at the fine windows above his restaurant across the square. Would Edward ever return there, he wondered? Would his children gaze down one day upon the varied delights of market day, as Edward had done, and his friend Bender's children had done, so long ago, when horses had clip-clopped across the cobbles and Edward the Seventh was on the throne?

He turned to look with affection at that monarch's mother, small and dignified, surveying the passing traffic from her plinth.

'No one like her,' exclaimed Sep involuntarily. 'No one to touch her, before or since.'

Two schoolgirls, chewing toffee, giggled together and nudged each other. What a silly old man, talking to himself! They passed on, unseen by Sep.

He entered the shop, glad to be greeted by its fragrant warmth after the raw cold outside. For four reigns now he had served in this his own small kingdom. Sometimes, lately, he had wondered if he could rule for much longer, but now, with Edward's good news ringing in his ears, he felt new strength to face the future.

'I'll take some crumpets for tea,' he said to the assistant behind the scrubbed counter.

He mounted the stairs slowly, bearing his paper bag to Miss

Taggerty. This, after all, he told himself, was the right way for a baker to celebrate.

The wedding was to be in January, and meanwhile Edward searched for a house or a larger flat than the one in which he now lived. Maisie accompanied him as often as her school work would allow.

It was a dispiriting task. New houses had gone up in abundance near Edward's factory, but neither he nor Maisie could face their stark ugliness, the slabs of raw earth waiting to be transformed into tiny gardens and the complete lack of privacy. Older houses, in matured gardens, never seemed to be for sale.

Back in Edward's little flat after an exhausting foray, Maisie kicked off her shoes and gazed round the room.

'What's wrong with this?' she asked.

'Why, nothing,' said Edward, 'except that it's hardly big enough for one, let alone two.'

'We haven't seen anything as comfortable as this,' replied Maisie. 'I'll be happy here, if you will. Let's start here anyway. If it becomes impossible we'll think again – but I simply can't look at any more places just now. I can't think why we didn't settle for this in the first place.'

Edward agreed, with relief. It might not be ideal, but the flat was quiet with an outlook upon grass and trees, and it would be simple for Maisie to run. He would like to have found something more splendid for his new wife, but their recent expeditions had proved daunting, to say the least. Maybe, in time, they could move much further away, to the pleasant greenness of Buckinghamshire, perhaps, where property was attractive and the daily journey to work would not be too arduous. Meanwhile, Edward's tiny flat, refurbished a little by Maisie, would be their first home.

There was snow on the ground on their wedding day, but the sun shone from a pale-blue cloudless sky. Steps and window sills were edged with white, and the pigeon's coral feet made hieroglyphics on the snowy pavements. Edward and Maisie emerged from the registrar's office into the market place, dazzled with the sunshine, the snow and their own happiness.

'I suppose,' said Mrs North to Bertie, as they followed the pair, 'that it's *legal*. I mean they *really are* married?'

'Perfectly legal, mamma,' Bertie assured her.

'It seems so *quick*,' protested the old lady. 'I do so hope you're right, Bertie. It would be terrible for them to find they were living in sin.'

The registrar, coming upon the scene and overhearing this remark, gave a frosty bow and marched stiffly away.

'Now you've offended him,' said Bertie, smiling.

'Hm!' snorted the old lady, unrepentant. 'Marrying people without even a surplice! Small wonder he hurries away!'

It was a gay party that gathered in Sep's restaurant. The wedding cake stood on a table by the windows which overlooked the snowy garden. The dark waters of the Cax gleamed against the white banks, and a robin perching upon a twig peered curiously at the array of food inside the window.

Edward gazed contentedly about him. Sep and his grandmother were nodding sagely across the table. Her wedding hat was composed of velvet pansies in shades of blue and violet. She had certainly succeeded in finding a beauty, thought Edward affectionately.

His mother and Bertie were in animated conversation. Aunt Kathy, gorgeous in rose-pink, glowed at the corner of the table, her children nearby. If only Joan could have been here it would have been perfect, but he and Maisie were to see her before long as they returned from their honeymoon.

He turned to look at his new wife. She wore a soft yellow suit and looked unusually demure. He laughed and took her hand. Another Howard had joined the family in the market square.

Far away, the quiet waters of Lough Corrib reflected the bare winter trees growing at the lake side.

There was no snow here. A gentle wind rustled the dry reeds, and the three white skiffs lay upside down on the bank, covered by a tarpaulin for the winter. The grey and white geese converged upon the back door of the inn, necks outstretched, demanding food.

A plume of blue smoke curled lazily towards the winter sky. Timeless and tranquil, 'The Star' gazed at its reflection in the water, and awaited its guests.

16

Harvest Loaves

ONE BRIGHT Sunday morning in April, Sep awoke with a curious constriction in his chest. He lay still, massaging it gently with a small bony hand. He was not greatly perturbed. A man in his eighties expects a few aches and pains, and Sep had always made light of his ailments.

It was fortunate, he thought, that it was Sunday. On weekdays he continued to rise betimes, despite his family's protests, but on Sunday he allowed himself some latitude and Miss Taggerty prepared breakfast for eight o'clock.

Always, when he awoke, his first thoughts were of Edna. He lay now, remembering just such a shining morning, when he and Edna had taken the two boys for a picnic in the woods at Beech Green. Robert and Kathy were not born then, and Jim and Leslie had frisked before them like young lambs, along the lane dappled with sunshine and shadow. They had picked bunches of primroses, and eaten their sandwiches in a little clearing. Sep could see the young birch trees now, fuzzy with green-gold leaf. A pair of blackbirds had flown back and forth to their nestlings, and a young rabbit had lolloped across the clearing, its fur silvered and its translucent ears pink, in the bright sunshine.

Perhaps he remembered it so clearly, thought Sep, because they so rarely had a day out together. The shop had always come first. Edna must have found it a great tie sometimes, but he could not recall her complaining. She had been a wonderful wife. He missed her more and more. It was hard to grow old alone.

He sat up, suddenly impatient with his own self-pity, and a spasm of pain shot through him. It was so sharp and unexpected that he gasped in dismay. When it had abated a little, he lay back gingerly against the pillow. The bells of St Peter's were ringing for early service. It would soon be seven-thirty.

'Indigestion,' Sep told himself aloud. He tried to remember if he had eaten anything unusual on the previous day, but failed. His appetite was small, and he had never been in the habit of eating a heavy meal in the evening. Perhaps he had put too much sugar in his Horlicks. As he grew older he found himself becoming increasingly fond of sweet things. He must not be so self-indulgent.

He sat up carefully. The pain was dwindling, and he crossed slowly to the window. A few church-goers were mounting the steps of St Peter's. A milkman's float clanged and jangled on the opposite side of the square. It was a typical Sunday morning in Caxley – a scene which he had looked upon hundreds of times and always taken for granted.

But today, suddenly, it had a poignant significance for Sep. Would he see many more Sundays? Death must come soon, and he was unafraid – but Caxley was very dear, and hard to leave behind.

He shaved and dressed carefully in his sober Sunday suit in readiness for chapel, and in his mind there beat a line of poetry which he had heard only that week.

> *'Look thy last on all things lovely,*
> *Every hour—'*

It was good sense, Sep decided, descending the stairs slowly, as well as good poetry.

In the weeks that followed, the pain recurred. Sep found that his head swam sometimes when he bent down, or if he lifted a heavy pan in the bakehouse. He told no one of the disability, dismissing it as a passing ailment, unworthy of serious attention. He brushed aside Miss Taggerty's anxious enquiries. There was little affecting her master which her keen old eyes missed, but natural timidity kept her from expressing her fears to the rest of the family. Sep would brook no tale-telling, she knew well.

But the secret could not be kept for long. One warm May evening Sep set off along the tow path to see Kathy and Bertie. Half a dozen naked boys splashed and shouted by the further bank. Clouds of midges drifted above the river, and swallows swooped back and forth, like dark blue arrows. From the oak tree near Bertie's garden gate, minute green caterpillars jerked on their gossamer threads. It was sultry, with a mass of dark clouds building up menacingly on the horizon. Soon there would be thunder, and the boys would scramble for home, leaving the placid surface of the river to be pitted with thousands of drops.

Bertie was in his vegetable garden, spraying the black fly from his broad beans. Sep heard the rhythmic squish-squish of the syringe. Bertie was hidden from sight by a hawthorn hedge which divided the lawn from the kitchen garden. A blackbird flew out, squawking frenziedly, as Sep brushed the hedge. There were probably a dozen or more nests secreted in its length, Sep surmised, looking at it with interest. He turned to watch his son-in-law, still unaware of his presence, intent on washing away the sticky black pest.

Bertie wore well, he thought affectionately. His figure had thickened slightly, and his hair, still plentiful, had turned to silver. But his complexion was fresh and his blue eyes as bright as ever. He was becoming more like Bender as he grew older, but would never have the girth, or the bluster, of his father. Bender's ebullience had made Sep nervous at times. There was nothing to fear in his son.

At last he straightened up, and started when he saw Sep's slight figure at the end of the row.

'Good heavens! I didn't hear you arrive! How are you? Let me put this thing away and we'll go indoors.'

'No, no, my boy. Finish the job. There's rain on the way and there's no hurry on my account.'

Obediently, Bertie refilled his syringe and set off along the last row, Sep following. A flourishing plant of groundsel caught the old man's eye and he bent to pull it up. Immediately, the pain in his chest had him in its grip with such intensity that his head thumped. The rosette of groundsel, the damp earth and the pale green stalks of the bean plants whirled round and round together, growing darker and darker, as the blood pounded in his head.

Bertie ran to pick up the old man who was in a dead faint and gasping alarmingly. His cheek and the grey hair at one temple were muddied by the wet soil. With difficulty Bertie managed to lift him in his arms and limped towards the house, calling for Kathy. Sep was as light as a bird, Bertie noticed, despite his agitation – lighter by far than his own young son, Andrew.

They put him on the couch and Kathy ran for smelling salts, while Bertie chafed the frail hands and watched him anxiously.

'We must call the doctor,' he said. As he spoke, Sep opened his eyes and shook his head slowly and wearily.

'No. No doctor,' he whispered.

'Some brandy?' urged Bertie.

'No, thank you,' said Sep, with a touch of his old austerity. Bertie realised that he had blundered.

'Some tea then?'

Sep nodded and closed his eyes again. Kathy ran to the kitchen and Bertie followed her.

'Whatever he says, I'm ringing for the doctor. This is something serious, I feel sure.'

Within ten minutes the doctor had arrived. There was no demur from Sep who, with the tea untasted, lay frail and shrunken against Kathy's bright cushions, with a blanket tucked around him. The examination over, the doctor spoke with false heartiness.

'You'll see us all out, Mr Howard. Just a tired heart, but if you take care of yourself, you'll be as sound as a bell for years yet. I'll write you a prescription.'

Bertie accompanied him into the lane, well out of ear-shot.

'Tell me the truth, doctor. How is he?'

'As I said. If he takes his pills regularly and avoids excessive exercise, he can tick over for a few more years. Your job is to persuade him to take things easily.'

'That's one of the hardest things in the world to ask me to do, but I'll try. Should he spend the night here?'

'It would be best. Tell him to stay there until I call again in the morning.'

Sep submitted to the doctor's orders with unusual docility, and as soon as he was settled in Kathy's spare room Bertie hurried to the market square to tell the news to Miss Taggerty.

It grieved Sep, in the months that followed, to lead such a comparatively inactive life. True, he rose at the usual time and supervised the shop, the restaurant, and the bakehouse, as he had always done, but he walked from place to place more slowly now, and tried not to mount his steep stairs more than was necessary. The doctor had advised him to rest after his midday dinner, and now that the weather was warm, he took to sitting in the old arbour by the river at the rear of the restaurant. This had been his old friend Bender's favourite spot, and Sep had made sure that it was kept as spruce as Bender would have wished.

Jasmine starred and scented its rustic entrance, and an Albertine rose added its splendour. Kathy made the rough seat comfortable with cushions, and provided a footstool and rug. It was a perfect sun trap, and as she went about her affairs in the restaurant, she could watch Sep dozing in sheltered warmth, or gazing at his life-long companion, the river Cax.

The family called to see Sep more often than usual. Hilda North took to paying Sep an occasional afternoon visit. Winnie drove her down the hill from Rose Lodge and left her to keep the old man company while she shopped in the town.

The two old people, who shared so many common memories, were closer now than ever they had been, and as they took tea together in the arbour they enjoyed reminiscing about their early days in the market square when their children had played together in this same garden, and floated their toy boats on the river before them.

184

Edward and Maisie spent as many weekends in Caxley as they could, but both were busy, for Maisie had taken a part-time teaching post. Miss Hedges, the middle-aged headmistress who lived in a neighbouring flat, had soon discovered that Maisie was a trained teacher, and had no difficulty in persuading her to accompany her three mornings a week to school. Here Maisie helped children who were backward in reading and thoroughly enjoyed the work.

'But we don't call them "backward" these days, my dear,' said Miss Hedges with a twinkle. ' "Less able" is the most forthright term we are allowed to use in these namby-pamby times!'

Maisie was glad to be doing something worthwhile again. She and Edward were blissfully happy, but he was off to work before half-past eight, the tiny flat was set to rights soon after, and Maisie was beginning to find time hanging heavily on her hands when Miss Hedges had appeared. It was a happy arrangement for them all.

Maisie found her new life absorbing. She looked back now upon her doubts and fears with amusement and incredulity. How right Joan had been, and how lucky she was to have found Edward! They had much in common. As a Londoner, Maisie shared Edward's love of the theatre and they spent many evenings there. Aunt Mary, going from strength to strength as she became better known as a character actress, saw them frequently, and was loud in her approval of Edward's choice.

'And when are you going to Caxley?' she enquired one September evening, after the play. She was in her dressing-room removing make-up with rapid expert strokes.

'The weekend after next,' replied Edward.

'I meant for good,' said his aunt. She noted Edward's surprise.

'Hadn't really thought about it,' said Edward frankly. 'This job is growing daily, and the journey from Caxley would take too long. We're still hoping for a house in the country somewhere, but it will have to be nearer than Caxley.'

Aunt Mary did not pursue the subject. How it would come about she did not know, but in her bones she felt quite sure that Edward and his Maisie were destined for Caxley one day.

She rose from her seat before the dressing table and kissed them unexpectedly.

'Give the old place my love,' she said. 'And all the people who remember me there. Particularly Sep – yes, particularly Sep!'

The last Friday in September was as warm and golden as the harvest fields through which Edward and Maisie drove to Caxley. It had been a good crop this year and the weather had been favourable. Most of the fields were already cut, and the bright stubble bristled cleanly in the sunshine.

Winnie was staking Michaelmas daisies in the garden of Rose Lodge when they arrived. Edward thought how well she looked, and his grandmother too, as they sipped their sherry and exchanged news.

'And Sep?' asked Edward.

'Fairly well,' said his grandmother. 'I had tea with him yesterday afternoon and he's looking forward to seeing you.'

'I'll go and have a word with him now,' said Edward. 'Coming?' he asked Maisie.

'Tell him I'll look in tomorrow morning,' she answered. 'I'll unpack and help here.'

'Don't be long,' called Winnie as he made for the car. 'There's a chicken in the oven, and it will be ready by eight o'clock.'

'That's a date,' shouted Edward cheerfully, driving off.

The long shadow of St Peter's spire stretched across the market place, but the sun still gleamed warmly upon Sep's shop and the windows of his house above it. Edward parked the car and looked around him with satisfaction. Choir practice was in session and he could hear the singers running through the old familiar harvest hymns. Queen Victoria wore a pigeon on her crown and looked disapproving. At the window of his own flat he could see old John Bush, peering at a newspaper held up to the light. This was the time of day when Sep's house had the best of it, Edward thought, and remembered how, as a boy, he had explained to his grandfather why he preferred Bender's old home to Sep's.

'It gets the sun most of the day,' he had told the old man. 'You only get it in the evening.'

But how it glorified everything, to be sure! The western rays burnished Sep's side of the square, gilding steps and doorframes and turning the glass to sheets of fire. Edward ran up the stairs, at the side of the closed shop, and called to his grandfather. Miss Taggerty greeted him warmly.

'He's pottering about downstairs, Mr Edward, having a final look at the Harvest Festival loaves, no doubt. The chapel folk are fetching them tomorrow morning for the decorations. Lovely they are! He did them himself. You'll find him there, you'll see.'

Edward made his way to the bakehouse. There was no-one about at this time of day and the yard was very quiet. He entered the bakehouse and was greeted by the clean fragrance of newly-baked bread which had been familiar to him all his life. Ranged against the white wall stood two splendid loaves in the shape of sheaves of corn, with smaller ones neatly lined up beside them. There were long plaited loaves, fat round ones, Coburg, cottage, split-top – a beautiful array of every pattern known to a master baker.

And sitting before them, at the great table white and ribbed with a lifetime's scrubbing, was their creator. He was leaning back in his wooden arm chair, his hands upon the table top and his gaze upon his handiwork. He looked well content.

But when Edward came to him he saw that the eyes were sightless and the small hands cold in death. There, in the centre of his world, his lovely work about him and his duty done, Sep rested at last.

Dazed and devastated, an arm about his grandfather's frail shoulders, Edward became conscious of the eerie silence of the room. Across the square the sound of singing drifted as the boys in St Peter's choir practised their final hymn.

'*All is safely gathered in*,' they shrilled triumphantly, as the long shadows reached towards Sep's home.

17

Problems for Edward

IN THE bewildered hours that followed Sep's death, the family began to realise just how deeply they would miss his presence. He had played a vital part in the life of each one. He had been the lynch-pin holding the Norths and Howards together, and his going moved them all profoundly.

After the first shock was over, Edward and Bertie spent the weekend making necessary arrangements for the funeral, writing to friends and relatives, drafting a notice for *The Caxley Chronicle* and coping with the many messages of sympathy from the townsfolk who had known Sep all his life.

As they sat at their task, one at each end of Bertie's dining-room table, Bertie looked across at Edward. The younger man was engrossed in his writing, head bent and eyes lowered. His expression was unusually solemn, and in that moment Bertie realised how very like Sep's was his cast of countenance. There was something in the slant of the cheekbone and the set of the ear which recalled the dead man clearly. Age would strengthen the likeness as Edward's hair lost its colour and his face grew thinner.

There was also, thought Bertie, the same concentration on the job in hand. Edward had assumed this sudden responsibility so naturally that, for the first time, he felt dependent upon the younger man. He had slipped into his position of authority unconsciously, and it was clear to Bertie that Edward henceforth would be the head of the family. It was a thought which flooded Bertie with rejoicing and relief. It was all that Sep had hoped for, in his wisdom.

The chapel in the High Street was full on the occasion of Sep's funeral. Edward had not realised how many activities Sep had taken part in in the town. He was a councillor for many years. He had been a member of the hospital board, the Red Cross committee, the Boys' Brigade, and a trustee of several local charities. All these duties he had performed conscientiously and unobtrusively. It was plain, from the large congregation, that Sep's influence was widely felt and that he would be sorely missed in Caxley's public life.

The coffin, bore the golden flowers of autumn. The chapel was still decorated with the corn and trailing berries of Harvest Festival. Edward, standing between Maisie and his mother, with Kathy beautiful in black nearby, was deeply moved, and when, later, Sep was lowered into the grave beside his adored wife, the dark cypress trees and bright flowers of Caxley's burial ground were blurred by unaccustomed tears. Sep had been a father as well as a grandfather to him. It was doubly hard to say farewell.

But, driving back to Bertie and Kathy's after the ceremony, he became conscious of a feeling of inner calm. This was death as it should be – rest after work well done, port after storm. Death, as Edward had met it first during the war, was violent and unnatural, the brutal and premature end of men still young. Sep had stayed his course, and the memory of that serene dead face gave his grandson comfort now, and hope for the future.

*　　*　　*

He and Maisie said little on the journey back to town, but later that evening Maisie spoke tentatively.

'Did you wish – did you feel – that your father should have been there, Edward?'

'Yes, I did,' replied Edward seriously. 'As a matter of fact, I wrote to him and told him.'

'Where is he then? I'd no idea you knew where he was!'

'I haven't. Mother would never speak of him – nor, of course, would Sep. But I found an address among his papers when Uncle Bertie and I were putting things straight. Somewhere in Devon. Heaven alone knows if he's still there, but it might be sent on to him, if he's moved. I felt he should know.'

It was the first time that his father had been mentioned, though Maisie knew well the story of Leslie Howard's flight with an earlier love when Edward was only four and Joan still a baby in arms.

'Do you remember him?'

'Hardly at all. I can remember that he used to swing me up high over his head, which I liked. The general impression is a happy one, strangely enough. He was full of high spirits – probably slightly drunk – but willing to have the sort of rough-and-tumble that little boys enjoy.'

'And you've never wanted to see him again?'

'Sometimes, yes. Particularly when I was about sixteen or so. Luckily, Uncle Bertie was at hand always, so he got landed with my problems then. And I knew mother would have hated to see him again, or to know that I'd been in touch. As for Grandma North, I think she would have strangled my father with her bare hands if she'd clapped eyes on him again! He certainly behaved very badly to his family. Sep minded more than anyone. That's why he never spoke of him. He was such a kind man that I always thought it was extraordinary how ruthlessly he dealt with my father.'

'Sep was a man with exceptionally high principles,' said Maisie. She crossed the room to switch on the wireless, and paused on her way back to her chair to look down upon Edward. He was so solemn that she ruffled his thick hair teasingly.

'And a Victorian,' added Edward, still far away, 'with a good Victorian's rigid mode of conduct. It must have made life very simple in some ways. You knew exactly where you were.'

'You're going grey,' said Maisie, peering at the crown of his head, and Edward laughed.

'It's marriage,' he said, pulling her down beside him.

One morning, a week or so later, a long envelope with a Caxley postmark arrived for Edward. It was the only letter for him, but Maisie had a long one from Joan, full of news about the baby and Sarah's recovery from measles. Sipping her breakfast coffee, and engrossed in the letter from Ireland, she was unaware of the effect that Edward's correspondence was making upon him, until he pushed away his half-eaten breakfast and got up hastily.

He looked white and bewildered, and rubbed his forehead as he always did when perplexed.

'Not more bad news?' cried Maisie.

'No. Not really. I suppose one should say quite the opposite – but the hell of a shock.'

He handed her the letter and paced the room while she read it.

'He's left you *everything?*' queried Maisie in a whisper. 'But what about Aunt Kathy and your father and the other grand-children? I don't understand it.'

'They're all provided for – except for my father, which one would expect – by incredibly large sums of money. But the two businesses are for me, evidently.'

'Didn't he ever mention this to you?'

'Never. It honestly never entered my head. It's amazingly generous, but a terrific responsibility. I thought everything would be Aunt Kathy's, with perhaps a few bequests to the others. He'd already given me the house above the restaurant. This is staggering.'

'But lovely,' exclaimed Maisie. 'Dear Sep! He always wanted you in the market square.'

Edward paused in his pacing and looked at her in astonish-ment.

'Do you seriously suggest that I should run the business myself? I don't know the first thing about baking – or catering for that matter.'

'You could learn,' pointed out Maisie. 'And running one business must be very like running another. And just think – to live in Caxley!' Her eyes were bright.

Edward continued to look distracted. His eye caught sight of the time and he gave a cry of dismay.

'I must be off. This will need a lot of thought. Lovejoy wants to see me anyway to sign some papers. We'll talk this over this evening, and go down again this weekend.'

'Don't look so worried,' comforted Maisie. 'Anyone would think you'd been sentenced to death! In fact you've been sentenced to a new life.'

'Not so fast, please,' begged Edward, collecting his belongings frenziedly. 'There's a great deal to consider – Sep's wishes, the family's reactions, whether we can cope with the business ourselves or get people in to manage it properly – a hundred problems! And what about my job here? I can't let Jim down after all he's done for me.'

Maisie pushed her agitated husband through the front door. 'Tell Jim what's happened,' she said soothingly. 'And calm down. I'm going back to celebrate in a second cup of coffee.'

The day seemed to drag by very slowly for Maisie. There was no school for her that morning, and although she was glad to have some time to collect her thoughts, she longed for Edward to return so that they could discuss this miraculous news.

For her own part she welcomed a return to Caxley. To live in the market square, either in Edward's house or in Sep's, would give her enormous pleasure. Her friends were there, and the thought of living so near all her in-laws, which might daunt many young wives, did not worry Maisie who had known the Howards and Norths now for so many years. She longed too to have a sizeable house to furnish and decorate. Here, in the tiny flat, she had found small scope for her talents. It would be lovely to choose curtains and wall-paper and to bring either of the two fine old houses to life again.

And what better place to raise a Howard family than in the heart of Caxley where their roots ran so deeply? This would mean too the end of the fruitless house-hunting which depressed them both. As she went mechanically about her household tasks, Maisie hoped desperately that Edward would be able to wind up the job satisfactorily here, and return to

Caxley with a clear conscience and zest for what lay ahead.

Edward returned, looking less agitated than when he had departed for the office that morning.

'Jim is as pleased as if it had happened to him,' said he. 'We've gone into things as thoroughly as we can at this stage. He's quite happy for me to go whenever I like, but we've all sorts of negotiations going on at the moment, started by me mainly, and I must see those wound up before I'd feel free.'

'And when would that be?'

'I can't say. Probably in a few months' time.'

'A few *months*!' echoed Maisie, trying to keep the disappointment from her voice.

Edward looked across at her and laughed.

'You want to go back very badly, don't you?'

Maisie nodded.

'I'm beginning to think that I do, too, but I must clear up things at this end first. We'll see what Lovejoy says at the weekend, and how the family feels. Who knows? We may be back in the market square by the New Year. That is if I've mastered the bakery business by that time!'

As they drove to Caxley that weekend, Edward had some private misgivings. How would Aunt Kathy feel about the will? She had taken an active part in the business, and it seemed hard that no share in it had been left to her. It was true that Sep's bequest to her and her children had been characteristically generous, and of a magnitude which staggered Edward, but it was not quite the same as having a part in a thriving concern. And how would the rest of the family view his amazing good fortune? Edward had seen many united families rent asunder by wills, and could only hope that the Howards and Norths would be spared this ignominy. He approached Caxley with some trepidation.

His mother and grandmother greeted them with unfeigned delight.

'Which house will you settle in, dear?' asked Mrs North with the shattering directness of old age. She refused to believe that Edward did not know yet if he would be able to return to Caxley at all.

'But you must have known, dear, that Sep intended you to have the business?'

'I hadn't a clue, grandma, and that's the plain truth.'

'Neither had I,' said his mother.

'Well, he spoke to me about it, towards the end,' maintained Mrs North trenchantly, 'and I agreed that it was an excellent idea.'

'Grandma, you are incorrigible!' exclaimed Edward, amused.

'It's high time you came back anyway, to look after your mother and me. And what about your own family? Married for nearly a year and no baby on the way! It's deplorable! What you need is some invigorating Caxley air.'

Edward and Maisie exchanged delighted glances.

'Yes, grandma,' said Edward meekly.

He walked up the familiar path to Bertie and Kathy's house with a nervousness he had never felt before. Kathy opened the door to him, put her arms round his neck, and kissed him soundly. All Edward's worries fled in the face of this warm embrace.

'We're all very pleased about it,' Bertie assured him, when they were settled by the fire. 'Although Sep never said a word about his settlements we guessed that this would be the way he wanted it.'

'Would you come in with me as a partner?' asked Edward of his aunt. She smiled and shook her head.

'You're a dear to think of it, but I'm fifty-six next birthday and shall be quite glad to be away from it all. Father's left us money, as you know, and I'm glad the business is yours – still in the family, with "Howard" over the door – but not giving me any more worries.'

They talked of Edward's plans, and he explained the necessity of staying in town to clear up his affairs at the factory.

'And I'm still not absolutely sure if I ought to come back to run the shop and restaurant myself, or whether I should try and get someone to manage them.'

'John Bush and I can hold the fort until you decide,' offered Kathy. 'But *please* think about taking it on yourself. You could do it easily, and think how pleased Sep would have been.'

'And Maisie will be,' added Bertie. 'Off you go to your appointment with Lovejoy! See what he advises.'

Mr Lovejoy, pink and voluble, succeeded in confusing Edward even more, by presenting him with a host of incomprehensible documents to peruse, and a torrent of explanation.

From amidst the chaos one thing emerged clearly to Edward. He was going to be a man of some wealth. Death duties would amount to a considerable sum, but if the business continued at its present rate he could expect an income far in excess of that which he now earned. He had no doubt, in his own mind, that with some rebuilding and more modern equipment, the two businesses could become even more lucrative.

He thanked Mr Lovejoy for his help and emerged into the pale October sunlight. Hardly knowing what he was about, he passed Howard's Restaurant and crossed to Sep's old shop. It was strange to think that all this now belonged to him.

He stepped into the shop in a daze. A young new assistant, unknown to him, asked him what he would like. Edward tried to pull himself together.

'Oh, a loaf,' he said desperately. 'Just a loaf.'

She picked out a stout crusty cottage loaf from the window, shrouded it in a piece of white tissue paper, and thrust it into his arms like a warm baby.

Edward gave her a florin, and she slapped some coins into his palm in return. He studied them with interest. It was time he knew the price of bread.

Still bemused, and clutching his awkward burden, he made his way towards the Cax. What had possessed him to buy a loaf, he wondered, exasperation overcoming his numbness!

He strode now with more purpose towards the tow path. The families of mallards and moorhens paddled busily at the edge of the water, as they had always done. Today, thought Edward, they should celebrate his inheritance.

He broke pieces of the loaf and threw them joyfully upon the Cax. Squawking, quacking, piping, the birds rushed this way and that, wings flapping, streaking the water with their bright feet, as they fought for this largesse.

Exhilarated, Edward tossed the pieces this way and that, laughing at the birds' antics and his own incredible good fortune. What was it that the Scriptures said about 'casting thy bread upon the waters'? He would ask Grandma North when he returned.

He thrust the last delicious morsel into his mouth, dusted his hands, and walked home, whistling.

18

Edward Meets His Father

THE FIRST frosts of autumn blackened the bright dahlias in the suburban gardens and began to strip the golden trees. Children were scuffling through the carpet of dead leaves as Edward drove to the factory one morning.

In his pocket lay a letter from his father. It was the first communication he had ever received from him, and it provided food for thought.

He studied it again in the privacy of his office. It was written on cheap ruled paper, but the writing was clear and well-formed. It had come from an address in Lincolnshire, and said:

'My dear Edward,

Thank you for writing to tell me of the death of your grandfather.

To be frank, I had already seen a notice of it in *The Caxley Chronicle* which has been sent to me ever since I left the town.

I could not have attended the funeral, even if I had wished to do so, as the expense of the fare to Caxley made the trip impossible. I live alone here, in very straitened circumstances, my second wife having died two years ago.

I should very much like to see your mother again and, of course, you too, but I shall understand if it is not convenient.

The contents of your grandfather's will are unknown to me, but I take it that he was stubbornly against me to the end.

Affectionately,

Leslie Howard'

It was pretty plain, thought Edward, from the letter before him, that his father was as bitter as ever against Sep. Not once did he speak of him as 'my father' – but as 'your grandfather', and the final reference to the will disclosed a disappointed man. Nevertheless, Edward experienced a strong feeling of mingled pity and curiosity. His father must be getting on in years. He was certainly older than Uncle Bertie, and must now be approaching sixty. He sounded lonely too, as well as hard up.

He began to wonder how he lived. There had been two children by the second marriage, as far as he remembered. Was he perhaps living with one of them in Lincolnshire? He felt fairly certain that his mother would not wish to meet his father again, but he himself was suddenly drawn to the idea of seeing him. He turned the notion over in his mind, deciding not to do anything precipitous which might upset the family.

At the weekend, when he went once more to Caxley, he showed his mother the letter when they were alone. The vehemence of her reaction astonished him.

'He wrote to me at much the same time,' she told Edward, her face working. 'I tore up the letter. He's hurt me too much in the past, Edward. If anything, the bitterness has grown with the years. I wouldn't lift a finger to help him. He treated us all abominably, and if it hadn't been for his own father we should have been very hard up indeed. And now he has the nerve to

approach us and – more than that – to expect money from
Sep! The whole thing is despicable.'

It was obviously not the moment to tell his mother that he
felt like visiting his father; but before he and Maisie left for
home he broached the subject tentatively. He had already told
Kathy and Bertie about Leslie's letter, and about the possibility
of travelling to Lincoln to see how his father fared. They had
both been sympathetic towards Edward's project, but had no
desire to meet Leslie themselves.

'He's a charmer – or was –' said Bertie plainly, 'and a
sponger. So be warned, my boy. And if your mother objects, I
advise you to chuck up the idea. No point in opening old
wounds.'

'I see that well enough,' responded Edward. 'But I don't like
to think of him in want, when Sep has left us all so comfortably
off.'

'Your feelings do you credit,' replied Bertie, 'but don't let
yourself in for embarrassment in the future. Leslie might well
have developed into an old-man-of-the-sea, always demanding
more and more.'

As his nephew vanished up the lane to the High Street, Kathy
looked at Bertie.

'Will he really go, do you think?'

'He'll go,' said Bertie. 'He feels it's his duty. He's Sep all over
again when it comes to it – and the sooner we all realise it, the
better.'

Luckily, Winnie's reactions to Edward's proposal were less
violent than he had imagined.

'I can understand that you want to see him,' she said, rather
wearily. 'He is your father after all. But I absolutely refuse to

have any more to do with him. And nothing of this is to be mentioned to Grandma. She is too old for this sort of shock.'

Edward promised to be discreet, kissed his mother good-bye and drove back to London well content.

The next few weeks were unusually busy for Edward, and it was early December before the trip northwards could be arranged.

The clearing-up process at the factory was going well, but Edward was to remain one of the directors and there were a number of legal matters to arrange. Every other weekend he spent at Caxley, studying the business, and going through the accounts and staff arrangements with Kathy and John Bush. It was clear that they longed to hand over the responsibilities of the shop and restaurant which they had so bravely borne, and Edward hoped to move back to his own house as soon as the tenants in the floors below could find alternative accommodation. John Bush had been offered the little cottage where Edward and Joan had been born. A daughter, recently widowed, was to share it with him, and the old man made no secret of looking forward now to complete retirement.

Maisie was in her element choosing papers for the walls and material for curtains and covers. She went with Winnie to one or two furniture sales and acquired some fine pieces. Old Mrs North gave her the tea service which had graced her own table at the house in the market square, and Maisie liked to think of it in its own home again.

At the end of November she was delighted to discover that she was to have a baby in the early summer.

'We *must* get in before long,' she implored Edward. 'I

must get everything ready for it while I'm still mobile.'

The family was as pleased as they were themselves at the news, and Mrs North's comment amused them all.

'At last,' she cried, 'we'll have a *christening* at St Peter's. Don't tell me you've anything against that?'

She was reassured, and set to work to knit half a dozen first-size vests with enthusiasm.

Edward set out alone on his journey, starting very early, as he wanted to make the return trip in the day.

It was cold and overcast when he set out, and rain began to fall heavily after an hour or so on the road. He had looked forward to this visit, but now a certain depression invaded him, due in part to the dismal weather and to general fatigue. Although he had made up his mind to return to the market square and to take up the duties laid upon him by Sep, he still had moments of doubt.

True, as Maisie had said, running one business was very like running another, but he was going to miss his trips abroad and his growing skill in designing. Life in London had been pleasant. Would he find Caxley too parochial after wider horizons? He could only hope that he was doing the right thing. In any case the thought of the baby being born in Caxley gave him enormous pleasure, and he looked forward to introducing it to all the varied delights of the Cax running through the garden.

He reached the town where his father lived a little before noon. Rain slashed against the side windows, and passing vehicles sent up showers of water across the windscreen. Wet grey-slated roofs and drab houses stretched desolately in all directions. Bedraggled people, bent behind dripping umbrellas, looked as wretched as their surroundings. Edward drove through the centre of the town and followed the route which his father's last letter had given.

He found the road, the house, switched off the car's engine and sat looking about him. It was less gloomy than parts of the town he had just traversed, but pretty dispiriting, nevertheless. The houses were semi-detached, and built, Edward guessed, sometime in the thirties. They were brick below and pebble-dash above, each having an arched porch with a red-tiled floor to it. The front gardens, now leafless, were very small. Here and there a wispy ornamental cherry tree, or an etiolated rowan, struggled for existence in the teeth of the winds which came from the North Sea.

The sharp air took his breath away as he made his way to the door. It was opened so quickly that Edward felt sure that his arrival had been watched. A plump breathless woman of middle-age greeted him with an air of excitement. She wore a flowered overall and carried a duster.

'Come to see your dad?' she greeted him. 'He's been waiting for you. Come in. You must be shrammed.'

Edward, who had never heard this attractive word, supposed, rightly, that it meant that he must be cold, and followed her into the small hall. An overpowering smell of floor polish pervaded the house and everything which could be burnished, from brass stair rods to the chain of the cuckoo clock on the wall, gleamed on every side.

The door on the right opened and there stood a slight figure, taller than Sep, but less tall than Edward, gazing at him with the bright dark eyes of the Howards.

'Your son's come,' announced the woman. The words dropped into the sudden silence like pebbles into a still pool.

'Come in, my boy,' said Leslie quietly, and they went into the sitting-room together.

The meeting had stirred Edward deeply, and for a moment or two he could find nothing to say. His father was fumbling at the catch of a cupboard.

'Like a drink?'

'Thank you.'

'Whisky, sherry or beer?'

'Sherry, please.'

Edward watched his father pouring the liquid. He was very like Aunt Kathy. His hair was still thick, but now more grey than black. He had the same dark, rather highly arched, eyebrows, and the pronounced lines from nose to the corner of the upper lip which all the Howards seemed to have inherited from Sep. He was dressed in a tweed suit, warm but shabby, and his shirt was so dazzlingly white that Edward felt sure that his landlady attended to his linen.

The room was over-filled with large furniture and innumerable knick-knacks, but a good fire warmed all, and old-fashioned red wallpaper, overpowering in normal circumstances, gave some cheer on a morning as bleak as this.

'You seem very comfortable here,' ventured Edward, glass in hand.

'They're good people,' said Leslie. 'He's a railway man, due to retire soon. I have two rooms. I sold up when the wife died. Came up here from the west country, and took a job with a car firm.'

'Are you still with them?' asked Edward.

'No,' replied Leslie briefly. 'Tell me about the family.'

Edward told him all that he could. He appeared quite unaffected by Robert's tragic end and his father's recent death, but Edward noticed that mention of his mother brought a smile.

'But she won't see me, eh?'

'I'm afraid not. I hope you won't try.'

'Don't worry. I treated her badly. Can't blame her for giving me the cold shoulder now. I shan't come to Caxley. I thought of it when I read of the old man's death, but decided against it. If there were any pickings I reckoned Lovejoy would let me know.'

There was something so casually callous about this last utterance, that Edward stiffened.

'Did you imagine that there would be?' he enquired. There must have been an edge to his tone, for the older man shot him a quick glance.

'Can't say I did, but hope springs eternal, you know.'

He placed his glass carefully on the table beside him, and turned to face Edward.

'This looks like the only time I'll be able to put my side of the story, so I may as well tell it now. You knew my father well enough, I know, but only as an older man when he'd mellowed a bit. When Jim and I were boys he was too dam' strict by half. Chapel three times on Sundays and Lord knows how many Bible meetings of one sort or another during the week. Jim stuck it all better than I did – and then, as we got older, he didn't have the same eye for the girls as I had. He was more like Dad – I was like Mum. I don't think I ever loved my father. He said "No" too often.'

'But I know he was fond of all his children,' broke in Edward.

'Had a funny way of showing it,' observed his father bitterly. 'He drove me to deceit, and that's the truth. He was a narrow-minded bigoted old fool bent on getting to heaven at any cost. I can't forgive him.' He was breathing heavily.

'He was also brave, honest and generous,' said Edward levelly. His father seemed not to hear.

'And he poisoned Winnie's mind against me later. There was no hope of reconciliation while Father was alive.'

'That's not true,' said Edward, anger rising in him. 'My mother's mind was made up from the moment you parted!'

'Maybe,' replied Leslie indifferently. 'She was a North – as obstinate as her old man.' He laughed suddenly, and his face was transformed. Now Edward could see why Leslie Howard was remembered in Caxley as a charmer.

'Don't let's squabble,' he pleaded. 'We've a lot to talk over. Let's come out to a pub I know for our grub. Mrs Jones here is a dab hand with house-cleaning but her cooking's of the baked-cod-and-flaked-rice variety. I told her we'd go out.'

Edward was secretly sorry to leave the good fire and over-stuffed armchair, but dutifully drove through the relentless rain to a small public house situated two or three miles away on a windswept plain. Over an excellent mixed grill Edward learnt a little more of his father's life.

'My boy was killed in France,' said Leslie, 'and the girl is married and out in Australia'.

It was queer, thought Edward, to hear of this half-brother and sister whom he had never seen. His father spoke of them with affection. Naturally, they were closer to him than he and Joan could ever have been.

'And then Ellen was ill for so long – three or four years,

before she died. I got to hate that place in Devon. We had a garage there, you know. Dam' hard work and mighty little return for it.'

'What happened to it?' asked Edward.

'Sold everything up when Ellen went. Paid my debts – and they were plenty – and found this place. I wanted a change, and besides, the doctor told me to live somewhere flat. I've got a dicky heart. Same thing that took off my poor mum, I daresay.'

Gradually, Edward began to see the kind of life which was now his father's lot. He had fallen out with the car firm. It was obvious that he disliked being an employee after running his own business. It was also plain to Edward that if he did not have some regular employment he would very soon drift into a pointless existence in which drink would play a major part. Nevertheless, it seemed that there were grounds for believing that he had some heart complaint. The woman behind the bar, who seemed to be an old friend, had enquired about 'his attacks' with some concern, and both his parents had suffered from heart trouble.

For the past week he had been without work for the first time. He had heard of two book-keeping jobs in local firms and proposed to apply for them. Edward thought it sounded hopeful. As far as he could gather, his father's financial resources consisted of fifty pounds or so in the bank. This amount would not last long even in such modest lodgings as Mrs Jones'. This urgency to earn was a spur in the right direction, Edward surmised.

He paid the bill and drove his father home. The matter which had been uppermost in his mind was more complicated than he had first thought. He was determined to see that his father was not in want. Now that he had met him he was equally sure that this was not the time to offer financial help. If he did, the chances of Leslie's helping himself grew considerably slighter. Prudently, Edward postponed a decision, but made his father promise to let him know the outcome of his job-hunting.

'I'll write to you in a week or so,' said Leslie as they parted. 'I don't suppose we'll meet again, my boy. Better to make this the last time, I think. It was good of you to make the journey. Tell those who are interested how I am. I've got a soft spot for old Bertie. I wonder if he ever regretted marrying a Howard?'

'Never,' said Edward stoutly, driving off, and left his father laughing.

Driving back along the wet roads Edward pondered on the day's encounter. He was satisfied now that he had seen his father. He was well looked after, in fairly good health, and obviously as happy as he would be anywhere.

As soon as heard that he was in work again he would make adequate provision against the future. He wanted to feel that there was a sum in the bank which would be available if the old man fell on hard times. But he must have a job – no matter how small the return – which would keep him actively occupied. His father's worst enemy, Edward saw, was himself. Too much solitude would breed self-pity and self-indulgence. He could see why Sep had never had much time for him. There was a streak of weakness which Sep would never have been able to understand or forgive.

'A rum lot, the Howards!' said Edward aloud, and putting his foot down on the accelerator, sped home.

19

Return to the Market Square

EDWARD FOUND a surprising lack of interest in Leslie's welfare among the family. Aunt Kathy was perfunctory in her enquiries. His mother refused to discuss the matter. Maisie, naturally enough, was only vaguely interested in someone she had never met. Uncle Bertie alone seemed concerned, and listened attentively to Edward's account of all that had happened. He approved of Edward's decision to wait and see if a job materialised.

In the week before Christmas the awaited letter arrived. Leslie wrote enthusiastically. The post was in a large baker's. 'Back where I began,' was how he put it. He not only looked after the accounts but also took the van out twice a week to relieve other roundsmen. His weekly wage was modest but enough for his needs, he wrote.

Edward replied congratulating him, and telling him that he was paying the sum of two hundred and fifty pounds into his bank account which he hoped he would accept as a nest-egg and a Christmas present. He posted the letter with some misgivings. Was he simply trying to salve his conscience by handing over this money? He hoped not. What would Sep have thought? Well, maybe Sep would not have approved, but Edward had his own decisions to make now, he told himself firmly. He felt sure that it was right to supply his father with a bulwark against future storms. He felt equally sure that it had been right to wait until he was established in a suitable job before providing that bulwark. Now it was up to his father.

Everything was now planned for their removal from the flat to the market square. After innumerable delays, the old house was free of workmen and, freshly decorated, awaited its owners.

Maisie had enjoyed refurbishing the fine old rooms. The great drawing-room, with its three windows looking out upon the market place, was painted in the palest green, a colour which would show up well the mahogany pieces which she had bought at the sales. It was a splendid room, high and airy. Bender North had always appreciated it, admiring its fine proportions and its red plush furnishings, after a day in the shop below. Now his grandson would find equal domestic pleasure in the same room.

On the same floor, at the back of the building, were the dining room and kitchen, overlooking the small garden and the river Cax. Above them were three bedrooms and a bathroom, while on the top floor, in the old attics, Edward's flat remained much as it was, except that his sitting-room had been converted into a nursery for the newcomer.

'You'll have to put the window bars back again,' said Uncle Bertie when he inspected the premises. 'There were three to each window when I slept there. You took them out too hastily, Edward my boy!'

Edward and Maisie spent the last weekend in January at Rose Lodge. She was to see the furniture in on the Monday, with Winnie's help, while Edward would return to the flat to arrange things at that end. It was bitterly cold, and as she and Winnie directed operations on Monday morning, and dodged rolls of carpet and bedsteads, Maisie was thankful that they had faced the expense of central heating for the house. With the open market square before, and the river Cax behind, it had always felt cold. Now, with new warmth, the house seemed to come to life.

She took a particular interest in the larger of the back bedrooms, for here she planned to have the baby. She was determined that it should be born in the old house in the market square, and had already engaged the monthly nurse who was to sleep in the bedroom adjoining her own.

The view from the windows on this bleak January day was grey and cheerless. The pollarded willows lining the Cax pointed gaunt fingers towards the leaden sky. The distant tunnel of horse chestnut trees made a dark smudge above the river mist, but Maisie could imagine it in May when the baby was due to arrive. Then the willows would be a golden green above the sparkling water. The chestnut leaves would be bursting from their sticky buds. The kingfisher – harbinger of good fortune – should be flashing over the water, and on the lawn below the window the crocuses, yellow, purple and white, would be giving way to daffodils and tulips.

It was past nine o'clock when Edward arrived. Both of them were excited but exhausted, and went early to bed in the bedroom overlooking the market square. Maisie fell asleep almost immediately, but Edward lay on his back watching the pattern on the ceiling, made by the lamps in the market place.

Now and again the old house creaked, as wood expanded gently in the unaccustomed heat. Someone crossed the cobbles, singing, pausing in his tune to call goodnight to a fellow wayfarer. There was a country burr in the tone which pleased Edward.

How often, he wondered, had Grandfather North lain in this same room listening to the sounds of the square by night? He thought of Uncle Bertie and his own mother, sleeping, as children, on the floor above, where soon his own child would be bedded. It gave him a queer feeling of wonder and pride.

Tomorrow, he told himself, he must wake early and go downstairs to the restaurant and then across to the bakery. He was a market square man now, with a reputation for diligence to keep up! Smiling at the thought, he turned his face into the pillow and fell asleep.

Caxley watched Edward's progress, in the ensuing weeks, with considerable interest. On the whole, his efforts met with approval. He was applying himself zealously to the new work, and people were glad to see a young man in charge.

The assistants in the shop and restaurant spoke well of him, and the grape-vine of the closely-knit little town hummed busily with day-to-day reports – mainly favourable. Young Edward was taking on two new counter-hands. He was going to enlarge the storage sheds at the back of the bakery. He was talking of keeping the restaurant open later at night. He was applying for a liquor licence. Think of that! The more sedate chapel-goers could imagine Sep turning in his grave at the thought, but the majority of Caxley's citizens approved.

Edward himself was beginning to enjoy it all enormously. The years of solitary living, which had been all that he desired after the break-up of his first marriage, were behind him. He began to flourish in this new gregarious life and found pleasure in joining some of the local activities and meeting boyhood friends again. The Crockfords, grandchildren of the famous Dan who had painted Edna Howard so long ago, lived within walking distance and were frequent visitors. William Crockford, the present owner of the family mill which supplied Edward with much of his flour, introduced him to the Rotary Club and Edward became an energetic member. He also took up cricket again. He sometimes went dutifully with Maisie to concerts at the Corn Exchange which she, who was musical, thoroughly enjoyed, while Edward, who was not, leant back and planned future business projects while local talent provided mingled harmony and discord.

For there was, indeed, a great deal to plan. Edward, the product of two business families, saw clearly the possibilities of the future. Times were becoming more prosperous after the lean forties. People were buying more, and demanding more luxurious goods. Caxley families were prepared to dine out in the evenings. Caxley business men took their lunches in the town much more frequently. What is more, they brought their clients, and talked over deals at Howard's Restaurant.

There were more cars on the road, more wayfarers travelling from London westward, and from the midlands southward. Caxley was a convenient stopping-place, as it had been in the days of the stage-coach. The restaurant trade was booming. It could become even more thriving with judicious re-organisation.

Edward was so engrossed with his present commitments and his plans for the future that a letter which arrived for him one April morning came as a bolt from the blue. He could hardly believe his eyes as he read the document.

It was from the managing director of a firm of departmental

stores well-known to Edward. They were proposing to set up several more branches in provincial towns. The two sites belonging to Edward would be suitable for their purpose. The larger site would be used for their drapery and furnishing departments. Their Food Hall would probably be accommodated on the present bakery site. Perhaps Mr Howard would consider taking up a position of responsibility in this department, the salary to be arranged by mutual agreement? Naturally, there was a great deal to consider on both sides, but his firm had in mind the sum of – (here followed a figure so large that Edward seriously wondered if a nought or two too many had been added) and their agents were Messrs Ginn, Hope & Toddy of Piccadilly who would be glad to hear from Mr Howard if he were interested.

Edward handed the letter to Maisie in silence.

'Well?' she said, looking up at last.

'Some hopes!' said Edward flatly, stuffing it in his pocket. 'This is ours. We stay.'

As a matter of interest he showed the letter to the family before replying to it. As he expected, Bertie whole-heartedly agreed with his decision, but Kathy and the two ladies at Rose Lodge had doubts. This surprised Edward. The two properties had been their homes and livelihoods for so long that he had felt sure that they would be as forthright in their rejection of the offer as he was himself. How strange women were!

'It's such a lot of money,' said old Mrs North. 'After all, with that amount you could start up another business anywhere, or go back to the plastics place, dear, couldn't you?'

'Or simply invest it, and have a nice little income and a long holiday somewhere,' said his mother. 'There's no need to feel tied to Caxley simply because the business has been left to you.'

'But I *want* to be tied to Caxley!' Edward almost shouted. 'This is *our* business – the *Howard* business! Dammit all, it's the work and worry of three generations we're considering! Doesn't that mean anything?'

'Really,' tutted Mrs North, in some exasperation, 'men are so romantic about everything – even currant buns, it seems!'

'All we're trying to say,' said Winnie, more patiently, 'is that we should quite understand if you felt like accepting the offer, and I'm sure the rest of the family would agree.'

'Well, I don't intend to, and that's flat,' retorted Edward. He had not felt so out of patience with his womenfolk for years, and took a childish pleasure in slamming the front door as he departed.

He walked back through a little park, and sat down on one of the seats to cool off. Beds of velvety wallflowers scented the evening air, and some small children screamed on the swings, or chased each other round and round the lime trees. A few middle-aged couples strolled about, admiring the flowers and taking a little gentle exercise. It was the sort of unremarkable scene being enacted a hundred-fold all over the country on this mild Spring evening, but to Edward, in his mood of tension, it had a poignant significance.

Here, years ago, he had swung and raced. Before long, his own children would know this pleasant plot. These people before him, old and young, were of Caxley as he was himself. They all played their parts in the same setting, and with their neighbours as fellow-actors. And the centre of that stage was Caxley's market square. How lucky he was to have his place so firmly there – his by birthright, and now by choice as well! Nothing should make him give up this inheritance.

A very old man shuffled up to Edward's bench and sat down gingerly. His pale blue eyes watered, and a shining drop trickled down his lined cheeks into the far from clean beard which hid his mouth and chin.

His clothes were shabby, his boots broken. Edward guessed that he was making his way to the workhouse on the hill. He held a paper bag, and thrusting a claw-like hand inside, he produced a meat pasty. He gazed unseeingly before him as he munched, the pastry flaking into a shower of light crumbs which sprinkled his deplorable beard and greasy coat.

But it was not so much the old man who engaged Edward's attention as the blue and white paper bag which he held. It was very familiar to him. He had seen such bags since his earliest days – bright and clean, with 'Howard's Bakery' printed diagonally across the checked surface. Tonight, the sight of it filled him with a surge of pride. Here he was, face to face with one of his customers, watching his own product from his own paper bag being consumed with smackings of satisfaction! Who would give up such rewards? He felt a sudden love for this dirty unknown, and rising swiftly, fumbled in his pocket and pressed half a crown into the grimy paw.

'Have a drink with it,' he said.

'Ta, mate,' answered the tramp laconically. 'Needs summat to wash this muck down.'

Edward walked home, savouring the delicious incident to the

full. It warmed the evening for him. It added to his growing zest for life in Caxley, and to the enjoyment he felt, later that evening, when he pulled a piece of writing paper towards him and wrote a short, polite, but absolute rejection of the store's offer.

It was dark as he crossed the square to post it. He balanced the white envelope on his hand before tipping it, with satisfaction, into the pillar box. Now it was done, he felt singularly light-hearted, and walked jauntily back across the cobbles, smiling at Queen Victoria's implacable bulk outlined against the night sky.

At his doorway he turned to take a last breath of fresh air. The moon slid out from behind a ragged cloud, and touched the market square with sudden beauty.

Edward gave the scene a conspiratorial wink, opened his own door, mounted his own stairs and made his way to bed.

20

John Septimus Howard

IT WAS six o'clock on a fine May morning.

The market square was deserted. Long shadows lay across the cobblestones, reaching almost to the steps of St Peter's church. At the window of his bedroom, in a crumpled suit, and with tousled hair, stood Edward. It had been one of the longest nights that he had ever known, but now peace, and the dawn, had arrived.

The monthly nurse, Mrs Porter, had been in the house with them for eight days. That she was expert in her profession, Edward had no doubt, but as a member of the household he had found her sorely trying. Her shiny red face and crackling starched cuffs and apron dominated every meal. She ate very slowly, but needed a large amount of food to keep her well-corseted bulk going, so that Maisie and Edward seemed to spend three times as long at the table.

Maisie was worried because the baby was overdue. Nurse Porter added to her anxiety by consulting the calendar daily and talking gloomily of her timetable which might well be completely thrown out by Maisie's tardy offspring. Her next engagement was in a noble household in the shires, a fact which gave her considerable satisfaction.

'And the Duchess,' she told Maisie daily, 'is *never* late. The two little boys arrived on the dot, and the little girl was two days early. You'll have to hurry up, my dear, or the Duchess will beat you to it.'

But yesterday, when Edward returned from the shop after tea, Maisie and the nurse were in the bedroom, and all, according to Nurse Porter was going well. Maisie's comments, in the midst of her pains, were less euphemistic.

'Shall I stay with you?' asked Edward solicitously.

'Good heavens, no!' exclaimed Maisie crossly. 'It's quite bad enough as it is, without having to put a good front on it. Go a long way away – to Rose Lodge or somewhere, so that I can have a good yell when I want to.'

Thus banished, Edward took himself to the restaurant below, and pottered aimlessly about. Thank God, he thought honestly, Maisie was not one of the modern brigade who wanted a husband's support at this time! Although he intended to stay with her had she so wished, he was frankly terrified of seeing her in pain, and squeamish at the sight of blood. Dear, oh dear, thought Edward, rubbing his forehead anxiously, what poor tools men were when it came to it!

He had no intention of going to Rose Lodge, or anywhere else for that matter, until the child was born. He would stay as close as he could while it all went on. He suffered the common terrifying qualms about his wife's safety, and to calm his agitation set himself to such mechanical tasks as sorting out the cutlery and inspecting the table linen for possible repairs.

He could settle to nothing for long, however, and walked into the little garden on the dew-wet grass beside the river, looking up at the lighted window where the drama was being enacted. Every so often he mounted the stairs quietly and listened, but there was nothing to hear. On one of these sorties he encountered the nurse, and she took pity on him.

'She's doing splendidly,' she said. 'Come and have a look.'

Maisie looked far from splendid to Edward's eyes. She looked white and exhausted, but seemed glad to see him.

'Not long now,' said Nurse Porter, with what, to Edward, seemed callous indifference to her patient's condition. 'It should be here by morning.'

'By *morning*?' echoed Edward, appalled. The hands of the clock stood at a little before two. Would Maisie live as long, he wondered desperately?

'Go and make us all a nice pot of tea,' suggested the nurse, and Edward obediently went to the kitchen to perform his task. How parents could have faced ten, fifteen and even twenty such ordeals in days gone by, he could not imagine! He decided to have a whisky and soda when he had delivered the tea-tray to his task-mistress.

Later, as the first light crept across the countryside, he dozed in the arm chair, dreaming uneasily of white boats floating upon dark water. Could they be the little boats he floated as a boy upon the Cax? Or were they the white boats 'that sailed like swans asleep' on the enchanted waters of Lough Corrib? And where was Maisie? She should be with him. Had she slipped beneath the black and shivering water? Would he see her again?

A little before five Nurse Porter woke him. Her red face glowed like the rising sun, broad and triumphant. She held a white bundle which she displayed proudly to Edward.

'Want to see your son?' she asked. 'Six and a half pounds, and a perfect beauty.'

Edward looked upon his firstborn. A pink mottled face, no bigger than one of his own buns, topped by wispy damp hair, was all that could be seen in the aperture of the snowy shawl. Nurse Porter's idea of beauty, Edward thought, differed from his own, but the child looked healthy and inordinately wise.

'How's Maisie?' said Edward, now wide awake. 'Can I see her?'

'Asleep. You shall go in later. She's fine, but needs her rest.'

At that moment the baby opened his mouth in a yawn. Edward gazed at it, fascinated. There was something wonderfully clever about such an achievement when one considered that the child was less than an hour old. Edward felt a pang of paternal pride for the first time.

'He seems a very forward child to me,' said Edward.

'Naturally!' responded Nurse Porter with sardonic amusement, and took her bundle back to the bedroom.

That was an hour ago. Since then he had seen his Maisie, well, but drowsy, drunk a pot of coffee and tried to marshal his incoherent thoughts. As soon as possible, he would telephone to Rose Lodge, but six o'clock calls might alarm the household. He must let Bertie and Kathy know too as soon as they were astir.

Meanwhile, he gazed upon the market place, pink in the growing sunlight. A thin black cat, in a sheltered angle of St Peter's porch, washed one upthrust leg, its body as round and curved as an elegant shell, and suddenly Edward was back in time, over ten long years ago, when he had stood thus, watching the same familiar scene.

What a lifetime ago it seemed! Since then he had experienced war, an unhappy marriage and personal desolation. He had watched Robert's tragic decline and death, and lost Sep, his guide and example. He had shared, with his fellows, the bitterness of war, and the numbing poverty of its aftermath.

But that was the darker side of the picture. There was a better and brighter one. He had found Maisie, he had refound Caxley, and in doing so he had found himself at last.

A wisp of blue smoke rose from Sep's old house. Miss Taggerty was making up the kitchen boiler, thought Edward affectionately. In the bakehouse, work would already have started. The little town was stirring, and he must prepare, too, for another Caxley day. It was good to look ahead. It was good too, to think that John Septimus Howard, his son, would be the fourth generation to know this old house as home.

What was it that Sep used to say? 'There's always tomorrow, my boy. Always tomorrow.'

And with that thought to cheer him, Edward went to look, once more, upon the new heir to the market square.

M I S S R E A D is the pen name of Mrs. Dora Saint, who was born on April 17, 1913. A teacher by profession, she began writing for several journals after World War II and worked as a scriptwriter for the BBC. She is the author of many immensely popular books, but she is especially beloved for her novels of English rural life set in the fictional villages of Fairacre and Thrush Green. The first of these, *Village School,* was published in 1955 by Michael Joseph Ltd. in England and by Houghton Mifflin in the United States. Miss Read continued to write until her retirement in 1996. In 1998 she was made a Member of the Order of the British Empire for her services to literature. She lives in Berkshire.

T 552957

The Fairacre Series *Available in Paperback*

"Miss Read, a gentle soul with kindly interest in all around her, is the master of the kind of detail that shows place and character in delicate focus . . . there's no underestimating the power of rural English charm." — *Publishers Weekly*

Village School ISBN 978-0-618-12702-3

Village Diary ISBN 978-0-618-88415-5

Storm in the Village ISBN 978-0-618-88416-2

Over the Gate ISBN 978-0-618-88417-9

The Caxley Chronicles ISBN 978-0-618-88429-2

Fairacre Festival ISBN 978-0-618-88418-6

Miss Clare Remembers and **Emily Davis** ISBN 978-0-618-88434-6

Tyler's Row ISBN 978-0-618-88435-3

Farther Afield ISBN 978-0-618-88436-0

Christmas at Fairacre ISBN 978-0-618-91810-2

Village Centenary ISBN 978-0-618-12703-0

Summer at Fairacre ISBN 978-0-618-12704-7

Mrs. Pringle of Fairacre ISBN 978-0-618-15588-0

Changes at Fairacre ISBN 978-0-618-15457-9

Farewell to Fairacre ISBN 978-0-618-15456-2

A Peaceful Retirement ISBN 978-0-618-88438-4

VISIT OUR WEB SITE: WWW.HOUGHTONMIFFLINBOOKS.COM.

Available from Houghton Mifflin Books